The Highlanders

A Smitten Historical Romance Collection

Night Fox by J'nell Ciesielski

A Tender Siege by Naomi Musch

The Year Without Summer by Janet Grunst

The Violinist by Jennifer Lamont Leo

SMITTEN
HISTORICAL ROMANCE
LIGHTHOUSE PUBLISHING of the CAROLINAS

Other Smitten Historical Romance Titles by *The Highlanders* Authors

Among the Poppies – J'nell Ciesielski

Songbird and the Spy – J'nell Ciesielski

Mist O'er the Voyageur – Naomi Musch

A Heart Set Free – Janet Grunst

A Heart for Freedom – Janet Grunst

You're the Cream in My Coffee – Jennifer Lamont Leo

Ain't Misbehavin' – Jennifer Lamont Leo

THE HIGHLANDERS BY J'NELL CIESIELSKI, JENNIFER LAMONT LEO, JANET
GRUNST, NAOMI MUSCH
Smitten Historical Romance is an imprint of LPCBooks
a division of Iron Stream Media
100 Missionary Ridge, Birmingham, AL 35242

ISBN: 978-1-64526-063-9
Copyright © 2019 by J'nell Ciesielski, Jennifer Lamont Leo, Janet Grunst, Naomi Musch
Cover design by Elaina Lee
Interior design by Karthick Srinivasan

Available in print from your local bookstore, online, or from the publisher at:
ShopLPC.com

For more information on this book and the authors visit: http://www.jnellciesielski.com/,
http://jenniferlamontleo.com/, https://janetgrunst.com/, https://naomimusch.com/

Brought to you by the creative team at Lighthouse Publishing of the Carolinas
(LPCBooks.com): Eddie Jones, Shonda Savage, Pegg Thomas, Stephen Mathisen,
Sue Fairchild, & Kelly Scott.

Library of Congress Cataloging-in-Publication Data
Ciesielski, J'nell, Leo, Jennifer Lamont, Grunst, Janet, Musch, Naomi
The Highlanders / J'nell Ciesielski, Jennifer Lamont Leo, Janet Grunst,
Naomi Musch 1st ed.

Printed in the United States of America

PRAISE FOR *THE HIGHLANDERS*

A bonny collection of four uniquely told tales with four thoroughly Scottish heroes. Skillfully woven romance and adventure spans centuries to create a heartfelt, poignant historical tapestry. The Highlanders is not to be missed!

~Laura Frantz
Christy award-winning author of *The Lacemaker*

From a village in 1717 Scotland to a Scotsman living in 1915 Sandpoint, Idaho, this delightful collection of stories will draw you into the richness of the Scottish culture. The characters in each story live and love from the heart of their heritage. You can hear the accent leap off the pages!

~Jan Cline
Author of the *American Dreams Series*

Night Fox

By

J'nell Ciesielski

Miss S.

Like this story, you're small but pack a mighty burst of excitement.
One day we promise to take you to the land of where all Mama's
stories come from and see why she wants Daddy to move us there.

Chapter 1

Scotland, 1717

ANOTHER CARRIAGE ON PARADE, another plump pheasant ripe for the plucking.

Rooney Corsen crouched in the bushes and edged the mask over her face. She pulled the dark hood of her cape over her hair, careful to tuck back the unruly springs that were her telltale feature, and waited as the carriage creaked up the dusty road. Judging by the braw set of grays with jingling harnesses that would have cost a village merchant ten years' wages, it looked to be His Excellency Arthur Logan, Druimbeath's own procurator fiscal.

Excitement fluttered in Rooney's chest. "The fattest purse of them all."

Sunlight dappled the gleaming carriage as it moved closer. Securing her pistol in her waistband, Rooney readied to move. The carriage rolled by. Leaping out of the bushes, she launched herself at the back and flipped onto the roof, her petite body landing without a thud. She gripped the edge and swung in through the window, landing with a neat plop on the seat.

"Good afternoon, yer Excellency."

The old toad's eyes bugged out of his fleshy face. "Y-you!"

Rooney frowned at his uncovered head and slipped into her accent ruse. "I dinna ken ye were bald."

Logan lunged for the tightly curled, gray wig on the bench next to him and slapped it atop his head. One pudgy hand reached up to rap on the roof.

"Wouldna advise that."

"You think to stop me, boy?"

Shrugging, Rooney pulled out her pistol. "My dag will have something to say about it." She'd never had to fire it before and prayed today wouldn't be the first time.

Logan lowered his arm and scowled. "I know who you are. Night Fox."

"Good, then ye'll ken why I'm here."

"Pilfering, looting, robbing, and making a mockery of my official robes."

"Have no fear, yer Excellency. Yer robes are under no threat from me. They'd swallow me whole if I were to take them." She leveled the pistol at his face. "But I will partake o the others where it concerns yer purse. If ye dinna mind."

"I do mind!"

Rooney pulled back the hammer. The deadly click resonated within the cushioned confines. "'Tis a shame, for that's a bonny jabot ye're wearing. So crisp and white."

With a choking sound, Logan pulled a small box out from under his feet and flipped off the lid. Inside nestled two plump bags. He lifted them and tossed them to Rooney. "One day they'll finally catch you and string you up a tree. When you cry out for my mercy, I'll turn a deaf ear as I muse over my dessert. One less miscreant I have to judge."

"Ye fatten yerself o'er the misfortunes o others. Too bad the villagers canna pickle ye in broth. They'd feast for months." Rooney shook her head. "Nay, I shouldna said that. Yer juices are too foul for anyone to stomach."

"Why you little—"

"Tsk, tsk. Ye're purplin and it isna a good color for ye. As I believe I may be the culprit, I shall have to remove myself from yer bulging presence. Thank ye kindly for the offerings."

"Laird Glèidh returns today, and he'll not stand to have a thief on his lands!"

"Then I shall have to pay him a visit and welcome him home." Securing the bags and her pistol to her belt, Rooney sailed through the window and on top of the carriage. Twisting around, she stuck her head back through the window. "Dinna think to stop and have yer driver come after me. I'm a crack shot and will be watching from among the trees. Farewell, yer Excellency. Until we meet again."

Rooney caught hold of a tree limb as the carriage passed under its boughs and swung into the leafy sanctuary. The carriage disappeared from view. She took an unsteady breath. As her plundering fame grew so did the danger. It wouldn't be like this forever. Only until the debt was paid.

Skinning down the tree, Rooney pulled the stifling black mask and hood from her face. Bothersome thing, but if anyone discovered she was the eldest daughter of a deceased laird thieving money from her neighbors, the hangman's noose would come fast around her neck. Her sisters would have no one to protect them, and that was a fate Rooney would never allow to happen. Not while there was breath in her body.

And the procurator fiscal's money bags in her hands.

Every battle-weary bone in Deven McLendon's body ached as he crossed the threshold of his bedchamber and slammed the door on fiscal Logan's blustering. Silence. It fell blissfully on Deven's ears after a year of booming cannons, clanging swords, and death screams on the fields of combat. Another spent in hiding.

He was finally home.

Two years ago, to the month, he'd ridden off with the McLendon chieftain to fight for King James and his right to the throne of England. It had been a disastrous defeat for the Jacobites. Now, Deven wanted nothing more than to put the English and the horrid memories of war and death behind him.

But that would never be. Every gray stone of his home, each turret and chimney, now belonged to him because of that fateful musket ball that had slain his father on Preston field. Over three hundred years of McLendon ancestry now weighed on Deven's shoulders.

Crossing the room to his desk, Deven ran his hand over the worn surface. It was dusted, and the books kept precisely where he'd stacked them before joining the cause. He adjusted the quill feather that faced the wrong way. Tomorrow he would have his things moved into the laird's chambers. Not tonight. His father's spirit could rest there one final time.

Deven pulled a fresh sheet of parchment from the drawer and smoothed it over the desk then dipped the quill in the newly filled inkwell to scratch out an itemized list. First thing in the morning, he would look over the estate's account books to see how badly it had been managed in the master's absence. Then he'd ride out to inspect the crops for the coming winter and begin repairs on the tenant's homes. Too many things neglected over the years, but no longer. He was home to set them right.

He laid down the quill as exhaustion blurred his vision. It had been a long, hard ride back to Strathmoore, crossing the Great Glen and the Cairngorms, avoiding detachments of British soldiers and their loyalists eager to turn in Jacobites for coin. The Indemnity Act passed two months prior, pardoning all those who'd participated in the Rising, but news was slow to reach the Highlands. A boon for the British.

Deven rose and opened the window. A late September breeze swept in, cooling the stuffy air. Somewhere in the darkness, an animal cried. A fox.

Night Fox.

Propping his hands on the windowsill, the conversation with Logan backed up like the aftereffects of a bad meal. Two weeks of hard riding to be welcomed home by the fuming procurator demanding his money be returned and justice ignited against this roving band of thieves which the Night Fox led. His Excellency had then drunk all of the best whisky and ordered a chamber to be made up for him, having no desire to be robbed again on his return trip home.

Deven pushed away from the window and paced. Something must be done about this Fox. As laird of Strathmoore, he could not allow lawlessness to beleaguer his estate and people. Nor could he take one more unannounced visit from the fiscal. His whisky storage wouldn't survive it.

"Trouble sleeping?"

Deven grabbed the dirk at his hip. A small figure cloaked in black crouched in his open window. "Should've thought twice afore climbing into this window, laddie."

The shadow flipped back the edge of his cloak. A pistol pointed directly at Deven.

"I did, but I couldna resist an openin. Thank ye kindly for makin it so easy. Customarily, I'm obliged to break a glass or two."

Deven removed his hand from his dirk but didn't relax his stance as he stared at the masked intruder. He was small with the unchanged voice of a lad and speech of the unschooled. He sat in a comfortable squat of one who'd crouched in many windows. Survival in the Highlands had always been meant for the strongest, and those among the weak had too oft succumbed to less scrupulous occupations. But weak or strong, none were exempt from the law. Nor were the young. "Ye're the one they're calling the Night Fox."

"At yer service, Lord Glèidh. *Ceud mile fàilte.*"

Deven snorted at the proper Gaelic greeting. "A hundred thousand welcomes. Is that what ye say before ye reive people? Rather polite for someone of yer ilk."

"I see no reason why this shouldna be a pleasant experience for all involved. Stealing or not."

"So said with a dag pointed at my heart."

"Precautions must be made. Ye canna imagine the skelloch some raise when asked to hand o'er their coin purse."

"Ye and yer band of thieves are making quite the impression across my lands."

"My band? Nay, ye're mistaken, my lord. I work alone. More profit that way."

"I suppose the fiscal was distraught when he recounted being robbed by an entire troupe of hooded bandits. A pistol aimed at the heart will do that to a person."

The Fox's head tilted to the side. "Canna blame the auld toad. Must be a cut to his pride to have been waylaid by only the one. To survive a band sounds much more the menacin escape."

"I leave for a rebellion and return to find bairns thinking they ken how to play a man's game. Sorry, lad, but ye'll not be taking from me. Not this night and not any other. Nor from any of my people."

The Fox's small feet shifted on the windowsill with the balance of a cat. Naught but the whites of his eyes shone through the cloaking blackness. "Allow me to put yer mind at ease. I've no intention o takin from yer people, at least not the ones yer powerful hand seeks to protect. 'Tis the fattened ganders that should sleep with one eye open."

"Yer presence here tonight confirms I'm one of those corpulent geese."

"I come to bid ye welcome home, though it be under saddened conditions as the new laird. Yer father was always a kind and fair laird."

The simple words cut like a blade. Ever a gracious man who put his tenants and clan first, Father had never gotten over Deven's leaving to attend Oxford for law. One of their many contentions. "My father's ways are not mine. There is only the law of right and wrong. Anyone caught crossing the line will be handled with the swift arm of justice."

"Ne'er cared o'ermuch for lines. More fun dancin across them."

"Ye've been warned, Night Fox."

"As have ye, m'laird." The Fox pulled an object from the folds of his cloak and held it out for inspection. "Bonny bauble. Ye shouldna leave it layin about for anyone to pick up."

Candlelight winked off the ruby studs beveled into the silver disk. Father's brooch. The birthright of the laird. Deven shook with anger. "Ye'll be giving that back."

"I think not just the now, but I do look forward to our wee dance. Catch!" Pocketing the brooch, the Fox extracted another object and tossed it across the room.

Deven caught it. A bundle of green foxtails tied with a red ribbon. He looked up. The window was empty. Throwing the bundle to the floor, he raced to the window and scanned the ground and trees. Laughter floated above him. There, dangling from a rope tossed over the roof was the Night Fox.

"Laugh while ye can, lad, for I have caught yer scent. The hunt is on."

Hoisting himself onto the roof, the Night Fox laughed again. "I do hope so, for I've no doubt ye'll be a worthy adversary!"

Deven slammed the window shut and bolted it tight. Let that scoundrel go. Let him flee into the night with the carefree wind at his back for tomorrow the chase began.

Chapter 2

IT WAS THE MOST exquisite thing Rooney had ever taken. A silver brooch with deep ruby stones curving around it like studs on a warrior's shield. With the amount she could get for it, this piece could be the final answer to her family's prayers. Never again would she have to steal.

On the other hand, she'd miss the chance to spar with Deven McLendon.

Last evening's grab was meant to be a quick in and out, but he'd made things rather difficult. Challenging her without fear. Most of her victims didn't know how to find their mouth without a fork to guide them much less pull a blade on her. She couldn't leave the brave man standing there in an attempt of defending his property without giving him a proper foe.

If he wanted to hunt the Fox, then a chase she would give him.

Flipping the piece over, she traced a nail over the Gaelic inscription. *Valor of my ancestors.* A beautiful sentiment.

Bang. Thump.

"Nay!"

Rooney sighed. Never a moment's peace. Stuffing the brooch into the small box of other confiscated treasures, she slid it behind the splintered wardrobe. She swiped the dust from her skirt and flung open the curtain separating the sleeping quarters from the living area. "There better be a reason ye two are waging a kerfuffle instead of filling the baskets as I told ye to."

Ruby, her twelve-year-old sister, pointed an accusing finger at their youngest sibling. "She's skipping around with the rope, and when my back is turned, knots it around me as if I'm some common cow."

An impish light glowed in eight-year-old Rose's eyes. "Not some common cow. A braw hairy coo. Moo!" Rose made horns with her fingers and wiggled them at her sister.

Red surged across Ruby's face, highlighting the freckles on her cheeks. Raising her tome of poetry, Ruby chased Rose around the tiny set of table and chairs.

Rooney grabbed them by the arms on their third pass and held them apart. "Enough of that. If anything, we're all to be red-pelted deer." She tugged a lock of russet hair on each of them, identical to her own. "Get the baskets ready before the buying hour is past. Hurry."

Stuffing baskets full of their woven wares, they made their way to Druimbeath's market square where the other villagers plied their goods. Passing a stall of beets, Rooney took her customary place just opposite of the blacksmith shop. The place of lowest prominence.

Rooney smiled at the woman selling beets. "Good morn, Mistress Kerry. Yer beets look particularly fine this day."

Mistress Kerry flipped her pug nose up with an indelicate sniff. "As if ye ken anythin aboot 'em." She rotated her broad backside to Rooney and smiled sweetly at a potential customer.

Had the rude woman forgotten so quickly that her prize beets once adorned the Corsen's table? Of course she had, as did all of Druimbeath when Rooney's father fell from grace at the gambling tables, forcing her family to sell everything and move from their home to a tiny cottage on the edge of the clan lands. Social outcasts.

Labeled an outcast was not any easy burden to bear, but it was not as terrible as watching her sisters live hand to mouth on the meager earnings they received from weaving heather rope and rushes to be trod upon by the wealthy. But not for much longer. A few more heists with the added weight of that brooch would set them safe once more. She could pay off the remaining debt and have their home back.

Snapping out a wool blanket, Rooney arranged their goods in an enticing arrangement then greeted a passerby. "Good morn, sir. Are ye in need of a sturdy rope? Made from the finest heather in the Highlands. No? Rushes for yer floors then. Their sweet smell drifts up with every step ye take. No more dirty floors to tread on after a long day. Well, good day to ye. Ah, good lady! Would ye care—no? Thank ye."

The villagers walked by in a wide berth without so much as a glance.

"Try lying down in front of them next time. They canna ignore ye that way," Ruby said from behind her book.

"They'd take more pleasure in walking directly over me."

"Who would dare to walk over such a beautiful woman?" The distinguished voice crawled over Rooney's skin. Dressed in the finely spun silk and wool of his beloved English court, Sir Leslie Milford was a peacock preening among the grouse.

Rooney dipped into a small curtsy as he stopped before her. "Sir Leslie."

He waved a slender hand as if to indicate that she may rise. Which she already had. "My dear Miss Corsen. How lovely you look from last we met. I trust things are … well?" He raised a brow at the coarse ropes.

Heat climbed Rooney's neck. She and her sisters had spent days twisting and braiding plants into submission. "Aye. We have plenty to keep our hands from idleness."

Taking her elbow, Sir Leslie led her away from the beet stall. Solemn concern darkened his muddy eyes. "You may tell me the truth, my dear." He lightly squeezed her elbow. "You are not accustomed to a life of pulling weeds on the moor or living in a dirty hut with naught but a smoky peat fire to keep you warm at night. You were born to be lady of a manor."

A manor. *Her* manor, but Father had bet their estate's deed of sasine in a desperate gambling match. Sir Leslie had won, and the title and property now belonged to him.

Rooney took a step back, dislodging her elbow. "The only manor I wish to be lady of is my family's home. I nearly have enough to repay my debt to ye."

"Nearly enough? I did not realize ropes and brooms claimed such profit." He snatched her hand and clasped it between his. "It pained me to watch your father's gambling sink him into debt. Only out of concern for you, your mother, and your sisters did I extend credit to him. Not even his gambling away the manor could repay what he owed me. A debt, I'm afraid, that fell to you. If I had known the disastrous path all of this would lead to … well, what's done is done though you must understand the delicate situation it puts me in. Asking a woman to repay her father's debts is terribly uncouth, but I look forward to the day it's behind us. Then you and your sisters may reside once more in your family home. With rent, of course."

Rooney had wanted to buy back the deed to her family estate, but Sir Leslie had laughed, claiming it was beyond a woman's limits to preside over property and she was better suited to merely renting the house from him. Thankfully, he required only the amount she sold her goods for at market. She loathed the idea of being a tenant in her own home, but a deal with the devil was worth the risk to keep her sisters from poverty. "I thank ye again for agreeing to an otherwise impossible arrangement."

"It needn't be so impossible. My other offer still stands."

Disgust dropped into Rooney's stomach.

Marriage. One of the few exchanges of payment offered to women. At least the more respectable of payments. She yanked her hand free. "As I said, all debts will be paid in full at the earliest convenience."

The concern dropped from Sir Leslie's eyes. Running a hand over his sleekly wigged head, he gave a short bow. "Then I shall look forward to our future transactions. Good day, my dear."

He disappeared into the market crowd. The air eased back into Rooney's lungs.

"Why doesna he return to England where he belongs and leave us alone?" Ruby peeked over her book.

"Because the king granted the loyal Milfords land here in an attempt to tame the natives generations ago. As if a *Sassenach* stood a chance of succeeding."

"If ye marry him, I'll run away into the woods and never come back."

Rooney wiped her hand against her scratchy skirt, but Sir Leslie's touch clung like a rotting disease. "I'll join ye."

"Rooney!" Rose crashed through the throng and landed on the blanket, overturning the baskets. Her braid had come undone, and springs of red hair stuck out every which way.

"Watch where ye're going. We've only the one—"

"They want us gone!"

"Who?" Rooney stuffed the spilled ropes into a basket.

Eyes wide, Rose pointed over her shoulder. "The village."

Rooney's heart leaped in her throat as a mob descended on them.

"The shame to show their faces."

"Thinkin they can mingle with respectable folks."

"Taintin our village with immorality."

Herding her sisters behind her, Rooney tried to appear serene despite the thudding of her heart. "Might there be a problem?"

A woman with frizzy brown hair and severe crow's feet pushed her way to the front of the mob and pointed a gnarled finger in Rooney's face. "Aye, 'tis ye. Makin a mockery o us. Standin here and takin good folks' money."

"We've the right to sell our wares at market same as everyone else."

"Takin coin to gamble with." The woman looked over her shoulder, prodding agreement from her fellow accomplices. She sneered at Rooney. "Black-hearted wagerin be in yer bad blood. Away with ye afore ye taint the rest o us."

Rooney gritted her teeth against the unsavory retort burning on her tongue. "My father's sins are not that of me and my sisters. We desire only to live in peace and to put food on our humble table."

The crowd jeered. They surged forward, kicking her baskets over and stomping on the brooms. Bristles splintered and ropes unraveled. Standing far back from the crowd was Sir Leslie with a smirk tilting his thin lips. Fury tumbled through Rooney, curling her hands to fists that could only feel blessed relief by punching him in his aristocratic nose. Foul man.

Rose and Ruby whimpered as they huddled together. Tears streamed down their faces.

"Girls, move away." Rooney lunged for a torn rope. "Stop! Please." Hands shoved her backward. She hit the ground. Pain shot up her tailbone.

"Miss, are ye all right?" A tall figure blocked out the weak sun. Arm around her waist, he took her hand and pulled Rooney to her feet. "Are ye hurt?"

The air stuck in Rooney's throat.

Deven McLendon. Coming to her defense.

Rooney shook her head as she gazed up at him. "Only my pride." Her gaze fell to the crushed baskets. "And my things."

He released her and rounded on the crowd. "What is the meaning of this?" His voice rocked over the market square, stilling everything in its authoritative path. "Have ye no shame for attacking lassies?"

"'Tis Lord Glèidh." The acknowledgement rumbled through the crowd, and they backed away, giving wide berth to Rooney and her weeping sisters. McLendon stood in the center of the wreckage with legs braced far apart and staring down each villager with the ferocity of a hawk.

At last, he pivoted to Rooney. The gray eyes pierced her like the edge of a sword. "Why was this done?"

Rooney slipped her arms around her sisters and bent to check them over. No injuries, praise be, but the day would linger in their fears for a time to come. She looked up at McLendon. "My sisters and I come weekly to sell our things. We never seek to cause trouble."

The frizzy-haired woman scowled at her. "Seek it or not, ye bring it with ye." Glancing at the laird, her face melted to contrition. "We're no but simple, good folk here, m'laird. Ye ken us all yer life, but immorality snaps at the lassies' heels, and we dinna care to have it."

Rooney returned the harpy's scowl. "Our father's doings were not ours. Or mayhap ye care to have yer ancestors' wrongdoings heaped upon yer head for judgment."

"At least I dinna have the likes o Richard Corsen in my blood."

"Aye, ye've only hooked-nose old sheep."

The woman jumped at Rooney with hand raised. McLendon stepped between them, the wide expanse of his chest a cordoning wall. "Enough. If no laws have been broken and every transaction remains respectable, anyone is free to trade here. Good day to ye all." The crowd grumbled with indecision. He skewered them with another look of steel. "I said good day."

The mob drifted back to their own stalls, the frizzy woman grumbling over her shoulder. Sir Leslie had disappeared.

McLendon's rigid stance didn't ease. "What is this they accuse ye of?"

"My father's gambling debts. It ruined my family." Rooney knelt and gathered the fragmented remains of their wares into a basket. Another day without a coin. Sleep would evade her this night as she stayed awake to make new ropes.

McLendon squatted beside her and scooped the silver birch broom handles into a pile. "Corsen. I've heard the name."

Rooney's fingers fumbled. She'd been more than careful to keep hidden the Night Fox's true identity. Billowy black clothes to disguise more than her figure, flipping about like a boneless fish so her gait would not be recognized, even changing her speech. One slip could give her away. Secrecy was absolute to survival, not only for her but for her sisters.

She chanced a glance at the man beside her, his hair darker than revealed in last evening's candle glow. Black as a starless night, it waved away from his face tied back with a black ribbon. His nose was long with a slight dent at the bridge as if it had been broken. A shadow of beard dusted his jaw though it was clear he'd shaved recently. Perhaps it was the thrill of adventure speaking, but she preferred the growth of dark whiskers he'd sported last night.

"Mayhap ye've heard my name because scandal travels faster than goodwill," she said at last.

"So it does, but I have heard it. A time before I left."

"Ye left a long time ago. I was but a girl when ye shook off the dust of Scotland to enter Oxford. My father was the neighboring laird then."

"Was."

The word was a single arrow shot straight to her heart. Its poisoned tip seeped deep into wounds that refused to heal. Gathering her basket, Rooney stood. "He died seven years ago." From shame. Her mother followed a year later from a broken heart, leaving Rooney as sole caregiver to Ruby and Rose, wee bairns then.

McLendon stood. His black eyebrows drew together over smoky gray eyes. "I'm sorry for yer hardships, Miss Corsen, and sincerely hope ye're not placed in a situation such as this again." He swept his hand over the jumble of broken heather bits. "Ignorance of the law will not be tolerated. Nor will those who openly taunt justice."

Mere hours ago, she'd teased him about dancing across such lines. His countenance was much more serious in broad daylight. And handsome. "Do ye know of any such taunters, sir?"

"I hunt a criminal calling himself the Night Fox."

"The Night Fox." Rooney strung the words out as if uncertain. "Does he reive chickens?"

McLendon's eyes hardened to steel once more as he drew up to his full height. Rooney had to crane her neck to meet his gaze. "A blackguard highwayman that swoops into carriages and windows to steal items of considerable worth."

"Carriages and glass windows. Not likely I'll cross his path when he seeks such wealthy accommodations."

"How do ye know they were glass?" That stare. It was as unrelenting as a tempered blade.

Rooney took a tiny step back, her pulse racing. "Oh, well … what else would they be? When ye're as poor as we are, we improvise with cracks in the wattle and daub." She offered a smile that dashed like rain on his thorny expression.

"Whatever his tastes, the fool's days are numbered. 'Tis my duty to protect my people. The criminal will be caught. May God have mercy on his soul." Deven held out the other basket. Rooney took it, brushing his fingers. They were large and calloused, no doubt strong enough to tie a noose around her neck if he ever caught her.

She tucked the basket to her chest. "Mayhap mercy is what's called for, to begin with."

"There can be no mercy for a lawbreaker. Our laws are clear. Without them, we have no order."

Crivens! Why did the attractiveness generously applied to his physical appearance not extend to his narrow manner of thinking? Never had she met a man so unbending. "Not every situation can be judged right or wrong."

"A man's actions show his true character."

"If there's one thing I've learned in this world, 'tis that things are not always as they seem. We need only to look past the surface to find the truth."

"And if there is anything I have learned, 'tis that human nature canna be suppressed."

"Ye have a rather bleak outlook on people."

"Nay, I simply do not fall for their façades. No matter how charming and well-meaning." Extracting a pocket watch from his simple yet well-made waistcoat, he frowned at the hour. "If ye'll excuse me, Miss Corsen. I have more inquires to see to."

"I wish ye luck on finding yer fox."

"Luck is not required. Merely patience." With a short bow, McLendon strode away, the crowds parting before him like the staff of Moses and the Red Sea.

Rooney grinned. The first steps of their dance were proving delightful, and a more remarkable partner she couldn't ask for. Now to see if he could reel.

Chapter 3

THE WOOD CRACKED UNDER the ax's blade. Two even halves tumbled to Deven's feet. His muscles ached in satisfaction. Months of leading charges with broadsword and shield, slogging from one muddy battlefield to the next, and hiding had left him bereft of an honest day's work. There was nothing pretentious about wood, no hidden agendas, no side to choose. It was simple and straightforward. Unlike people and their mysterious facets.

None more so than Rooney Corsen. Try as he might, Deven couldn't forget the image of her standing in the market square defiant to all of Druimbeath. Those old corbies descended on her as a feast for their vile craving of humiliation, uncaring if she was in the wrong or not. He couldn't allow the lass to suffer such treatment.

Wiping the sweat from his face, Deven gathered an armful of wood and marched into the kitchen.

His cook kneaded dough and eyed the wood in his arms. "Och, master. Ye dinna need to fash yerself with such work."

"Gets me outdoors instead of under yer foot." Deven unloaded his burden near the fireplace and dusted the splinters from his palms. "Smells good."

"Aye, venison stew for the midday. I've pheasant and roasted quail eggs for supper along with a thick puddin. Ye need fattenin after all that army marchin."

"I look forward to yer efforts."

Leaving the fragrant warmth of the kitchen, Deven made his way to the main part of the house. A quick change from his dirty clothes and then he'd settle in with the accounts. Rent day for the tenants was fast approaching. From the brief glance he'd given the ledger, Father had recorded more credit in the tallies than actual payment. It wasn't easy earning a farmer's wage, but Strathmoore couldn't exist on charity alone. If Deven didn't pay the estate's rent on time, their chieftain would turn the land over to someone who could. He would never allow such ruin to befall his people.

Feminine voices drifted down the corridor. Jean, his sister, and—nay. Anyone but her. Pumping with dread, Deven bounded for the stairs.

"Deven." Jean's voice cracked from the front room. "Is that ye, brother?"

Caught. Fixing on what he hoped was a polite smile, Deven smoothed the front of his filthy kilt and stepped into the front room. Light streamed through the large windows onto the blue furniture with its spindly chairs.

Jean perched on one of them. Across from her sat Helen Logan, the fiscal's daughter. Her eyes widened at the sight of him, and a small gasp escaped her thin lips. Her thick figure threatened to split the seams of the girlish pink gown that was cut too low for appropriate daywear.

"Deven, surely ye remember Helen?" Jean pinned him with a threatening stare of politeness. What did she think he was going to do? Snort and toss the baggage out? Unlikely. One erroneous move and that dress would spill secrets he'd rather not see.

Deven gave a short bow. "Miss Logan. It's been some time. How well ye look."

Helen tittered behind a pudgy hand. "Lord Glèidh. Always such a tease. Ye have not changed one bit except to say how well the mantle of laird suits ye. That is, God rest the soul of yer dear departed father." Her eyelashes fluttered down in a show of sympathy.

Deven gritted his teeth. "What might we owe the pleasure of yer visit?"

Dropping the sympathy, excitement blazed across her face. "To extend an invitation of dinner on Thursday next for our honorable hero."

"Hero is hardly the title to associate me with."

"Oh, but it is. Ye answered the call to defend our glorious land against the English invaders. Fighting alongside our rightful sovereign, King James."

Never mind she woefully neglected the fact that it was the Scots who did the invading. While winning at first, the Jacobites had returned home in mournful defeat. There had been nothing glorious about killing men simply because they stood opposite the field of your sword.

Deven clenched his hands behind his back. "The only heroes are the ones who fell in defense of their beliefs. 'Tis their memory and love for Scotland that I honor."

"Ever so modest." Helen simpered to Jean. "How do ye manage such a dashing brother?"

Jean stared at her brother with a deceptively smooth brow. "With great difficulty, I assure ye."

"Perhaps because a sister can only do so much when another woman's hand could gain more ground." Helen's gaze fluttered at Deven. With the aim of an expert archer, invisible shackles shot across the space, seeking to capture him.

The last thing Deven desired was a vacuous woman. He backed toward the door. "Extend my apologies to the fiscal, Miss Logan. I will be unable to attend next Thursday. Jean, of course, will more than make up for my boorish conversation with her lively chatter."

"Papa is most eager to speak with you." Helen's voice screeched with desperation. "So many thefts in the area. This Night Fox has us all in quite the tizzy."

The hairs sprang up on the back of Deven's neck, halting him in retreat. "The Night Fox."

"Yes, Papa may have new information on the scoundrel."

"*May*?"

Helen flushed. "I mean, he does. He wishes to discuss a plan with you." Whipping a hankie from her exposed bosom, she threaded it between her fat fingers. Particularly around the fourth finger of her left hand. "Only last night Sir Leslie was robbed. Again. He found a bundle of foxtails resting on his pillow. Can ye imagine the indecency? We're not safe in our own beds."

Deven clamped his arms across his chest to keep from reaching to his shoulder where the laird's brooch should have been pinned. His stolen heirloom. After everything he'd gone through to get it back after his father's foolishness only to find himself at the receiving end of another trickster's hand was a wound of the deepest kind to his pride.

The sooner the Night Fox was caught, the sooner integrity could be upheld.

"I accept yer father's invitation to discuss the matter." Deven moved to the door. "I'm off to speak with Sir Leslie. Dinna hold supper for me, Jean."

An hour later, Deven sat in Sir Leslie's study surrounded by suffocating luxury.

"More tea?" Sir Leslie gestured to the teapot sitting on the low table between them.

Deven glanced at the untouched brew filling the delicate cup next to him. Might as well drink loch water strained through bark. "Thank ye, nay." Restless, he stood and walked to a large diamond pendant on display under glass. It was exquisitely cut with hundreds of facets shimmering over its pale surface. A small notch was cut at the top as if it once held a chain. An unusual treasure to find in the remote Highlands. "What was taken?"

"My serving spoons. Gifted to my grandfather upon his knighthood by the Lord High Chancellor himself." Sir Leslie smoothed his satin cuff.

"Did he leave any clues?"

"I should say not. The Chancellor has been dead close to twenty years."

"The Night Fox."

"Oh, yes. A bundle of those prickly weeds, but I tossed it in the fire. A ghastly reminder of such impertinence."

And quite possibly their only evidence. "May I look around?"

"Of course." Sir Leslie guided him to a formal chamber on the second floor that boasted more lavish taste than the rooms below.

Deven strolled around, examining each wealthy item on display, the precise folding of the blanket across the bed, the silver candlesticks with beeswax candles—no cheap tallow here—and engraved plates of honor from the court of King George. No denying where the man's loyalties lie. Nor that a quarter of the wealth could feed the man's hungry tenants for a year. Deven had passed more than one gaunt face on his ride across Sir Leslie's land.

"Why were the serving spoons kept here and not in the kitchen?"

Sir Leslie scoffed. "A precious token should never be used in service by common hands. I keep them safe unless I am entertaining a distinguished guest who deserves the best I can offer."

Deven recalled no silver serving upon his arrival. Then again, if he had to wear a powdery wig and swear loyalty to a throne usurper to claim such an honor, then he preferred to eat with a wooden spoon. Crossing to the window, he threw up the sash and stuck his head out. No nearby trees. Most likely the Fox used a rope from the roof as he had done with Deven's chamber.

"Where did ye keep the spoons?"

"In a chest in my second wardrobe." Sir Leslie pointed to the upright armoire. "Difficult to display."

"Despite being yer prized possession."

Sir Leslie straightened. His angular shoulders creaked under the tight satin jacket. "No, that honor belongs to the diamond pendant that once belonged to Queen Elizabeth. You seemed quite intrigued with it in my study."

"Yer family receives impressive gifts."

"Rewards for generations of loyal service."

Scanning the room, an intangible itch crawled up Deven's neck. Each item sat in a place of prominence within easy reach. Anyone entering would immediately see the objects, their worth evident even to the untrained eye. Why go through the trouble of unlocking a wardrobe to steal a set of spoons when the grandest prize of all sat untouched downstairs?

A servant girl appeared at the door. "Excuse me, sir. There's a lady at the door."

Sir Leslie waved a distracted hand. "Instruct her to come back."

"Nay, sir. 'Tisn't—it be Miss Corsen."

Sir Leslie's eyebrows jutted up. "Show her to the sitting room. Bring a fresh pot of tea." Anticipation glittered in his eyes. "Is there anything else I can show you, Lord Glèidh? I hate to keep you from other appointments."

Deven's stomach twisted unexpectedly. What business was it of his if Rooney Corsen came to call on this milksop? Their estates had been adjacent for years though Sir Leslie owned them both now. No other reason to prolong his visit, Deven shook his head. "The Night Fox is canny. Leaving no clues save foxtails, and those can be traced to any field in Scotland. He'll make a mistake soon enough. All criminals do."

"A downfall to a swift hanging, I hope." Sir Leslie ushered him downstairs. "I wish you the best of luck in catching the scoundrel. Now, if you'll excuse me, I have business to—ah! Miss Corsen. A pleasure as always, my dear."

My dear. Sourness curled in Deven's stomach.

The lady herself stepped into the hall, a flame of light striking against the dark paneled walls. Her eyes widened at Deven. "My lord. Ye certainly are making swift rounds after yer arrival home."

Deven bowed slightly. "I was just leaving."

"Yes, he was." Sir Leslie sidestepped him and placed a hand under Rooney's elbow in an effort to guide her back to the sitting room. "I shall alert you if anything else has been taken."

"Aye, and in the meantime, ye might wish to lock away yer valuables.

Though that doesna seem to deter our fox."

Rooney pulled out of Sir Leslie's grasp and clutched her basket close. "The Night Fox has been here?"

The skin around Sir Leslie's thin mouth pinched white. "He has, but Lord Glèidh is close on his tracks. Don't let us keep you from your task, my lord. Miss Corsen and I have much to discuss."

Rooney ignored him as fascination danced in her unusually-colored eyes. "If ye're as close as ye claim, ye must have an idea of who he is."

"I have more understanding of who he is not, and that can prove a great deal more useful," Deven said.

"Can it?" Smiling, Rooney took a small bag from her basket and thrust it at Sir Leslie. "I believe ye'll find everything in order as agreed upon for the month."

Sir Leslie weighed the bag in his palm. "Surely you wish to come into the sitting room where we may discuss it. I ordered us tea and biscuits. Straight from London."

"I'm afraid I dinna have time for frivolities today. Ruby and Rose expect me back soon." Tucking her basket against her hip, Rooney let herself out the front door. "Good day, gentlemen."

"That girl …" Sir Leslie's knuckles whitened around the bag. Glancing at Deven, he eased a smile across his mouth. "You may join me for biscuits if you care."

"Thank ye, nay." Deven stepped outside of the grand manor and gathered the reins of his horse from the stable boy. He swung into the saddle and looked down at Sir Leslie standing shadowed in his doorway. "Send for me at once if the Fox returns."

Deven spurred his mount to a trot. The descending sun rested above the treetops, burnishing their leaves to gold and orange and sprawling shadows across the road. He breathed in the clean air. A stark contrast to the stuffy powder of Sir Leslie's. A rich man, could he not afford windows that opened to allow in a fresh breeze?

Rounding a bend, a flash of color brightened the dirt road. Rooney. Or more accurately, Rooney's red hair. She smiled at his approach. "Did ye not care to stay for tea and biscuits?"

Deven dismounted. "I dinna mix business with pleasure. Sir Leslie—"

"Is hardly pleasurable. Ye needn't tell me." A thin line puckered between her eyebrows for a brief moment. Shaking herself, she continued walking. "What did ye discover about the Night Fox? Or should I ask what did ye *not* discover as ye claim that provides more insight?"

Deven fell into step beside her as he led his horse along. "That he has excellent taste if not a wee bit unorthodox."

"Perhaps he's selective."

"Or he's sending a message."

"That sounds rather attentive for a common thief. One would think him to take the most valuable objects he can find."

"Only if value is all he cares about. A message is personal. A statement made to the victim not necessarily about the object."

Rooney stumbled. Deven caught her arm. Her thick braid swung across his fingers, igniting a sudden desire to run his hand up her arm, over her shoulder, and into the thick curls of copper and russet. She was a temptation he did not need.

Releasing her, Deven took tight hold of the horse reins once more. "The Fox's reasons mean naught to me, only that he's breaking the law."

"He steals only from the rich. Surely there's a compelling reason for that."

"There's no reason to steal from the poor. They haven't anything to tempt him."

"Or because the rich are less likely to starve with a few coins gone."

"Why do ye defend him so?"

She toyed with the basket's handle. "Before committing this Fox to the pillory for his offenses—I agree that what he's doing is wrong—I think it important to look beyond the crimes before naming him a dredge beyond redemption."

Redemption. A much sought-after concept with so few achieving it. Deven had learned firsthand that criminals never changed. Certainly, they may put on the appearance of contrition as that con man had done when Deven finally tracked him down after ten years. The laird's brooch had been retrieved, but the criminal walked free that day.

Their ilk was too slippery for justice.

Lacking all honor, they slinked back to the depraved hole from which they'd crawled to await their next victim. Victims like his father who had always been too trusting, too eager to see the goodness in people at the expense of their blatant faults. Deven had spent half his life trying to right the mistakes.

"Will ye come to the field with me?"

Deven jerked out of his thoughts as amber eyes stared at him. "I beg yer pardon?"

"To pick heather. More pleasant to have company out on the moor."

He preferred the moor for its quiet solitude. He preferred even less leaving Rooney on her own with the Night Fox prowling. The wealthy set may have been his primary target, but there was no guarantee against a bonny lass ripe for the picking in a lone field. "Lead the way."

Rooney stepped off the road and disappeared into the woods, and he followed. The heavy scent of pine and wet earth lightened as the trees thinned and gave way to a moor that spread up to a crest of rolling green braes in the far distance.

A generous smile curved Rooney's full lips. "Bonny, is it not?"

"Aye." White and purple heather swayed over the ground in thick tufts of vibrant color with splotches of green grass weaving between. The sun's golden rays skipped off the tops as it sank closer and closer to the hills. "Strathmoore lies beyond the braes there, but never have I been here."

"My sisters and I call it the Bodach Glen. The myth of the scary auld man helps to keep unwanted guests out." Rooney dropped her voice. "In particular, Sir Leslie."

"I canna imagine Sir Leslie has much preoccupation for anything outdoors."

"Ye're right about that. 'Tis a shame for he owns a wee slice of heaven here. Though he'll not be happy until he has everything under his thumb."

"Why do ye say that?"

Her face clouded briefly. "'Tis true. Have ye a knife on ye?"

On alert, Deven's left hand dropped to his sword as he scanned the area for threat.

Laughing, Rooney laid a small hand on his. "Calm yerself, soldier. It's to help me cut heather, but it'll do us no good if ye undertake the plants all as foes. Perhaps ye can hold my basket instead."

Obliging, he took her basket as she knelt and pulled a wee *sgian dubh* from her boot. She sliced through the slim stalks with precision and tucked them in the basket.

"Do ye oft have business with Sir Leslie?"

The lines around her mouth tightened. "Once a month for rent and payment."

"Yer father was a laird. How came ye to be Sir Leslie's tenants?"

"My father gambled away our estate. Sir Leslie owns it now but offered us a small cottage to live in at the edge of his property for rent.

I'm saving every coin I can to repay our debts at which time Sir Leslie will allow us to return to our family home. To rent, of course."

"How generous of him."

"My sisters canna live in a mud cottage with mice skittering about for the rest of their lives and naught but a peat fire to keep their bones from quaking in the winter."

Her desperation touched his mercy, but it was her determination that earned his respect. "Then I pray yer debts are quickly paid."

"Thank ye." Her knife jerked through a thick stalk of heather, scattering tiny white petals across her skirt. "Thank goodness I dinna listen to my mam when she told me learning to make rope was an unladylike pursuit."

"Uncommon to find a lady with knowledge of such a thing."

"We're never too grand to learn new things. Our old parish priest came from a farming village in the Hebrides. He taught me the best fishing spots, how to tie a knot, and where to climb the highest tree to see the sun setting over Loch Garry."

"D'ye mean Father Lewis?"

"Aye."

"I didna realize he hailed from the Hebrides."

"Did ye ever ask him?"

"Well, nay."

"Mayhap next time ye should. Might be surprised what ye find." Tucking her wee blade in her boot, Rooney stood and dusted leaves from her hands. "There. That should be enough to keep me busy tonight."

"Why take only the white heather?"

"It brings good fortune as the fallen tears of a woman who lost her lover in battle. Though it brought her sorrow, she prayed it would bring goodness to others."

Deven shrugged. "Seems as good a reason as any."

"Och, nay. Instead of sinking into her grief, she used it as a blessing. There is nothing more beautiful than that."

"I agree 'tis a braw story."

"But ye dinna believe it."

Enchanting as she was telling her tale, Deven had no place for such lore to take root. "Anything to be gained in this world is done through honest, hard work. A discipline that must be fought for, not plucked on the wild moor."

"If ye do nothing but fight for discipline, ye'll miss the beauty of spontaneity." Reaching into her basket, she took out a single stalk of heather. The white flowers dangled like tiny bells from the end. She tucked it between the buttons of his waistcoat.

He touched the delicate blossoms as her spell threatened to weave over him. "Spontaneity does not agree with me."

A smile curved her lips. "A statement that doesna surprise me in the least."

Leaving the moor, they walked in silence until coming to a small cottage. The pungent scent of peat smoke rose from a hole in the thatched roof as flickering light slipped through the cracks of waddle and daub walls. A blanket hung in place of a door while a broken fence surrounded a sagging chicken coop. Anger flashed through Deven. The dwelling was common enough among Highlanders, but surely Sir Leslie could have given the lassies a more suitable place. Why had he not seen to the simple repairs?

Rooney picked at the basket's handle, averting her gaze from his. "Ye are welcome to come inside, but I'm afraid our hospitality offerings are lacking of late."

"I must decline for I need to return home, but I look forward to accepting yer invitation at another time."

Relief flitted across her face. Her eyes were not amber as he'd first thought. Here in the last light of day green, gold, and amber swirled together. The perfect complement to the freckles swathing her cheeks and nose. "Then I'll be saying good night to ye."

The parting filled him with regret like a light snuffed out before he was ready for the darkness. "Stay inside. No need to draw the Night Fox's attention."

"Something tells me with all the sneaking about of late, he may be in need of an evening's rest."

"As ye say." But Deven knew better. He waited until Rooney entered her home before mounting his horse, his hand never leaving his sword.

Chapter 4

A BEE BUZZED IN Rooney's ear. She swatted at it and shifted on the heather-stuffed mattress, her mind drifting back to sleep. A heathered moor. Deven McLendon walking with her in the gloaming.

The bee buzzed again. "Rooney."

Rooney buried her head under the pillow. "Go away."

"Wake up."

"Nay. Just went to sleep."

"There's a man outside."

Sir Leslie. He threatened to come by that day. Rooney groaned. "Tell him to go jump in the loch."

"Not that mozie auld poutworm." Rose flung herself on Rooney's back. "'Tis that man with the black hair. The one who brought ye home last night."

Rooney bolted upright, knocking Rose to the floor. Deven McLendon ... here?

Her little sister rolled around laughing. "Told ye that would get her up!"

"And I told ye to let her sleep." Ruby held up the curtain that separated their sleeping pallets from the main area. A stern frown crossed her face. "She was up till nearly cock crow finishing those ropes."

"About the same time he arrived."

Staggering to her feet, Rooney wiped the bleariness from her eyes and lurched to the window. McLendon stood with his back to her, a linen shirt stretched taut across his broad shoulders as he hammered nails into a flat board. Tools and long-split wood were laid out in neat piles on the ground. The chicken fence no longer sagged. In fact, it appeared to be new. Why was he repairing her things?

She flung aside the blanket serving as the door and took a step outside. Ruby yanked her back and blocked the entrance. "Ye canna go out there. Ye're not dressed."

Her sister was right. She couldn't very well confront the lord and master of the land wearing her nightrail. She slipped into her clothes with lightning speed, then marched outside. "May I ask what ye're doing here?"

McLendon didn't bother to turn around as he raised the hammer. *Whack. Whack.* "Making a door."

"We have a door."

"Ye have a blanket. I'd wager it doesna keep out the rain."

Rooney bristled. "It's served us well enough."

"Well enough when the snow comes?"

Braw or not, he had no right. *She* was taking care of her family. "I'll thank ye for yer concern, but—"

"Dinna step there!"

She teetered on one foot, the other mid-step.

"I've nails all about." He frowned at her bare feet. "Ye've not even the sense to put shoes on."

Rooney reared back. "And ye've not the sense to ask for permission before ye barge in and make repairs where ye think necessary. We've gotten along perfectly well on our own."

"I didna want to see ye cold when winter comes. 'Tis the responsibility of a laird to see his people cared for."

"But I'm not one of yer people."

"Nay, but I'll not ignore a problem that can be righted. Ye deserve such consideration whether ye're mine or not."

Her bluster evaporated on an extinguished puff of pride. No one had ever thought to provide for her like that, at least not without something in return. She met his eye squarely. "I'll repay yer services as soon as I've sold enough at market."

His unblinking silver gaze swept from her toes peeking out from under the homespun skirt to her head. Rooney self-consciously touched the wild hairs springing out in every direction. Why had she not bothered to comb it? Why did he suddenly make her think about such things? Too often she'd found pity or disgust in other's assessments. He had a way of looking without reproach. A way of making her feel worthy of his attention. It was an unusual sensation, but not altogether unpleasant. Aside from the twinge of guilt over stealing his brooch.

At last, he turned back to the door. "I dinna want payment, but I could use a hand." He glanced over his shoulder, a quick smile tugging his lips. "And shod feet."

"Oh." Cheeks flaming, Rooney dashed inside and tugged on her hose and shoes. She tied a kerchief over her hair, pinched her cheeks for a spot of color, and raced back out. Ruby and Rose stood on either side of McLendon.

"A door will be lovely." Ruby sighed.

"Look at the fence. We willna have to chase the chickens when they've gone too far in the woods again." Rose pranced around flapping her hands.

"This is no work for bairns. Back inside with ye." Rooney shooed them away. "Make a tray of bannocks, cream, eggs, and figs for Lord Glèidh. Skedaddle."

"Dinna say anything interesting until we get back," Rose called as the girls scurried away.

Rooney shook her head. No matter the circumstances, they were a bright spot amidst the world's gloom. "Apologies. My sisters have forgotten how to behave in front of guests."

"They came out earlier when I startled the chickens. I told them not to wake ye." McLendon bent over several of the shorter boards before selecting one. "Did ye finish the ropes?"

"I completed what I had, but several more will need to be made if I'm to turn a profit. The last batch of heather honey didna set right. Honestly, I think those bees despise me."

"Never have I tasted heather honey. Heather ale, aye. The brewmaster must've left clumps of dirt in it." He shuddered. "Hold the board there. Aye, keep it even."

Rooney held the cross board that lashed the planks together at the top as he hammered in nails. He'd rolled back his shirt sleeves to expose forearms covered in thick, dark hair. Corded muscles rippled beneath the tanned skin. No landowner she knew boasted such a physique with their rounded bellies and sallow complexions. McLendon had not an ounce of fat. Nor did he surround himself with pretensions. He was honest and straightforward. Traits she longed to find in a man, but a luxury she could no longer afford for herself. Soon she could put away the mask of the Night Fox. Until then, the weight of deception weighed on her. No more so than when she looked into his clear eyes.

Rooney cleared her throat as nonchalantly as possible. "Has the Night Fox dared to poke his nose into any new windows, or did he keep safely to his den last evening?"

"The people slept in peace. I'm grateful to report. If the Fox is wise, he'll remain in hiding for a time now that word has spread of my searching for him. If, however, he is as foolish as I think him to be, he'll not resist the thrill of the hunt."

"Mayhap 'tis not foolishness. The Fox is canny, aye? Who's to say he's not sporting with ye?"

"I'm betting on that."

Rooney's breath caught. "Does that mean ye have a plan to capture him?"

He looked at her, confidence in his eyes. "*Beag air beag.*"

Little by little. So he would like to think, but Rooney had promised him a chase, and a chase was precisely what Lord Deven McLendon would get.

"I'm carrying it." Ruby charged from the cottage with Rose clipping at her heels.

"Nay, me!"

"Ye'll drop it, and there willna be anything to eat. Bring the jug."

Rose raced around Ruby and plonked a stoneware jug in front of McLendon. "Drink up." She stuck her tongue out at Ruby who carefully placed her tray on the door that served as an impromptu table.

He raised the jug to his lips. Eyes widening, he sputtered and swallowed. He held the bottle away from him as if poisoned. "That's … I've never tasted anything of its kind."

Rose beamed. "*Sgathach.*"

Groaning inwardly, Rooney took the bottle and smelled the sweet pungency. "Thickened sour milk under cream that's been churned to froth. A common drink among the crofters to cool a parched throat." She offered him an apologetic smile as shame burned her inside. He would be accustomed to fine wine, not a poor man's swill. "Ye needn't drink it. Ruby will fetch fresh water from the creek."

McLendon grabbed the jug from Rooney and tipped it back. He took several deep swallows before coming up for air. His face only twitched once. "The crofters ken what they're about. Keeps the dust from collecting on yer tongue." Setting the bottle down, he looked over Ruby's tray. "Bannocks, fried herring, and what's this here? Crowdie. Haven't had that cheese since I was a lad." Taking a bannock, he scooped the soft white cheese and shoveled it into his mouth. And smiled.

The pent-up breath eased from Rooney's lungs. At least there was one thing they could offer that didn't taste vile.

"Ye're Ruby which makes ye Rose." He pointed to each sister then slid his gaze to Rooney. "Yer parents enjoyed the letter R, did they?"

"Aye, well, when ye're born the color of a red deer pelt 'tis best to make the most of it." Rooney tugged a spring of hair that had slipped from her kerchief's confines.

"A deer, no. More like red squirrels. Because they're so wee." Catching her loosened hair, he tugged it straight before realizing it, his fingers brushing the bottom of her ear. Delight fluttered in Rooney's stomach, like butterflies stretching their wings for the first time. If she were to linger in this moment, would he wish to also?

Clip clop. Clip clop.

All cheerfulness scattered at the sight of Sir Leslie perched atop his dappled gray horse.

Squinting from under his fashionable hat, he trotted his horse forward. "My dear, I came to discuss unresolved matters from yesterday, but I see I've waited too long to call on you at a proper time. Your guest has me at a disadvantage."

Why did he insist on showing up where he was least wanted? And calling her that ridiculous name. As if she would ever consent to becoming his dear. "The rent was paid on time, and I saw no reason to prolong my visit. Surely ye have more important things than to tally accounts with tenants."

Sir Leslie flicked the lacy jabot tied about his scrawny neck and narrowed his stare on McLendon. "I might inquire the same for Lord Glèidh. Yet here I find you. You certainly are a man who gets about. The other day at market, yesterday at my home, and now here. Wherever shall I find you next? His majesty's court?"

"I doubt the palace doors are in need of repair, but the Misses Corsens' did. Were ye unaware they have nothing to keep the weather out?" McLendon picked up the hammer. "I ken ye've spent much time in England, but have ye no pride in keeping yer land from ruin?"

"I have numerous tenants, each with a list of complaints the length of my arm. My man has fallen behind in reaching them all. If I'd known the state of affairs, I would have sent him post haste."

Rooney held back a bark of laughter. There was no man as there was no list. The tenants had learned to do for themselves or go without. Sir Leslie never lifted a finger unless it was in his own interest. He was all too aware that the people living on his land had no place else to go and weren't about to complain for the dreary accommodations least they be turned out on their ears.

"Ye need not worry, sir. Lord Glèidh has things well in hand,"

Rooney said.

McLendon stepped forward, arms braced across his chest that finely put on display the wealth of muscle beneath his shirt. "Since yer man finds himself overworked, there are plenty of strong backs in the village in need of work."

"Yes, well. I trust my man and not unknown villagers." Sir Leslie sniffed. "I'm putting together a dinner party for the local gentry next week. Lords and ladies, a fellow baron or two, and a visiting acquaintance while the House of Lords is in recess. A proper covey of associates for you to mingle with as befitting your status, McLendon."

"My status is as servant to my people."

"Even so, surely you wish to visit with other land owners. After all, 'tis easy to succeed all together. Helping one another in common interests."

"I doubt my interests are the same as the other lords and lairds. Too many believe the crofters are there to serve their laird's whims when 'tis we who serve them."

"The Night Fox is of interest to us all. His capture is a task that should be left to local authorities and the Kiliwhimin garrison soldiers."

McLendon shook his head. "The Fox trespasses on my land. I willna leave such an interference in the hands of others. 'Tis my duty as laird to protect my people."

If he didn't speak of her as a common miscreant, Rooney could almost admire his tenacity. It was an odd sensation, and one she wasn't quite ready to sort out. Finding safety with McLendon on watch yet prickled with dread knowing it was she he hunted.

"You are hardly the only laird dealing with this nuisance," Sir Leslie said. "Lord Dalryple informs me that the Fox's reach extends past Lochaber and Inverness-shire to Argyllshire and Perthshire. A few believe reports that he's gone as far as Edinburgh."

Rooney snorted, quickly covering it with a cough. Argyllshire? She'd never stepped foot off of Logan clan lands much less trekked all the way to Auld Reekie. If she wasn't careful, her reputation could leak to London. The Hanovarian Elector George would be quivering in his kingly bed. Because of her! What a wee coupe that would be to steal the crown jewels.

"My, my. He must sprout wings to cover such ground." Rooney held back a laugh. "Not one of us can hope for escape."

"Precisely what Helen Logan was saying when she informed me

that Lord Glèidh has accepted an invitation to dine with her tomorrow evening. I felt it only right to have her and the fiscal to my dinner party. She'll make an excellent dinner companion for you, McLendon. Among other things." Sir Leslie's lips tilted with meaning before he looked at Rooney. "My dear, I would be the happiest of men if you would sit as my companion."

An immediate and resounding *no* leapt to Rooney's lips. Not only would she be forced to suffer Sir Leslie's presence, but all the other preening peacocks as well. She being no more than a bland field mouse amidst all their gowned finery. And jewels. That crowd never left home without a diamond or two strung about their fleshy necks. One priceless necklace would fill the pantry for years to come. Her sisters would never go without again. She bit back the *no*.

"I accept," Rooney said.

"I know you don't think—I beg your pardon?" Sir Leslie stared at her as if she'd spoken from another head.

"I should be delighted to join yer party."

Blinking several times as if to understand her meaning, a smile slicked across his face. "Wonderful."

"Can we go?" Rose clasped her hands under her chin. "Please, oh, please! I've always wanted to sit at a long table with lots of food. Will ye serve swan?"

Ruby smacked her on the back of the head. "Swans are difficult to come by this far north. If ye read more, ye'd know that."

"I dinna need yer musty books." Rose pinched Ruby's arm, eliciting a howl of pain.

Rooney should've sent them inside, but there was a chance the squabbling would frighten Sir Leslie away. "Girls. Wheesht yerselves."

Sir Leslie's lip curled in disdain. "There isn't room for children, I'm afraid. Perhaps another time."

Rose's eyes widened in eagerness. "Next month then?"

His mouth opened and closed like a trout on the line, desperate to free himself from the hook.

"I accept yer invitation as well," McLendon said.

Sir Leslie sighed in relief as he slipped from Rose's expertly cast hook. "Then I shall send round the formal letter soon. Rooney, dear, my man will come by tomorrow to inspect for other problems in need of repair." Touching a boney finger to his plumed hat, he spurred his horse away.

Shaking off his departing presence, Rooney stared at the cottage. The sagging angles, the wall cracks, the warped timber. "Do ye think we can finish today?" She looked at McLendon. "If we dinna, some poor man will be forced to come here and serve as Sir Leslie's spy."

"A fate I would wish on no man." He held up his hammer. "Ye get the nails, and I'll hammer."

A few more hours spent with Lord Deven McLendon. Rooney couldn't stop her smile as she retrieved the bag of nails from the grass and plopped them atop the door. She handed him one. "Helen Logan, eh?"

Whack. His gaze shifted to her then back to the nail. *Whack.* "She talks too much."

"Apparently about ye."

He grunted. *Whack.*

Jealousy flashed through Rooney. She tamped it down. Or tried to. "Sure'n she'll make a lovely dinner companion."

"As lovely as Sir Leslie."

Rooney rolled her eyes. "They should pair up."

A muscle ticked along his jaw. "Then why did ye accept his invitation?"

"Why did ye?"

"I think it best to discover what these lords and ladies have to offer."

Images of sparkling rubies and glittering emeralds flashed before Rooney's eyes. "Oddly enough, that's my reason too."

Chapter 5

He needed air. Deven pushed into the corner of the carriage, but Helen and her perfume followed him.

"Have ye ever tasted anything as succulent as those pigeon pies at dinner?" She pressed against him. "Or the candied pears?"

Deven pulled his arm across his lap before it was swallowed by the folds of ample hip and bosom. "It was unnecessary to prepare so much food for me when I came only on yer father's invitation to discuss the Night Fox." Yet not one word had been spoken on the subject the entire evening.

"I shall tell Father to put together more evenings like this. Good food and excellent company. I can only hope Sir Leslie's upcoming party is just as stimulating." Helen tittered and ran a jeweled finger down his arm. "All those months at war have left ye too thin. No woman around to ensure ye receive a proper meal."

Deven turned his face to the window for a gulp of fresh air. Why were women always concerned with stuffing his wame? And why did the carriage crawl along at a snail's pace? "Yer father should not have summoned a carriage to bring me."

"Nonsense. A laird must ride in the manner befitting his status."

"Status is for those with a desperate need to prove something. Quite often a deficiency in themselves."

"I hope ye do not find deficiencies within me."

"Yer qualities will make for an excellent lady of the manor someday, however—"

The carriage swerved and jerked to a stop, flinging Helen across the seat. She sprawled half on top of Deven. Horses whinnied.

Deven shoved Helen upright and reached for the pistol in his belt. "Stay here."

"No! Wait." Helen grabbed his arm, locking herself around it.

The carriage jostled, and a second later the door cracked open to reveal the driver's face. "The doubletree cracked, and the horses canna pull any further. I'll have to double back to the house and fetch a new one, Miss Logan."

"Oh, dear. How terrible." Helen laid a hand to her flushed cheek. "I suppose Lord Glèidh will have to wait until ye return. I'm certain Father will understand the urgency of our unchaperoned state. Hurry along, Carter."

Deven wriggled out of her grasp and moved to the door. "Mayhap there's a way to repair it."

"Nay!" Carter and Helen screeched at the same time.

"Nay, my lord." Carter's gaze darted to Helen then back to Deven. "With all the rain of late, yer boots will be ruined in the muck. And 'tis too dark to see much. I know this carriage and its equipment better than anyone. Trust me when I say there's naught to be done." He slammed the door, his footsteps retreating.

Deven sat still long enough for Helen's skirt to brush his kilt. He sprang up. "I'll see to the horses. They needna be out there alone."

"But *I* needn't be in here alone." Helen's nails clawed into his arm. "The horses have each other for company. Besides, I'm frightened. The dark woods are most sinister."

"Aye, m'lord. Ye ne'er ken what may be lurkin in the shadows." The door on Helen's side cracked open, and the shiny muzzle of a pistol peeked in, followed by a hooded figure.

"Aieee!" Helen screamed.

"Wheesht yer kine there, or I'll be forced to silence her meself."

"Cease yer hysterics, woman." Deven unhooked Helen's fingers from his arm. "Night Fox, we meet again."

"Ye make it easy, m'lord. Leavin windows open has become a bad habit for ye, but a fortunate one for me."

"One I should like to correct immediately." Deven reached for his pistol.

"*Tsk, tsk*. None o that." Night Fox pointed the muzzle at Deven's hand. "Ye'll not be wantin me to make a mess in this bonny carriage, would ye? Not in front o the, ah … lady. Toss yer dag o'er here along with the dirk."

Deven calculated the odds. They weren't in his favor. He still had the *sgian dubh* hidden in his boot if need be. He slid the pistol and dirk across the floor.

Night Fox grabbed them and tossed them outside. "The wee blade in yer boot, if ye please."

How did the swine know where Deven kept his knife? Swallowing back a curse, he retrieved that one as well and flung it. It hit the doorframe an inch above Night Fox's hand. He grasped the quivering handle and jerked the embedded tip from the wood, tossing it outside with the others. "An impressive collection o' death for a dinner party."

"They're of more use than jewels, so ye'll be disappointed to discover that I've no valuables on me tonight."

"Do ye not?" Night Fox tilted his head at Helen.

Helen screeched again. "What is it? Why is he looking at me? Make him stop! Oh, what do ye want?"

"'Tis ye m'lady. I had to see ye for myself after hearing ye've caught the attention o the most sought-after laird in the land." His hooded head moved as if examining her. "I should say ye dinna disappoint my curiosity."

Helen fumed. "How dare you!"

"I dare all I please which will serve ye well to remember. Yer hankie, if ye please."

"I do not please."

"Hand it here all the same."

Pulling a bit of square lace from her bosom, Helen tossed it at the Fox. The Fox caught it and sniffed. "Whew! Ye'd drown a coo in that amount o perfume. I'll have to scrub it clean afore I dare blow my nebbit." Holding it away from his nose, the Fox tucked the piece up his sleeve.

Deven seized the distraction and kicked. The Night Fox jerked his hand back and slammed the door on Deven's foot. Pain ricocheted up his leg, and he fell against the seat.

The window curtain brushed aside as the pistol muzzle slid in followed by the Fox's mask. "Why ever would ye do such a thing? I only came to pay a friendly call as ye're so oft wantin to do with the ladies."

"Next time, face me like a man."

Night Fox shook his head. "'Tis more fun this way."

Deven clenched his hands atop his knees. It wasn't the first time he'd had a musket ball trained on him, but never in front of a lady.

"Whatever does he mean by 'ladies'?" Indignation bypassed fear in Helen's tone.

"Dinna assume ye're alone in his attentions," Night Fox said. "I counted three lovely redheads last week."

Deven half rose off the seat as air hissed through his teeth. "Stay away from Rooney—Miss Corsen."

The Night Fox's head cocked to the side as he considered Deven for a long moment. The movement was unsettlingly familiar. At last, the Fox sighed loud enough to stir the strip of material about his mouth and nose. "I've no reason to proddle an honest lass. As I said afore, fatted calves be what I'm after."

Helen snorted. "Rooney Corsen. That disgraced laird's daughter?"

What did Helen understand of disgrace and the sting it left on a person's soul? "Miss Corsen canna help the failings of her father. 'Tis her upright character that should be judged without blemish."

"Well, well," said Night Fox. "Ye've an understandin for the unfortunates, m'lord. Seems we've more in common after all."

"Do not think to compare the two of us, Thief."

"I am merely a reflection o what is born in every man. Many keep it cleverly hidden, but 'tis there all the same. The spirit to do what is needed. Which reminds me, Miss Corsen's thatched roof has taken to leakin from all the rain o late. Seein as how ye havena been there in a while, I thought ye might wish to know. Now, with my curiosity satisfied, I'll be on my way. Miss Logan, ye've been more than I could ever hope for."

Darkness shrouded the Fox's features. Like a faceless ghost set to haunt him. "Running like a coward again. Enjoy the freedom while ye can."

"More threats. If I had a silver doit for every time ye handed me one o those, I'd be a verra rich man." The Night Fox laughed. "Mayhap next time when I havena the advantage on ye. Come to think on it, if I wait that long, I'll be a long time dead." Withdrawing his pistol, the curtain fell back in place. His voice drifted from the other side. "Oh, there's no crack in the doubletree. Yer driver is sittin just around the bend havin a wee smoke on his pipe. Good evenin to ye."

Chapter 6

WEAVING PAST ANOTHER INSISTENT server carrying a tray of wine glasses, Rooney sidled along the back wall to where a potted fern on a pedestal provided the perfect hiding spot from Sir Leslie's dinner guests. She discreetly tugged on her low-cut bodice that somehow made her feel more exposed than when taking a swim in the loch. Why had Mam bought a dress in dusty rose? Didn't she know pink and red hair mixed like vinegar and water?

For the hundredth time since arriving, she looked at the door. All guests accounted for save the one she wished to see. Where was Lord Glèidh? Deven? Her face warmed at thinking of him by his given name, as she had ever since that evening in the carriage.

Violin and harp music floated around the sitting room as small groups mingled. Men in their refined Lowland cuts of satin breeks and women in splashes of color with glittering jewels adorning their necks and hands. Enough baubles to feed the villagers for months ... years.

She patted her silk evening bag. It would have to be after dinner when the fatted calves were glutted with food and drink and merriment. Spilled wine on a lap could provide the distraction needed to slip off a bracelet or ring.

The ornate gold clock on the mantel showed eight forty-five. The invitation said dinner would be served promptly at nine. Why did rich people insist on eating so late? Was it a testament to their greatness to see how long their empty stomachs could withhold from food? Rooney's stomach growled. She'd hoped lacing herself into tight stays would stop the noise, but her stomach rumbled in fierce protest.

"Not hiding, are you, my flower?" Sir Leslie appeared at her side dressed in black velvet with a ruby boulder stickpin resting in the lacey froth of his jabot. He touched a tapered finger to her ruffled sleeve. "Like a rose in a garden of milkweed."

Rooney angled away. She'd kept her mother's dress as the only nice frock she had to wear, but after tonight she'd decide whether or not to burn it. "A bonny turnout ye have."

"Indeed, but only because I have the most extraordinary hostess."

She smiled but kept her thoughts to herself. Let him think what he would if it kept her family in his good graces.

"You may have shied from your duties to greet our guests, but why are you not mingling? It's bad manners to hide your delightful self away," Sir Leslie said.

It was also bad manners to force one's guests into uncomfortable situations. "I'm afraid my social skills have rusted from lack of use."

"Then we must sharpen them if you are to take your place once more. Sharpening comes with practice. Ah, here are Lord and Lady Branaugh." Sir Leslie gripped Rooney's elbow and pulled her away from the wall toward a middle-aged couple. "My lord and lady, allow me to present Miss Corsen."

The man's eyebrows furrowed together. "Corsen ... Corsen. Where have I heard that?" His wife whispered in his ear, and his eyebrows shot up. "Of course. That laird's daughter. How'd you do?"

Without waiting for a reply, they walked away.

Rooney edged back toward the plant. She was a fool to come here in the open. The promise of jewels had begged too much of her attention. Slipping into their carriages as the Night Fox after the party would have been a wiser move.

The door opened. Rooney's heart tripped as she stood on tiptoe to see who entered, but even in Mam's heeled shoes, she couldn't rise above the gaggle of women flocking to the newcomer.

"Late." Sir Leslie clipped beside her.

The crowd parted, and Rooney's breath caught as Deven stood in the doorway. He was magnificent in kilt, gray long coat, embroidered waistcoat, and plaid in the McLendon blue and green sashed across his chest and held at his shoulder with a silver brooch. His eyes cut through the crowd like a sword and stopped on her. With a tilt of his mouth, he approached.

"Sir Leslie. Miss Corsen." Stopping directly in front of her, he inclined his head in a courtly manner. A black wave of hair swung over his forehead. Straightening, he brushed it back. "How beautiful ye are this evening." His gaze never left her face.

She touched her neck to cover the tell-tale blotches of flustered red that would give away her excitement. "My Lord Glèidh. I was beginning to doubt yer arrival."

"With such company, never."

A ball of lace and butter yellow barreled through the crowd and catapulted itself at Deven. Helen Logan. "I thought ye would never come. How handsome ye look. Have ye received yer invitation to the chieftain's masked ball? I'm planning to go as a Norse queen." Straightening her curled wig, she clutched his arm and narrowed hawk eyes to Rooney. "I presume ye're Corsen. Oh, I apologize. That was yer father. *Miss* Corsen."

Rooney cracked a small smile. "Miss Logan."

"For now." She purred and stroked Deven's sleeve.

Deven pulled away and inched closer to Rooney.

Jutting out her lip, Helen latched on to Sir Leslie with a swish of her taffeta-swathed hips. They bent their heads close together and moved off, whispering furiously.

"I do hope I'll be invited to yer wedding," Rooney whispered. "Save a piece of the cake for me."

"I dinna care for cake," he grumbled.

"Everyone enjoys cake. Ye simply need to find yer flavor."

"What flavor might ye suggest? Something frothy and sweet or mayhap with a dash of spice?"

"A taste unexpected. With one bite ye'll not understand how ye've missed it yer entire life."

"What about me tells ye I fancy the unexpected?"

"Nothing, which is precisely why ye need it."

"Need and want are two verra different things."

"Not always." Rooney's gaze moved to the piece pinning his plaid. "A bonny brooch ye have there. Is it stag horns locking together?"

Lips flattening, he touched the silver circle at his shoulder. "Aye. Stags. My other is ...well, is unique."

His father's ruby brooch. Guilt gripped Rooney.

Double doors opened behind them to reveal the dining room glowing with candlelight and heralding the rich scent of awaiting food.

"Dinner is served," a servant announced.

"I hope 'tis not *sgathach*," Rooney whispered, recalling the soured milk drink.

The corners of Deven's eyes crinkled as he offered her his arm. "Shall we?"

Heart racing, Rooney placed her hand lightly atop his arm. For the first time all evening, she felt at ease.

"I'll take her from here, McLendon." Sir Leslie snatched Rooney's hand and clamped it on his own arm, locking it in place as he dragged her into the dining room.

Rooney glanced over her shoulder. Helen attached herself to Deven and gave Rooney a smirk of satisfaction. Resisting the urge to scowl, Rooney flashed Deven a smile he boldly returned. Sir Leslie escorted her past the customary hostess's chair at the far end and swept her to the left-hand side of the head of the table, imprisoning her at his side for the entire evening.

Jewels glittered the length of the table. *That* was why Rooney had come. Let Sir Leslie attempt to display her like a show horse, she would walk away with the grand prizes. Deven and Helen sat at the other end of the table. Not only would she walk away with the jewels, she'd be the only one to receive a smile from Deven. A reward if there ever was one.

By the end of dinner, Rooney was stuffed with more than she'd eaten in the past year while her ears gathered wool from the dull conversation. Politics, happenings at court, land agreements. How did they not fall asleep in their soup?

"Miss Corsen?"

All eyes fastened on her, especially Sir Leslie's. "Pardon?"

He smiled apologetically at his guests. "Forgive her. Miss Corsen is not accustomed to the delicious rumors of court life."

"Nothing from the last twenty years I'd wager." Helen dabbed the corners of her mouth with her linen napkin and swept her gaze over Rooney's dress. "The fashion for turned back skirts and wide, ruffled sleeves was best saved for our grandmothers, God rest them."

Snickering erupted down the table. Heat flushed Rooney's face. She ran a hand across her lap. Mama had always looked beautiful in this dress. "Fashion has never carried much weight with me. Not when there are so many other intelligent interests to pursue."

Helen's eyes glittered with ice. "A pearl choker or cascade of sapphires would set off yer hair to perfection. A distraction from the other ... ah, failings. But how dare I be so unfeeling? Of course, ye have no fine jewels to comfort yer appearance with. If my father were to gamble away our family finery, I should never be as brave as ye to show my face in public again."

Several seats down, Helen's father grunted as he licked his pudding spoon clean. "Nay fear, daughter. I would never be so careless to jeopardize our standing in the community. Ye and yer mother may hold yer heads up proudly."

Heads nodded in approval.

Deven's hand came down on the table, a solid thunk that garnered silence. "Miss Corsen has every right to hold her head proudly. Weaker constitutions may have crumbled, but never have I seen a stronger character as she works to care for her sisters."

Helen threaded a lace hankie through her fat fingers. It was identical to the one Rooney had swiped from her that night in the carriage nearly a week ago. "A lady should not have to work, but then, that doesna seem to concern ye. Does it, Miss Corsen?"

Rooney smiled past the humiliation choking off her air. "Not when it keeps me from growing thick around the middle and sagging about the jaw. Excuse me, Sir Leslie." Rooney pushed back her chair and rose.

Deven stood. The only one. "Miss Corsen—"

She walked from the room, keeping her chin tilted so the threatening tears didn't shame her further. Outside, she found sanctuary in a small sunken garden bordered by trailing ivy, out of season rose bushes, and ash trees. Perfect for climbing.

She sank onto a stone bench and blinked heavily against the cool evening air. Those people would not squeeze one tear from her. After watching her mother cry herself into an early grave, Rooney had vowed never to allow wretched people to twist her emotions. For years she had locked herself away from the shame that followed, but tonight the rusty key had cracked open a portal to the rawness still buried inside.

She took a deep breath. Slowly, her heart resumed its rhythmic pace. If she had any hope of achieving what she came here to do, she'd have to go back inside. A few tears in the eyes and she could beg a handkerchief from one of the men. Many a gold watch had winked from the insides of their jackets. A simple enough lift. As for the women—she refused to call them ladies—it would take more finagling. Nobles required stroked egos, and a sobbing, repentant heart in need of advice would prove irresistible to them. The thought sickened her. Groveling at their skirts as if she truly desired their grace. In front of Deven. Her stomach churned. There had to be another way.

Surging to her feet, she paced the grass. Spill wine on their dresses for distraction? No, it would draw too much attention. Help them on with their coats? No, that was a servant's task though it was clear they thought her low as one. A tour of the house? Aye, possibly. The tight staircases and halls were ideal for crowding close. The guests wouldn't give much thought to Rooney jostling among them.

A twinkle caught her eye. She moved to the glass window. Sir Leslie's prized diamond pendant which he claimed once adorned the white neck of Queen Elizabeth. Her buyer would sell his own mother to get his greedy hands on such a gem. It would be the finest she'd ever brought into his shop to exchange for silver and gold.

Sconces glowed on the walls, arching a halo over the pendant's case like a shrine. Thousands of facets twinkled at her like rainbow stars. How easy it would be to take. She traced the teardrop shape on the glass. No one inside could catch her. Except Deven. She pulled her hand back as the memory of his touch warmed through her fingers. She didn't want to lose that feeling nor did she want to evoke the absolute disappointment when he discovered her duplicity. If luck prevailed, her soul alone would carry the secret of the Night Fox to the grave.

"Beautiful, is it not?"

Rooney jumped, icicles slithering down her back. Sir Leslie stood next to her. Close, much too close. She tucked her arms against her sides. "I should be afraid to display it so without armed guards."

"No one would dare to lay a finger on it. The dogs would be loosed before the culprit reached the end of the drive."

Hounds must have been a recent acquisition for in all of Rooney's nightly escapades she'd never encountered such beasts on her trail. "I find it a testament to the Fox's canniness to slip by yer hounds time and time again."

Sir Leslie stiffened. "They have closed in on him on more than one occasion. When he came for my silver, one of the dogs caught his ankle as he made out of the window. I told McLendon that we are now looking for a thief with a possible hobble."

"Oh my." How many rumors were there swirling about her?

"My dear, let us not speak of dogs or foxes. Not when there are so many other appealing topics. Such as how enchanting my pendant would look on a chain about your slender throat, the diamond glistening just there in the shallow hollow of white skin." His eyes drifted to a spot barely above her cleavage. "The first of many jewels I will shower you with as Lady Milford."

Rooney stepped back, eager to put as much space between her and his loathsome presence as possible. "Hear me, Sir Leslie. My obligations are to my sisters and repaying the debt owed ye for our home."

"As my wife, your debt would be paid in full. Your sisters free to live there for all their years. Think of all we could be, Rooney. Think of all we could do." His last words rolled on a purr of lust. He snatched her hand and pressed it to his dry lips.

"Nay."

"Always saying one thing when I know you truly mean another."

"Do not delude yerself on that account."

His grasping arms came around her as his lips fell to her neck.

Rooney shoved against him. "I said nay."

Chapter 7

DEVEN STUCK HIS HEAD into the front sitting room. "Rooney?" No answer save the crackle of a well-tended fire in the marbled hearth. She'd looked beautiful standing in this room hours before surrounded by candlelight and soft music. Her fiery hair had caught each spark of light and spun it to copper.

That was before the insults and cutting looks. She had born them with pride and grace, but there was only so much assault one's armor could hold defense against. Why had he not shielded her better? Why had he allowed her to withstand the offense in the first place?

He snagged a servant passing in the hall. "Has Miss Corsen left for the evening?"

"Nay, my lord. Or if she has, she's left her cloak."

Deven stalked away and peered into more rooms, stopping last in Sir Leslie's study where that horrid pendant shone on its display. An altar for the greedy man to bow before. Shadows moved outside the window. Rooney? His heart skipped. And Sir Leslie. Standing too close. Cursing under his breath, Deven threw open the door and charged outside.

"I said nay."

Deven grabbed Sir Leslie by the collar and yanked him off of Rooney. *"Mac an muice!"*

Sir Leslie reeled, stumbled, and toppled to the grass. Disbelief slackened his sallow face. "McLendon? How dare you call me such a thing?"

"'Tis a name ye deserve with no morals. Attacking a lady in the middle of the night." Rage burned through Deven's curled fists.

Bright red splotches marred Rooney's pale cheeks. "It comes as no shock to me."

Sir Leslie scrambled to his feet, brushing off his coat. "Is it improper for a man to steal a moment with his intended?"

"Intended?" Rooney moved toward Sir Leslie with hand raised. "There is only one thing I intend to do."

Deven caught her hand as it swung through the air. "Dinna give him the privilege of yer touch again." He stared at Sir Leslie. "If ye ever lay a finger on her again, be assured that I'll use more than the flat of my hand on ye."

"This is none of your affair," Sir Leslie hissed.

"I'm making it my affair."

"'Tis perfectly acceptable for a gentleman to steal a few alone moments with the lady he is wooing."

"I came here to be alone," Rooney said through clenched teeth.

"Ah, yes. And so, we were alone. Very much so. Long enough for the guests inside to wonder at your absence without a chaperone. One might even suggest you lured me out here for that very purpose." His threat coiled in the air.

"If ye think to utter one word about my compromised reputation, I'll tell everyone how ye threw yerself on me while I screamed nay. Yer lords and ladies willna socialize themselves with a lecher."

"Do you really think they'd believe you over me?"

Deven stepped in front of Rooney, blocking her from the man's evil stare. "Nay, but ye'll look the fool when I say it never happened. I've been here the entire time. D'ye wish to find out what they'll think then?"

Sir Leslie's eyes narrowed. "It's a lie."

"Aye, but only one to cease yer mischief. The next time I'll use more forceful means to ensure yer silence. Back inside with ye."

Rooney sidestepped Deven, hands on her hips and glared at Sir Leslie. "Since ye find yerself in need of something to get handsy with, try the pearl hairpins ye keep locked in the wardrobe. Might be as close to a woman as any would allow ye."

Sir Leslie's eyebrows shot up. "How did you—" His lips pressed into a white line. "Very well. If that is how it is to be." He spun and stalked into the house.

Deven slowly uncurled his fists, willing the haze of red to recede from his vision. Once more in control, he looked at Rooney. "Are ye all right?"

Swiping the front of her skirt with an agitated huff, she raised one delicate eyebrow. "Did ye really call him a son of a pig?"

"I apologize. I shouldna have spoken so in front of ye."

"He deserves much worse."

"Mayhap he does, but to recall a more explicit name would require me to think on him. A task I'd rather avoid."

"Thank ye for coming to my aid." She smiled, and the righteous burn of anger in his chest diffused. How did such a small woman hold sway over his reactions? His reins had been tightly in control for most of his life, but she made him forget direction as he eagerly awaited her next move. A thrilling and terrifying adventure.

"I'm here should ye ever need me, Rooney."

Her smile faded as she knotted her fingers together. "My lord—"

"Deven."

"Deven, there's something ye should—" Wind ruffled through the trees, splaying chill bumps across her skin. She shivered and rubbed her hands over her bare arms.

"Ye're cold. Let's go inside."

"Nay, I'd rather not."

"Then I'll fetch yer cloak."

"I think I should like to go home. Nothing good can come from staying here."

"I'll take ye. Wait here." Slipping inside, Deven rounded up their cloaks and hurried back outside where Rooney had taken shelter under a drooping ash tree. He wrapped her cloak over her slender shoulders.

A silky curl brushed his knuckles as she looked at him. The hesitancy in her expression from moments before disappeared into a coy grin. "Did ye say good night to Miss Logan? She'll wonder where ye've gone."

"Would ye like me to usher ye inside to find out?"

"Nay." Rooney laughed and took his arm in the most natural way. One minute smiling, the next fearful, and the next teasing. Like masks she slipped on at appropriate intervals. Who was she truly beneath all of it? And why was he impatient to tear through them all to discover it for himself?

Rounding to the front of the house, Deven requested his horse which was brought from the stables in a matter of minutes. Without waiting for permission, he fitted his hands about Rooney's waist and lifted her into the saddle. He swung up behind her and tapped his heels against the horse's flanks. Rooney's shoulder snuggled against his chest, her hair caressing his jaw. It took every ounce of willpower to not bury his face in its fragrant softness.

She tugged at the edges of her cloak.

"Still cold?" Deven's own skin and bared knees were impervious to the weather, no matter the season. Scottish stubbornness, his father had called it. Highlanders were born with it, and if they weren't, they perished soon enough as a matter of survival.

"Velvet is well enough to look at, but it doesna stave off the wind."

With a quick flick of his fingers, Deven undid the brooch at his shoulder. He pulled his plaid around him and Rooney, cocooning them in its woolen folds. Rooney stiffened, but as their warmth built, she settled against him. He took a shaky breath, certain she could feel his heart pounding at the nearness and her sweet scent filling the air.

All too soon they arrived at her cottage. She didn't move. Neither did he.

"He'll be angry." Rooney's fingers twisted the edges of his plaid.

Deven stiffened, all musings of calming warmth gone. "If he comes to ye again, send for me at once."

"That's not what I'm afraid of." She shuddered as she looked at the small cottage. Yellow light slipped through the crack at the bottom of the door. "He'll come for this next. That's what he does. He brings people to the end of their rope before lopping it off. Falling into the abyss of despair and ruin, the person will stretch out their hand and grasp Sir Leslie's offer of help. Too late do they realize they've grasped a snake."

He tightened his arms about her. "Ye needna fear such a thing for I willna allow it to happen. Ye and yer sisters are under my protection now."

"Ye lied tonight. In the garden." Her voice was low, like the whispers of wind over a deep loch that rippled into Deven's soul.

"Reputations are worth preserving."

"More so than yer word of honor?"

Deven's honor meant more to him than life. To not uphold it would mean death for him, the death of everything he believed in. Such a code was decidedly simpler to live by with an unbending line of right and wrong. Mangled emotions held no sway nor cast doubt. Until tonight when he'd bent his own rules. Because the truth would have destroyed an innocent's integrity. It would have destroyed Rooney. "My honor is bound in truth. I may not have been present in the garden, but that fact is overshadowed by the lies Sir Leslie would have spread."

"Ye lied to tell the truth. For me."

Yes. He had lied for her. "In a manner of speaking."

"Deven McLendon, there are perhaps more shades to ye than black and white." She lifted her face to his. The wide, amber eyes reflected his features like swirls in a dram of whisky. "If I look closely, will I detect a faint pink?"

His pulse quickened. He smoothed her hair, the silky springs catching between his fingers. "All I see is red."

Her breath caught, the small hitch igniting his blood. She was nothing he'd ever wanted, and she'd become everything he needed. He lowered his mouth to cover hers.

The front door banged open. Deven and Rooney jumped apart. Rose and Ruby stood in the doorway, peering into the darkness.

"Rooney, is that ye?"

"I told ye she was back. How was it? What did ye eat?"

"What were the ladies wearing?"

"Wheesht ye wee rattens and back inside." Rooney turned to Deven with an apologetic smile. "We willna gain a moment's peace with those two, so I'll bid ye goodnight. And thank ye."

Before Deven could respond or offer his hand, she slid off the horse in a whisper of satin. Raising her hood over her head, she dashed to her cottage door. She stopped briefly in an eerily familiar silhouette.

The light footsteps quickly covering the ground like a shadow, the petite height, for a moment he saw the hooded figure crouched in his window, the ruby glow of his brooch in the gloved hand.

He blinked hard as Rooney disappeared inside. A long night indeed when he began to see a charming lass lurking about as an infamous thief.

Chapter 8

"Good morn, Mistress Kerry. Yer beets look particularly red amidst the morning dew." Not even the sour-faced woman on market day could diminish Rooney's cheerfulness. She plucked a lock of hair from her braid and wound it around her finger. It looked redder today. Not orange or copper, but a bright titian that sparked like light glinting from garnets. She'd never appreciated the unruly mess before, considered by all an unlucky omen.

That was before Deven had run his fingers through it with the reverence of a man touching the Stone of Destiny. When he had almost kissed her.

"Rooney!"

Rooney's smile flattened at Rose's shriek. "No need to raise a skelloch for all the village to hear. I'm here." Her sister pushed through the market crowd and stopped in front of their baskets. Dirt caked her face and dress. "Where have ye been, and what pigsty have ye been rolling in?"

"Behind the tanner's shop. We wanted to find the piglet with the curliest tail." Rose thumbed her chest. "I won."

"There's consolation in that, I suppose. We canna have muddy and losing." Rooney narrowed her eyes. "Who is 'we?'"

"Me and Hamish. I told him to come join me for a game of obblyonkers, but he needed to get the midday meal for his mam." She swiped her forehead, smearing more mud. "I think he was afraid to lose again."

Why was Hamish fetching food in the middle of the day? Rooney had brought him and his mother food not a week before. Surely supplies hadn't run out already. "Stay here."

Rooney hurried to the baker's shop where the enticing scent of warm bread beckoned her inside. It was empty save the baker who stood at a table kneading dough.

He glanced up from his task. "Can I be helpin ye at all, miss?"

"I was looking for someone, but I must have been mistaken." Then a grimy hand reached from under a table and grabbed a roll.

"Ye!" The baker pointed a flour-encrusted finger as Hamish scrambled out the back door. "Thief! Stop there, ye wee clatty imp!"

Rooney raced after Hamish. A tall figure stepped out from around the corner. The man grabbed Hamish's shirt front, lifting him to his toes as the lad tottered backward.

Rooney skittered to a halt. "D—Lord Glèidh."

Deven's brow lifted in surprise. "D'ye ken the lad, or are ye about a stretch of the legs?" He glanced down to the roll in Hamish's grimy hand. "In a bit of trouble, are ye lad?"

Hamish struggled in Deven's unrelenting grip. "Let me go, ye black-hearted worm!"

"There's no need for name calling, Hamish." Rooney stepped forward. "Nor for stealing."

Deven's gaze cut back to Hamish. "There's a penalty for thievery."

"Not the pillory." Hamish sagged as tears spilled down his gaunt cheeks. "Please, my laird. The pain is too great for me to bear again." His left earlobe was torn in two from having been nailed to the pillory a year ago. It had taken him nearly three days to work up the courage to tear himself free.

"There's been a misunderstanding. One quickly rectified." Rooney reached into the coin pouch tied at her belt and extracted a silver bawbee. She walked back inside and handed the payment to the baker and returned outside.

Deven's frown didn't flinch. "It may be paid for, but the boy has committed a crime."

"Because he is desperate."

"That doesna change the facts."

"Nay, the facts dinna change, but perhaps how ye see them can. Come with me." When Deven didn't release Hamish, Rooney sighed and placed a light hand on his forearm. "Please."

Deven uncurled his fingers from Hamish's sark. The boy ran off as fast as his short legs could carry him. "I'm finding it rather difficult to refuse ye."

His words curled through her, settling in her heart with pleasure. "Is that such a terrible thing?"

"Dinna ken, but it keeps my days busy."

Rooney looked into Deven's face in hopes of catching a glimpse from last night. A flicker of reassurance that his lips so close to hers had not been a dream. His gaze dropped to her mouth, his eyes warm as molten silver. Rooney edged closer, prompting him to end the distance between them with a kiss.

He pulled in a breath, then stepped back. "Take me to the lad's home."

Rooney blinked in surprise. "Now?"

"Aye. I think it best."

"What will ye be needing with Hamish?"

"Will ye trust me? Please."

There was no retribution in his eyes. She did trust him, more than anyone she'd allowed herself to trust. Though she would've liked the kiss as well.

Shaking off her disappointment, Rooney led Deven out of the village and through the sanctuary of the woods to a cluster of mud bothies with scrawny chickens pecking the barren ground. The scent of cramped living conditions choked the air. Keeping to the trees, Rooney pointed at the last bothy that resembled a decaying mushroom slowly sinking back into the earth. A woman little older than she hung tattered clothing on a line. She was no more than skin and bones. Hamish raced down the path and flung himself around the woman's legs, nearly toppling her. He held up his roll, as fat tears shimmied down his cheeks. The woman smoothed the hair from his face and led him inside the mud hut.

"These homes were once under my father's care. Sir Leslie now owns them," Rooney said. "Hamish's father was killed in the Rising. Caitrine tried to find work, but her lungs are weak. I bring them food every week. Sometimes 'tis not enough."

She leaned against a tree as the familiar ache of painful understanding rippled through her. "'Tis not right what Hamish did, but circumstances often bring people to a point of desperation they thought never to cross. Because they canna see another way in caring for those they love."

Deven stared at the poor dwelling. "I am not immune to the hardships of this world, but I believe in order. Turning a blind eye to wrongdoings is no way to seek justice."

Where was the man from last evening? The man whose compassion had saved her reputation while spiriting away a piece of her heart. "Can ye honestly look at this and think so coldly?"

Genuine surprise lifted his black eyebrows. "Ye think me cold."

She had indeed, but as she looked closer, beyond the harsh detachment of reason, she saw the true hold it had on him. Not as a mantle of strength with which he perceived the world, but shackles he was unable to break free of. More than anything she wished for a hammer at that moment. "I think ye imprisoned by yer own ideals. The world can be cruel and unforgiving, but we've been gifted with the ability to show mercy."

"My father showed mercy. It cost my family nearly everything. Took me years to recover what had been lost." Deven crossed his arms over his wide chest, the leather baldric holding his broadsword creaked in protest. "He was never good at running a large estate. Money disappeared through the cracks. Tenants always owed but never paid. Accounts never tallied, fields left barren. Riches weren't everything he would tell me until it became necessary. Even he couldna deny that. He took the one thing left of value my family owned, the laird's brooch, and brought it to a man for appraisal." Deven snorted. "The crook stole our most precious possession and ran. Ten years it took me to track him down. Made me buy it back at thrice the price."

Coldness crept over Rooney at each word. "Why did ye not turn him in for theft?"

"Because he'd wormed his way into becoming the town's magistrate. His word against mine." Deven's hands clenched into fists. "I've lost the brooch by another black hand. The Night Fox."

"This brooch is an h-heirloom?"

"Passed from one laird to the next for generations. A legacy of the McLendons. Gone."

Valor of my ancestors. The brooch's inscription burned Rooney with guilt. A taunt really, against the new laird who dared come after her. She had been mistaken to think he was like the spoiled others and their riches. The fiscal would hardly miss a few coins, but the brooch was a piece of Deven. And she had stolen it without a second thought.

She swallowed hard. "Not truly gone, merely … misplaced."

"The Fox misplaces nothing. He kens precisely what he's about." Deven leaned a forearm against the oak tree, curling his fingertips into the bark. "I've done everything I can to abide by the rules. I expect others to do likewise. Unfortunately, circumstances exist beyond our control and the rules are broken. Items are stolen. Fathers killed. Lives forever altered. 'Tis my responsibility to repair them as much as I am able."

"Ye place too much burden on yerself."

"Not nearly enough. But some wrongs can be fixed. Ye've helped me see that shades of gray are permissible." He stroked her cheek with the tip of his finger. "Starting today."

Whirling, he strode from the trees toward the small bothy. Rooney wrapped her arms around her middle as her legs began to shake. What had she done?

Chapter 9

"WILL THAT BE ALL, my lord?" Hamish asked as he cleared the plates from the dining table.

Deven nodded. "See that the kitchen is in order, and ye may retire for the evening."

Hamish's little chest puffed up as if he were truly given charge of the kitchen and off he scampered with his loaded tray.

"He's too wee for carrying such things," Jean said from across the table.

"He'll grow." Deven stood and pushed his chair in. "How is Caitrine settling in?"

"Well enough as a kitchen maid. At least there she can taste the food and put a bit of meat on her bones." Jean rose, the slightest smile curling her lip. "If I dinna ken better, I'd say that redheaded lass had some persuasion with yer decision to bring them here yesterday. Dinna look at me like that. There isna a villager who hasna noticed ye with her. Helen Logan is practically spitting grisses in her morning parritch."

That was a sight Deven would give his sword arm for, as long as she didn't spit the nails at him. However, the village putting him and Rooney under glass for observation was another thing entirely.

"Miss Corsen is ..." Deven searched for an explanation, but no mere words could express her spirit, or charm, or unrivaled heart. Nor the affect she had possessed on him. "Captivating."

"Ye mean to say she's the only one to scale that insurmountable wall of defense ye've built around yerself."

"Good night to ye, Jean." Deven ducked out of the dining hall as her verbal darts hit with irritating accuracy.

"Bring her 'round. Mayhap to the McLendon's ball the night after next," Jean called after him. "I want to meet this woman who dares to brave ye."

Deven bounded up the stairs to his chamber, thoughts of Rooney trailing after him. Closing the door, he leaned his head against the smooth wood. She was never far from his mind. Prodding him to think beyond his governing restrictions to seize opportunities with grace and compassion. The sensation was unknown, like a creature stretching into its new skin after winter. Not quite uncomfortable, but it would take time before he understood the intricacies of it.

Rooney had gifted that to him. He could spend a lifetime showing her his gratitude.

A figure moved near his armoire.

"Hamish, is that ye? Told ye to go to bed, lad. No need to tire yerself out the first day."

The figure darted for the window. A small, round object fell to the floor. Ruby stones winked in the candlelight. The laird's brooch. Anger bolted through Deven. "Night Fox."

The Fox slipped out the open window and shimmied up a rope tied to the roof. Deven followed, the rope damp between his palms and the stones slick beneath his feet as he heaved himself on the roof. The night air hung heavy with thick mist as the Fox raced ahead of him.

"Canna run now, Fox. Not when ye've returned to the scene of the crime. Was once not enough?" Deven sprinted after the thief who was no more than a smudge of darkness through the fog. "Stay and face me like a man, ye wee *gealtair*!"

The Fox tripped. Deven closed in fast. Scrambling to his feet, the Fox sprinted the last few feet to the edge of the roof and leaped with arms stretched wide to the towering rowan tree leaning on the side of the house. He hit a branch with a small cry.

The sound punched Deven in the gut. Air ripped from his throat, he stumbled to a stop.

The small figure dangled from the branch with gloved hands gripping tight. Twisting his legs, the Fox swung himself onto the branch in a crouch. The figure stared at Deven from within the hood's shadow. In a flash, the Fox disappeared into the leaves. Deven moved stiff-legged to the edge of the roof and watched in numb silence as the shadow slipped to the ground and raced across the grass toward the woods.

"Rooney."

Rooney peeled off her black cloak, wincing as the rough fabric dragged across the scratches on her arm. She'd never lost control on a landing, at least not since a bairn learning to swing from branch to branch. Rolling up the Night Fox's clothes, she stuffed them into the small chest between the rocks and pulled her shift and gown on. Her arm burned where the tree bark had scraped her. As long as she kept it covered with sleeves, her sisters would never notice.

She shouldn't have lingered in Deven's chamber after replacing the brooch. She couldn't keep it after learning what it meant to him and the anguish he had endured to retrieve it once before. But then the glow of candlelight had fallen on a stalk of heather placed on the nightstand. The same flower she'd gifted him that day out in the field. Surrounded by stark order, Deven kept a piece of wildness near him. A piece she had given him.

Then Deven had burst in and chased her across the roof, calling her a coward. Would he have called her such a thing if he knew she was behind the mask? Rooney dug her fingernails into her palms. Did she want to find out?

No. She did not.

Deven had built his life on the truth. She'd built hers on lies. He thought her worthy of esteem—and the guilt of it broke her heart.

Stepping from behind the cluster of trees, Rooney walked toward her cottage with heavy steps. The mist had thickened, hazing angles and edges to shapeless outlines in the blackness. Without a doubt, the wet chill had seeped inside and dampened the walls and floors, to say nothing of the bedding. Rooney swept aside her guilt and shouldered her resolve. Her sisters deserved a dry roof to sleep under.

"Dreary night for a stroll through the mist." Sir Leslie's voice crept out from the dark.

Rooney jumped, hand reaching for her dag. She'd left it at the rocks with her other Night Fox accessories. "What are ye doing here?"

He emerged from the shadowy corner of the cottage. The pale outline of his face shone like wax under his wide-brimmed hat. "To make you an offer."

"I've already told ye. I willna marry ye." She brushed past him, but he caught her arm and twisted her around. Rooney yelped.

"You have not heard it yet."

"I doubt 'tis changed from the last time. Any new caveats ye've placed on it have my utmost revulsion."

A sparkling white object flashed in front of Rooney's nose. A diamond bracelet she'd taken from Lady Flincher two months prior. Horror slithered into her stomach.

Sir Leslie brushed the cold stones over Rooney's cheek. "Do I have your attention now?"

Rooney ceased her struggles and took a shaky breath. "I see no way to avoid it."

"How did I not know it was you all this time? A girl of your meager means should never have been able to scrape together a monthly rent, much less repay a debt. Then that comment about the pearl hairpins. No one knew they existed except me and whoever took my spoons. My clever little fox." He held the bracelet up. The diamond facets shone like starlight in the drops of rain. "How brilliant of you to pay me back in stolen treasure."

"Ye've no right to go through my things." Panicking, she yanked her arm, but he held tight. "Where are Ruby and Rose?"

"Safely inside with my manservant while we have our private tête-à-tête."

"Keep them out of this. I willna have them linked to what I've done."

"Calm yourself, my dear. Arrangements can be made to the satisfaction of all."

"What do ye want?"

"For you to keep doing what you are doing, but instead of exchanging your treasure for gold coin—I assume you have a middle man with whom you trade—you will give me the trinkets directly. I, in turn, will give you my silence."

"What will ye do with bracelets and pocket watches?"

"That is my concern." He pocketed the diamond band, giving it a comforting pat. "I can see in your face that silence is not enough. Ah, yes. Your family's house. Your sisters may return to it once we are married. Rent free."

"Married! I will never—"

Sir Leslie grabbed her chin and jerked her head up. She tried not to gag on his brandy-soaked breath. "You are not in a position to refuse my magnanimous offer. One word from me and you'll be hanged as a common thief. Your sisters flung out onto the streets for men to leer at and rats to gnaw at, but with you as my wife, they will have the entire protection of my position."

Rooney's retort died.

Protection, food, a roof that didn't leak. Ruby and Rose deserved safety after hardships no children their ages should have to endure. But to marry Sir Leslie in order to obtain it? Rooney's stomach convulsed.

She'd rather spend a lifetime of running from the hangman than pledge herself to such a loathsome creature. Was her pride truly worth more than her sisters' happiness?

"Ye've made yer offer, now I offer mine," she said. "In two nights, the McLendon is hosting a masquerade ball where all the lairds and their ladies of the land shall be in attendance."

"The McLendon. Wasteful tradition if you ask me, all these barbaric clans ruling themselves under a detestable Scot deigning himself as chieftain."

"The guests will be dressed in their finest, dripping with jewels and expensive baubles. Enough riches to pay ye back tenfold over."

"The Night Fox strikes again." Sir Leslie's eyes glittered beneath the brim of his hat. "Bring me the payment, and I shall consider all debts paid in full. If you fail, you belong to me."

This is what it had come to. A deal with the devil. Rooney could turn herself over to him or risk herself one last time before the noose.

Everything balanced on the edge of her success. Even her chance with Deven. For years she had locked her heart away, but the first moment with him had sprung it free. Life could begin again. Her only burden left to carry would be guilt from the lies—a silent penitence. She pushed away all thoughts of Deven before she could change her mind. "Do we have an agreement?"

Sir Leslie grabbed her hand and pressed cracked lips to her palm. "We do. One I most eagerly anticipate collecting on."

Rooney yanked her hand away. "Ye are despicable."

"I'm a man who knows how to win no matter the circumstances."

Rooney spun away, leaving the serpent to crawl back into his hole. She had a ball to prepare for.

Chapter 10

SHE SHOULD HAVE CUT the tail smaller. Rooney swept her furry train out of the way as another guest disguised as Robert the Bruce slashed his sword in a show of weaponry for his giggling companion who flitted about in a flurry of swan feathers.

Skirting around a court jester attempting to juggle empty goblets, Rooney walked the perimeter of the great hall. The chieftain of the McLendons had created a magical night filled with candles, sumptuous food, caskets of drink, and merry music spilling from the minstrels' gallery high above. She'd had no difficulty in slipping in unnoticed without an invitation.

Leaning against the stone wall, she watched as couples spun in an intricate dance before her. Peacocks and troubadours, medieval ladies and knights, a sun and his companionable moon. They dripped with jewels in every color under the rainbow as they floated in whispers of silk and satin. Any other night, Rooney would have loved nothing more than to enjoy the wondrous spectacle, perhaps even learn to dance, but tonight she could afford no distractions. She had a single purpose for being here, and not one thing could keep her from—

A man dressed in black with a wide hat walked toward her. Rooney's heart lurched. He winked from behind his mask and kept walking. A cockernonny of blond hair swished across his back. Rooney slumped. Not Deven.

Concentrate. How was she to perform when he brushed her every waking thought. Those keen eyes piercing her, twisting further the guilt of what she was about to do. She pushed it away, pushed *him* away. Nothing mattered beyond the task.

Across the hall, a woman costumed as a pale pink rose downed cup after cup of wine. Her falcon-feathered companion whispered in her ear, and she doubled over in a fit of laughter that sent wine sloshing from her cup. Never once did she glance down at the drops staining her bottom petals. Pink stones clustered around her thick neck and arms.

Perfect.

Rooney readjusted her mask and took a deep breath to calm her jittering nerves. She'd done this a hundred times. Only tonight she didn't have her hood, her pistol, or the cover of darkness. Taking another breath, Rooney slipped between the dancing couples as if she belonged here among the finery. She moved neither fast nor slow, a small smile on her lips so not to draw unwanted attention.

She approached the food table and took an offered cup of wine. Pretending to sip, she strolled around the table and stood behind the rose. A simple clasp held the choker in place. A quick flick of the thumb would undo it. The bracelets could prove a challenge as they would need to be pulled directly off. The woman's gloves should help ease the friction of dragging stones over her pudgy hand. Rooney glanced at the woman's elbows and determined the left was better to stumble against.

Rooney reached forward with her cup as if to place it on the table and knocked into the woman's elbow. "Oh, no! Do pardon me." Rooney lifted her hand to the woman's neck. Her fingers brushed the cold stones. She drew back. "I apologize."

The rose turned to her and blinked. "Think nothing of it. We're entitled to a fumble after indulging on the McLendon's wine." She tipped said contents into her mouth and smiled. "My, my, what red hair you have. Oh! It's part of your costume. How delightful to find a red fox among us."

If ye only knew. Rooney forced a smile. "Be careful, the Fox is cunning."

The woman laughed, the diamonds twinkling at her throat. "Charming. Utterly charming." Grasping her partner's wing, she pulled him to the middle of the dancers and swung into an off-rhythm reel.

Rooney twisted her hands together. What was wrong with her? She never hesitated. The setup had been perfect, and at the last second, her conscience decided it was high time to prick her. She reached back and tugged at the strings tying her mask.

A hand closed around hers. "Careful now. Wouldna want to give away yer identity."

Rooney spun around to find her conscience standing behind her. "Deven. I—I didna expect to see ye at the party."

"I fought alongside the McLendon chieftain during the Rising. It would be an insult to refuse his invitation." Deven wore head-to-toe black with thick gold embroidery spiraling across his chest and down the sides of his breeks. It was the first time Rooney had seen him without a kilt, and she didn't much care for it. A black cape hung from his shoulders, and a simple cloth of black covered his eyes. Darkly dangerous. And standing much too close.

Rooney took a step back as the air thickened between them.

"Would ye care to dance?" Deven held his hand out.

She forced her gaze from the fingers she knew would curl around hers like a glove. A distraction if there ever was one. "Surely there are other ladies here more suited to accompany ye in the skirl."

"I dinna want another lady. I want ye."

Rooney ducked her head, away from those penetrating gray eyes. "Dancing skills ... elude me."

"I dinna believe that. Ye've the agility to dance around anything." He tweaked one of the fox ears atop her head and trailed his fingers over her hair and down her arm to take her hand. "Dance with me, Rooney."

She couldn't stop him from pulling her along. Anything to linger in the warmth his touch brought.

The music slowed, and the men and women split into two separate lines. Dryness coated Rooney's mouth as Deven took his place opposite her at the end of the lines. At the far end, couples began to twirl. She should never have agreed to this. Light on her feet up a tree was one thing, but precise steps in pinched shoes was another. Before she knew it, Deven beckoned her forward into a spin. He moved as if on glass and she a reflection of his guidance.

"Ye look bonny tonight. Only fox I've seen."

Rooney swallowed and tried not to think about her feet. "Corsen means fox."

"Does it now?"

"My father used to call us his wee fox cubs." Deven took her hand and placed it on his shoulder as they twirled around another couple.

It felt right to be in his arms as if she belonged there all along. She could spend a lifetime there and never want to leave. A sparkle drew her gaze to the brooch attached to Deven's shoulder. The rubies glowed like dark wine. A thrill ran through her seeing it where it belonged. "Yer brooch. 'Tis been restored to ye."

"Aye. Seems the Night Fox took pity on my plight."

"Or didna realize its true value lay beyond a monetary price."

Deven ran his hand along her arm. Rooney jolted at the sting of pain from her scratches. "Have I hurt ye?"

"'Tis not yer fault. A mere scratch from the woodpile."

Deven's arms circled her waist, drawing her closer. He bent his head and brushed his lips against her ear. "I ken it was ye, Night Fox." Rooney yanked back, but Deven held her tight. His gaze hooked into the deepest part of her and forced her to stare into the pain of truth. "I ken it was ye, Rooney. All this time."

His arms fell away. Rooney fled. From him, from the mockery of joyful music, and the glittering of jewels. She raced across the great hall and out a set of double doors onto a small balcony. It was a short drop to the ground below and only a few yards out to the protective cover of the woods. Hoisting her skirts, Rooney climbed onto the rail.

Knocking dancing couples out of the way, Deven sprinted after Rooney. She stood on the balcony rail, skirts bunched in her hands, and knees bending to jump. He grabbed her around the waist and hauled her off. "Not that easy, ye dinna."

"Let me go."

"Now that I've finally caught the elusive Night Fox? I think not." She kicked the air, threatening to knock them sideways. Deven clenched her tighter. "Cease yer struggling. There's no tree for ye to leap into."

"I dinna always need a tree."

"Aye, well, there isna carriages or windows about either."

A half-hysterical laugh tumbled out of Rooney. "Of course, it would be ye to find me out. Ye with the eyes that miss nothing."

Deven eased her to the ground though he kept his arms about her. Each curve fitting perfectly against him, warm and soft. "I missed the signs that were directly in front of me. Ye held me bewitched."

Rooney inhaled sharply. She turned in his arms and fixed an unfathomable gaze of gold and green on him. His pulse pounded as he waited for her to speak. For two nights he'd not slept as every second of her lying betrayal stabbed him anew. Weakness had prowled him, taunting another failure to a con. Finally, as his blood cooled long enough to clear his mind, he realized Rooney was nothing like the man who'd tricked his father and taken the laird's brooch. She was not a common criminal who deserved the pillory despite her wrongdoings. She deserved another chance. A chance from him for as improbable as it seemed, he'd fallen for a thief. And so, he waited for fate to decide their outcome.

Her head tilted. Moonlight slanted silver across her red mask.

"What are ye going to do now? Turn me in?"

"Nay. I'm going to marry ye." The words echoed in his head, their meaning pounding louder and stronger until he could no longer deny the truth in them. More solid than any conviction he'd ever had, Rooney Corsen was his destiny.

Rooney jumped out of his arms, every line in her body rigid. "W— what did ye say?"

"I'm going to marry ye. No matter where ye hide or how far ye run, I'll catch ye. As many times as need be until the only place left for ye to turn is to me."

"I am a thief. I lie, cheat, and steal. Everything ye abhor."

"As do ye. 'Tis why ye dinna take that woman's bracelets tonight. Was the perfect opportunity, and ye decided not to at the last."

"How did ye ken?"

"I've watched ye since the moment ye stepped into the hall."

She clenched her hands together. "I dinna wish to be here, but there are reasons ye canna understand."

"Rose and Ruby." He longed to reach for her, to reassure her that she could trust him, but he stood still. Waiting. "Will ye not confide in me?"

"I do it all for them. My sisters deserve a life beyond what we've fallen to. I hate what I do. The only comfort is kening I take from those less likely to notice a few stolen coins and jewels." She ran an agitated hand through her hair, springing loose curls in every direction. "Tonight's earnings would have provided enough so that I never have to steal again. When the time came … I couldna go through with it. 'Tis yer fault." She glared at him.

"Mine?"

"Seems my conscience takes ye into consideration now. Little good it does me."

"Give up the Fox. Yer sisters can live with us at Strathmoore." Reaching behind her head, he untied the strings of her mask and tossed it off the balcony. "Ye need never more wear the mask."

Rooney laughed, a mirthless sound in sharp contrast to her spirit. "Simple as that? Ye, whose ingrained principles could rival an exasperating saint, can ignore everything I've done these past years. Why? Pity for my plight?"

"Because ye're the only woman to challenge me to be a different man. A man beyond rigid rules with the capability of understanding the fallacies of people and not judging them on it."

"I never wanted ye to be different."

"Aye, and that's what challenges me to be better." Stepping closer, Deven traced a finger over the satiny curve of her cheek as the weight of truth lifted its burden. "Return all of the items and—"

"I canna. I've traded most of them for coin. My exchanger is not in the business of extending refunds."

Deven pinched the bridge of his nose. "On the black market, was it?"

Rooney nodded. "I ken well what ye're thinking, but I'll not allow ye anywhere near that depravity. Not after what it's cost ye in dealing with thieves." She touched his brooch.

Deven closed his hand over hers and squeezed. "I'm already involved and plan to be for yer entire future."

She pulled back, the defiant mask slipping into place once more. "Ye dinna understand what's at stake. I canna and willna marry ye."

"There isna one good reason ye can give me that—"

"She's going to marry me." Sir Leslie stood in the doorway wearing a mask of glittering gold. "I appreciate it if you did not squire away my betrothed to darkened corners. I will be forced to defend her reputation."

Deven moved in front of Rooney. "The irony in that comment is a long way from threatening."

Sir Leslie's thin nostrils flared white. "Come, Rooney. The evening is young with many guests to attend to. We wish for tonight to be a success, do we not? Remember our deal, my dear."

It hit Deven like a punch to the gut. Of course. He spun to Rooney. "How long has he been blackmailing ye?"

Sir Leslie hissed. "That is a dangerous accusation."

Deven ignored him, locking his attention on Rooney. "Desperation breeds dealings with the devil. Even so far to agree to unholy matrimony."

Fear sprang to her eyes. "Ye dinna understand."

"Oh, I think I do. Ye've agreed to marry this snake in exchange for expunging yer debts. Yet ye still feel the need to find payment, hence tonight. Which can only mean a loophole to this farce of a match. Full payment or a wedding band." The rage that should have flooded Deven drowned in sorrow. "Why dinna ye come to me?"

Rooney shook her head. "Not every problem is yers to repair, Deven. The wrongs are mine. I must be the one to right them. A thief ruined yer life. I willna be responsible for that again."

"That choice no longer belongs to ye." Grasping her shoulders,

Deven pulled Rooney to him and kissed her. It wasn't a gentle kiss, more one to prove a point, but the instant his lips touched hers Deven knew there was no going back. She'd claimed his heart, and he had no intention of taking it back.

Sir Leslie screeched behind them. "How dare you put hands on my wife?"

Rooney pulled back, gaze crackling with ice as she stared at Sir Leslie. "I am not yer wife. Nor will I ever be. Tonight my debt is settled."

"As if you could have succeeded in paying me back or continued to afford rent once I raised the price. I razed that eyesore to the ground months ago just as I'm doing with the surrounding crofts that supported it to make ways for sheep pastures."

Rooney's mouth dropped open. "Ye lied to me. All this time. Ye made me believe—"

"You didn't think I would actually allow you to succeed tonight? I told you that you were meant to be my wife one way or another. Now I have you." Sir Leslie swerved around Deven and grabbed Rooney by the arm, yanking her toward the door. Rooney cried out as she dug her heels into the stone.

Fury boiled Deven's blood as he dropped his hand to his sword. "The Stirrling Stone."

Sir Leslie stopped dead cold. "What did you say?"

"The great diamond of the Stirrling family. Surely ye've heard of it. It shines like a thousand stars with a wee notch at the top where it once dangled from a chain. None other like it in Scotland, or all of Great Britain for that matter. It went missing twenty-five years ago. Rumored to have floated on the black market before a wealthy lord snatched it for his own collection." Deven smiled as panic suffused Sir Leslie's face. "I took the liberty of examining yer diamond and found an exact notch at the top. D'ye care to explain how the Stirrling's family stone came to be in yer possession?"

"The diamond is mine."

"Ye're a crook, though I willna wish to be in yer shoes when the Stirrlings find out. They're not a forgiving lot."

Sir Leslie sneered. "You tell anyone and I'll not hesitate to lead her straight to the hangman. Your darling Night Fox."

Deven kept his hand relaxed despite the urge to run his blade through the man. "Night Fox? Her? A slip of a lass climbing into windows. Holding men at gunpoint. Look at her. She couldna lift a pistol much less ken how to fire one. The Fox is canny and prevails in feats too grand for a woman."

"It's her. She knows where my silver hairpins are kept."

"A set of missing hairpins were reported last year in London around the same time ye journeyed there for the House of Lords session. More dealings on the black market."

"No one will believe you. I am a lord, recognized by His Majesty King George."

"Ye can make such claims before the magistrate. Guards." Three armed guards of the McLendon stepped onto the balcony and took hold of Sir Leslie. "Thank ye for the confession."

Face paling, Sir Leslie sputtered curses. "Rooney Corsen! She's the Night Fox! Arrest her."

Sir Leslie's shouts died as the guards hauled him away. Silence descended, cloaking Deven and Rooney in uncertainty. Rooney moved to the railing.

"Yer costume needs imagination." Her voice shook. "If ye're to dress as a magistrate, ye need the curly wig."

"Dinna care for wigs. I thought this would suit well enough."

"In an ironic twist."

Deven eyed Rooney's fox tail as he joined her at the rail. "Ye above all people should approve."

Her gaze slanted to him. "I'm in yer debt for what ye've done, but I willna marry ye."

"Nay? Ye think to find another man so understanding of yer light-fingered habits?"

"Habits? Ye've done more lying tonight than I have the entire time playing the Fox."

"Every bit about Sir Leslie was the truth. Law University did help me sort the criminals from the more or less innocent."

Rooney snorted. "Now ye call me innocent."

"Certainly not. Ye'll have to return everything to its proper owners."

"Impossible. Some of those trinkets I took years ago. The man I sell them to for coin doesna keep his stock for long."

"Aye, but ye forget I'm well adapted at tracking items down." Deven moved his hand closer to hers, brushing against her little finger.

"My family home. Everything I promised my sisters. Gone." Rooney pummeled the rail. "That lying, two-faced, conniving, sneaking, wretched excuse for a rat!" Tears fell down her face in silvery tracks.

"I've risked my life, broken morals, and committed sins to bring back what was rightfully ours. My soul has been blackened for nothing."

Her pain seeped into Deven until all he could think about was removing her from it. He took her hands in his. "I'm sorry for the home ye've lost, but if it's a place full of love that ye long for, then I can promise ye that and a lifetime more with me."

Tears studded her long lashes as she looked at him. "I'm not worthy of yer love. I've nothing to offer ye."

"There is but one thing I seek from ye. Yer heart. Any other offering pales in comparison and is of no use to me."

"What about my past?"

"Yer past belongs to yesterday. Yer tomorrows are my privilege."

What seemed a thousand lifetimes hung in the ensuing silence as she looked him over head to toe. Her gaze settled on his face, and her full lips curved up at the corner. "I've one request."

The ticking seconds warred against Deven's sanity. "D'ye drive me mad on purpose?"

She wiped away a tear and smiled fully. "A carriage ride. I've spent more time on the roof than properly inside, and Helen Logan claims ye to be quite the charming companion to ride with."

Deven's pent-up breath rushed out in relief. "Taking advice from her now, are ye?"

"She shouldna enjoy an experience that ye're not willing to share with me."

"There are many experiences I'd like to share with ye and no one else." He reached for Rooney, eager to taste her wild sweetness once more. "Come here to me, my wee fox."

Laughing, she slipped nimbly from his reach. "The Fox isna so easily caught. No matter how charming the captor."

Pinning her against the rail, he brushed kisses over her forehead, nose, and each cheek. She smelled of heather and grass and Rooney. A lifetime would not be enough of her. "I told ye once before that I will catch ye, no matter how far ye run or how long it takes, for ye're the fox who has stolen my heart."

"A thievery I'm not the least bit repentant of." Rooney wrapped her arms around his neck and leaned up to kiss him.

"Neither am I."

A big huge thank you to Linda, Pegg, and the whole team at LPC for believing in me and making this the best story it can be. And for thinking of me when it came time to write a story about Scotland. That's probably the biggest compliment I can get. My dear friend Kim, who spent hours and hours drumming up a plot with me when the only inkling of an idea I had was a lady thief, I owe you a big heart-shaped box full of chocolate caramels. To my amazing husband who seems to enjoy this wild adventure we call life together and has yet to call me crazy for living in my imagination. Destiny is all.

And to Scotland. My heart's in the Highlands wherever I go. *Sláinte mhath*!

Believing she was born in the wrong era, J'nell Ciesielski spends her days writing heart-stopping heroes, brave heroines, and adventurous exploits in times gone by. Winner of the Romance Through the Ages contest and Maggie Award, J'nell can often be found dreaming of a second home in Scotland, indulging in chocolate of any kind, or watching old black and white movies. Born a Florida girl, she now calls Virginia home, along with her very understanding husband, young daughter, and one lazy beagle. Find out more at www.jnellciesielski.com.

A Tender Siege

By

Naomi Musch

Dedicated to my grandma, Marie Rose (Gilbert) Schoechert, out of whose bloodline comes the only bit of Celtic blood I can lay claim to. Residing in the presence of the Lord for some years now, she held no earthly fame, but her life of dedication, perseverance, and love for family left an imprint on the generations that knew her, including me. She taught me more than she ever knew.

Chapter 1

His Majesty's Forces at Bushy Run, Pennsylvania
August 6, 1763

LACHLAN McRAE PRESSED HIS chest to the earth behind a fallen chestnut tree. His heart throbbed against the musty leaf litter, sending further pulses of pain into his leg where a musket ball lay embedded.

He hadn't a true will to live, yet neither did he wish to have his skull laid wide by a tomahawk blade. Sweat trickled into his eyes as he turned his head just enough for a desperate glimpse into the forest. He hovered between two worlds. In the present one, his warm flesh still bled. In the future world, where Moira waited with their child, her unfelt touch was all that mattered.

He splayed his fingers across his tattered kilt and pressed it to the bleeding wound on his thigh. Wetness leeched through. Lachlan gritted his teeth. How far had the others in his regiment gone?

"Nab." His friend's name was a rasp between gasps of agony. "Nab, are ye there?"

Deathly silence answered all around. Lachlan had not seen Jesse Nab since the ambush yesterday when their battalion of light infantry charged forward to support the advance guard. The Indians had reappeared in another position on the neighboring heights. Soldiers had dispersed in varying directions seeking cover as the Indians assailed them from over the ridge, first coming from one side of the draw and then another. Many of his comrades had fallen. Lachlan, Nab, and a half dozen others broke off and had hunkered in a small depression in the hillside, but were later separated during the melee.

Lachlan's Brown Bess lay beside him, powder damp from his tumble into Bushy Run, but the bloody bayonet remained affixed. Small comfort it offered, while his thigh lay torn through the flesh. When the ball from an Indian's musket struck his leg, Lachlan hadn't even discerned the direction the shot had come from, yet he'd managed to halt the sudden appearance of his assailant with his bayonet. This morning, the firing had begun again, and since then, the last Highlander he'd seen lay dead somewhere east or south of his current position.

Now, as eerie stillness engulfed the land, he couldn't be sure whether Bouquet's entire army had been wiped out or if the Indians had been pushed back. He dare not drag himself onto the road toward the smoke rising in the distance to find out. His only recourse was to move to deeper cover.

He gritted his teeth and forced himself upright. The effort stole his breath. He disengaged the bayonet and pulled himself to stand on one foot, using the musket as a crutch. He must get free of this place or bleed out while he tried. If any of Bouquet's army remained—the 60th Royal Americans, the 77th Highlanders, or his own 42nd Highlanders—they would still be headed to relieve the siege at Fort Pitt, as had been their mission before the Indians attacked.

Lachlan staggered forward peering left and right. After twenty rods, he pinched back a groan and fell to a stop. He huffed for breath. A humid breeze fluttered the leaves along a deep swale, the rustling sound able to cover moccasined feet. Lachlan tightened his jaw. Sweat trickled down his temple and stuck the shirt beneath his brick-red waistcoat to his back.

Blood continued to trickle down his leg, soaking into the red and white crisscross pattern of his hose. With gory fingers, he removed his belt and grimaced as he cinched it at the top of his leg near his groin. Tremors shook him from head to feet. For a moment he questioned his sanity in not letting himself bleed out. *Moira.* He could almost taste her name on his lips. Perhaps if he closed his eyes and lay here a bit longer, she would come to him and take him away.

Go on, Lachlan.

He shook his head. "No, Moira. I want to come to ye."

Go on, Lachlan.

He opened his eyes. Blue skies peeked down through the treetops.

Again, he pushed to his feet, and this time he did cry out.

"I canna keep going. I've gone on enough."

Go on, Lachlan. The voice in his head was no longer Moira's, but whose? God's?

"I beg Ye to take me."

This time, not even a leaf rustled in reply.

He stepped forward and bit his cheek against the fire racing up his leg. Then began the slow, miles-long journey over hill and rock and gully. He dragged himself on, eating the bits of jerky he carried in his pouch and chewing on withering berries. He sensed no fever, only weakness, pain, and hunger. Bushy Station stood abandoned. Moccasin footprints in the mud outside showed frequent visits by the ranging natives.

As the hours passed, his leg swelled, but the bleeding hole had hardened to a seeping crust. He suspected infection setting in and smirked. Such a way to finally die. Did any of his comrades even now suffer so? How many lay dead in the bush 'neath the hot sun? He prayed not many and that Nab was not among them, but his heart held bitter doubts as he laid his head on the ground.

In the morning, he awoke. Alive still, he glimpsed toward heaven. "So this is what Ye intend, then?" He dragged himself on, step by tortuous step.

Lachlan moved northwest, each footfall its own agony, keeping the main trail within a distance of twenty rods or so. Still, by the third day since the battle, he sensed he'd not covered more than a handful of miles. The forests and gullies lay endless. He collapsed in a thicket. "God! What would Ye have me do?" He panted and rubbed his torn sleeve across his grizzled chin.

His ears pricked. Footsteps? He crouched lower. No. Not footsteps but the trickle of moving water. Lachlan moved his parched tongue across cracked lips. He had not passed a creek since yesterday, and his canteen was empty. Now the hope of quenching his thirst nearly put away caution. He slung back his head with a gasp, then leaned forward and pushed to his feet again. Perhaps, at the water, he would loosen the belt and lay his leg in the shallows. Mayhap the coolness would numb the pain. Mayhap, he'd lie there until Moira came again.

He was out of breath and strength when he reached a stream a little further on. Breaking through the trees, it flowed along over shale and rock. He scanned the area, seeking danger, but as he'd not come across another human being, either red or white, he shuffled to the water and stepped into the black mud along its edge. He laid aside his musket and withdrew his sword, setting both weapons on a flat stone. Gently, he eased himself down. He stripped off his shoes and hose and set his feet into the water. With teeth clenched, Lachlan leaned back on his arms and gasped as the water washed over his wound. It did not numb but, rather, enlivened the pain. He struck the water with both fists. Gritting against the burning, he stripped off the belt and let his circulation flow. After some moments of nearly blinding pain, it began to ease. An ugly redness stitched lines around the hole making a ragged opening in the meat of his thigh. Surely, it was a good thing to clean out the debris embedded in the wound.

For what seemed nearly an hour he lay there. His leg soaked to white, shriveled flesh, and his kilt too was soddened. The stream of red thinned to nearly clear water again. He'd removed his coat but left his waistcoat and shirt in place. If he could find a rock touched by the sun, perhaps he would lie upon it and sleep while he dried and dreamed.

He'd only considered the idea when a new sound, like a mourning dove's notes, reached him. His heart punched inside his chest, for he knew 'twas no bird. He scrambled for his sword and gun, jerking his leg from the water in a manner that brought new agony. Clasping the items against his chest, he scooted backward toward the trees.

Ah! His shoes and hose. There was nothing for it. They would have to remain in the open, and hopefully whoever came would take no notice of them.

The red of the stockings seemed like flares to Lachlan's eyes, however. As the sound of humming drew closer, he willed blindness on the intruder. With a narrow oak to his back, Lachlan peered behind, over his shoulder. A movement on the opposite bank of the creek captured his attention. A flit of deerskin. A shine of dark hair. He held his breath and froze, his hand on the hilt of his sword.

The humming ceased abruptly. A bird warbled in the treetops and another answered. Lachlan glanced at his bare leg where a pink ooze issued from the wound. Did someone creep close? Were these to be his final moments? Would his scalp be lifted while his feet yet kicked the earth? He adjusted his grip on the sword and turned his head enough to see the water flowing and that no one crept up behind him. He turned another inch, then two, and then he saw her. A woman stared at him from across the stream, her eyes fixed and bright. She crouched at the water's edge, a string in her hands, and on one end, lifted from the water, a fish wriggled.

He ducked back and clenched his eyelids shut. Memories of the clearances at home in Scotland threatened. Of Moira's suffering. He didn't want to kill a woman, but if she thought to attack him ... *God. Dinna force my hand.*

He peered once more, and she was gone. Lachlan's heartbeat quickened as he searched the forest around him. There was no sign of her. But for how long, and would she return with a war party?

He glanced to the place he had seen her with the fish, and his stomach tightened. Perhaps she dropped it, and it lay there still on its string. Would he be able to cross the slippery rocks in the stream and find out? In answer, his belly groaned. He maneuvered out of the woods and retrieved his stockings and shoes. Rinsing one of the stockings, he used it to wrap his wound and then stepped barefooted into the stream.

Inches turned to a journey over the rocks, slick with wet moss. Sharp stones poked the tender flesh of his soles. The rushing water made him wobble. Then, just when he was within feet of the embankment, his stronger leg slid out on a stone, and he tumbled. His hip crashed into a rock and Lachlan flipped over. He dropped the Bess, and as he clamored to retrieve it, he slid on another rock and fell, bashing his skull.

Moira stood there on the shore, holding out her hand. Oblivion crept around the edges of his vision, narrowing his view of her. "Dinna go." He moved his mouth, but whether or not he spoke aloud, he didn't know. Perhaps it didn't matter, for she tilted her head as if she listened. He urged words, but they were mist. *Ye must come get me, darlin, for I canna come on my own.*

Wenonah dropped the stringer holding her catch of fish and shoved her cabin door shut. She slid down against it, breathless. Pressing her hands to her stomach, she fought against rising panic. What was she to do if the soldier found her here, as he might if he continued down the river? What would prevent him from doing just as the raiders had done, stealing her things and destroying what little remained? How would she then survive the ordeal ahead of her, and what of the supplies she must keep for her coming journey?

She lowered her hands and stared at the empty pot sitting at the hearth. *He is wounded or ill.* She could tell it easily enough. Anguish lay in his eyes, and the way he held himself proved pain of some sort, for he had barely been able to stand on his bare feet. *He is hungry.*

Hunger made a dangerous enemy. Hunger and desperation could kill. At least the raiders had let her live, but would this man?

Wenonah swallowed against bile knotting in her throat. To fight her fear, she must take action. Resolved, she pushed to her feet and cracked open the door. Her breathing calmed as she peered out. Light rain fell, and darkness would come soon. The soldier was weak. He would not find her tonight.

And tomorrow she would not let him.

Slipping her knife from its hilt at her hip, she picked the stringer off the floor and carried the fish outside. Tonight, she would eat and gather strength. Tomorrow she would rise early and return to the river's edge.

Wenonah cleaned the fish and spitted them. Then, choosing a few well-dried sticks of oak from her supply of wood next to the hearth, she built a small, nearly smokeless fire and cooked the fish above the glowing red coals. There was no sense sending out a beacon to the soldier. Perhaps others of his kinsmen still roamed the forest. Hopefully, they had all moved on to the English for, but she could not be sure of such. And what if they returned this way? Between the soldiers and Shawnee warriors with their allies of half a dozen nations passing to and fro, Wenonah's safety was nothing but a brittle reed that might easily be crushed.

As darkness fell, she sharpened her knife. She set it beside her as she settled on the furs covering her rope bed. Gentle rain on the rooftop turned heavy at times then lightened again, but continued half the night, assuring Wenonah that the soldier must have sought shelter. Yet, she slept the dreamless sleep of the wary, her eyelids springing open at the sound of a field mouse scurrying in the corner, and her thoughts waking her with plans for the coming day.

She would move out at morning's light, and if the stranger had gone, then so be it. Surely, he hoped to reach the fort. If he remained at the river, she would offer him the kindness of food. Perhaps her gesture would soften his heart, and he would continue on in peace. If not ... Wenonah laid her hand on the buckhorn handle of her knife. She would defend herself, stopping him completely if necessary.

Chapter 2

PAIN SEARED HIS HEAD. The throbbing forbade him opening his eyes. He curled onto his side, but sharp tentacles wrapped hold of his leg and gripped. *Alive.* Lachlan felt like weeping.

He passed into blackness again, and the next time he woke, the dark of night lay thick, and rain fell softly. Moira had not stayed with him. Neither had he gone to her.

He shivered. Had a woman really been here, watching him at the riverside today, or had it only been Moira's spirit, taunting him? At least sleep had lessened the pain in his head. He gently prodded his skull with his fingertips and found a tender welt. The skin was intact. The last thing he needed was another place leaking blood. He squeezed the bones in his shoulders and arm and bent his head to be certain his neck worked. Lachlan didn't remember climbing out of the water after he'd fallen, but he must have, for here he lay on the creek bank.

Forcing himself to sit up, he peered deeper into the darkness. Where had he dropped the gun? He would not find it in the dark. And his sword, did it lay in the creek bottom too?

He felt around him. Nothing he owned lay within reach. No shoes, no stocking, not even the canteen. He would simply have to wait for dawn and hope that when it came, a party of Indians would not be waiting to finish the job they'd started at Bushy Run.

He dragged himself further from the bank, up against a hollow in a gully wall protruding with green rock and roots. He leaned against it and closed his eyes. It was not a cave, but it offered the merest shelter and a screen from anyone coming up the trail on this side of the creek.

As the gray mist of dawn wet his skin, Lachlan woke again, weak with hunger and cold. His clothes had never fully dried, and now more drizzle fell from the sky. There was nothing to be had in his pouch. The jerky had long since been eaten. He pulled back the kilt and examined his leg again. The hole had filled with a plug of dried blood, but the rest of the area was a swollen mass. Gently, he moved his fingers along the edge and beneath wherever the pain radiated. The musket ball had not exited, and the muscle felt mutilated inside, but Lachlan was fairly certain it hadn't damaged his bone. He leaned forward. He could lie here and die, but instinct urged him to keep moving. He planted his palms on the earth to heave himself up when the sound of a cracking twig stopped him. He glanced around him. He'd no weapon. Even his tomahawk had been lost in the battle. He flexed his hands and pushed to his feet, but the pain almost sent him to the forest floor again. He sucked in his breath and waited. Footsteps shuffled on damp ground sounded only feet away, just beyond the edge of the rock. Lachlan held his breath.

The woman from yesterday stepped into view carrying a bucket made of stiff, tanned hide, with the end of a stick protruding out of it. Her head jerked around, and her eyes widened at the same moment that Lachlan's heart jumped. He raised his hands to brace for an attack.

She took a step back toward the water's edge, and her stance shifted revealing the protrusion of her belly at the front of her dress.

She carries a bairn.

She fled, and Lachlan leaned forward. "Wait!" The woman kept moving and glanced back for only a second before disappearing completely into the woods.

Lachlan slumped back against the promontory to ease the pain. After a few moments' rest, he straightened and limped toward the stream. He could not go on without the musket, and it must lie somewhere beneath the riffles of the stream. He soon spotted it beneath the surface amongst the rocks. His sword and canteen lay sparkling in the mud of the shallows nearby. The drizzle had turned to rain, and Lachlan was already soaked through as he eased himself into the water. He slid one foot across the bottom and dragged his wounded leg.

At last, he retrieved the weapons, but he could not find his shoes. The whole procedure had drained him beyond his limits. He needed food and rest, or he would never make it to Fort Pitt.

He rolled onto his back, limp and without hope, until sleep called again.

Some inner sense pricked him back to life. His eyelids sprang open. Shafts of sunlight angling from the west filtered down through the dripping crown of oak and maple, hemlock and pine, but his heart pumped painfully inside his chest as awareness sent his senses tingling.

Not alone ... He didn't look, not right away. Let them think he was unaware. His hand lay next to the pommel of his sword. He drew his fingers over it. Then he turned but a fraction and shifted his eyes.

The woman again.

She stood rigid upon the far bank, a dozen rods or so upstream, watching him. When he didn't move, she took a step toward the water. With one foot stretched before her and then the other, she made her way across a pair of stones and onto a wide, flat rock. She looked up again, guardedly. With one hand cradling her belly, she lowered something to the ground.

Lachlan swept the woods behind her with a sharp look. What trap did she lay?

She straightened, and with the deftness of a deer, returned to the other shore. Her glance caught his once more before she slipped into the forest.

Lachlan stared for a good long time, awaiting the attack he was sure would follow. Whatever she had laid on the rock near the closer bank remained. Did the Indians wait for him to approach it? Yet they must see he was wounded. Why would they wait?

Why would they send a pregnant woman to bait him? Or was it all a dream ... just like Moira?

Lachlan raised himself using the musket again as a crutch. His body tightened with wariness as he inched along toward the mysterious object on the rock. Grass lay matted against the ground. The Indians must use this place often. The hairs on his forearms tingled. When he reached the rock's edge, he stood still for as long as he could bear the weight of his body. The wound had begun to throb with a hard burn, and every part of his skin below the belt tourniquet stretched tight and hot. He dragged himself one step forward and then another. The blackened object was attached to a stick. He craned his neck to study its shape.

Fish.

Had the woman brought him food? He urged his step faster. He scanned the area between fish and trees, still expecting to be ambushed, but the lure of food lying within his grasp was a powerful contender with his safety. After all his fear of being bashed in the head by a tomahawk and stripped of his scalp, if he could die without starving, it might be worth it.

The fish broke apart in his fingers, tender and flaky beneath the charred skin. He coughed as he shoved morsels of it into his mouth and licked it off his fingers. He was unwilling to lose even a crumb. When it was gone, but for a few bare bones, he made his way off the slab of rock. Finally gaining the ground, he sat down to rest. He no longer cared if he was murdered in his sleep.

A powerful thirst drove him back to the water, as the evening sun cast long shadows over the ravine. Dragging himself to the edge, he lay on his stomach and drank long and deeply. He was still weak, still hurting, but good sense told him he must move. He might die in trying, but it would be better to die in the comfort of a warm bedroll.

Lachlan smirked. Had one small fish in his belly given him the notion that such a thing as a comfortable death was possible?

He studied the route ahead. Dare he cross the river again, or should he continue on this path? The woman had made it look easy using the boulders as stepping stones. Yet shouldn't he move further away from the river? He was loathe to leave it, especially without his shoes. How far north would it take him, and how many twists and turns would there be, slowing him from reaching his destination? He braced the musket beneath his arm. He would stay with it for tonight. He might not get far in the dark, but at least the river would keep him from losing his way until daylight returned.

As another night blackened to pitch, only the moon's glow on the water guided his steps. With each dragging step he relived the battle, hearing again the cries of his comrades. Questions filled his head without answers, and more than once he begged God for Moira to comfort him. He'd gone about an hour, moving slower than a porcupine, when he heard voices. A guttural language. Indians. Heart hammering, he crouched in the tall grass. A campfire's acrid smoke reached him, heightening his senses. He glanced to the water. The river had narrowed. He must certainly cross it now.

Lachlan braced the Brown Bess stock against the river bottom. It was sandier here. Good. The flow of water would cover the sound of his movements. He made his way as quickly as he dared, feeling for any stray stones that might trip him. He reached the other bank without incident. There he had no choice but to go deeper into the woods away from the water's edge. He peered back, and from this side, the flicker of a campfire shone through the trees. Yes, he must go deeper.

He limped blindly into the dark woods. Branches snapped against his face, and briars clawed his bare legs and feet, pulling at his kilt and the makeshift stocking bandage. He tripped once and bit back a cry. He had gone as far as he could, yet not far enough. It would have to do. He crawled behind a deadfall and waited, while mosquitoes feasted on his exposed skin.

In the morning, Lachlan floundered in a half-sleep that weighted his mind and limbs alike. He could not move, could not come fully awake. His body was hot. He thought he fought with his coat, but perhaps he dreamed it.

Sickness.

Moira was there again, shaking her head and turning her face away. *Help me, Moira!* He pleaded, but she faded anyway. He pried his eyes open, heavy as though a heated iron pressed down on them. A blur of green filled his vision, and then the blur separated into branches and leaves. Something flitted between them as birdsong chirped nearby. The burning of his body and the weight of his wounded leg pinned him down. Lachlan could only turn his head and that with great effort.

The woman stood close, not two arms' lengths away, watching him. Or was this the fever, tricking him? Lachlan felt for his sword, but no metal lay within his reach. The Brown Bess, too, was nowhere in sight. Had she crept so close and taken them, and he'd not heard? He blinked hard to clear his vision.

She gripped a knife.

"Go ahead then." His throat was thick around his words, unused to speaking. "Get it o'er with, will ye?" Resigned, he let his eyelids close. He would die the moment her blade touched him, without resisting.

Insects buzzed around his ears. He must look a sight. Black hair a knot, his face and body covered in blood, sweat, and filth. Moira might not recognize him when he came. He could not hold their baby thus.

The stillness lengthened, and finally, he cracked an eyelid open again. He had to swallow before pushing more words out of his throat. "What do ye wait for? I've no fear of dyin'."

Then he saw that in her other hand she held his canteen. She took a step, remaining just beyond his reach, and swung it close. It landed in the leaves beside him, and then she stepped back again.

He let out a laugh, though it sounded more like a cough. Did she not intend his death? What kind of enemy was this woman? Her chin lifted as he narrowed his focus, bringing her into his vision again. The thought of cold water made him ache in a new way. He glimpsed the canteen then stretched shaking fingers to it. He could barely lift it. It wobbled in his hand as he labored to bite out the cork. Finally, he managed to get it to his lips and swig. His body lurched into a fit as he coughed and spat. Lachlan let his head drop back again. The canteen balanced precariously on the ground beside him. When next he eyed the woman, she frowned. She took a step, her knife at the ready. He closed his eyes.

The cool trickle of water touched his lips. He blinked his eyes open and swallowed. The woman's nostrils flared, but she remained beside him giving him small swallows until he'd had his fill.

Chapter 3

As the stranger's eyes cleared, Wenonah set the canteen down and scooted back on her knees. He was too weak to harm her at the moment, but she would take no chances. Perhaps she had been unwise. She should have used the knife instead of letting her heart soften at the man's suffering. He might yet try to hurt her and her unborn child. He was her enemy, after all. Still ... her heart could not hate him any more than it could hate her father, who had given her as wife to the trapper. She had learned to live in two worlds.

This man's words were strange. She understood in part, but he was different than her husband or the other white men she had met before. Even though he'd spoken so little, she noted how the sounds of his speech rolled off his tongue. His dress was different than the trappers and fur traders. Those warriors he traveled with were not like the other redcoats she'd seen either. They were of some other people. Her glance flicked to the woolen breechcloth—if such it could be called, for it was like a skirt—then back to the warrior's face. He had closed his eyes again, and his breathing had calmed. His skin was burned from the sun, and dirt lined the creases at the corners of his eyes. His hair was black and clipped short like the other whites, but those eyes before they closed had been green like the forest. He was not old, perhaps not many seasons beyond her twenty-four summers.

She looked to his dress and wounded leg again. The man would not live long if he was not treated. The sickness in the swollen flesh would creep through his body, if it wasn't already doing so, and kill him. The water would comfort him for a while, but soon enough the fever would take him.

Wenonah laid one hand atop her rounded belly and, with the other, braced the knife against the ground to push up. As she moved away the babe kicked. This man was not her problem, and she'd no intention of watching him die. She turned her back and walked into the woods.

After only a dozen steps the man groaned. She faltered. Her

heartbeat sped when she peered back over her shoulder.

He had risen to a sitting position and was trying to stand. She hurried on a few more steps, her nerves tightening, but he cried out again. She stopped and turned. He stood against a tree, his face a grimace of agony. He huffed for breath, and his eyes sought her out.

"*Fuirichibh dàbhiog.* Won't ye wait?"

Now her own chest rose and fell in quick breaths. Did he mean to follow her? He wobbled forward, and she took another step away. Though there was distance between them, and he could barely stand, she battled the unreasonable fear that suddenly he would run at her. She pinched her lips and forced her feet to root.

"I beg ye." He stumbled toward her. The wounded leg collapsed. He cried out again as he pitched forward, catching himself on the smooth trunk of an *ininaatig* tree, the kind she might collect the sugar sap from in the spring.

With a quick look around, Wenonah spotted a straight branch about two inches in diameter poking up from a deadfall. She broke it free. She ran a hand along its length, considering what she was about to do. *Foolish … foolish!* Shaking, she ignored the warning. Showing him what she intended, she used it as a staff, and with cautious steps, approached the man. She stopped the pole's length away and stretched it to him. He took it from her, muttering something she thought to perhaps be his thanks, in that unfamiliar language.

As Wenonah turned away, her mind knotted with worry. Should she lead him away to the trail the whites called Braddock's Road, a place where his people would find him? With the many Shawnee, Wyandot, Delaware, and Mingo warriors lingering about, they would certainly find him first and kill him unless she intervened. Did they still hold the British, along with their women and children, in the English fort called Pitt? This man would not survive going there if they did, even though he was closer to the place than he probably realized.

But if she took him to her own lodge, what would happen then? Her cabin, with its one burned-out wall, was no place for this man. He would certainly bring her harm if he lived, and if he died, what was she to do with him? She would be better off to leave him here now, as she should have done from the beginning rather than bring him the food or succor his thirst.

She glanced again. He still followed her, though his face sagged with pain. His steps were so slow that, even in her pregnant condition, she could out-pace him easily. Yet she abated her pace, giving him time. Perhaps ... perhaps she could treat his wound, and it would be enough. Then she could send him on his way. Whatever happened to him then— whether he lived or died—was of no concern to her. Her babe would come soon. That was all she needed to worry about.

She cradled her belly, her instinct to love and protect filling her with hope.

The old trapper's cabin was not far. It lay only a short distance from the Monongahela River to the west, but Wenonah preferred the safer haven of the small creek where she'd found the stranger. Too many traveled the bigger river, friend and foe alike. Her husband had chosen the spot to build his cabin between the two places where he could hunt and trap as well as have access to the bigger waters that carried his goods to the fort and to the white man's village called Pittsburgh.

She expected the man to teeter and fall at any moment, but he staggered on, surprising her. When her cabin came into view just off the riverbank, he seemed to find a reserve of strength and quickened his step. Her heart beat *caution, caution,* but she could not change her mind about helping him now.

The cabin nestled among the trees, a squat, one-room building hewn of pine, oak, and ash, strong except for one wall. Using a store of hides her husband had hidden in a cache buried in the woods, Wenonah had stretched them over the side of the cabin a raiding war party had burned, enclosing a gaping hole. A mud-daubed chimney took up the corner supporting the sagging roof where part of the missing wall met singed logs. The door remained intact as well as the rest of the cabin. It would do to shelter her from the elements until the baby was born. Then Wenonah would return to her people up north. For now, she would let the man rest inside. She would offer to treat his wound. If he showed any sign of aggression, she would go away and leave him there. Wenonah rested her hand on the hilt of the knife in her belt. She could defend herself if necessary.

The doorway faced west. Wenonah paused and squinted at the foreigner before lifting the latch and stepping aside. She gripped her knife handle and withdrew it from her belt, her watch steady upon him lest he get the wrong idea about her invitation.

He nodded. "I ken yer meaning." He hobbled closer. She stepped back as he ducked through the doorway.

Wenonah remained where she stood and watched. He scanned her dwelling from side to side by the shaft of sunlight falling through the doorway. He spied a narrow space along the north wall and limped toward it. With the aid of his walking stick, he lowered himself to the floor and dropped against the wall, a gasp escaping him. His face was pale, and he lay trembling.

Wenonah left him there. She went into the forest and gathered some yarrow and other wild plants.

When she returned, she filled a pot and set it over a fire. The man slept while she worked. When the water boiled, she poured half into a wooden basin and set it aside. To the rest, she added herbs and bits of jerky. By the time she finished, the man had awakened again. He watched her while she ladled the broth into a carved bowl and brought it to him. He accepted it with a nod and drank it down hungrily. If he had eaten nothing since the fish yesterday, he would make himself sick. Hopefully, he would keep the contents of his stomach inside.

Now for the difficult task. Wenonah unrolled a bearskin on the floor and directed him to scoot onto it.

"Ye want me to lie on that? 'Tis yer own."

Though she understood his words, she gave no indication. She pointed again and folded her arms over her protruding belly.

"If ye insist. I'll likely leave a nest of lice behind."

She frowned, but it was not right to take back the offer now. He would need a comfortable place to lie while she worked. Wenonah gathered the kettle of hot water and a cloth of soft rabbit skin. Standing before him, a new uncertainty washed over her. Now she would have to touch the man.

Their eyes locked. She raised her brow. He would understand what she intended.

He set his empty bowl aside and lay down on the rug, cringing as he settled his wounded leg. "Get on about it then." He squeezed his eyelids tight and blew out a deep breath.

Wenonah kneeled before him. Only now did she realize her knife lay out of reach. Her heart quickened. His leg lay stiff and dirty, a third the size of the other. *He has no strength.* She steeled herself and plucked at the thing binding it. At closer inspection, she recognized a man's stocking, though it was discolored with dried blood and soil, making it almost unidentifiable. She peeled it back, and he huffed another breath as it came free of the ugly wound. She flung the ragged, filthy thing aside.

As Wenonah laid the hot rabbit skin rag over the wound, his jaw bulged and he flinched. She pressed the rag down, and he drew up his good leg at the knee. His fists clenched at his sides, but after a few moments, he opened his hands and lowered the leg again, quivering. She rinsed the rag in the steaming water and repeated the procedure many times, sometimes dribbling water over the wound.

The man shuddered, and eventually he opened his mossy-green eyes, staring at her, but he said nothing as she continued her ministrations. When she'd cleaned the wound as best she could, she took the steamed, wilted leaves of the yarrow and packed them against the bullet hole, then wrapped them tightly in clean bindings. Wenonah had no doubt a lead ball was inside, but it would stay there tight against his bone. She would cause more damage trying to remove it.

Wenonah backed away and let out a long breath of her own. He needed to rest now. She took the bowl of dirty water and carried it toward the door. Earlier this morning, she'd caught a rabbit in a snare, and it still waited to be skinned and cleaned. She would cook it for her and the man. He would need the strength of food to promote healing.

Wearily, she swung the door open and stifled a gasp. Coming toward her cabin was Catahecassa, a Shawnee warrior. She turned and set the bowl of water inside the door, then stepped out to meet him as she pulled the door closed behind her. Hopefully, the man inside would make no sound. She lifted her face without smiling at the Shawnee.

"Wenonah." He smiled. He was a handsome man, but there was a hardness about him that did not warm Wenonah. He bowed his head. When he raised it, he let his look linger.

"Greetings, Catahecassa."

"You look well today."

Wenonah stroked a hand over her unborn child without reply.

"I bring a gift." He lowered a sack from his shoulders and pulled it open. "It is a venison haunch for you. Last night I brought down a deer with one arrow. Now you will have plenty to eat until the child comes." His gaze roved to her belly and slowly slid upward.

Wenonah folded her hands over her child. "It is a kind thought, Catahecassa, but unnecessary. I have plenty to eat. In fact, I was about to clean this rabbit." She raised a hand and pointed toward the stiff creature hanging by its legs from a tree branch only yards away.

"But it is my offering to you. You can dry the meat and save it for later."

"I am too busy to do that now."

He frowned. "With what do you busy yourself?"

She shrugged, hoping he didn't think her nervous. "Oh, many things. I make clothing and collect moss for my baby. I ready the cradleboard. Many things ..." She spread her hands as if the list were too long to name.

"My sister has things she no longer uses now that her children are older. You have only to tell me, and I will bring you whatever you need."

Wenonah blinked away the offer as she glanced down to her feet. With a gathered breath, she looked up again. "Thank you for your thoughts, Catahecassa, but I can think of nothing I need. My husband left me with some things the raiders did not spoil." She frowned slightly, reminding him that his own brothers were among the warriors who murdered the trapper and burned her cabin.

"Still, you must accept the venison."

She dare not accept it. Since her husband died, Catahecassa had made his interest known, and he had brought gift after gift, which she had declined. This venison haunch—however much the thought of roasting it made her tongue long for a taste—was the largest yet. If she were to accept it, it would be a sign of her acceptance of his suit.

"No, thank you, Catahecassa. I cannot. Now, if you will excuse me, the sun is hot. I must take care of the rabbit."

His expression stiffened, and her refusal left a cool glitter in his eyes. He gave a sharp nod. "I hope that when you hunger, you will remember my offer. I will come then if you call. You would not go hungry with Catahecassa providing for you." He shot another glance at her belly. "Nor would this trapper's child."

Anger boiled up inside her. "My child shall be healthy and provided for. I will see to it."

His eyes softened as he seemed to realize his error. He dipped his head in a nod. "Yes. You will be a good mother."

"Thank you." She turned to attend the rabbit, indicating he should leave.

He picked up the bag of venison and slung it again over his shoulder.

"*Minawaa giga-waabamin,* Wenonah. I will see you again."

As he turned and strode up the trail, she lowered the rabbit, and her shoulders slumped. The warriors had spared her when they burned out her cabin and killed her man. Would they do so again if they discovered she harbored one of their great enemies? No. Catahecassa's dark, broad shoulders disappeared through the foliage of the forest. She knew him well. He would be back, and if he discovered the white soldier in her care, he would kill them both.

Chapter 4

"MOIRA," LACHLAN WHISPERED HIS golden-haired wife's name as he had so many times before, loving her, but the cool touch on his forehead lifted. He opened his eyes. *Not Moira.*

The dark-eyed woman knelt beside him, and for a moment some scent softer and sweeter than his own stink brushed past him. She stared into his eyes then moved back, giving him room. The feathery brush of her hair swept across his arm, sending a life-giving sensation rushing over him.

He closed his eyes and reached for his voice. "Thank ye, lass."

The sense of her moving again made him open his eyes. She had only reached for the bowl. She held it to his lips again. One gentle hand moved beneath his neck and helped him raise his head.

He was more awake now, and he breathed in deeply of her scent, but it was quickly spoiled by the broth which this time smelled like fresh meat. The multiple sensations swirled through his brain, and the result made him hunger. He drank greedily so that she had to tip the bowl faster.

She murmured something in her tongue, the tone a bit like scolding. Her brow bent as she pulled the bowl back. He forced a smile.

"I ken. Ye've ne'er seen such a glutton."

"Hunger good. Food give strength." She nodded at his leg.

His chest tightened, and he knew his surprise must show. "So ye ken what I'm a-sayin."

She gave a nod then rose and took the bowl away.

"How long has it been?"

"Two day. Fever break today."

He must be improving, yet his leg ached like it had been cut off, hot and heavy. He laid a hand on it and touched an unfamiliar wrap. He stared at the cabin roof over his head then looked around the room. It was constructed in the English way, with notched logs joined at the corners. He barely remembered coming inside. A disaster of some type had charred one wall and the edge of the roof straight through, but hides covered the hole.

"Whose place is this?"

She glanced over her shoulder. "It belong to my husband, Abraham Wolsey." She turned away again and busied herself with some task on a mat on the floor.

"Yer husband, aye?" No man had been about. Was she lying? In his earlier delirium, he'd thought he heard voices somewhere distant. Perhaps it was her man. Yet the words had been indistinguishable, foreign. Would an Indian woman make up such a name as *Abraham Wolsey*? "Where is he then?"

She worked with a tool, punching holes in leather, and did not look up or answer for some time. He finally rested his head on the floor, staring at the ceiling. She must have her own reasons for not answering.

"He is there." Lachlan turned to see where she spoke of. She nodded toward the door. "In ground."

He squinted as he took her meaning and swallowed against the pinch in his throat. She abruptly laid aside her work and rose. In three short steps, she was at the door and disappeared through it.

Lachlan sighed. What had happened to the man? That he was dead, and that Lachlan had upset her by asking pressed against his conscience. Moira's sigh drifted through his thoughts, the one she gave when he had blundered. Or ... maybe he interpreted the situation wrongly. Who knew whether or not she'd killed the man herself? He could not have been dead long, for the woman had not gotten pregnant by herself.

A while later she returned carrying her hide bucket. She brought a dipper and lowered herself before Lachlan. He held up a hand, stopping her. With a struggle, he pushed himself upright on the bearskin and leaned against the wall. He cleared his throat and allowed her to offer him a sip. Her eyes fastened on him but lowered once he finished drinking and raised his head. Who was she? She moved aside.

"Do ye have a name then?" His question stopped her from rising.

"I am Wenonah."

"Wenonah,"—he dipped his head—"thank ye for saving my life."

"It is not yet saved." She dropped the dipper into the bucket and pushed to her feet.

No, not saved yet.

He thought of the voices again. They had seemed real, but he usually only dreamed of Moira. "Ye have no one to help ye here? Are there others somewhere about?"

She returned to her work on the mat, but her glance flicked his way. "I need no help."

Stubborn woman. Moira had been like that. She'd insisted that it was too soon to call for the midwife. Little did either of them know the bairn intended to come so early.

Lachlan shook off the painful memory. Did this woman Wenonah understand what was in store for her? "Yer to have a wee one."

Wenonah paused in her work and laid a hand on her stomach. Her brow tweaked ever so slightly, hinting at a moment's uncertainty. She nodded. "Yes. Abraham will not see his child."

"'Tis sorry I am."

"Sorry?"

"For yer loss."

She gathered her tools from the mat and put them away. "He was old and did not think a child would yet be his."

His age must've taken him. "I thought I heard voices while I slept."

She jerked around, and her eyes darted over him and to the door. "Catahecassa. Shawnee. Very dangerous. He come back."

Lachlan sat straighter, his nerves tingling. "Ye're certain of this?"

She nodded. "He want ..." Her dark skin turned an even richer shade, and she moved to the fireplace. A few small logs and branches lay beside the hearth. She arranged them neatly inside. No wonder she did not fear him. She had this other man, this dangerous Shawnee warrior, watching out for her. Lachlan needed more information, and he could think of only one question to draw it out.

"Ye get a new husband, eh?" He grinned when she looked back.

Her fist tightened on a stick, and she scowled. "I no want Catahecassa. He keep coming. Bring gifts. I take baby and go away where he never find me."

So ... this Catahecassa was a plague to her then. Still, her description of the man, that he was dangerous, did not ease his concerns. "When do ye expect to have the bairn?" Lachlan allowed a tender inflection to creep into his voice.

But this time she kept her back to him and did not answer. *Wise girl, Wenonah. For I am your enemy still.*

The day passed away as Lachlan woke for periods but slept much.

Wenonah changed the dressing again, and this time the marks around the bullet wound seemed less livid. Ugly all the same, but not as frightening as at first. She talked little, only telling him when to shift or what she intended to do—if words were necessary. Lachlan did not broach the subject of her child or the Shawnee again.

The next day, Wenonah disappeared for a long time. He began to think she had made good on her word to go away. Perhaps she would do so now, before the baby came, thereby avoiding any further contact with either him or the Shawnee. Loneliness descended, which he tried to ignore. He had been strangely comforted by her presence, yet it was best she left him alone. He would heal well enough in time. Soon he must get to Fort Pitt and discover if any of his brigade survived—or if, indeed, the fort still stood.

Just when he believed he truly would be left to tend himself, she returned with a batch of fish in a basket of reeds. She moved slowly, her expression wan as she retrieved a trencher. "I go clean fish." A moment later, she slipped outside again.

Lachlan ground his jaw. Not only did she have herself to care for, but now she was taking care of him too. He was the one who needed to move on, sooner rather than later. Tomorrow he would leave this place and continue to Fort Pitt. Better to put the pregnant woman and the Shawnee behind him. If the warrior came again, as Wenonah said he would, Lachlan would be nearly defenseless. He'd not seen his Brown Bess or sword since he lay in the woods. She must have taken them, but where had she hidden them? He shifted his wounded leg and grimaced. No weapon and little strength. The Shawnee would have little trouble overpowering him. Then what would happen to Wenonah? What would the Shawnee do to her when he discovered she'd harbored his enemy?

Lachlan shifted his leg again. Moving carefully, he turned to his side and reached for the staff. Beads of sweat formed on his brow as he pulled himself upright. His blood rushed, and he had to pause, gripping the staff with whitened knuckles until his leg stopped burning and the pain settled into a more temperate throb. With halting steps, he walked across the floor and pushed open the door. The daylight nearly blinded him. He blinked a moment then saw her standing there at a makeshift table, watching him. The cabin sat in an area of tall trees and a few stumps scattered amid matted grass. A couple of hand-made tools hung on the side of the building, and a hoe leaned against it. To the west, a small garden patch was turned and growing scraggly vines. Corn stalks lay crushed on the ground.

He looked to her again, and Wenonah faced him, as if she'd been following his perusal of her things.

"They trample garden."

"Who?"

"Raiders who kill my man."

He jerked with surprise. So age hadn't taken her husband.

She laid a fish on the table where some flies buzzed around entrails. With a push of her knife, she slit its glistening belly.

"Where is my Bess? My gun?"

She stuck her fingers into the slit she'd made and drew out the fish's insides.

"I willna hurt ye, but if there are raiders about—even this Shawnee ye told me of—then I must have my gun."

Now her dark eyes flashed up. She poured a stream of water over the fish, rinsing it clean, and laid it on her trencher.

"Yer in no danger from me, Wenonah. I only want my gun. Tomorrow I'll leave ye in peace."

She paused and gave him a slow study. She nodded to the north. "I bury under leaves behind cabin."

He nodded and took a step in that direction.

"I get gun and long knife." She swiped her hands down her dress and hurried on silent feet around the cabin while Lachlan leaned on his staff. She returned hauling the weapons as well as his powder supply and—perhaps most surprising—his shoes. She paused for a moment as if considering her wisdom then stepped forward. "I put inside."

He gave a nod.

Lachlan took a slow walk toward the fish table as he waited for her to return. His leg had more strength than before. If she redressed the wound in the morning, and if he were careful, he could make it to Fort Pitt by the next nightfall or perhaps the following. The fort couldn't be far away now. They'd been less than thirty miles from it when the Indians ambushed the regiments. Now he must not be half that distance. Wenonah would know.

When she returned, he offered his thanks with a smile. "Wenonah, do ye ken how far away Fort Pitt is?"

She pointed into the distance and arched a hand a portion of the way across the sky. "A walk of the sun from so ... to so." She looked at him. "Without wound."

Only a few hours without his wound holding him back. But with the wound? She moved past him and retrieved the trencher of fish. Lachlan picked up the empty basket and followed her. The fish smelled better than he did.

"Wenonah, have ye a pot of water I could wash with?"

They ducked inside the low door frame, and she set the fish down next to the hearth then turned to him. "I fetch water."

He nodded. He hated having her run another errand for him, but what else could he do? She seemed happy to help. Maybe she wished he smelled better too.

An hour later, the water had been sprinkled with a generous amount of dried herbs and heated over the fire. Lachlan carried it outside. He scrubbed the grime from his body and doused his head. He also washed out his shirt and splashed the remaining water over his feet. His bandage wasn't wetted too badly, and Wenonah had promised to change it when he finished anyway.

Tired from the exercise, Lachlan felt better, nevertheless. His shirt would take some time to dry. Wenonah would have to endure a half-dressed man lying about her cabin for the remainder of the day. He entered to the scent of fish baking in the hot coals.

"Well now, that feels better, and isna that fish yer cookin makin my stomach yearn?"

She glanced up and away quickly, and Lachlan suddenly felt self-conscious for embarrassing her with his chest bared naked in front of her. But her skin flushed becomingly, and he could understand the Shawnee's interest in the lass. He caught his own gaze lingering.

Pulling it away, he spied the gun and sword leaning against the wall by his bed, and hobbled over to inspect them. He set aside his staff and lowered himself then picked up the Bess and inspected the mechanisms. Nothing appeared damaged from its time in the river or wood. He would find a bit of cloth to clean her and pour out his powder to dry in the meantime.

Wenonah rose from the fireside and brought him a trencher of food. He looked up at her as she held it out. "Yer a God-send, lass. I mean it." He smiled and accepted the food.

She returned to her own meal, and they ate in silence. With furtive glances, Lachlan watched her. She was a comely woman, young, and healthy despite her current situation. That she had married some old trapper puzzled him. How had such an arrangement occurred? Had she been in dire straits, depending on him for aid? Lachlan would never know. After tomorrow morning, they would never meet again.

When they'd finished eating, she cleaned up from their meal, scrubbed the trenchers, and set them by the hearth until tomorrow. Finally, she went to her bed and lay down. Lachlan had already lowered himself to the bearskin, resting shirtless on the soft fur. The fire had died to ash, and only a coal or two glowed. Lachlan watched them until he fell asleep.

Moira came to him then. Ah, but it had been too long since he'd seen her. Too many hours. Tonight, her eyes were playful again, and her long blond hair blew around her shoulders. *Moira, darlin, yer wearing yer weddin dress. Let me dance with ye.* He twirled her around, lifting her off her bare feet. Her laughter bubbled out, and Lachlan laughed too. He nuzzled her neck with his beard and kissed her. Yet it wasn't as though he could taste her enough. She groaned, or was it him? Lachlan frowned. The edges of the dream blurred, and panic rose in his chest as it always did when their time was over. *I'm not done lovin ye, Moira. Please dinna leave just yet.* But she released his hands and floated away, her bare feet dancing over grass and wildflowers. The moaning grew louder.

Lachlan opened his eyes to the darkness of a log cabin.

"Aaaah ..." Panting came from across the room.

Wenonah.

Lachlan sat up, staring into the darkness. His heart crashed against his chest. He groped for the staff and wrapped his fingers round it. Wenonah quieted. Did she dream too?

He listened for another minute before shifting his hip to lay himself back down when she groaned again.

"Wenonah." He pulled himself upright, ignoring the dull ache in his leg, and moved to the fireplace. He felt for the green stick she used to stir the coals and pushed around the ash until he found one. Then, locating the tongs, he picked it up and lit the single candle she used inside the dark cabin. With a heavy limp, he carried it to her beside.

Her eyes were wide upon him, her face a sheen of sweat. Fear enlarged the whites around her irises, and she twisted her body as another pain came upon her.

Chapter 5

LACHLAN STARED, FROZEN, BARELY able to let out his own breath as Wenonah first panted then gritted her teeth. *Not this!* Her brow curled in agony, but she did not speak, only watched him as she reached out to her side and coiled her fingers around the hilt of her knife. He raised the candle higher. She writhed as she pointed the knife at him. Then her face deepened in dark color, and she gave a guttural cry.

He came to life and locked his mind against the past. "Dinna fear, Wenonah. I will help ye." He pressed both hands toward her, palms open, encouraging calm. Then he dragged the stump that served as the cabin's only chair and set the candle on it. Sweat beaded his brow, and he pushed a hand through his hair. He hadn't even put his shirt back on, but there was no time for it—at least he didn't think so.

Wenonah had lowered her hand and dropped the knife, focusing now on the pain. She reached down and tugged upward at her dress.

Lachlan swallowed down a knot of terror. Moira's image reappeared before him. Never had he seen such blood, not even during battle. Such a merciless flow of life.

"Peace, Wenonah. I will guide the bairn with my hands. I willna bring ye harm nor the bairn"—he pushed his knuckles across his mouth—"if God will strengthen me." Lachlan begged God's aid as he stumped about the cabin gathering a soft hide for swaddling and his shirt from where it hung dry on a peg. Perhaps Wenonah or the bairn would need it.

"Trust me." Slowly he bent and helped her with the dress, his eyes steady upon hers.

The fear in them remained until another pain clenched her, then she nearly rose off the bed, and he quickly scooted the garment back. Water gushed out, and he smothered a hand across his face. *Help me, God. Dinna fail this woman.* He rejected the thought, *As Ye did my Moira.*

"All right, steady now, Wenonah. Soon ye'll hold your bairn."

With the next pain, Wenonah pushed, and again with several

more. Lachlan focused all his being on the crowning head, when with a sudden gush it emerged, dark and wet. With one more push, the child was born. Her warm, soft body filled his strong hands, and Lachlan's heart beat now with some emotion he didn't know what to do with. He released a gasp of gladness.

"Ye've a bonny wee lassie." He looked up to see Wenonah watched him, wonder in her expression overcoming her exhaustion. *Thank Ye, God. She seems well. They both do.* He gently lowered the baby atop her, and her arms came up to cling the child. "We've a wee more work to do." Lachlan moved to Wenonah's feet again, and in a few more moments the afterbirth came free. He tied the cord with a piece of gut string and used Wenonah's own knife to sever it.

Wenonah shuddered.

"Not much more. Ye'll be all right soon." He helped her wrap the infant, and then he proceeded to clean Wenonah's legs with the clean cloth, careful not to go beyond any further bounds of trust as his throat clenched tight. She had bled but not as badly as Moira. The child had come without hesitation. Not so his own child. Heaviness and joy co-mingled. How could it be that he could still sorrow over his loss after four years, yet rejoice at this moment for a woman he didn't know.

The child gave a soft mew, and Wenonah looked to Lachlan again. She tugged at the top of her dress. "She hungers." Her voice was shy.

"Aye ... I'm sorry. I'll help ye remove it if ye wish, and I'll go outside the cabin while ye take care of her."

She nodded. "There is moss in the corner—and more cloths."

"I'll get them."

He moved behind her and helped her lift the soiled dress over her head, turning his face as much as he could. The shape of her bare back stamped on his mind, nevertheless. He cleared his throat and reached for his clean shirt. "'Tis a warm night. I dinna need this." He laid it beside her and hastened to the door with the wooden basin of soiled water.

Lachlan latched the door behind him and dropped down among the grass and trees. A gray light filtered from the east. He'd seen more than he should, and Lachlan had not seen a woman in a long time. Yet he would not harm her for all the world. He scrubbed his hands over his face, as the long hours washed over him until the stain of tears filled his palms. He had stopped asking God why Moira died. Perhaps this was why—so that he would be here tonight, to help this woman in her hour of need. He shook his head. Sometimes answers didn't bear knowing. He could only trust that God understood his weeping and bore his sorrow too.

"Ye would ha' been proud, Moira. I dinna let her down." He closed his eyes. "Tell her, God. Tell my Moira she would ha' been proud."

He stayed outdoors for an hour as the sun rose, and when he returned, Wenonah wore his white shirt. Moss and soft cloths were removed from the stack, and she was asleep beneath a trader's blanket, the child swaddled in her arms.

Lachlan could watch her now. The tallow candle had burned low, but by its flickering light, he gazed upon Wenonah's face. She was a strong, brave woman, an inarguable fact. She had planned well for this birth, despite having her plans upended by the arrival of a Highland soldier, lost and wounded, who required her to draw upon her reserves. Now, though, she needed that strength returned. He could not just depart in a few hours and leave her to make her way all alone. What had she said? Something about returning to her people? Who were they? How far away did she hope to travel? And what of the Shawnee warrior who had intentions of his own?

Dangerous.

Her word, not his. Lachlan laid the back of his knuckles against the long tress of her hair that fanned out on the bed and stroked it. She slept deeply, her face free of fear, worry, and sternness. Not a line to show her beyond his age, but younger. Too young to carry such burdens. Yet old enough to be a wife, a mother.

Wenonah ... He caressed her name silently, studying the way her jaw curved and her dark brows lay in a slightly arched line over her closed eyes. *A beauty ye are, and 'tis certain the Shawnee will have ye if he can.* The babe stirred, and Wenonah's hand folded instinctively over her. Long fingers, delicate and able, draped over the covering on the child.

Lachlan backed away. He would find them something for their breakfast. It was his turn to give aid, to thank her for all she'd done. He wouldna be leaving for Fort Pitt this day. He must remain, and later count the cost.

Chapter 6

WENONAH MARVELED AT HER tiny daughter nuzzling her breast. How beautiful she was. How perfect. She brushed her fingertips over the velvety dark crown of her head. When the child finished nursing, she lifted her to her shoulder and drew her shirt closed. His shirt. She caressed the worn fabric. It was clean but still bore a scent of the strange man who had been kind to her. He had not treated her as an enemy but had shown mercy to her and to her babe. How carefully he had guided her child into the world, and the look on his face when he handed Waaseyaa to her the first time ... She lingered over the memory, the unguarded look of tenderness in his eyes, and when he had turned away, a bit of moisture. Tiredness, perhaps, from the long night.

The door opened, letting in the bright light of day. He propped it wide so sunshine would spill over the room. His face lifted in a smile. "Yer awake then." He carried her bucket of water and the empty basin, nodding toward the fireplace. "I've heated water for yer bath and extra if ye wish to clean the babe. There's a bit o' gruel in the pot for yer breakfast as well."

She turned her head to see whereof he spoke then nodded. Her kettle hung by the fireplace. Self-consciousness stole over Wenonah at the man's kindnesses. To conquer it, she looked toward his leg. "You pain? Leg better?"

He raised his brow with a slight grimace. "'Tis been better I can tell ye, but I can walk easier than before. I'm right thankful to have my shoes again." He gave her a nod.

"You must rest."

He set down the items and stirred the pot of gruel warming by the fire. Then he approached her bedside and spoke softly. "I've time to do that later. Ye must rest as well." He indicated the babe with a nod. "How is our wee darlin doing?"

Wenonah laid the baby back with a smile. "She perfect."

"Does she have a name then?"

She smiled. "Her name Waaseyaa. First Light of Morning Sun." She spoke the name reverently as the man leaned closer to peer at her daughter. He examined the babe, his own face a hand's breadth from Wenonah's, and Wenonah shifted to study him. The growth of beard on his face looked soft rather than grizzly. His skin was darkened by days in the outdoors. Lighter creases spread out from the corners of his green eyes, eyes that sparkled with admiration as he looked at Waaseyaa. He wore his waistcoat without the shirt so that the generously proportioned muscles of his shoulders were bare, exuding strength along with his gentleness. His short hair, nearly as black as her own, smoothed back along the side of his head to tuck behind his ears. He was of handsome face and form, this foreigner.

She drew her forehead back with a breath, aware that if he looked up, he might notice her deep perusal. He backed away too. "If ye like, I can hold her for ye while ye break yer fast or take care of yer other needs."

She tucked at the baby's swaddling as she considered his offer. What else was she to do? He had proved she need not fear him. She nodded, but her heart beat harder as she handed him her child. If felt as though he held her very life in his large hands. Then he bent his head and smiled down at Waaseyaa. He began to croon. *"Fhuar mi lorg an laoigh bhric dheirg ..."*

Her lips bowed with a peace settling through her, and she shifted to rise. *The man is kind.* He appeared wholly content as he continued to sing softly to Waaseyaa and rock her in his arms. Wenonah took slow steps toward the door as the strength returned to her limbs. At the doorway, she paused and turned to him. "You name?"

He smiled at her. "Aye, lass, my name is Lachlan. Lachlan McRae."

"Lac-lan."

He nodded and repeated the name, his throat making a soft, burring sound. "Lachlan." His smile widened, so his teeth showed smooth and white.

A strange pleasure at his smile filled her, and Wenonah warmed. She slipped out the door. Why did she feel content in the presence of this stranger who should mean her nothing but harm? Yet, everything inside her felt peace and happiness at his presence. Quite a different sentiment than Catahacassa's nearness lent her. Even now, she glanced through the trees, wondering when the Shawnee would appear again, and what would keep him from coming into her cabin if she weren't outside to prevent it—to prevent him from discovering Lac-lan. She practiced his name again, grinning when she tried to form the sound in her throat that he did, but it was not the same.

Wenonah roamed into the edge of the woods until she came to a place to make her water. Afterward, she walked down to the river. She would wash there then return to the cabin to tend Waaseyaa.

She was gone only a short while, but she was weary by the time she returned. Weakened by the exertion, she stepped inside, anxious to lie down. There, seated on the stool stump, Lac-lan still cradled Waaseyaa peacefully in his broad arms. Wenonah reached for her. Lac-lan hesitated, as if reluctant to let her go, but his hands moved gently until he'd released the babe. His knuckles brushed Wenonah's arms as he laid Waaseyaa against her, and the brief moment's touch was like the breath of a gentle breeze to her senses. Her glance flew up to meet his, but he was watching the babe.

And then he wasn't.

His forest-green eyes met hers, and their gazes locked, yet nothing in the exchange frightened Wenonah—no threat, no lust. The eyes that only days ago were shadowed with pain came alive with something bright and hopeful. She dared not stay locked in their hold long. She stepped back and settled onto her bed to nurse the baby.

Lac-lan turned away too. He rose from the stump and limped to his bearskin rug where he lowered himself and examined his leg.

"Tomorrow, I fix new medicine."

"Dinna ye worry none about me." He gave a nod. "Ye just tend to the wee First Light of Dawn. Waaseyaa needs yer attention more than I. I am strong enough to tend myself."

"You stubborn man."

He glanced up sharply, and she grinned, then ducked her head again so that her hair draped over both her and Waaseyaa.

"Aye. So I've been told."

By wife? Wenonah wanted to know but could not ask. She swallowed the question before it edged too far out on her tongue to withdraw.

He checked his bandaging, and something about the set of his shoulders told Wenonah that his thoughts had turned inward.

The next day Wenonah felt stronger, and Lac-lan appeared rested as well. They spoke of a meal. Wenonah thought of the venison haunch

Catahacassa had offered. Nursing her daughter increased her appetite. The rabbit she'd snared on the day Lac-lan came had long since been devoured. There was some pemmican and jerky, and a few bits of dried fish, but little else. Barely enough for her to get by on with a hungry infant. Certainly, an insufficient supply for a grown man to subsist on.

"My powder is dry," Lac-lan said. "I will hunt. Something will come along. Perhaps even a deer or a bear."

"There is the risk of the Shawnee or others."

"I willna take more than a single shot, and I will go far enough from the cabin so they willna come here. They will think 'tis another Indian hunting."

"Perhaps." Her nerves tightened. "Perhaps not."

Lac-lan shrugged. "I must try. Ye need more to eat for yer milk."

A flush crept up her throat that he should say so, yet his words were true. "I go too. I get more plants for medicine and for food."

He took up his gun and cocked his head, but he did not argue it. He only nodded.

Wenonah gathered up the baby and swaddled her. She would not require the cradleboard yet. The babe was tiny and light enough to carry as she searched for the plants. They would not be out long. If Lac-lan wandered farther in search of food, she and Waaseyaa would return to the cabin.

They left a short time later, and Wenonah turned to the pathway that led toward the river. Lac-lan walked with a heavy limp deeper into the brush further on. Wenonah found the patch of yarrow she had picked from before. The baby slept soundly while she searched for wild carrot and other roots they might put into a pot over the fire.

Lac-lan was still out of sight, so Wenonah stepped down to the river for a drink. When a shot fired, she jumped, and the baby whimpered. "Sh ... Is Lac-lan hunting us some meat." She drew the back of her hand across her forehead and pushed her hair over her shoulder so that she might stoop for another drink of cold water. She glimpsed up as was her habit while she squatted down, and her heart jerked against the baby when she spotted a man watching her on the trail across the water. A man in a red coat who was not Lac-lan. A sneer curled his lip.

She jumped to her feet and spun away, just as the splash of the man's feet plunged into the stream. Wenonah flew through the forest, the baby clutched against her. Her moccasins left hardly a sound as they struck the earth, yet each *whoosh* of her breath and slap of a branch sounded like a shout that would lead him to her. *Lac-lan!* She clamped her throat around the cry she wanted to release, afraid of what would happen if the soldier reached them. She gripped Waaseyaa tighter and pleaded for the Great Spirit to protect her daughter.

Suddenly a crack hit the tree beside her, followed almost instantly by a gun's report. She ducked her head with a gasp and ran on. The cabin lay just ahead, and soon the soldier would see it too. What should she do? Shut herself inside? Run past it into the woods? Where was Lac-lan?

Then he stepped out from the forest to her left, and her heart bolted. She stifled a cry. It was not the soldier. Only him, her Lac-lan.

She ran toward him, and he shouted past her. "Halt!" He lifted up his gun like a flag.

Wenonah spun around. The approaching soldier sidled closer, his musket drawing a bead on her, his lips twisting. "Looks like ye won't be goin far, now does it?" The soldier didn't look past her at Lac-lan. "We've got ye between us, and there's no gettin by us."

Lac-lan shouted again. "I am Lachlan McRae of his Majesty's 42nd Foot! Put down yer gun!"

The soldier stiffened. The hot, angry look on his face twitched into surprise, and his glance moved past Wenonah. Sweat streamed down his face as his eyes widened.

"McRae? Is it ye?"

Lac-lan beckoned her with his free hand, his eyes trained on the soldier. "'Tis me, Jesse Nab."

The man's gun dropped lower as he stared at Lachlan.

Wenonah moved behind Lac-lan, guided by his hand, but her heart continued thrumming.

"Yer alive." The soldier's words sounded dumbstruck.

Wenonah tucked herself and the babe against Lac-lan's back, his strength a wall between her and the child and their assailant.

"That I am, thanks to this woman ye nearly scared to death."

She would not peek from behind Lac-lan, but the weight of the other man's long silence hung in the air. Then his voice was closer. "The savage there behind ye?"

Lac-lan reached behind and gently gripped her arm, drawing her out and holding her close. "Aye, Nab, only no savage. More a savior. I'd be dead and rotting away if not for this lass."

The man's gaze drifted from Lac-lan to Wenonah and blinked. Wenonah raised her chin higher. Her racing heart slowed. She glanced up at the man beside her, and her heartbeat shifted yet again. It shifted, and it cracked open wide.

Chapter 7

NAB BLINKED AGAIN AND gasped. "Yer alive. I canna hardly believe it."

Lachlan extended his hand and stepped toward Nab. "'Tis warming my heart to see ye again, my friend." He braced a hand on Nab's shoulder, but his glance quickly took in the surrounding woods. "Did ye come to this place alone?"

Nab nodded. "Aye, except for one of the scouts returning to Fort Bedford." He stuck his fingers in his mouth and gave a sharp whistle.

Lachlan's grip on Nab's shoulder dug in. "Ye'll have the Shawnee and who knows what others down on our heads."

Nab gave a cockeyed grin and shook his head. "They've cleared out. Gone. Did ye not ken that we won the battle?"

"What? Nay! Tell me what happened. I was killed, but not dead. When I woke up, I couldna tell the lay of things, and I dragged myself off. I feared all was lost."

Nab sought Wenonah again, and Lachlan drew her near. Her arm trembled in his grasp, and he longed to reassure her. He offered a gentle squeeze.

"This is Wenonah. I meant what I said. She saved me. Took care of my wound and kept me fed." A flash of movement caught his eye as a ranger stepped out from among the trees beyond Nab. He was close enough to have killed them if he'd had a mind. He stalked as silently as an Indian.

Jesse set the stock of his Brown Bess on the earth and swiveled to follow Lachlan's notice. He addressed the newcomer. "Look who I've found. My friend McRea whom I thought dead. Turns out, he's of stronger Scot's stuff than even his brethren could have imagined." Nab grinned at Lachlan again and looked him up and down, from Lachlan's bandaged leg to the way he leaned on his gun again. "Are ye able to travel?"

"Only slowly. I thought to make it to Pitt as soon as I dare. Is the fort secured then?"

Nab nodded. "'Tis." The ranger remained silent, eyeing them from his position at the wood line. "We are quartered there for the time being. Bushy Run may have turned the tide of this native rebellion."

"How did it happen? I was separated, and those around me killed. I couldna figure a way back toward the others without crossing paths with the Indians, and me bleeding out a trail easy to follow." Lachlan gave a shake of his head. "I thought I was done for."

"As did we all. Each time we charged, the Indians vanished into the woods, until the troops were broken apart."

"Aye ..." Lachlan rubbed his chin. 'Twas precisely what happened to him and a handful of men with him.

"Bouquet ordered a fort built of the flour bags where the wounded were given cover. 'Twasna much for protection, but we defended the hill as best we could when the fighting resumed the next day. I searched for ye among the men. 'Twas then I feared the worst.

"When morning came, Bouquet formed an audacious plan." Nab grinned and draped one arm over the end of his barrel. "He's an old Indian fighter, ye ken. The Indians had left a hole in their circumference— an escape route for their defenders—as they often do. They were a-tightening the noose around our forces, but Bouquet realized there had been no attacks from down the gully to the east. He pulled out two of our own companies of the 42nd, and we slipped through the gap. We ran across the open and took cover in the forest beyond—ye recall that wide swath of open ground—well, the Indians thought we were on the run, and they took the bait." Nab's chuckle rumbled. "We filled our guns with double shot and turned the ambush on its end."

Nab was deep into the tale now. He raised his brows and studied the area around them as though seeing the terrain from that day. He drew a circling motion with his finger. "Then Campbell brought his Highlanders around the hill in a fishhook, and before long, they closed the trap on the right flank of those screechin beasts. They flushed out and broke cover. As ye can imagine, the hill exploded." He gave a slow shrug and puffed up his chest. "Nothin more to it. The savages have scattered to the west. I doubt they'll be able to round up enough fighters to prolong the troubles."

Nab eyed Wenonah again. "None of 'em are likely to come 'round here to bother us now that we've chased 'em off."

She stiffened beneath Lachlan's touch, and he grazed his thumb in a soothing caress against her arm. "That would bode well for Wenona as well as the rest of us then," he said.

Nab's pupils disappeared inside his narrow gaze.

"What are Bouquet's plans now?" Lachlan's question drew Nab's attention from Wenonah. He glanced at the scout, who remained at a passive distance, his eyes alert around them.

"Bouquet intends to remain here in this godforsaken wilderness, keeping down uprisings around the forts." Nab turned his head and spat. "He'll have a hard time keeping his army together. The enlisted Royal Americans want to return to their homes."

Home—a thing no longer to be grasped by Lachlan. "And what is to keep them from goin?" he muttered.

Nab's look drifted again to Wenonah and settled on the babe. The gleam in his eyes held unasked questions. Lachlan refrained from encircling Wenonah's shoulders with a protective arm.

"They'll go if they're keen on doing so," Nab said. "Perhaps they're more of a mind to protect their families from these uprisings than to worry over a scatterin of forts in the wilderness."

Lachlan felt Wenonah's nearness. Who would shield her and her child? He searched the area. "Perhaps." He forced a small smile and adjusted his weight on the musket. "Have ye had anything to eat? If not, there should be a rabbit lying amid some brush over yon, waiting to be skinned." He spoke softly to Wenonah. "Go on back now. We'll come." He gave Nab a nod and hobbled past him, expecting he would follow.

"Hold a moment." Nab strode toward the scout. They spoke in tones Lachlan could not hear, then the scout melted into the forest. Nab's feet crunched along behind Lachlan. "He'll go, now I've found ye. I'll stay with ye until ye can make the trek to Fort Pitt, if ye don't mind my intrusion."

Lachlan's shoulders tightened with unease, but there was nothing to be done for it. He thanked Nab, and they wandered about the brush for several minutes until Lachlan discovered his quarry. He plucked the dead rabbit up by its long, hind legs. "Let us see if there's still a fire burning in the hearth."

Nab raised his brows, his questions sealed behind his lips as Lachlan led the way. When the trapper's cabin came into view, Lachlan glimpsed Nab's squint.

"So, ye've been set pretty well then."

"I was almost killed dead when Wenonah found me and gave me aid."

"What inspired her to do it, I wonder?"

"Her husband was English. This is his place."

Nab rubbed his jaw. "I see now."

Lachlan took out his knife and slit the creature's skin. As he cleaned their dinner, Nab strode about, looking over the cabin's exterior. "What happened to him?"

"Killed by raiders."

Wenonah stepped out the door and looked to Lachlan, pointedly ignoring Jesse Nab. "I look at wound then cook rabbit."

"A'right." Lachlan called to Nab, "Come on then."

Nab peered about as they entered, taking in the small but tidy lodging, the pot of herbs steaming over the fire, the tiny babe nestled on the rope bed on the side of the room, and Lachlan's own pallet of hides on the floor. He looked over the array of small tools and other bare essentials hanging from pegs on the wall. "'Tis tight and cozy enough, I reckon."

Lachlan settled on his pallet, and Nab took the log stump near Wenonah's bed. His attention flicked to the babe, and Wenonah's fingers coiled atop Lachlan's leg. He reached out and gently patted her hand. "The babe is called Waaseyaa. First Light of Dawn."

Nab leaned over and looked closer at the child. "I wonder how it was the woman was able to find you and still take care of the *bairn*."

"Jesse ..." Lachlan flinched as Wenonah tightened the bindings over his leg, her eyes darting to his. "I was here when she birthed the child. I didn't plan to say so, but ..."

Nab's chin dipped. "I ken ye've come to care for them."

Wenonah's glance shot between them and lowered. Her lips pinched tight, but a flush on her skin deepened its lovely color. Lachlan touched her hand again. "Aye. I reckon I 'ave."

"*Hatito*, Wenonah!" A deep shout came from outside the door, and all three of them lurched. Wenonah jerked back from Lachlan, and Nab jumped to his feet, his tomahawk already in his hand.

Wenonah scrambled past Nab with a hurried shake of her head and spoke through the closed door. "*Hatito! Thah-kee-chee nee-sah-hah.*" Her dark eyes turned to them, and she laid a finger to her lips. Nab stepped back against the wall, and Lachlan reached for his gun as he pressed himself into the corner.

Wenonah edged the door open only far enough to slip outside, but Lachlan glimpsed the well-muscled Indian standing in the sunlight before she closed them in again.

"She'll betray us," Nab whispered with a hiss.

Lachlan shook his head and pressed his lips together. He grimaced as he rose to his feet. Then he hoisted the gun.

Outside, native speech leeched muffled tones through the door, first the big man's voice then Wenonah's. She'd drawn him further away. Lachlan limped forward and pressed his ear to the door.

The big Indian's voice was smooth, wooing. His deep, throaty chuckle sent a shard of jealousy through Lachlan. He couldn't hear Wenonah's response.

There was quiet. Lachlan tensed. Then Wenonah gasped. With a racing heart, Lachlan eased up the door latch.

"What are ye doing?" Nab's whisper cut across the room.

Lachlan opened the door a crack and peered with one eye into the bright forest. Wenonah and the Shawnee stood down the path. Catehecassa held onto Wenonah's upper arm as she attempted to veer from him. He breathed words against her ear. Wenonah tugged. Even from where Lachlan peered out the crack, he could see Catahecassa's grip tighten, refusing to release her. He inched the door open further.

Wenonah's face was set. Lachlan didn't understand her language, but her expression was clear. The Shawnee's nostrils flared. His eyes burned bright with intent as he ground out more words, all wooing gone from his tone.

Wenonah shook her head.

Lachlan's heart raced as the Indian man jerked her closer. Lachlan pushed through the door. The Indian's gaze shot up. With one hand on her still, Catahecassa drew his tomahawk.

Lachlan leveled his musket, and the man's eyes widened. "Get yer hands off her."

Catahecassa dropped his hold on Wenonah, and she stumbled clear. The Indian jerked the tomahawk back with a shout, and Lachlan squeezed the trigger.

Click. The metal hammer snapped without percussion.

"McRae!"

Lachlan twisted sideways as Catahecassa's tomahawk spun past and ricocheted off a tree. The Shawnee charged. Lachlan caught Nab's musket. Catahecassa leapt, knife drawn in an arc above his head. The gun exploded, and a cloud of smoke filled the space. The Indian's heavy body struck Lachlan with a force that knocked him to the ground. Lachlan scrambled to push him off, but suddenly Nab was there. With a grunt, the other Highlander yanked Catahecassa free by his scalp lock. The Shawnee blinked twice at Lachlan, then his eyes rolled back. He sputtered once. Blood spewed down his face and mingled with the pool running out his chest before he died.

Lachlan fell back and closed his eyes. He heaved for breath. A shadow fell upon him, and then a touch. He opened his eyes again and raised his head. The throbbing in his leg was forgotten as Wenonah bent over him and grasped his shoulders. Fright in her eyes slowly eased away as she saw that he was well, but a tear escaped down her cheek and dripped off her chin.

"I'm a'right." He looked down over his shirt, covered in Catahecassa's blood. "My leg pains me something fierce though." He searched out Nab. "Thank ye for saving my life. Seems providence brought ye to us at just the right time."

Jesse Nab retrieved the fallen musket and glanced between Lachlan and Wenonah. His mouth turned up on one side. "I reckon 'tis you who done the savin."

Wenonah's lips arched in a smile.

Chapter 8

WENONAH KNEELED AT THE stream and scoured Catahecassa's blood out of Lachlan's waistcoat. If she got rid of the blotch in its entirety, she might forget the fearful events of this day. Catahecassa had been a stain to her as well, a man she would not have, but a man who would not accept her answer. He had threatened her there on the path. Told her he would take her against her will if she did not accept him. Said he would pay her father the bride price if he must. He even insinuated he would harm the trapper's child if she refused.

She clenched her lips and scrubbed harder. She would have murdered Catahecassa herself were she strong enough. Dropping the waistcoat in a puddle on the rock before her, Wenonah leaned back on her legs and closed her eyes. Just as the water washed out the blood and carried it away, so she must let go of her anger. Holding such scorn inside would only seed a great hatred. It was not right. Catahecassa was dead. There was no reason to hold onto bitterness. Her husband, Abraham Wolsey, had been old and dull but always kind to her. He had read to her of the great God who carried away sin. Her hatred was sin.

And yet ... she was not sorry Catahecassa was dead. The stranger Jesse Nab had buried him in a shallow grave while Wenonah tended Lac-lan's injury. Lac-lan had grimaced and spoken tenderly of Waaseyaa while she cleaned and redressed his leg. Now, Lac-lan cradled her daughter while he spoke with his friend, and Wenonah slipped away to clean the waistcoat.

Her stomach tightened at the thought of his leaving, for he would surely do so now that the other soldier had arrived.

What were the words that Lac-lan's friend had been saying right before Catahecassa's arrival? Something that made her blush ... something that made her yearn for the words to be true.

"Ye've come to care for them." And Lac-lan had nodded. *"I reckon I 'ave."* Lac-lan had touched her hand and looked into her eyes. The simple gesture had warmed her in a way she had never experienced.

Ever. Even now, with eyes closed at the memory, she felt that touch, the kindness in those words.

Could they have been more than kind? How could she ever know? He would leave soon, and she must begin the long journey back to her people.

Wenonah's eyes fluttered open at the stinging thought. She would return to her father's lodge with nothing to offer and a child to care for. What would keep her father from selling her again, perhaps this time to someone less gentle than Abraham Wolsey? He might easily accept a bid for her from someone like Catahecassa.

She would rather remain with Lac-lan.

Her heart fluttered. If not for fear of injuring him further, she would have thrown herself into his arms when he lay sprawled on the ground after Catahecassa's attack. She would have pressed her head to the heart beating in his chest and inhaled his warmth. But she had not dared.

And now she did not dare look directly at Nab, whose eyes narrowed in study.

Wenonah moved the soiled garment aside. She leaned over the water and washed her face. She combed fingers through her hair and tied it into two long tails. Then she wrung the sopping waistcoat and rose to her feet, her body sore, and more so to think of the coming weeks when she would be alone again. She must accept her fate. Nab would take Lac-lan away.

She carried the damp clothing back to the cabin. Lac-lan and his friend stood outside. Lac-lan leaned against the wall, relieving the weight from his leg.

Wenonah lifted her chin. "Where baby?"

"She's inside, asleep."

Relieved that the child slept, Wenonah turned aside and hung the waistcoat from a branch. The day had grown hot once again, and the coat would dry quickly. She stepped toward the cabin and lowered her eyes as she strode between the men. Nab's hand shot out, stopping her. Her heart jumped, and she frowned.

"I've something to say. It involves ye, so you'd best hear." He looked at Lac-lan. "I don't think it's good that ye travel yet. I'll go back to the fort alone. You stay with her." His glance swept over Wenonah. "Let her tend ye a while longer. I'll give a report, and then I'll fetch ye when the time is right." He focused again on Lac-lan, and his voice deepened.

"When you've healed."

Nab wanted Lac-lan to stay with her? To have her tend him longer? Her own long journey lay ahead of her. In a few weeks, the weather would begin to turn. Time would have been lost. But if Lac-lan agreed with Nab, could she refuse?

No. She could not.

Lac-lan bowed his head and didn't answer right away. He must disagree with his friend's plan. He shifted his stance, and still he did not look at them … at her. He murmured something in that strange, rolling tongue she could not clearly understand.

"Amen," Nab said. "Are ye in agreement then?"

Lac-lan nodded. Wenonah's heart thumped. She did not understand, but the moment his forest green eyes met hers, her heart slowed, and her journey ceased to matter.

"I will wait as long as I need to keep the wound from putrefying. If the Indians have cleared off as ye say, and ye return as guide before too many days, I see no reason against resting a while longer. Wenonah has plans of her own. It is up to her if she will stay." His voice was soft, accepting, while at the same time some flicker of hope edged from it into his eyes. At least she thought so.

Wenonah clenched her hands into fists, her decision made. She gave one nod. "I stay here. I take care of Lac-lan."

His lips twitched, and the corners of his eyes eased into a smile. "And I'll make sure ye don't lack for rabbits."

She blushed and could not hide it. She turned away and moved through the doorway to check on Waaseyaa, though there was no need. She left the door open to their voices.

"I'll be goin after I've had a share of that rabbit turning on the spit then," Nab said. "I wish ye both well while I'm away."

Chapter 9

JESSE NAB HAD FINALLY ceased his talking now that food lay before him. He no longer sent Wenonah suspicious glances. He had promised to return and guide Lachlan back to the fort later. *When ye've healed.* Given space to think, Nab's remark echoed in Lachlan's head. The look on Nab's face when he said it was laden with memories of Scotland. For the first time in two days, Moira's image visited him as he ate. Her long blond hair, so different from Wenonah's, wrapped about her shoulders. Her hands clasped together behind his neck, with her fair, freckled arms warm and welcoming. Wenonah's skin was dark, rich as maple syrup, and just as smooth. Even with her life of hard work, her hands felt like cream beneath his touch.

He shifted a glance at her where she plucked meat off the rabbit and nibbled at it in small bits. Her narrow hands and wrists were able. Shapely arms disappeared beneath the sleeves of her deerskin dress. She was sturdy like a sapling, but with the look of having born a child. Full breasts and ... The image of her back facing him the night she'd given birth now surfaced in his memory. Though she was fully clothed, Lachlan had to look away. He chewed on the meat and sucked off the bone.

The baby stirred and whimpered. In a flash, Wenonah was beside the child, shushing her. She drew Waaseyaa into her arms and laid a kiss on the velvety cheek. Then she turned away from the men and nursed.

An urge to walk over and lay a hand on her shoulder nearly overpowered Lachlan. Nab paid no attention, for which Lachlan was grateful. Yet he could hardly be still, and he could not hold onto the image of Moira. He wiped his hands on his pants and breathed a silent prayer that God would clear his thoughts.

Nab dropped a clean bone on his trencher and pushed himself to his feet. "I'd best be on my way. I can make it back by nightfall and give my report."

"When should I expect ye to return?" Lachlan asked.

Nab glanced at Wenonah and jerked his head toward the door. "Why not walk outside with me if ye've the strength, and we'll discuss it."

Lachlan's leg felt better after he'd rested and eaten. His limp was slighter than before as he followed Nab outside.

Nab walked a few paces clear of the cabin. When he spoke, his voice was low. "I don't plan to rush my return. Yer no good to the king's army until yer well. Bouquet can make do without ye for a while yet, I swear. I'll carry word back that ye'll be well enough by month's end."

Lachlan startled. "Month's end? That long? I thought perhaps a week."

"We'll say two then." Nab pulled in a breath and sighed. "Ah, Lachlan ... Can't ye see what a chance ye've been given?"

"What do ye mean?" He thought he knew, but he wasn't sure he could yet admit it.

"I mean *her*." Nab glanced toward the cabin. "Both of them. She's a comely lass. Surely the thought has crossed yer mind that she might be good for ye—a salve for yer heartache."

Lachlan looked away. He wrestled with his memories of Moira. He'd loved her since she was but a girl of fifteen. He would always love her. Nevertheless ...

"I see the way ye look at her." Nab drew out a pause then added with a deeper voice, "And the way she looks at ye. Yer not going to let her travel through the wilderness back to her people, are ye? Not when we'll probably be stuck in this country for the whole of winter? Perhaps, by springtime, the war will be settled at last, and we can all get what was promised."

Lachlan rubbed a hand across his jaw. They'd passed through countless miles of rugged country, some not unlike their own Highlands with its mountains and glens. They had been promised the option of returning to Scotland or receiving a land payment in the colonies. Lachlan studied the green forest about them. The stream trickled faintly in the distance. "'Twould be as good a place to put down roots as any, I reckon."

Nab grinned. "Call it roots, if ye want. 'Twould be a good land for marrying and raising yer own bairns is what ye mean. A whole clan of wee McRaes."

Lachlan felt a stab, but it didn't prick as deeply as it used to. "If I found another woman foolish enough to marry me ye mean."

Nab grasped Lachlan's shoulder. "Now ye ken my meaning." He lowered his hand and clasped Lachlan's. "Fare thee well, McRae. I'll be back before ye know it, and then ye'll be certain, one way or t'other."

"Two weeks."

Nab shrugged. "Inside of three anyway." He turned away and whistled a tune as he strode up the trail. "Or four!" he hollered. Then his voice echoed back in song as he disappeared through the trees.

> *"He looked high, he looked low,*
> *He cast an under look;*
> *And there he saw a fair pretty maid*
> *Beside the wat'ry brook."*

Lachlan could not help but smile. He returned to the cabin just as the door opened. Wenonah stood inside the frame. *A fair pretty maid indeed.* Her lovely dark eyes caught his and caused his breath to tighten in his chest. Lachlan cleared his throat. "Nab has gone on. He'll be back in time."

She raised her pert chin and gave half a nod. One brow arched over her doe-like eyes. Lachlan's heart kicked with a sudden longing, one he barely remembered. It was not the same as the lonesome ache he'd borne like a mantle for months over Moira. This craving was fresh and filled with something akin to hope—hope stolen from him for such a long time, he'd forgotten its pull. Now it tugged at him with yearning. Could feelings that had been driven only into dreams become real again?

He approached her and stopped a few feet away. "I owe ye further thanks."

"What for?"

He took another step. "For offering to stay and tend me, when it is ye and wee Waaseyaa who need tendin. I'm sorry to keep ye from yer people."

Her eyelids fluttered. "It not matter. My people, they ..." She shrugged.

Lachlan had known her so short a time. Were days enough? Were needs and loneliness enough? His heartbeat lost rhythm. "They what?"

She shook her head. "I know not what will happen when I return to my father's lodge."

"I suppose there's no use tryin to guess the things we canna see.

There is only what we can know of today."

She nodded. "Yes, Lac-lan. So it is. You, too, return to the soldier fort and know not what will happen next."

He didn't like to think of it. He would return to soldiering. He had no choice. "Aye, but for now we will worry only about our next meal, and ye will only worry about our wee First Light of Dawn." He offered her a smile, and her shoulders relaxed. Her lips spread too, moving him with her beauty. He cleared his throat when he realized he'd been staring at them. "Did yer husband have any traps or leave anything else that the Indians dinna take?"

She shook her head. "They take all his things. I make trap for fish and snares for rabbit."

"Ye are a good woman."

Pleasure teased the corners of her lips. She turned aside. "I show you."

Lachlan followed her around the cabin to where the trapper's woodpile must have stood. The ground was littered with wood chips and a few rotted wood chunks. Lachlan would have to come by a good ax once he received his parcel of land. A good ax and many other things. He thrilled again at the thought of these new ideas. When had he last laid plans of his own?

Wenonah showed him the trap she'd woven of sticks and reeds. As good a fish trap as any he'd seen. They could use some of the rabbit entrails as bait. "We'll take it to the river later."

She turned a demure glance his way, accepting his idea.

"Tomorrow morning I'll take my Bess and see if I can hunt us some larger game."

"You not walk far?"

"Nay. I'll be careful of my leg. I promise."

"Lac-lan must take great care. Bullet stay in leg. Must have chance to heal."

The tiny cry of the baby came from inside the cabin. Lachlan placed a hand gently on the small of Wenonah's back. "She's calling for her *màithair*."

Wenonah hurried off.

Lachlan turned up his palm and stared at is as she disappeared around the cabin. The feel of her dress lingered there. She was real. Living. As fine a woman as ... as Moira.

A sacred wonder filled him as he pulled in a deep breath. His lungs expanded, and his chest thrust out. The rich flow of his life's blood rushed through his veins.

The following morning, Lachlan unwrapped his thigh and examined his flesh. The wound had closed. He carefully probed the spot where the bullet had settled deep in his muscle near the bone. Whether or not a surgeon would ever open the leg again to remove it remained to be seen. He doubted such would happen. He would likely feel the pain and pressure of it to his dying day, but it would not keep him a cripple.

The leg ached as it did each morning, but he could gently stretch it now. He cast aside the medicinal dressing and wrapped only the light, clean cloth around his thigh. It was enough to protect the tender flesh from debris or snapping twigs while he hobbled into the forest.

Wenonah slept soundly with Waayesaa tucked in the crook of her arm, their foreheads touching. Lachlan moved near and took a long moment to study them both. His heart swelled. He could love this woman and her child, and perhaps he already did. He slipped out the door before he did something rash, like bend to kiss her brow.

Daylight barely touched the forest. Dew lay heavy on grass and fern, and it dripped from every weighted leaf. He stole over the padded ground, soundless despite his limp. Every dozen rods he stopped and listened as he made his way to the river's edge. He followed the flow north until it came to a grassy glen spotted with deer droppings. He surveyed the area where hoof tracks carved sharp edges in mud along a well-worn trail that crossed through the middle of the clearing then disappeared again into the thick growth on the other side. 'Twas a fair good place to wait, and likely to yield game if he was patient.

Lachlan skirted the edge of the glen, keeping downwind from the trail. He found a recently fallen tree upon which he could sit. He barely needed to bend his sore leg and still remained hidden behind the foliage of the crown. Settling onto the rough-barked seat, he checked the powder in his pan, then he stilled. Silence lay thick about the land, broken only by the occasional rush of bird wings or the buzzing of an insect near his ear. The smell of earth rose from the ground mingling with the scent of foliage—spicy fern and damp leaves. He inhaled and released a slow, silent breath. Then again. For the briefest moment, Lachlan closed his eyes, savoring the dawn and life itself. Did Wenonah stir? Even now did she wonder where he'd gone? She would recall their conversation of last night. Would she prepare to break her fast? No, first she would bare her breast and suckle the babe.

He opened his eyes at the warmth of the thought squirreling away through his insides and lighting like down in his conscious, soft, tickling, welcome. Wenonah ...

The tiny snap of a twig sharpened his senses. He refused to flinch, but his ears strained while he focused hard between the branches and leaves of the trees. Soon he spotted a brown leg, then two. His heart pounded, and his body tightened with anticipation. Every sound and movement magnified as a doe stepped further into view. Her head rose from the waves of grass, and she stiffened. One ear twitched. Then she bent her head again, and Lachlan raised his musket. Her head bobbed upward. Her shoulder muscles flinched. And Lachlan fired. Thick, acrid smoke clouded between him and his quarry. He turned off the tree trunk, pain in his leg forgotten as he sought for any sign of the deer. He stood still and waited until at last, he saw the thick grass move. She was down.

Lachlan's breath rushed in and out with the throbbing in his chest. Perspiration trickled down his temple, even as the sun glinted its first bright rays through the dewy trees. The glory of it turned his heart to thanks and to Wenonah and to the wee babe named after the dawn.

Thank Ye, God. Thank Ye.

Chapter 10

"WENONAH!"

Wenonah jumped as Lac-lan burst through the door. She quickly pulled her dress closed. "Something is wrong?" Fear scattered her wits.

His face was flushed, but a smile spread across it, showing white beneath his dark beard and mustache. His green eyes were wide. "I've taken a big doe." He gestured at his leg. "I'll not be able to shoulder the weight yet. Have ye a length of rope?"

Wenonah nodded as her breath eased out in relief. She retrieved the rope from behind her bedding. A doe. She would smoke and dry the venison, and today she would put a loin on the spit for their supper. Her mouth watered in anticipation. "I come help too."

His glance shifted warmly over her. "I'd be happy for yer help, but ye've Waaseyaa, and ye mustn't overdo it."

"Wenonah strong. Able."

"Aye. I won't argue with that. Ye've waited on me hand and foot, all while ye've had yerself and a newborn to care for, but I won't have ye draggin the deer. Ye can come if ye want, but I'll draw the load. I am well enough."

His consideration touched her, and she agreed. Were he a man like Catahecassa, he would have expected her to handle the work alone.

Ten minutes later, with Waaseyaa in her cradleboard and Lac-lan carrying a pack Wenonah had retrieved from her cache, the two set out to bring back the venison. Wenonah smiled inwardly at the way Lac-lan strode through the woods, his limp not keeping him from pressing on to the task. She offered him her skinning knife, and he grinned in thanks as he took it and slit the belly of the animal.

The deer was cleanly shot, her hide barely damaged. Later, Wenonah would soak it in ash lye and prepare it for scraping. The skin would make a nice hunting shirt. Lac-lan's shoulders stretched and bunched his waistcoat across his back as he worked over the deer. Wenonah sized him up. Yes, she would make him a shirt from this hide as a gift.

"Hand me the pack."

She set it beside him, open at the top. Lac-lan carefully put the two long loins and heart inside. "This meat will feed us for some days, Wenonah. It'll help ye keep yer milk up for Waaseyaa."

Warmth spread through her to her fingertips at the expression of his thoughts. She doubted even Abraham Woolsey would have thought of her needs so.

Lac-lan soon had completed the dressing and had the hind legs bound together with the rope so that he might drag the deer back to the cabin. He tore off a clump of long grass and rubbed it between his hands. "I'll hoist it in that oak tree on the north side of the cabin. That'll make it easier to skin and quarter."

"Wenonah cut meat."

He shook his head. "I told ye—I'll do the work. Ye can do the cooking." One side of his mouth lifted in half a grin and he winked. "I've gotten used to it."

She blushed and let a smile slip out.

"I might let ye teach me yer tricks for smoking the hindquarters." He tossed away the grass and freed her of the inviting spark in his eyes as he shouldered the pack with the loins and heart. Grabbing the rope, he pulled the deer behind him.

Wenonah followed him with the baby. What would she do when he returned to the fort and left her? She had gotten used to him too. More than used to him in fact. Was this stirring he caused inside her alive in his own breast too? A stirring she did not wish to cease?

She studied him as he trudged ahead. Other than the effects of the injury that caused him to measure his steps, he was a strong man. Strong and broad-shouldered like an oak. His hair had begun to edge around his collar in a way that made her want to tuck her fingers beneath it. He was a handsome man too. Very handsome indeed.

Her heart fluttered, but this time she did not try to smother its wild beat. Then, with another thought, it nearly stopped. Did Lac-lan have a woman? He was a soldier, off to war. Did a wife wait for him somewhere far away in the land of his home? Perhaps Wenonah was wrong to welcome feelings for this man. Perhaps she should never have let them awaken.

Lac-lan paused when they approached the stream. He let go of the rope and dropped the pack to rest. Sweat coiled the dark strands of his hair against his brow. He lowered himself to the ground at the water's edge and washed the rest of the blood off his hands and arms until they were clean. Then he splashed water on his face and dipped his head. He slung it back, and water droplets fanned out around him.

Wenonah giggled. If Lac-lan did have a woman waiting for him, Wenonah would have to open her heart and let him fly from it, but for this moment, she would hold him inside and revel in his presence.

He smiled up at her, his mossy green eyes squinting against the sunlight. "What are ye laughing at?" He cupped water in his palm and dashed it at her.

She squealed and scooted back. Then, after they'd both laughed, she lowered herself beside him.

"Turn 'round."

She eyed him for a moment then did as he bid. He gently wrestled the cradleboard off her back and propped the sleeping baby against a shady rock. Wenonah stretched her shoulders and bent to the water to wash the perspiration from her face and neck. When she turned to him again, he was looking at her in a way that sent her heart back to beating wildly. If ever she would know the answer ...

"Lac-lan McRae ..." She swallowed against the squeezing in her throat. "You have wife?"

The water danced a woodland tune over the rocks beside them. The sky held not a cloud above the fluttering treetops. All the forest was keen and alive—like Lachlan himself. Had he really been so dead for the past four years? Wenonah's eyes, deep and questioning, dark and vivid at once, grasped hold of him without her touch. His breath eased out as they stared at one another.

"Nay."

Her brow relaxed ... in relief? Did she want to know because ...

When he reached for her hand, she let him twine his fingers with hers. They were cool and still damp. *Alive.* Now he needed to draw another breath.

He studied their fingers. "I had a wife, but she is in the ground, like yer husband. Our bairn is with her. Her name was Moira, and she died givin birth to our son."

Wenonah's fingers tightened, and he responded. He lifted his face to hers, and the sorrow in her eyes reached out to him, touched him as physically as her hand holding his.

"I am sorry, Lac-lan."

"'Twas long ago now, in Scotland. Much longer than the time that's passed since ye lost yer man."

Her gaze wandered up the river, then swept slowly back to him. "I am sorry Abraham was killed. He did not deserve to die in such a way, but he did not stay long inside my heart." She laid her free hand to her chest. "It does not sorrow in the way of yours."

When had he last dreamed of holding Moira? It used to be every night—even every day—but he had not dreamed of her since ... when? Not since before Nab's arrival. Not since his fever sought to bring him to the grave. He gave a small shake of his head. "She is at rest, and 'tis time that I am as well."

A question flashed through her eyes, and Lachlan's pulse jumped. He reached for her other wrist. His fingers trailed over her palm as he drew her hand into his until both were captured. He studied her face, from the smoothness of her brow to the dark lines arching her eyes. High cheekbones drew a line to a narrow chin, past full lips. There his gaze settled. Her lips parted slightly, and Lachlan tilted his head.

Shutting off the sky and trees, they leaned together, and he brushed his lips across hers. He felt their shape with the barest graze. Then again, until he found their purchase. A blaze coursed through him, and he yielded to the taste of her. Their hands parted, and Wenonah's slid around him. He stirred at the passion in her kiss. His hands slipped beneath her hair and tilted her face upward so that he might deepen the kiss in return.

Hunger such as he'd forgotten—hunger of which his dreams were only a weak reminder—consumed him. He wanted more ... needed more ...

And then Waaseyaa cried.

Wenonah pulled back. In an instant, they separated, both breathless, but Lachlan's need was unabated. Her hair was loose in its ties. She pushed a wisp off her flushed cheek as she withdrew.

Lachlan watched her tend the infant, her footsteps light in their moccasins, her shape calling to his desire. He had to turn away. He leaned over the creek and again splashed water over his face and neck, repeating the ablutions until the heat inside settled and his racing heart calmed.

"Wenonah ..." Her name was still an ache on his lips that sounded gruff to his ears. He faced her. She'd taken the baby from its bindings in the cradleboard and held her close, hushing her though there seemed no need. The bairn no longer cried.

Wenonah's expression had smoothed. She lifted her chin. "Lac-lan go back to Fort Pitt soon. No time for new woman. No place ..." Her eyes filled, and she shook her head, holding firm, though she trembled.

Lachlan rose to his feet, his sore leg stiff from exertion. He limped to stand in front of her. She turned her face away, and he touched her chin, drawing it back. "No. I want ... I *need* ..." He dropped his chin to his chest. This was not what he meant to say. He looked at her again. He stroked her hair then grazed a finger over Waaseyaa's downy cheek. "I will go to Fort Pitt when 'tis time, aye. But I want ye and Waaseyaa to go with me. There is a man there named Bouquet. He will bind us as one." He swallowed down a ball of unexpected emotion that went deeper than desire. "I want ye for my wife, Wenonah."

Her eyes widened, glistening even fuller.

"Do ye ken my meanin? Will ye marry me?"

Tears sat on the fringe of her lashes, and she bent her head to dash them away.

"Wenonah?"

He cradled her cheek, and she leaned into his touch. He bent his head and kissed the baby's crown. Waaseyaa stirred but slept on.

Wenonah raised her head and whispered. "You want I belong to you?"

"I want to be yer husband. I want"—he swallowed against the hunger returning—"I want to take care of ye and wee First Light of Dawn. I want to be her father. I want to love ye, Wenonah. I do love ye."

"I think ... I think I, too, love Lac-lan McRae."

The muscles in his body, in his face, relaxed. His heart filled up, and he grinned. "Ye love Lachlan McRea, do ye?"

She nodded and smiled despite a tear escaping down her cheek.

Lachlan moved closer over mother and child. "Ye love such a man as me, aye?" He spoke softly as his future opened before him with a surprising glory all its own.

She nodded.

"I do love ye, Wenonah." He took the sides of her face in his hands once more, and this time when he kissed her, the urgency released, and all that had held him captive fled. Heaven smiled. The gates of his heart fell open and free.

In acknowledgement and dedication to my Lord Jesus,
Who opens doors when there seems to be no door.

Naomi is an award-winning author who crafts her stories from a deer farm in the pristine north woods of Wisconsin, where she and her husband Jeff live as epically as God allows near the families of their five adult children. She enjoys roaming around on the farm, snacking out of the garden, relaxing in her vintage camper, and loving on her passel of grandchildren. Naomi is a member of the American Christian Fiction Writers, the Wisconsin Writers' Association, and the Lake Superior Writers. Though she has written in a variety of venues, her great love is historical fiction. Naomi would love to connect with you around the web. Visit her at:

Website: NaomiMusch.com
FB: Naomi Musch - Author
Twitter: @NMusch
Instagram: NaomiMusch
Goodreads: Naomi Dawn Musch
Bookbub: Naomi Musch
Pinterest: Naomi Musch
Monthly Newsletter: News of the Northwoods

The Year Without Summer

By

Janet Grunst

And we know that in all things God works for the good of those who love him, who have been called according to his purpose.
Romans 8:28

Dedicated to my ancestors from the villages of Inverness and
Tullochgorham, Scotland,
and from Aghadowey, County Londonderry, Ireland.
As a result of the famines, enclosures, and desire for a better future
they sought a new life in a faraway land—America.

CHAPTER 1

1816

COLD WIND BLEW OFF the loch as Grant Cummings headed toward Loch Ness Tavern, one of the inns in Fort Augustus that catered to the men working on the Highland's Caledonian Canal. His stomach growled, and he wanted nothing more than to enjoy a warm meal and head upstairs to his room. Pulling his woolen coat tighter, he crossed the cobblestone street.

"Cummings, ye goin in for tea?" Mac, a co-worker, ambled toward him.

"Aye, Mrs. Finlay promised Cullen skink, my favorite soup. Come 'n share some."

They entered the dark tavern. Mrs. Finley smiled and waved as they sat at a table. "I've been expectin ye. Still cold as the dickens out there? Who's yer friend?"

"Hamish MacDonald. He works with me on the canal locks. I been braggin about yer Cullen skink."

"Aye, some for me too, sweetheart." Mac's eyebrows lifted, his grin appeared hopeful as Mrs. Finley walked away. "She's a bonnie lass."

"And married, so mind yer Ps and Qs."

Mac tossed his cap beside him. "Workin every day leaves little time for courtin anyway." He laughed. "Bet a fine strappin fella like yerself likely has no problem."

"Not lookin for a lass till I settle someplace."

Mrs. Finley brought two bowls of the thick Scottish soup. "Plenty of smoked haddock in it today." She studied Mac as she set a plate of bannocks, Scottish oatcakes, in front of him. "Ye new?"

"Aye." Mac took one of the bannocks. "'Tis quite a project Telford's got goin here. I worked on the Craigellachie Bridge couple of years back."

"So, what do ye think of the Caledonian Canal?" She wiped her hands on her stained apron.

"I'm a stonemason, so this promises steady employment."

"Well, come back. We've got the best vittles."

Mac nodded. "Ta. Smells heavenly."

She wandered off just as a Royal Post driver came through the door carrying a thick bundle.

Mac shoved the first spoonful in his mouth as he peered at the post driver. "Not received any posts from my family in weeks. Makes me wonder what is happenin in Inverness. Hae ye heard from yer family? Ye said they lived south of Inverness."

Grant nodded. "In Tullochgorum near the River Spey and Cairngorm Mountains. Pa passed. He worked in the linen mills. But Ma is a flax spinner and still a crofter of sorts. 'Tis a fickle business though and they live at the mercy of a finicky laird. 'Twas why I took up construction. I could do more with my life 'n not rely on the whims of others."

Mac broke one of the bannocks and dipped it in his soup. "With Napoleon no longer at our heels, I'm thinkin the military will not need the canal for passage." He plopped the softened oatcake into his mouth.

"'Tis sixty miles through the Great Glen." Grant put down his spoon. "Travelers and cargo ships will use the canal even if the Royal Navy no longer does."

Mrs. Finley approached with what looked like mail. "'Tis for ye." She dropped the post on the table by Grant's bowl. "Ye wantin more soup?"

"Nay, 'tis enough for me," Grant opened the letter from home. He glanced at the bottom. 'Twas signed by a neighbor and dated late April, over a week ago.

Molly MacGregor mashed a creamy mixture of cabbage, leeks, and potatoes just as Scott came through the cottage door. "Is something troubling ye?" Her seven-year-old brother's red face was a stark contrast to his flaxen hair.

"Aye. Pa is grumpy again … and he is heading this way."

"Don't worry, lad. I can soften him up with the colcannon I'm mashing. Wash and get the bowls out, please."

"Just dinna want him to skelp me for not helping him in the fields." His eyes darted first to the door and back to her.

"Ye know Pa is more bluster than action."

"Molly, where are ye, lass?" Pa's voice carried through the open window.

"In here, Pa, fixing yer favorite supper." She wiped her hands on her apron and placed the large bowl and spoons on the table.

She squared her shoulders, ready for whatever Pa would blow up about this time. Had it been an argument at the mill with one of the other weavers or some other irritant?

Rory MacGregor came through the door. Jaw set, he slammed his hat on the table. His hacking cough had returned, piercing the quiet of the small stone cottage. He grabbed the damp dish rag to wipe his hands. "We need to go to America. Yer brother was right. There's no future here."

She fought the urge to roll her eyes. "Pa, don't go getting yer Irish up. We have been over this before. Just because Ewan left doesn't mean we must go. Ye have weaving work at the mill, an acre to tend, and I have the spinning. I just picked up another dress-making job for the landowner's housekeeper."

"Everything is changing." He continued coughing and having more trouble catching his breath than usual.

"I'll make ye some sow thistle tea with a bit of honey. 'Twill make it less bitter and soothe yer throat." She bit her lip. If he could breathe easier, he wouldn't be so hot-tempered.

Molly spooned the colcannon into bowls and passed them around. "Pa, yer favorite."

"Ta." He took a bite of the savory dish, then looked up. "Lad, we need to get to planting when we're done. 'Tis sure to warm up soon. Coldest May I can remember in many a year."

"Aye, Pa." Scott shot her a piercing look. Even a seven-year-old could see Pa was not up to planting flax.

She nodded at her brother. "Take a nap, Pa, and let us do it. I can do the spinning later."

Pa's eyes narrowed. "Hmph. Did I mention Séamus Macaulay is coming by to see ye?"

"Nay, ye didna." Molly put down her spoon and pushed the bowl away. "I have asked ye not to encourage him."

"Well, somebody needs to do the encouraging. Yer twenty-two years old. Ye should be married. The fellow not only works the mill but earns extra as an undertaker."

At that, rolling her eyes was unavoidable. She motioned to Scott when Pa started a bad coughing fit. "Help me get him to his pallet." She took one arm while Scott came and took the other. "I'm not marrying Séamus Macaulay, so ye can get that out of yer head."

CHAPTER 2

GRANT STARED AT THE letter on the table in front of him.

Grant,

Yer ma has taken ill, and I think ye needs to come home as soon as ye can.

I'm caring for her and Keith.

⸸Lena Simpson

His stomach knotted. *Ma sick? She was as strong as an ox.* His job on the canal would now be in jeopardy. He needed to let the foreman know he would be returning to Tullochgorum.

Mac cocked his head. "Somethin wrong?"

"'Tis news of home an I'm needin to leave."

An hour later, Grant had packed his belongings and settled his accounts at Loch Ness Tavern. He needed to find the foreman at the lock construction site to give notice. At least temporarily. Three or four days of travel through rugged and mostly uninhabited terrain was ahead. And still so cold for May.

How was Keith handling Ma's distress? Poor lad, only eight and still dealing with the loss of Pa but a year ago.

Grant reached Tullochgoram and the family's stone cottage after three long days of riding through rain-soaked bogs, rivers, and cold mountainous country. No one was at the cottage, a bad sign. A bitter taste rose in his throat. Perhaps Mrs. Simpson had taken Ma and Keith to their place. He rode the short distance to their nearest neighbor.

Lena Simpson opened the door and welcomed him into the cottage. The pungent smell of peat and heat from the fire was as much a relief as seeing his brother huddled on the dirt floor. Keith's eyes widened as he ran to him and buried his face in his side. Keith's arms wrapped around his waist.

He patted the back of his brother's head as he glanced about the room. His and Lena's eyes met. Only the low rumble of the peat fire broke the silence.

"Have a seat. I will git ye a cup of tea to take the chill off." As the small, slender woman moved toward the hearth, Grant lifted Keith's chin. Tears filled the lad's eyes.

Dread swept through him. "'Tis good to see ye, brother. Come and sit."

Lena poured them each a cup and sat at the only other chair around the small table. "Angus is off herdin sheep. Will not be back till tomorrow."

"Sheep? What's a crofter doin herdin sheep?"

"With the cold 'n the heavy rains, we fear an ill flax harvest ... the laird is evictin his tenants 'n shiftin toward sheep raisin. We are lucky. Angus knew shepherdin, so the laird kept him on."

Grant took a sip of the tea. "And Ma?"

"Isabella was failin for a while. She passed a week back, so we buried her side yer pa."

He swallowed hard. Tears would only make it harder for Keith, now staring at the tea in front of him. "Ta, Lena."

She stood and went to a shelf. "Yer ma left ye a note before she passed. Had the pastor write it." She handed it to him.

I'm sorry I could not see ye again. Ye were a good son. 'Tis time now for ye to care for Keith. The Cummings have been crofters in Tullochgorum, Invernesshire, for decades, but those days are bygone. Ye were right to find a different way, somethin better. Take Keith to Ireland where my sister Katherine Grant lives in Aghadowey, County Londonderry. There, ye can find buildin work, and my sister will help ye with Keith. Ye has an adventurous spirit, son. It may be God's plan for ye. Brighter days are ahead for ye there.

Remember, to keep God in yer heart 'n let Him guide yer steps. He works in ways ye canna ken.

Grant sniffled and wiped the tears he had fought to keep at bay. Ireland? So many Scots had migrated to Ulster over the past seventy years. She might as well have told him to sail to America where cousin Gavin had gone.

He was too weary to think straight.

Lena poured more tea. "I was with Isabella when she spoke those words to the pastor. We had talked about it before. Yer ma was fond 'n trusted Katherine. Yer aunt says work and life is better there in Ulster."

"Please take me with ye wherever ye go." Keith's eyes were full of pain.

"Dinna fret, lad. I'll not leave ye." He smiled at Lena. "I think we need to get home."

She packed a basket with bread and a couple of potatoes, onions, and turnips and handed it to him. "There is peat at yer home. Take some burnin peat with ye to get it started." She shoveled some of the hot bricks from her own fire into a tin bucket.

Grant took her hand. "Thank ye for takin care of Ma 'n Keith. Ye hae been a true friend."

"Dinna mention it."

Grant picked up the basket and bucket while Keith gathered his things. The lad hugged Lena before following him outside.

Grant held the horse steady. "Ye ride. I can walk. 'Tis not far." How was he to properly care for his brother and work? The lad was too young to leave alone.

The only sound now from Pa was a rattle in his chest. Molly sat on a stool by his pallet with Scott next to her on another stool. She reached for Pa's hand, and with her other hand, she held tight to Scott's. "We're right here, Pa." Could he hear her or was he too far gone this side of heaven?

Scott's eyes brimmed with tears. "Pa's not coughing anymore." The lad's free hand rested on Pa's blanket.

"'Tis because he hasn't much time left here, dearie. He'll be with Ma soon." She let go of Scott's hand. Struggling for a smile, she ran her fingers through his flaxen hair and caressed his damp cheek. "'Twill be all right."

The front door opened, and Katherine Grant came in carrying a kettle. "I came to spell ye if ye need a break." She set the kettle down on the table and went to the hearth. "Brought soup and I can pour us some tea."

"Yer a treasure." Molly offered as much a smile as she could muster.

"Pa!" Scott called out.

Pa's eyes flew open, and his hand tightened on hers—for just a few seconds. Then his eyes closed, and his hand went limp. The rattle stopped.

The air went out of her. Lips quivering, she reached over and kissed Pa's forehead. "He's gone."

Scott stood shaking beside her. She wrapped her arms around him and hugged him tight before he pulled away. Scott bent down and kissed Pa.

Molly took a deep breath. "Ye can go home with the angels now, Pa." Her voice cracked. She and Scott stood, looking up, each with an arm around the other's waist.

Molly greeted neighbors and friends as they came to pay their respects after Rory MacGregor's graveside service. Now Pa was gone, what was she to do? How would they get by without his wages?

Séamus Macaulay hovered, which only unsettled her more. How was one to avoid the undertaker at a funeral? "Scott, take the wraps and put them by the hearth, so they warm up before folks leave. 'Tis bad enough they're rain-soaked."

Loaded with coats, Scott approached the hearth where Katherine poured tea for the guests. "A shame some of the visitors are stuck waiting outdoors in the rain."

The minister's wife, grace Campbell, approached Molly with a mug. "Here, lass, ye look like ye could use it. I brought ye and Scott some scones."

"Bless ye, such a friend ye's been, and thanks for all yer help, and yer husband for his kind words at the service." She wiped a tear from her cheek.

"'Twill be over soon."

"Aye."

Molly received hugs and handshakes for an hour before the last of the mourners finally departed. All but Katherine Grant and Séamus Macaulay.

While Katherine quietly washed the cups and dishes, Molly searched the cottage and picked up any that were left.

Séamus still sat with Scott at the table when she brought the few remaining dishes to Katherine. "So many cups and plates to clean. How are ye going to remember who to return them to?"

"'Tis easy. I set them all out on my table and ask them to take their own."

She placed her hand on Katherine's back. "What would I do without ye?"

Katherine tilted her head in the direction of the table, her clear blue eyes full of warning. She whispered, "Ye know he has plans for ye?"

"Aye, and I have been avoiding private conversations with him as best I can," she whispered.

"Do ye want me to stay 'til he leaves?"

"Nay, I need to face up to all that lies ahead," she muttered, "even Séamus Macaulay."

Within fifteen minutes, Katherine had packed all the borrowed dishes into baskets and placed them in her wagon. "Now remember, I'm only a ten-minute walk, and I will help ye if I can." Katherine nodded at Séamus and Scott. "See ye later."

Molly stood in the doorway and waved as Katherine held the hood of her cape over her head for protection from the rain and dragged the wagon behind her. Molly closed the door and turned, almost bumping into Séamus. "Ye startled me, Séamus. I didna hear ye approach. I will get ye the money for yer services in the next fortnight."

"I'm not worried about payment, but I did want to talk over something with ye." He glanced back at the table where Scott sat whittling.

She pulled her shoulders back. Might as well get this over with. "What is it?" The man, older than her by a decade, could not have been even two inches taller than her five and a half foot frame. A reddish color rose to the top of his face while he held his shaking hat with both hands in front of him.

"Yer the prettiest lass with yer carrot-colored locks and yer blue eyes. Yer needing a fellow to care for ye now ... and the laddie ... of course. I'm thinking we should marry."

Scott got up, still holding his pocketknife and walked over to her, standing tall with a defiant look. "She does not have carrot-colored locks ... and I'm thinking that I will care for my sister."

Séamus' eyes flared, and she bit her lip. Out of the mouths of babes. The urge to laugh or smile was so strong, and so improper only a few hours after burying Pa. And 'twas certainly not a seemly way to respond to a marriage proposal. "I'm deeply honored by yer declaration, but I'm not even close to thinking about marrying ... anyone."

CHAPTER 3

A WEEK AFTER RETURNING to Tullochgorum, Grant was stacking peat while Keith emptied the root cellar when one of the laird's agents showed up.

He handed them papers. "Ye hae three days to vacate."

Grant slapped the eviction notice against his thigh as the agent rode off. "'Tis not a surprise. Been expectin that."

Keith sat on the three-legged stool by the front door of their stone cottage. "What do we do now?"

Grant wiped his other hand on his pants and placed it on Keith's shoulder. "We leave. Come, I have somethin to show ye." The eight-year-old needed hope. "There's more to life than workin at the mercy o a self-servin laird."

Inside the small cottage, Grant motioned for Keith to sit at the table. "Ever seen a map afore?"

"Nay."

Grant removed the rolled parchment from a shelf. He smoothed it out on the alder oak table, anchoring the corners with potatoes. Keith's pale blue eyes were wide with wonder and joy, something the lad had not displayed much lately.

"What's that?" Keith took off his cap and sat at the table, studying every inch of the document.

"'Tis a map of Scotland 'n' Ireland, 'n ... England."

"Where did ye get it?"

"I found it in some of Ma's things I was organizin this mornin. Maybe she got it from her sister 'n brother-in-law. Katherine and Henry must have left it fer Ma and Pa when they moved to Ireland years back hopin they would follow." He pointed to the cartographer's drawings. "These are the boundaries dividin the countries and bodies of water. "There are the Scottish Highlands 'n the Lowlands."

"Do ye know where we are?"

"Aye." He pointed to an area on the tan parchment. "Right around here in the Cairngorm Mountains."

Keith leaned both arms on the table, quizzing him on all the symbols, names, and defining areas.

"This is where in Ireland our kin bides." He pointed to an area south of Coleraine.

"Way up there, near the top?"

"Aye, the whole area is Ulster, where the Scots went when they left home. I'm thinkin we should go. Not much left for us here. Aunt Katherine was a Grant, like Ma, and she married a Grant, but Henry died. Their son, our cousin Gavin, left Ireland and went to America."

"Where is that?"

Grant knocked his knuckles on the far side of the table.

"That far?"

"Aye. So what do ye think? 'Twill be an adventure." He grinned and rubbed his hand on Keith's auburn curls.

"Aye, does not look so far."

He laughed and gave Keith a playful jab in the arm. "Not on paper, but ye will see, 'twill be quite a journey."

"What about the goat 'n the pony?"

"We will give the goat to the Simpsons. They helped ma 'n ye. We need the pony for ye to ride. When we reach the coast, we sell it 'n my horse. Then purchase other ones in Ireland." He rolled up the map and put it aside. "Go wash. 'Tis neeps and tatties for supper." And that was proof enough that they needed to leave, nothing left to eat here but turnips and potatoes.

Three days later and a day into their journey, they reached a few miles south of the remnants of Ruthven Barracks. A crofter in his field waved to them. "Where are ye headed?"

"Glasgow." Grant glanced at Keith. The lad was weary and cold. "Have any shelter for the night?"

"Aye, have a lean-to yer welcome to. And some hot porridge if yer hungry."

Keith's eyes lighting up was all the encouragement he needed.

After two more days of travel, they reached the market town of Stirling on the River Forth. Grant laughed. "Laddie, yer head is swivelin 'n yer eyes bulgin. Ye have never seen a village anythin like this afore."

The lad's mouth dropped open when he spotted Stirling Castle standing high atop a hill. "I never knew there was such a town."

"We are out of the Highlands now 'n into the Lowlands. Tonight, we will be at a tavern with a hot meal for a change."

The next evening, Grant and Keith crossed an arched bridge over the River Clyde and arrived in Glasgow. Keith's eyes searched the area when they entered the Tradeston district, his nose twitching. "The air is filled with smoke, 'n the buildins blackened with soot. Smells reeky."

"Town livin is crowded with industry, 'n progress. I prefer the moors 'n glens. Glasgow 'tis the farthest I've gone. Tomorrow will be new territory for me, too."

Keith patted his pony. "How many more days will it take?"

He pointed to an inn amongst the tenements. "We'll stay there. 'Tis about a hundred more miles till we reach Portpatrick. Then over the Irish Sea. We dock at Donaghadee, 'n then on to Belfast, 'n Aghadowey."

Molly sat at her spinning wheel, dipping her fingers in the cup of water and working the flax as she spun it. The clock chimed two. Scott would return soon to eat. She glanced out the small window and then at the soft blue wool fabric spread across the other side of the table. To have a dress made of it would be lovely, but there was no way of justifying the expense. She sighed looking down at the black muslin dress she wore. She needed to get back to work on Mrs. McGuire's dress while the light was good. They needed the income. The sooner she could pay off Pa's burial fees the easier it would be to avoid Séamus Macaulay.

Scott came through the door followed by Katherine Grant. "I finished the chores. May I go to Patrick's? We planned to fish."

"After we eat."

Katherine, tall and slender and still in black, set down the basket she carried. "I brought ye some stew and came to see how yer farin."

Molly walked to the hearth. "Have a seat. I will pour us some tea." She set out a plate of biscuits with the tea and resumed her place at the wheel. "If ye dinna mind, I will keep spinning. One of the weavers will be by later today to pick it up on his way to the mill. We are doing as best we can, right Scott?"

"Aye, but ye work well into the night on yer sewing and spinning."

Katherine dished up some stew for Scott and sat at the table beside him. "I understand Séamus is regularly comin by."

Scott put down his biscuit. "Séamus Macaulay is a nuisance."

Molly laughed. "Where did ye learn such a word?"

"From Patrick. The man is nasty." Scott's glare was comical. He shoveled some of the stew into his mouth.

Molly gave him a warning look. "Well, we need to be polite."

Katherine patted Scott's arm. "The man is fond of yer sister."

Scott ate the last of the stew. "He creeps up on her and says her hair is the color of carrots. Anyone can see her locks are a wee bit redder than mine, but not the color of carrots."

"Scott, if ye are finished, go on to Patrick's, but be back in a couple of hours."

"Aye, ta." He grabbed his cap, another biscuit, and said to Katherine, "Tell her not to wed Séamus."

When Scott left, Katherine took another sip of tea. "Ye need to eat something lass and keep up yer strength—even if 'tis just to keep out of reach of Séamus Macaulay. Ye cannot work round the clock."

"'Tis been weeks since Pa's passing and without his income ..."

"Have ye thought of lettin out the hut? 'Tis in good condition."

"Aye, it did cross my mind. It only has a wee hearth, perhaps it would do for a young couple starting out. If ye hear of someone trustworthy, let me know. I wouldna want just anyone so close. The hut was rethatched same time as the cottage two years back so should be plenty dry and warm." She shivered and wrapped her shawl tighter. "Are ye believing 'tis almost June and still so cold 'n overcast? Makes me wonder how the crops and flax fields will fare."

"Many folks are wonderin the same. So, what are ye goin to do about Séamus?" Katherine took the pot of stew and emptied what was left into an empty pot beside the hearth.

Molly continued spinning. "I told him I'm not interested in marrying. I'm eager to pay him for Pa's services, so he has no more reason to come round."

"If he learns of other lads comin around ye, he may not give up." Katherine set her pot back into her basket. "Is this for Mrs. McGuire?" She fingered the blue wool fabric on the table. "'Tis so lightweight and bonny."

Molly nodded. "I have no time or interest in the lads." She got up from the wheel and walked to the table. "I'm behind, and Mrs. McGuire is expecting a fitting next week."

"I will be prayin that the Lord would provide ye the time and resources ye need. Mention to Parson Campbell yer thinkin about lettin yer hut. He may know of someone with a need." Katherine hugged her.

"Good suggestion. Thank ye, sweet friend, for the stew … and yer prayers." She would see Grace Campbell that afternoon for a fitting. She could mention it then. Letting the hut wouldn't solve all her problems, but it would be something.

CHAPTER 4

GRANT SHIFTED ON THE horse to view Keith riding behind him. The lad studied the countryside. "We are almost there, laddie. Crossin the Agivey water means we will be at Aunt Katherine's afore supper."

"I'm thankful for that." Keith pulled his horse alongside Grant's. "Aunt will be surprised to see us."

"True. I'm hopin she kin direct us to someplace to stay ... 'n where I can find work."

When they entered the village, Grant spotted a man leaving the church. If he was the pastor, he might know how to find their aunt. "Excuse me, sir. We are hopin to locate our aunt, Katherine Grant."

The tall man's wide smile was a welcome sight. "Follow that road along the river about ten minutes. Just when the road veers off to the right, ye will see a clump of birch trees. The Grant home is the first stone cottage after that. Has a fine apple tree on one side and a pear tree on the other."

Grant nodded. "Much obliged, sir." They followed the man's instructions. "Looks like a pleasant village." The man seemed familiar with Aunt's home, but then it was just a village. 'Twas more populated than Tullochgorum but still rural.

Keith stretched and patted the horse's neck. "Another river. Wonder if it has good fishin."

Grant took a deep breath when they approached what fit the man's description of their aunt's cottage. The whitewashed, thatched roof dwelling with a blue dutch door the color of the Scottish saltire flag appeared welcoming. "Stay by the pony 'til we learn if she is home." He dismounted, tied his horse to a rail, walked to the door, and knocked.

A moment later, a tall, thin woman opened the top portion of the door. Her eyes widened, and her mouth dropped open. "Can it be?"

Keith approached, and he put an arm around him. "I'm Grant Cummings 'n this is my brother Keith. Are ye Katherine Grant, sister to Isabella Grant Cummings?"

"Aye. Ye looks so like yer pa, tall with yer blue eyes and brown curls. Come in, come in." She opened the bottom of the door. "Tie yer horses to the post. I'll make ye some tea."

"Ta." After securing their horses, they followed the woman into the small cottage. She took the kettle from over the peat fire and poured them tea. The aroma reminded him of home.

"Sit and tell me, how's yer ma?"

He and Keith sat at the table. "She passed about a month ago, but left a letter." Grant pulled the letter out and showed it to their aunt. Katherine was the same build and coloring as Ma with her soft medium-blonde hair. Her reaction to his news and then to the letter brought back his own loss. "The laird evicted the crofters since he's turnin to raisin sheep."

Their aunt wiped a tear from her cheek. "We always hoped yer folks would join us here. Ulster is filled with Scots, though most are Lowlanders like my Henry. Ye knew he passed?"

"Aye, we did. Sorry for yer loss." Grant glanced at Keith. An anxious look formed on the lad's face. "We are not here to impose, but we will need to find lodgins 'n a job for me. I worked on the Caledonian Canal afore comin here."

She placed her hand on Ma's letter on the table in front of her. "Of course, I will help ye out, but as ye can see, 'tis a wee cottage. Yer cousin Gavin left seven years back, but his pallet is not big enough for the both of ye." She sighed then smiled. "'Tis good that ye has experience in construction. There is talk of a canal, but most likely will be road and bridge construction around here."

Grant smiled and took a sip of the tea. It was the first encouraging news he had heard in weeks.

Katherine went to the hearth and returned to the table with the kettle. "Ye two stay here, let yer horses feed in the field over there. A stream runs beside the field that comes from the Aghadowey River." She pointed to a pasture on the other side of the cottage and picked up her shawl. "I may have a spot ye can board, but I need to check. There's bread and pear jam if ye are hungry." She smiled sympathetically. "I'm sorry about my sister, but I'm glad ye came here. Be back soon."

They followed her outside. She scurried in the opposite direction from where they'd come, glancing over her shoulder once. She evidently had a plan, hopefully, one that would bear fruit.

"Come, lad. Let's see to the horses."

CHAPTER 5

"KATHERINE, I LOVE YE like a mother, and I would like to help, but Highlanders?" Molly put down her shears and placed her hands on her hips. "Ye dinna even know these fellows. Surely ye dinna want me to house loud, uneducated, wild, haughty chaps. Highlanders think they are better than the rest of us." She crossed her arms in front of her. "The Reverend Mr. Campbell will have a better suggestion for a tenant for my hut as well as a spot for yer kin."

Katherine stood silently, a patient expression on her face.

Why had she been so harsh in her response? Her friend was only trying to help needy relatives. Had she not also recently benefited from Katherine's kindness and generosity? She offered a meek smile. "I'm sorry I didna mean to be unkind."

"Ye inherited yer pa's prejudice for Highlanders, lass. They are not oafs. They seem respectable, and the older one left a good job to take responsibility for his younger brother." Katherine pulled her shawl tight across her chest. "'Tis cold in here. Ye need more peat or ye shall take ill. The lad is about the same age as Scott. My nephews have little resources, and ye has a hut to let. Besides addin to yer funds, they could help around here, cuttin peat and workin the plot o land so ye could keep sewin and spinnin."

Molly wrung her hands then smoothed the fabric she had just cut. Katherine had an annoying way of bringing folks around to her way of thinking. But letting the hut to Highlanders sounded like more trouble than good.

Katherine pointed to the light blue wool dress draped over the chair. "Is that the lady's gown?"

"Aye. I'm just making the Spencer for it."

"And that one?" Katherine walked to the magenta colored dress hung on a peg.

"'Tis Grace Campbell's."

"Verra fine. I will bring the chaps to church in the morn. 'Twill give ye a chance to meet them and perhaps soften to lettin the hut to them. The older one, Grant, has been in construction so may look for road or bridge work."

Molly again folded her arms across her chest. "'Twould mean cooking for them."

"Aye, like ye does fer yer brother and yerself ... but with extra funds." Molly rolled her eyes.

Katherine glanced over her shoulder as she reached the door. "See ye in the morn at church."

Grant studied the tall spire on the front of a large rectangular-shaped church constructed of basalt. 'Twas old but finer than anything at home any closer than Inverness. Katherine introduced the clergyman and his wife to them outside the main entrance, and they seemed pleasant enough. He and Keith followed her into the church. The attendees seated in the pews numbered about twenty. There was a box seat in front for the local gentry.

Katherine whispered to him. "St. Guaire's. 'Twas in ruins but rebuilt almost ten years back." She led them to a pew halfway down the aisle from the chancel and smiled at folks around as they took their seats.

Grant studied the other parishioners. A good mix of couples, individuals, and families. Across the aisle and up a row was a lad about Keith's age who kept staring at them. Next to him was a lass who did not look old enough to be his mother. When she glanced their way, she had an irked expression on her face. A bonny lass, fair and in her twenties.

The service proceeded with the readings, prayers, and hymn singing. Grant relaxed despite the formality of the service. The peaceful expression on Keith's face reassured him. Perhaps Ma was right to encourage them to come here. If they could get settled nearby and if he could find work, this could provide a better future. As the congregation stood for the final hymn, the lad across the aisle turned and stared until the woman elbowed him.

At the end of the service, when he started to leave, Katherine grasped his sleeve. He put his hand on Keith's shoulder. There was obviously a protocol observed. They could leave after the clergy recessed. The gentry left the nave before the rest of the congregation.

Exiting the church, Katherine slipped her arm through his. A kindly gesture from a relative he had known less than twenty-four hours. Keith was gazing at the tall narrow windows in awe. The lad's world had truly expanded since they left home.

Katherine pulled on his arm. "Come, I want ye to meet some of the church members." She was definitely directing them this morning.

"Molly, Scott," his aunt called out as she approached the woman and lad he had noticed earlier in church. "I want to introduce ye to my nephews." The young woman faced them.

Grant pulled Keith alongside. One look into her sea-blue eyes took his breath away. What a stunner. The lass could not have been more than four and twenty, with fair skin and reddish blonde locks peeking out from beneath her bonnet. The expression on her face suggested she anticipated the introduction and was anything but pleased. The lad next to her eyed both he and Keith with wariness.

Outside, the five of them moved off to the side, away from the congregants, but still within the stone-walled churchyard and the adjacent cemetery.

"These are my nephews, Grant and Keith Cummings. And this is my friend Molly MacGregor and her brother Scott."

Grant nodded. "Nice to make yer acquaintance."

The lass had a stern look when she curtsied. "What brings ye to Aghadowey, Mr. Cummings?"

She was direct if not welcoming. "Evictions in the Highlands, so I'm seekin work here near our aunt." Her eyebrows raised at his mention of the Highlands. A Lowland snob? He had met enough of them in the past.

"Is there good fishin here?" Keith's question lightened the heavy atmosphere and distracted from the lass's reserved stare.

"Salmon 'n trout." The towhead seemed as suspicious as his sister.

Miss MacGregor's voice was soft but formal. "I understand yer looking for lodging. I have a hut we could let to ye on a trial basis, say for a month. If it works out for each of us, we could extend it."

Her reserve made sense now. The lass must have been who Katherine left to call on yesterday. Grant nodded. "Thank ye. Sounds like a fair agreement."

Katherine nodded, smiling as she looked between him and the young lass.

"Fine. Come around three today for tea. We can work out the details." She motioned for her brother, and they headed out of the enclosed churchyard and toward the direction of Aunt Katherine's home.

CHAPTER 6

MOLLY WALKED AS FAST as she could once out of eyeshot from the church. Had she lost her mind? Letting to Highlanders was rife with problems. For all she knew he was a drinking, brawling, cursing man. Pa would be turning over in his grave. Being charitable and putting up Highlanders made no sense, but she needed the income. She would have dismissed Katherine's plea entirely were it not for the Reverend Mr. Campbell's meddling in this morning's sermon.

"Verily I say unto you, Inasmuch as ye have done it unto one of the least of these my brethren, ye have done it unto me."

"Blessed is he that considereth the poor: the Lord will deliver him in time of trouble."

The wind kicked up, and she put one hand to her bonnet to keep it from flying off.

"Why are we running home from church?" Scott called.

"We need to get back and finish cleaning out the hut." Molly glanced to her right as they passed Katherine's cottage. Even Katherine's words had come back and bitten her. *"Ye have inherited yer pa's prejudice for Highlanders. My nephews have little resources and ye has a hut to let."*

Scott caught up to her. "Ye really going to let them live in our hut? The fellow said they were from the Highlands. Pa would skelp ye if he knew ye would house them."

"Well, Pa's not here, and neither are his wages." The wind was in full force now, and the clouds signaled rain. There would be no burning rubbish from the hut today. "When we get home, change out of yer Sunday clothes and help me."

"Aye." Scott, still shaking his head, raced to keep pace with her.

At the front walk, she grabbed Scott's arm. "When they get here, be well-mannered. We can show them how civilized folk behave. And be welcoming to the lad. He just lost his ma." She went inside and removed her Spencer jacket and bonnet. As she changed into her work clothes, she glanced at the table, half covered with her sewing project. "Humph!

Now we will need four spaces to eat. I'll be forever putting things aside."

Fifteen minutes later, she was tossing unneeded items from the hut into a crate. "Scott, fetch me a bucket of water and carry this crate and empty it into the burn pit." When they had done that, she carried the empty crate back to the hut.

Scott followed her. "The pallets look …"

"I know, I know. Help me bring them outside so I can swat the dust from them." When that task was completed, and the straw mattresses were returned to their wooden frames, she washed the small window adjacent to the door. Back at the cottage, she gathered blankets for the pallets, towels, and a cloth to cover the wooden crate. When everything was in place, she scanned the confined area. Not much of a table but it would do in such a small space. "Something for washing." She ran back to the cottage and found a bowl, and a pitcher of water to place on the crate.

"Are we done yet?" No mistaking Scott's annoyance.

"Aye, 'tis good enough. Wait, make sure the privy is presentable and go see to Gertie and Clara while I make some cock-a-leekie soup." She scanned the dwelling. *Ye needn't be concerned. They will be gone in a month or be looking for something better once they get established.*

At five till three, Scott, eyes wide, came scurrying through the door of the cottage. "They are coming down the road."

Molly peered out the window. Sure enough, Katherine walked alongside the older one. What was his name again? Agh! She whisked off her soiled apron then went to the mirror hanging in her bedroom. Some of her hair had fallen out of the braided knot fastened high on the back of her head. She scrambled for extra pins to tuck them in before returning to the main room.

Katherine entered with the Highlanders. The older one had to stoop to get through the door.

He nodded in greeting and handed her a fistful of heather. "We appreciate yer havin us."

She took the heather. "Ta. 'Tis June and about the only thing blooming yet. Have a seat, and I will pour ye some tea. We have cock-a-leekie if yer hungry."

Both brother's eyes lit up as if they had been offered a prize. The older one's smile was friendly. "'Tis most kind of ye."

Katherine set down a basket and helped dish the soup. "There are scones for ye in the basket. My nephews have been here but a day, 'n already Grant has helped with some needed repairs. Ye four sit at the table." Katherine sat on Scott's pallet with a bowl of the soup. "'Tis nice and soft."

Molly squinted at her neighbor. Katherine was not a bit subtle in suggesting the benefits of letting to these two. "I thought after we ate I could show ye the hut, and we could discuss terms."

"I'm obliged." He had a disarming way of looking directly at her.

She ate little as she observed the brothers. His name was Grant, same as Katherine's name, and Keith. Grant was a looker, tall, well built, nice smile, and probably full of himself. Best add no female guests to the rules.

"The cock-a-leekie is grand. 'Tis bin weeks since we had anythin this good."

"I'm glad ye like it." She best be wary. He was a charmer.

The freckle-faced lad seemed to like the soup, too. "How old are ye, Keith?"

He wiped his mouth on his sleeve and swallowed hard. "I'm eight."

Scott sat tall and put his chin back. "I'm seven, but turn eight in August, just in time for flax harvesting. Do ye work the flax where ye come from?"

"I helped." Keith pointed to the spinning wheel in the corner. "Ma was a spinner. She used one of them."

Scott nodded. "Pa was a weaver 'n worked in the mill till he passed."

Katherine came alongside her as she cleared the bowls from the table. "I will take care of these while ye show the lads around."

"Verra well." She walked around the table just as Grant stood. The cottage shrunk with him standing over her not two feet away. "Watch yer head." She led the way outside and in the direction of the hut.

The wood door to the hut had been left open to air the small room. They need not know how musty it smelled a few hours ago. "'Tis wee, but clean and dry." She stood outside while Grant ducked and entered.

"We have a horse and pony," he said as he came out of the small hut.

"There is a paddock yonder." She pointed to a small makeshift barn. "And a water trough and food there." She stood by the stone wall while the lads ran to where Clara and Gertie were feeding in the pasture. When they were out of earshot, she faced the man standing only three feet away and quoted a price for the month.

"'Tis agreeable."

"But there are some conditions to yer staying." She crossed her arms over her chest. "There will be no drinking on the premises ... or coming back here drunk. Ye are to use the privy to relieve yerselves. And there will be no cursing, brawling, loud ... caterwauling, and no female guests." The man's brows raised, his blue eyes widened. Was he stunned or was he fighting back a grin?

"We can agree to yer edicts. Canna even remember the last time I caterwauled."

CHAPTER 7

GRANT AND KEITH RETRIEVED their scant belongings from Katherine's and stowed them in the hut. Grant stood by the open door, gazing at the cottage, a stone's throw away. "'Tis a meager shack, but 'twill have to do for now. Aunt Katherine said ye could spend tomorrow with her while I search out employment."

Keith sat on one of the pallets. "Miss Molly seems nice, perhaps a bit stern." He examined the cramped quarters. "At least 'tis clean 'n the rain didna come in."

Grant laughed. "She is all business." He sat on the other pallet. "Her reserve might change when she gets to know us better." The lass definitely had an attitude and some odd notions about Highlanders. Had she ever even met one before?

"About tomorrow, what if Scott wants to go fishin'?"

"Dinna ye bring it up. See if he does. I say we ease in to these friendships. Aunt will be expectin ye." Grant ran his fingers through his hair. "Now let's go to the cottage. The lass said they would have a light supper for us."

Scott opened the door for them. His sister was clearing some fabric and sewing notions off the table. When they entered, she stopped and smoothed her skirt. "We have some bread and cheese with our tea. Please, sit." She motioned for them to sit at the table in the center of the room before placing a bowl of soft cheese and a round of bread. "'Tis not much but we only have one goat and cow."

Grant waited to see if she would offer a blessing while she eyed him like she was wondering the same. "May I offer a blessing?" He would show her they were not the heathens she took them for.

She nodded.

"We are thankful, God, for providing shelter 'n ask Yer blessings on this home 'n this meal ... 'n all who dwell here."

Her blue-green eyes still had that uncertain expression. Stange, she was too bonny to not be married. Perhaps she was promised.

"Do the young folk get any schoolin here?" Education was probably not something she expected him to inquire about. One side of her lip turned up. Was it surprise? Or disbelief?

"As a matter of fact, Scott and a couple of the local lads spend time with yer aunt several days a week for reading, writing, and sums when they are not busy with planting and harvesting."

He held back his laugh when Keith's shoulders sagged. "Just as we thought, lad, livin here wouldna be much different than the Highlands." He slathered some of the soft cheese onto a piece of bread. "So tomorrow, ye go to Aunt Katherine's, lad, while I look for work."

The next day Molly had been spinning for over an hour when the Cummings brothers came at half past six in the morning. "Help yerselves to tea, scones, and jelly." She dipped her fingers in the cup of water and continued to work the flax. The older one was studying the garments hanging on pegs near one of the windows. "I'm a spinner and a seamstress. That is why the area is in disarray at times." She continued spinning. 'Twould take some getting used to having them for meals, but the income was a necessity.

Grant nodded. "Yer work is verra handsome. Someone will be pleased with these."

"Since Pa passed, we are dependent on what I earn, so I dare not slow down." They may as well know, so as not to expect much from her.

Grant got up from the table. "Sorry to hear of yer loss. I will take Keith to Katherine's afore heading to Agivey. I dinna know what my work demands will be but I'm happy to help out where I can. Thank ye for the meal."

Grant helped Scott clear the table of the empty dishes. Pa had never done that.

Grant picked up his coat. "Ye want to come along with us, Scott, to our aunt's home? I will need the horse to get to Agivey, but ye two can walk."

"I will be there later, after my chores."

Grant motioned for his brother to follow. "Good day to ye then."

Keith smiled and waved when he reached the door. "See ye."

Molly rose from behind the wheel and moved her sewing materials back to the table. "Go now, get yer work done so ye can get to Miss Katherine's."

"I will." Scott stood by the table looking up at her, frowning as if he had a secret.

"Ye has something to confess? I'm not going to scutch ye."

He stood back. "They dinna seem so bad … for Highlanders."

"Hmm. We shall see. Be off with ye, now."

There was a knock at the door. Molly glanced at the clock on the hutch. Quarter past ten. Who could be calling when she had so much to do? Not Katherine, the lads were with her. She stood, smoothed her skirt, and opened the door. She curtsied. "Mrs. McGuire, come in." The small room was not as tidy as she would have it to welcome a guest of her rank. "I was not expecting ye. I thought I was to come to yer home for a fitting. Was there a misunderstanding?"

"Nay." The lady's generous figure was complimented by her printed linen day dress. Her plain Spencer and a straw bonnet provided the perfect balance. Mrs. McGuire scanned the room like she expected to find something. "I was curious to see your progress on my order." She came further into the room, and her brows lifted when she spotted her garments hanging on the far wall.

Mrs. McGuire felt the soft woolen fabric holding it out to better assess the progress. "'Tis lovely, and such fine tailoring on the Spencer jackets. You were right. The dark blue goes well with the lighter blue gown as does the plaid one."

Molly took a deep breath. Relief. The woman had not come to cancel her order. "May I offer ye some tea?"

"Nay, but thank you." Mrs. McGuire walked toward the hearth beyond the opposite end of the table and stared out the window.

There was more going on here than a visit to check on her sewing progress. Molly tapped her foot on the slate floor. "May I be of further assistance, ma'am? I am happy to bring yer garments for a fitting, say the day after tomorrow."

"Do I understand correctly, you are renting your shack to Highlanders?"

So that was it. News traveled faster here than the wind. "Aye, we are. Katherine Grant's kin arrived in town and needed a place to live. Her cottage couldna accommodate them, and I had a hut to let." Of what possible interest would that be to the landowner's housekeeper?

"'Tis very close, not fifteen feet away." A troubled expression formed on the lady's face. "Are you not concerned how it might appear?"

"Not at all. Many women find it necessary to run inns or boarding houses. Mine just happens to be a wee hut. I'm thankful I have such a spot to let and provide extra income for my brother and myself, particularly now that our father is gone." The woman's lips pursed. *Please, Lord, dinna let this rob me of her business.*

Mrs. McGuire glanced again at her new garments and shook her head. "You do very fine work, Miss MacGregor. Please bring them Wednesday at four for the fitting."

"Aye, ma'am."

With that, Mrs. McGuire walked to the door and stepped outside.

Molly stood in the doorway as Mrs. McGuire got into her chaise and turned onto the road. Why should letting the hut be anyone else's business? Was the woman's insinuation because they were Highlanders or that they were males? No matter. They likely wouldn't stay long anyway. Was letting to them going to bring more trouble than the coins they would furnish?

It was nearly seven when Grant returned to Katherine's cottage. A light shone through the window even though it would be a couple of hours before dark. Was Keith still there, or had he and Scott returned home? Home. What a thought. He was already thinking of the wee hut as home. Had the day gone well for the lad? He hoped so. All in all, it had been a successful day being taken on to work on the Agivey Bridge repairs. If this went well, there was the promise of other jobs ahead.

Katherine opened the door and greeted him with a grin. "Come in and tell me about yer day. Were ye able to find work?"

He surveyed the room. Where was Keith? "Aye, I did, Aunt, just as ye suggested … at the Agivey Bridge. What about Keith? Did he fare well the day?"

She smiled. "He did. We did some readin and sums so I could judge where he was in his learnin. Keith is a bright lad. Isabella, Duncan, and ye have done a good job raisin him."

"Ta. 'Tis to our parents' credit. I was gone for years. Is Keith back at the MacGregors'?" Had all gone well with the lass and her brother today? Working in Agivey, while only three miles away, would mean being gone long days.

"Those two were like bread and butter." Katherine laughed. "After a time of studies, they went back and forth about fishin and huntin. They left here after three, gabbin about goin back to the cottage to gather the gear and go to the river. The Aghadowey has grand fishin."

"I'm glad to hear the lad had a good day. He tries to be cheerful when at times I know he is down after losin Ma." He squeezed Katherine's hand. "Thank ye for all ye hae done for us, carin for Keith, locatin a place to bide, 'n suggestin where to find work. 'Tis been a successful day, and ye have been a blessin."

"'Tis the Lord. He knows what ye has been through and has gone before ye and made a way."

"Sure seems so. I best git back to the hut 'n see how Keith is farin. Doin well with Miss MacGregor, I hope."

"Molly's a good lass, upright, responsible, 'n kindhearted." Katherine tilted her head with a knowing look. "Smart 'n bonny, too."

"And opinionated when it comes to Highlanders."

"Hmm, that too. Good luck."

"Ta." Grant walked toward the door but stopped when he opened it. "How come the bonny, upright, responsible, 'n kindhearted lassie is not married? Or is she spoken for?"

"Not spoken for." Katherine winked then winced. "Molly is a wee bit bullheaded."

CHAPTER 8

SÉAMUS SLAMMED THE PAPER on top of the creamy linen on the table. "Ye cannot let the hut to those Highlanders. Think how it looks in town for ye to be having them living not fifteen feet away. Yer reputation would be besmirched in no time."

Breathing heavily, Molly grabbed the paper. She would not risk the ink soiling her fabric. "Yer insinuations are nasty, Séamus Macaulay. Folks let out rooms and dependencies all the time. With Pa gone, we need the income." She stood, head up, shoulders back, and her hands on hips. "I'm letting the hut out to them, so ye may as well go."

He pointed to the invoice in her hand. "I will be by in a week to get the payment for yer pa's services." His face was red right up to his receding hairline. "The landlord may appreciate knowing yer making money off his property."

"'Tis no different than selling from my garden. Yer just being vindictive because I wouldna marry ye."

Loud voices came from the cottage as Grant approached. *Please, dinna let it be about Keith.* He tied his horse to the rail and patted its side. "I will be back to care for ye in a bit." He hesitated a moment before knocking on the cottage door.

Molly, red-faced, opened it, her eyes blazing. "Oh, 'tis ye. Come in." She stepped aside so he could enter. Standing by the table, covered with her sewing notions and fabric, was a rather angry-looking chap.

Still looking annoyed, Molly faced the gent. "Séamus, this is Grant Cummings, Katherine's nephew ... and our tenant. Ye met his brother Keith before he left with Scott. Mr. Cummings, this is Séamus Macaulay, the town undertaker. He also works in the mill."

Grant stood silent a moment. What had he walked in on? "Good to make yer acquaintance." From the look on the chap's face, the sentiment was not returned. "I should find Keith."

"He is out back with Scott. They caught some fish and are gutting and scaling them. Supper should be ready in about twenty minutes." A caged bull couldn't have sent more angry signals than the lass.

"Ta. Sounds grand." Grant walked outside. *Glad to be free from whatever set them off.* Scott and Keith were laughing as they gathered the remains of their work into a pail.

"Looks like ye had a productive day, 'n I can almost taste those fish." Katherine was right, the lads were getting along fine. "I'm off to care for the horse."

Scott hefted the pail. "Go ahead, Keith. I can bury the remains and take the fish to Molly."

"Ta. See ye for supper." Keith came alongside Grant.

He rubbed the top of Keith's head. "How was yer day? Aunt Katherine said ye did well."

Keith grinned from ear to ear. "'Twas a good day, studied some, then went to the river 'n caught six trout."

"Remarkable." Just as they came around the side of the cottage and were headed to the hut, the door slammed. The gent, still in a huff, and with a frightful scowl yelled at them. "Ye will find another place to live if ye have any sense."

Grant pulled Keith close.

The chap got on a fine mare and left in a hurry.

Keith's eyes widened. "Is he scared of Miss Molly or mad at us?"

"Couldn't answer that, lad."

Molly cleared the table to set it for supper, her head pounding. *Dinna let that filthy-minded miser vex ye.*

Scott entered with the pail of fish, his forehead creased. "Why was ye fighting with Séamus? Sure sounded loud."

"'Tis Mr. Macaulay to ye, laddie. A disagreement but no need to give it another thought. Wash and I will get these in the skillet." She sliced potatoes and added them to some water in another pan.

Fifteen minutes later, when there was a knock at the door, she yelled, "Come in."

The Cummings brothers entered. Their hands were clean, and their hair was damp and slicked back like they had just bathed. *Must be trying to make a good impression.* Grant glanced at her untidy work area. Heat crept into her cheeks. *How embarrassing, but where else was* she to set her work?

Grant smiled at her as he took off his jacket. "Somethin smells mighty good. May I do somethin to help?"

"Aye." She handed him the platter of fish. The man's penetrating blue eyes were a distraction. She placed the drained potatoes in a bowl and handed Scott the plates. "Please put these and forks around. We can all sit now." She stared across the small table directly at Grant. "I will ask the blessing. 'Bless, O Father, Thy gifts to our use and us to Thy service; for Christ's sake. Amen.'" She cringed. She was speaking to the Lord, and her mind had wandered back to Séamus. *Forgive me, God.* It was worry enough how she would take care of them with so little funds, and now with Seamus making trouble.

"Please take the plate of tatties." Scott frowned, holding it out to her.

"Sorry." She took it and served herself before passing it to Keith. Their situation was dire. How would they keep the cottage and continue to put food on all their plates?

Grant took the plate. "Ye did well, lads, the fish is grand." Looking at her, "I will have the rest o this month's rent for ye at the end o the week."

His gentle gaze relaxed the tension in her neck. Fighting back tears, she swallowed hard. "Ta." That and what she had set aside would pay off Séamus. Good riddance. Mrs. McGuire and Grace would be paying her too. If only the weather would warm so their garden would produce. The man continued to stare at her. She cleared her throat. "So ye found work today? At the Agivey Bridge like ye thought?"

"Aye, 'n if it works out well, 'n I hae no reason to think otherwise, there will be more."

His engaging smile was impossible to ignore. But he had no worries about being turned out—well—other than already having been turned out in the Highlands. "Good for ye."

Scott pointed to the platter of fish. "May I have more?"

"Aye, have mine." She pushed her uneaten meal toward him. It looked and smelled tasty, but her appetite was gone.

Grant placed more potatoes on his plate. "I don't mean to intrude, but was there trouble with Mr. Macaulay? Ye seemed to be in a quarrel when I got here."

Scott, with a mouth full of trout, spoke up. "Nay, he is just a nuisance."

Her brother spoke his mind too freely. Still, laughter bubbled up, easing her soul.

Scott wiped his mouth. "He has been pestering Molly to marry him."

She scowled at him. "Ye talks too much. Now help me clear this away. I need to get back to sewing while I still have light." She got up and removed the dishes. When she wiped off the table, Grant was studying the bay window and her sewing mess again. Had he never seen the like before?

He went to the wash basin. "Thank ye for the meal. I can wash them so ye can get back to yer sewin."

Her jaw dropped. Neither Pa nor Scott had ever offered to do that. She closed her mouth and stared at him. "'Tis not necessary, but thank ye for offering."

CHAPTER 9

Days later, under an overcast sky, Grant stopped at Katherine's cottage on his return from Agivey. He pulled his coat close. Was June in Ulster always so chilly?

Katherine opened the door to him with a wide smile. "Come in. I have bin thinkin about ye and wonderin how ye was farin. One does not get much information from an eight-year-old."

He ducked his head as he entered the cottage. "I'm grateful to ye for suggestin I go to Agivey. The work is good 'n there is the promise of more in Ballymoney later. How has Keith been? The lad seems to be adjustin, but I wanted yer insight."

"He is doing well, and I think Scott and he have helped each other both with their studies 'n as friends, both losin a parent so recently. Can I pour ye some tea?"

"Nay, I want to get home, but wondered, have ye any wood to make a table 'n shelves or know where I could find some?"

Katherine smiled. "'Tis glad I am that yer settlin in. I do have some wood." She ushered him into the bedroom and pointed to the bed. "Henry saved some pieces from a broken table. They are under the bed."

He pulled out some oak pieces, then followed her around to the back to a covered three-sided lean-to. "Got some other odds and ends Henry found. If ye wants it yer welcome to it. Ye can use my cart to haul them away."

He studied what was available. "With some tools and nails, it should work. I can find them in Agivey. If Miss Molly allows it, I will be back for it 'n the cart."

"Cannot imagine why she wouldna let ye add to the hut."

He kissed her cheek. "Thank ye."

Grant fed the horse and put it out to pasture, then went to the hut. Keith was likely with Scott. The pitcher on the small table had been filled.

'Twas thoughtful of Keith or the lass, probably the lass. She seemed friendlier these past few days. He needed a bath. Tomorrow was Sunday and church.

Keith opened the cottage door and grinned. "Wondered where ye were."

"I stopped at Katherine's 'n washed when I got here." He entered the room. Molly was in the chair by the window in the bay sewing on some brown fabric. "Thank ye, for fillin the water jug."

"I was filling the trough so 'twas no trouble."

He nodded. "Was wondering where Keith 'n I could get a bath?"

Scott stopped setting the table and grinned. "Saturday evenings, spring and summer, I go down to the river for a swim."

Keith perked up. "Aye, we could go for a swim."

The lass stood and put her sewing aside. Was that a blush on her face? "We have a tin bathing tub by the root cellar. Ye can fill it from the well."

"Ta. If I remember correctly, services are at nine o'clock in the mornin."

Molly had a quizzical expression. "Aye, nine o'clock." She carried the dishes to the table.

When they had seated themselves, she blessed the food and ladled the cock-a-leekie into bowls. The lads finalized their plans to make a quick trip to the river. Grant only half listened to their conversation. The lass seemed to be deep in thought while glancing back and forth between Scott and Keith and avoiding his gaze. What was she thinking? And how would she receive his idea? He would tell her while the lads were off to the river.

Molly smiled. "I made a berry cobbler." She put a large scoop on each plate, then poured some tea.

His chest grew tight when her sea-blue eyes met his. She was a beauty, particularly when the suspicious look slipped away. Industrious and a good cook, too. No wonder the undertaker fellow resented male boarders, though she didn't seem so fond of him. Were there other chaps in town who had designs on her? When they finished the cobbler, he stood. "Ta. Enjoyed the entire meal."

She smiled again as she cleared the table.

Perhaps she was warming up to Highlanders.

Scott and Keith headed out the door. "Take some clean clothes with ye, Keith."

"Ye too, Scott." She added and poured Grant more tea.

"I'm needin a word with ye ... been thinkin about somethin to help ye."

She stepped away, but curiosity was written on her face.

He pointed to the bay window "What if ye had a table 'n chair here by the window? Ye would have plenty of light, 'n shelves to store yer things. Ye wouldna need to be movin yer work all the time."

Her eyes grew wide, and her mouth opened, but no words came out.

"Katherine has given me the wood 'n I could make it for ye."

Molly's fingers touched her lips for a moment. "I dinna understand. Why would ye do this?"

"I'm a builder. 'Tis what I do ... and ye seem to have a need."

"I ... I ... 'tis verra kind of ye."

"Ye helped us. I'm wantin to help ye. Now, I will be gettin that tub ... 'n a bath."

She blushed. "There is a bucket at the well, and I will bring some soap and hot water to add to it."

"Ta." He walked outside. The lass had promise—if she could get over her aversion to Highlanders.

Molly peered out the window. Grant carried the oblong tub from around the other side of the cellar. She had already filled another kettle and hung it over the fire. Two would better take the chill off the well water. When she went to get the lye soap, she spotted him carrying the tub toward the hut. She winced. He had to remove the crate to fit it in the hut. But he wanted privacy, and so did she.

Grant Cummings was an enigma. First, he helped in the kitchen so she could get back to her sewing. Then he wanted to bathe and go to church. And now the offer to build her a table. Either he was no normal Highlander—or she had misjudged Highlanders in general. He returned to the well with a bucket. She'd best take the water and soap out to him before he began disrobing.

His eyes met hers when she turned the corner of the cottage, a kettle in each hand.

"Here, let me take them."

This time she did not look away from the cleft in his chin and his blue eyes. She almost forgot the soap. Reaching into her apron pocket, she handed it to him. "I will leave ye now." For such a cool day it seemed increasingly warm.

"Ta. The lads should be back before long. I will wash our clothes after I bathe."

"Right." She walked back to the cottage. Inside she studied the bay window and paced back and forth. 'Twas a generous offer to make her a table. Surely his motives were honorable. She sank into her chair and picked up the piece she was hemming. A table just for her sewing right here under the window. And shelves to store things on. "Hmm." She rested her head against the back of the chair and closed her eyes. Perhaps Pa had been wrong about Highlanders. Grant was not such a rough chap after all. If only she could be sure. "A penny for yer thoughts, Grant Cummings."

CHAPTER 10

GRANT STEERED KEITH TO the graveyard when they arrived at the church. "Perhaps we should look here a for a while since we have time before the service."

"Why did we get here so early? We could have waited and come with the MacGregors."

"Look at the stones with me." An eight-year-old would not understand why it was best if they did not arrive with Molly and Scott. Villagers were notorious for gossiping.

Headstones of every shape and size covered the grassy lawn. He joined Keith at a recent grave with only a plain slate cross. "What has yer attention?"

"I think 'tis Scott's pa's grave. Says R. MacGregor died just two months ago."

Grant nodded. "I think yer right. 'Tis around the same time as Ma." Molly and Scott stood not twenty feet away, staring at them. In her hand was a sprig of posies and on her face, that suspicious expression again.

She approached them. "Scott mentioned ye left earlier, but I'm surprised ye are here … in the graveyard." She bent over and placed the flowers and sprigs of green down on the grave.

Grant placed his hand on Keith's shoulder. "Come, lad, time to go inside 'n give them privacy." They walked toward the large rectangular church and took their seats halfway up the nave. A few minutes later, Molly and Scott took seats two rows further up on the other side.

A well-dressed gentleman came in and sat in the box seat near the front set aside for the gentry. He greeted a few of the parishioners near his seat. He was followed by several others in fine garb who sat in pews directly behind him. Must be the local laird and his household.

Aunt Katherine slipped into the pew beside them right before the processional. "Good to see ye here."

The service was much like it was the previous week, and at the end, he placed his hand on Keith's shoulder. They would observe the local protocol and leave after the gentry.

Katherine cocked her head. "We can go now." As they walked down the aisle, she put her arm through his. "Would ye and Keith come over for dinner today? I have a stew to share."

"'Tis kind of ye. Let me tell Miss MacGregor to not expect us." After shaking the Reverend Mr. Campbell's hand at the church door, he stepped off to the side.

Katherine joined him. "I will go ahead. Molly is talkin with Grace Campbell and Mrs. McGuire, probably schedulin a fittin or a delivery."

"We will be there before long, Aunt."

Katherine passed Keith and Scott standing by the street. Grant walked up to them.

Keith kicked some of the gravel. "Scott says he is goin fishin this afternoon. May I go with him?"

"After we have dinner with Aunt Katherine." Was Molly finished yet? The clergyman's wife had gone. If she was conducting business with Mrs. McGuire, it did not appear the transaction was going well.

Molly, shoulders slumped, opened the door to the cottage and walked inside. She removed her hat and Spencer and placed them on hooks. Her home, this room, was filled with a lifetime of memories. The whitewashed walls, the darkened hearth that had provided warmth and cooked meals for as long as she could remember. The oak table, half covered with her sewing materials, the curtains Ma made so long ago, and the rocking chair Pa parked himself in at the end of each day. Could they really lose it all now?

Scott came through the door with a broad grin, peeling off his jacket. "Keith said they were eating at their aunt's, but when he gets home, we want to go fishing."

Good thing Scott was completely unaware of the serious situation they faced. "I know. His brother mentioned it after church. Get yer chores done and move the peat."

Molly poured water into a cup, sliced bread and cheese, and put it on a plate at the clear end of the table. "This should fill ye till supper."

She walked into her room and closed the curtain that separated it from the main area. Tears ran down her cheeks as she removed her church gown and put on her black day dress. Could Mrs. McGuire be right? Or had the woman only heard idle gossip? Would the landlord truly evict his tenants? Nay, 'twas foolish to fret about overheard conversations. She would just keep spinning for the weavers, growing their few garden crops, and sewing for the ladies in town. There would be time enough to determine what to do next if the situation changed. *Lord, please make a way for us.*

Molly returned to the main room and made some tea. Scott was no doubt rushing through his chores so he could be off to the river with Keith. 'Twas time to get back to work. Mrs. McGuire's fitting was tomorrow, and she needed to be ready. She passed the next hour and a half making significant progress on the linen dress. Keeping her mind from wandering to circumstances out of her control was a bigger challenge.

A rickety wagon creaked to a halt outside. Molly put down the trim fabric she was cutting and went to the window. Grant pulled a cart of wood with Scott and Keith walking alongside. She opened the door and placed her hands on her hips. "What have we here?"

Grant smiled, wiping his hands on his pants. "Wood for yer work spot, and two helpers to carry it inside."

When it was stacked inside, Molly poured cups of water for them.

"Ta." Grant took one of them. "Katherine had Some tools 'n nails, 'n I can pick up anything else I'm needin in Agivey tomorrow."

Scott drank his water and poked Keith in the arm. "We need to get down to the river. Those fish are calling us, Keith."

Grant set a canvas bag and hammer near the wood. "Go 'n change out o yer Sunday clothes first, lad, 'n bring us back some fish."

The lads left, and Grant examined the alcove for his project.

Molly smoothed loose strands of hair back from her face. "Do ye plan to start on it now? Ye can, but I will need to move the chair, lampstand, and clear the space." Why did the room always seem so much smaller when he was in it?

Grant stood not five feet away in silence. He had to be a foot taller, and his gaze enveloped her. Then, looking around the small room, he suddenly stepped back. "Nay … this wouldna be a good time. When the lads return, I could work on it for a while."

"Aye. That would be best." Her face grew warm. "Thank ye … meanwhile, I will clear the area."

He walked away, shutting the door behind him. The man rattled her. She closed her eyes and shook her head. He was a Highlander but … agh! What did she know about Highlanders but what Pa and others had said? That they were loud, boorish, arrogant, and prone to brawling and drunkenness. But Grant was none of those things. He chose not to be alone with her, to not place her in a compromising situation.

It was five-thirty when the lads returned. She opened the door to two grinning faces holding several trout. "Looks like ye both have some work to do if we are to enjoy them for supper."

Grant walked from the pasture toward them. "What a catch." The smile on his face warmed her. "I can get started if 'tis a good time for ye, but if not …"

"'Tis fine. The area is ready now." She stepped back as he came through the door. "If ye need anything …"

"Nay, this will allow me to get started 'n figure what else for ye I'm needin. Then I can work on it when I get back from Agivey tomorrow." He carefully measured the space, then moved an oak tabletop.

She wouldn't hover while he worked. Her time was better spent preparing for supper. Perhaps, while he worked in the cottage, she would grow more accustomed to his presence and feel less self-conscious. She looked out the window. The lads were coming around to the side with the fish, all gutted and ready to cook. If the landlord turned them out, it meant the Cummings would also be without shelter … and possibly out of her and Scott's lives.

CHAPTER 11

THE NEXT SUNDAY, MOLLY walked with him to Katherine's cottage for dinner with the lads following behind. Once inside, Molly wrapped her shawl tight around her shoulders. At least he could help to provide warmth for her body if not her heart. "I'll get more peat blocks from outside. Are yer summers usually this cool 'n overcast?"

"Nay," Katherine answered. "'Tis much cooler this year, and 'tis affecting the crops."

Grant patted his stomach. "The herrin was tasty and the boxty outstandin. Ye hae been so kind. 'Tis there anythin I can do to help ye, Aunt?"

"Nay, but lads, ye could clean up the garden. Pull the weeds and the dead plants. With the foul weather, 'tis not producin. Find the crate out back for the waste."

Keith and Scott left as Molly cleared the dishes from the table. "My garden 'tis no better, and word is most of the local crops, including flax, are doing poorly. 'Tis no wonder folks gossip about the landlord making changes."

Katherine poured them tea. "I can wash the dishes later. Come on back, lass, and sit with us." Katherine smiled at Grant. "I saw the way ye fixed up the table and shelves for Molly. 'Tis grand."

Molly returned to the table, sat and took a sip of tea. "Aye. And, as ye noticed, I've already filled every space. I cannot think why we never made better use of that nook." Her eyes locked with his. "'Twas verra kind of ye to do that."

Her appreciation and smile warmed his heart. "Ye needed it ... Katherine had the materials, 'n I could build it." He could hardly take his eyes off her.

Smoothing back a lock of her rose-gold hair, Molly's lips parted as she stared back at him.

Best look at somethin else before he made a fool of himself.

Katherine glanced back and forth between them. "Grace was

delighted with her new gown. And the dress yer makin for Mrs. McGuire is beautiful. I'm sure she's pleased."

Molly folded her hands and placed them on her lap. "She seemed content with it when she had her fitting last week. 'Tis almost finished."

Katherine poured them each more tea. "So why the anxious look on yer face, lass?"

"I can hardly utter the words." She smoothed the tablecloth with her fingertips. "Mrs. McGuire hinted, more than once, that the landlord has voiced making changes. With the potato tubers rotting and the failing flax crop, he may soon be evicting his tenants. Ye knows people at the manse, Katherine, and ye are always quick to hear what goes on in town. Is it true?"

Katherine's brows raised and she glanced first at him then at Molly. "I have heard the same ... and from more than one source."

A knot formed in Grant's stomach. The lass was clearly in distress. Clearances ... evictions he knew only too well. Just when things seemed to be going well—it would mean Keith and he would need to find another dwelling. But what would Molly and Scott do? Where would they go?

Molly's eyes grew moist. "What are we to do if that comes about?"

Katherine rubbed her fingertips around the rim of her cup. "Perhaps 'tis time for ye to make a change, lass. Yer brother is in America. Write to Ewan. I'm sure he would help ye and Scott make a new beginnin."

"Nay. Just because he took it in his head to go across an ocean to live amongst our enemies doesn't mean I'm so inclined." Molly stood and smoothed her skirt.

Katherine shook her head. Her son was in America. Molly's remark likely stung.

The lass paced back and forth. "I'm sorry. I know Gavin lives in Virginia and I meant no offense. But we have fought two wars with the Americans. Why would we go there? And where would we find the wherewithal? How would I care for Scott and myself?"

Grant finished his tea. "Ma said Gavin was doing well, and that many Scots have resettled in the Shenandoah Valley. Might ye join him there, Katherine?"

Katherine gathered the cups. "Aye, I'm thinkin I may. I'm sturdy and but forty-seven. Gavin and Lorna have a farm north of the village of Lexington. 'Twould be nice to know my grandchildren. He said makin that move was the best decision he ever made." Katherine gazed tenderly at Molly. "Ewan is in Philadelphia, a big city. Surely he could help ye find work there as a seamstress and help ye and Scott."

Molly shook her head. "Nay, I might go to Coleraine, 'tis not that far. Or some other large village to find employment. Now let me help ye wash the dishes." She placed the soiled dishes in the basin. "Then I need to get back to work."

How could he ease her distress? He joined her. "I can help Katherine with the dishes. Ye need to finish Mrs. McGuire's dress. I will bring the lads back with me."

She smiled at him and shook her head. "Seems I'm indebted to ye again." The lass was in turmoil but how to further aid her escaped him.

Molly wiped her hands and hugged Katherine. "I know ye are just trying to help us. I'm just ... confused and need some time to figure it out. We will find a way."

"I know yer uncertain about the future, and I will be prayin for ye. I know God will direct yer path," Katherine said.

"I hope so." Molly glanced his way, then left.

He took a wet dish from the basin and passed it to Katherine. "The lass sure has definite opinions. It appears that Highlanders are not the only folks she finds questionable."

"I warned ye." Katherine stacked the clean dishes. "Molly has a good heart. She is a strong and capable woman, but I think she's frightened. A couple of local lads perished in a battle in a bay near Virginia a few years back." Katherine placed her hand on his arm. "I'm not blind. Seems to me, there is something going on between ye two."

"Hmm." There was something going on, but he suspected it was all on his part. Was he that obvious?

Molly sat at the table Grant had made and picked up the creamy border to sew on Mrs. McGuire's gown. What was Katherine thinking, suggesting she and Scott go to America? Would she really move to Virginia? What a void her absence would leave in their lives. That Katherine had heard the chatter of evictions only made it seem more likely. If she and Scott were evicted and moved to Coleraine, they would be without friends like Katherine—and the Cummings. She sighed. No denying it, Grant and Keith Cummings had grown on her in the weeks they had lived here.

The shine on the oak tabletop caught her eye when she reached for her shears. Building the table might seem inconsequential to some folks, but his thoughtfulness and generosity were unexpected. Having him in the cottage while he constructed it had not been at all unpleasant either.

Scott came through the door. "Ye left Miss Katherine's without saying so." He walked up to her and rubbed his hand along the top of the new table. "'Tis good to have yer own space and nice of Mr. Cummings to build it for ye."

"Aye, 'twas. And it 'twas nice of ye to help Miss Katherine in her garden."

His eyes widened. "I never saw it looking so poorly before. The root plants are failing."

"Go check ours. 'Tis the cold and wet that threatens the potatoes and turnips. If yer hankering to pull the weeds and clear out the waste, I would have time to make a pudding." She winked at him.

"A half hour, and no more!" He rolled his eyes.

She blew him a kiss. "Ta. Did Keith and Mr. Cummings come back with ye?"

"Aye. They went out to the pasture to see to the horses."

Scott left, and she returned to her hemming. For the first time that day, she relaxed. Sunday services, a dinner with friends, and the gift of this table, all good reasons to be thankful. Fretting over the future was fruitless. She had been dwelling on the wrong things. Katherine obviously enjoyed having her nephews around. She surely wouldn't want to leave them since they had come so far to be with her. And they had made life more interesting for Katherine—and for them also. Aye, the Cummings arrival in Aghadowey may very well prove to have been providential.

CHAPTER 12

MOLLY FINISHED PULLING THE last of the rotten potatoes. It was already the end of June. Was there any hope for the rest of the crop? The flax field with its sparse growth appeared to be a loss. She removed her gloves and walked around the front of the cottage. Séamus Macaulay was approaching. About time he came for his payment. 'Twould be good to be done with it ... and him.

"Good to see ye, Molly." He tipped his cap at her, and she responded with a curtsy.

"I have yer payment inside." She opened the door, walked to the hearth, and pulled notes from the clay jar.

Séamus stood, cap in hand, by the dining table. "I regret being so harsh with ye when we last spoke. I was just concerned about yer well-being with having strangers boarding so close by."

"No harm done, Séamus." When she handed him the payment, he took her hand, and she yanked it back.

"Word is that next week the estate manager will be delivering eviction notices. What will you do?"

"I'm not certain yet, possibly go to Coleraine, and find work there."

"Ye do not need to leave Aghadowey. I live not fifteen minutes away. Marry me and ye can continue with yer sewing and ye and the lad can have a fit home."

Why had he not believed her before when she refused him? "Nay, I appreciate yer asking, but I'm not inclined."

"Is it the Highlander?"

"Nay, 'tis no one."

Séamus took a step toward her, and she backed up two. He followed. "I care for ye and will be a good husband to ye."

She should have moved to the side instead of backing herself into the kitchen alcove. He reached for her arms, drew her close, and just as he leaned in for a kiss, she ducked her head. "Let go of me, Séamus, and leave!"

Scott and Keith were in the doorway, eyes wide as saucers. Scott ran to Séamus. "Take yer hands off my sister."

Red-faced, Seamus pushed her away. "I'm leaving. Ye will be sorry ye turned me down when ye come to yer senses." He picked up his cap and stormed out the door.

"Did he hurt ye?"

"Nay, not at all. Mr. Macaulay has been paid for the funeral, and I dinna think he will trouble us anymore." She smoothed her hair back. "How was yer time at Miss Katherine's? Did ye learn much?" Best to get them all thinking on something other than what just occurred. She poured them each a cup of water and put a plate of ginger biscuits on the table.

Keith took one. "Aunt Katherine got a visit from the landlord's man. He gave her a paper 'n I could tell she was upset, even though she said 'twas nothing to worry about." He bit into the biscuit. "Tasty."

She smiled. Keith had his brother's charm.

So evictions had started. How soon would the landowner's steward come to their cottage? "If Miss Katherine said 'twas nothing to fret about, ye must not worry." She would go to Katherine's to find out for herself. "Lads, we should take Miss Katherine some biscuits to cheer her."

Ten minutes later, Molly strode down the well-worn cart path to Katherine's, with Scott and Keith in tow. The top of the Dutch door was open. Good. She was home.

Katherine answered her door with a grin. "I knew ye would be by within minutes."

Scott held out the small basket. "We brought ye ginger biscuits."

"Ta." Katherine eyed Scott and Keith with a pensive stare. "Lads, I forgot to feed the goats. Would ye mind doing that for me?"

"Aye." They walked toward the pen.

Molly followed Katherine inside to the table. "They told me about the steward bringing a letter. 'Tis it an eviction notice?"

Katherine passed her the document "Aye. I have until the end of the month. 'Twill seem odd not livin here anymore, but change can be good."

"How can ye say that? This was yer home with Henry and Gavin." She scanned the paper. "I suppose 'tis only a matter of days till we get ours. What will ye do?"

"I wrote to Gavin a fortnight ago tellin him 'twas expected and that I'm goin to find a way to get to Virginia." Katherine peered out the window to where the boys were. "Sit, lass, I will make us some tea. I didna tell the lads about goin to America. What will ye tell them when ye get yer notice?"

"I'm not certain. If I have till the end of June also, I should make a trip to Coleraine to secure work and lodging."

Katherine brought cups and the kettle to the table. "If that is yer choice, I have a friend in Coleraine ye might be able to stay with while ye search. And I can watch over Scott and Keith in yer absence."

"Ta, sweet friend. What will I do without ye? A better friend I've never known."

"Ye need not do without me. Come with me."

"Agh!" Molly shook her head. "Dinna be rash."

The door opened and in came Scott, Keith, and Grant.

Grant nodded at her. "No one was at the cottage. I thought I might find ye here."

Molly rose and put an arm around Scott. "I will take the lads home and start the supper so ye can talk with yer aunt."

His brow furrowed. "I will be there soon."

When Molly reached the door, she glanced over her shoulder at Grant with a hopeful smile. If only the bonny lass would follow Katherine's instincts to venture to America.

"Keith said the agent was here with a paper. Is it an eviction?"

"Aye. I have till the end of the month to vacate." She handed him the notice.

Grant read through it. "He sounds like he regrets needin to evict his tenants."

"I thought so, too. What do ye make of this sentence?" She pointed to the end of the page.

"Suggests he will be sendin more information soon. Not sure what it means."

Katherine offered him a ginger biscuit. "So, I best get things in order to leave in the next couple of weeks."

"I'm sorry. There are changes for all of us. Repairs on the Agivey Bridge are finished. But the foreman said there is work in Ballymoney."

"Agivey is halfway between Ballymoney and Aghadowey. What will ye do?"

"Bin thinkin Keith and I would accompany ye to Virginia."

Her eyes lit up. "'Twould be grand."

"Gavin will be glad when he gets yer letter. I should write to him and tell him we will also come."

"I wish we could convince Molly to join us, but the lass is inclined to go to Coleraine. She has always resisted change."

Grant nodded. "Ye knows her better than I. How do we convince her to go with us?"

A sly grin appeared on Katherine's face. "Marry her."

CHAPTER 13

"MARRY HER?" GRANT SHOOK his head. What was Katherine thinking? "Are ye makin a joke, Aunt? The lass is not fond of Highlanders 'n wants no part of Americans. If I asked her, Molly would laugh … or scream 'n evict us afore she even gets her own notice."

Katherine smiled and shook her head. "Nay, I think not. She cares for ye … but she may not know it yet. Molly is wary of change and the unknown and has some ill-informed notions. Until ye came, she had not known any Highland folk. Yet, in the past two months, her hostility toward Highlanders has waned."

"'Tis a long journey from hostility to affection, Aunt, 'n I'm not certain she has or wants to make it." He'd be a liar to deny he had pondered the idea. The fetching lass was never far from his mind, and he dreaded leaving her and Scott. He ran his fingers through his hair. "What makes ye think she might say aye?" Something must have put that bee in Katherine's bonnet.

"I'm not blind, man. I see the way she looks at ye and how flustered she is when she is round ye."

"I never planned to wed till I was settled in a job 'n could care for a wife. Now I must care for Keith."

Katherine smiled. "And the Lord tells us, *There are many devices in a man's heart; nevertheless, the counsel of the Lord, that shall stand.*"

"I best get home, or the lads will worry somethin is amiss." He started to leave, then took Katherine's hand. "Pray I will know what to do about Molly, 'n that her mind 'n heart might be open to me."

"I will pray ye will know what to say and when."

"'Tis a good prayer."

Grant walked toward home. He was a grown man so why was he in such a muddle? "Molly Cummings?" Sounded nice. How would he even begin to approach her, much less ask her to wed him? *Lord, I need a sign.*

Supper was ready when he arrived. After the blessing, the lads ate and chattered on about fishing in the morning. While he stirred the cock-a-leekie in his bowl, she sat across the table staring at him. His heart seemed to skip a beat looking into her sea-blue eyes.

"Is something wrong with yer soup?"

"Nay, I was … just thinkin. Smells grand." He took a spoonful and continued eating.

Were it not for Keith and Scott, the meal would have been silent. When supper was over, he stood. "When I was comin home, I noticed some border stones in the pasture had fallen. I will tend to it now." Her worried countenance aggravated his peace. "Thank ye for the soup. 'Twas tasty."

Once in the pasture, he stacked the rocks. How was he to woo Molly with the lads there? And what did he have to offer her? He had no steady work or place to live, just the hope of a better life in America. She was none too fond of Highlanders and had strong opinions about crossing the Atlantic to an unfamiliar land. Was he daft to think she'd agree? This was just the activity he needed to work off his tension.

With the border repaired, he wiped his hands on his pants. Molly was walking across the field toward him. Her hair glistened gold with the setting sun. They would be alone—one answer to prayer. So why was he so tongue-tied? "Ye looks like ye have somethin on yer mind."

"Aye. Yer aunt's eviction." She sat on the low stone wall. "Have ye a few minutes to talk?"

"Certainly."

"I have an idea, and I need yer help." Her smile gave him hope. Was this the sign he had prayed for?

He sat a few feet away on the same stone wall. "'Tis my pleasure to assist ye."

"I have no doubt my eviction will come soon. Katherine said she would care for the lads while I go to Coleraine to look for work. When we're evicted, Keith and ye will also need new lodgings. I'm hoping that ye might convince Katherine to move to Coleraine also." Her eyes took on a pleading look. "We might be able to find lodgings in Coleraine in close proximity."

He briefly glanced at Gertie and Clara, feeding near the tall oak tree. Not the sign he was hoping for, but she deserved a response. "Yer desire fer Katherine to be with ye is commendable, but it sounds like she wants to live near her son 'n his folk in Virginia."

She smoothed her skirt and leaned toward him. "There must be many opportunities for a builder in and near Coleraine. The lads have grown to be fast friends. 'Twould be nice if they could stay together and ye would have us to look after Keith while ye worked."

"I'm glad ye want to keep the families together. I was thinkin along similar lines ..."

A scream came from the direction of the cottage, and they both took off at a run.

Grant reached the yard first. He kneeled beside Keith laying on the ground near the well holding his leg and wailing. "What happened?"

Scott had a sheepish look. "He fell from the well roof."

Grant knelt and felt Keith's leg. "I fear 'tis broken."

Molly fell to her knees next to him and placed her hand on his back. "'Tis not long past eight, the doctor should be home. I can go for him. Can ye carry him inside?"

Keith groaned as Grant picked him up and carried him into the hut and placed him on his pallet. "What were ye doin up there?"

"I was tryin to save the kitten. The mother cat carried him up there, and I feared he would fall in the well. The roof was slippery, and I fell."

"Ah suppose we should be grateful ye didna fall in the well." He pulled up Keith's breeches and examined the swelling leg. "Scott, find some straight sticks for a splint till the doctor comes."

It was almost ten by the time the doctor left. He and Molly walked outside together. "Thank ye for yer help. The doctor said it 'twas not a bad break and will heal."

Molly walked toward the well. "I cannot believe he climbed up there, nor why the silly cat did either. Scott and I will watch over him. No need for ye to miss work tomorrow."

"My work in Agivey is finished. But I was planning to go to Coleraine 'n I might need a few days. I'm sure Katherine could help if needed."

Even though it was dark, he didn't miss her smile. Could Aunt Katherine be right?

"We will take good care of him. Ye go 'n see to yer business. Good night." Her eyes lit up as she headed into the cottage.

Perhaps Molly was warming to him.

CHAPTER 14

TWO DAYS LATER, GRACE Campbell came by the MacGregors' for a fitting and a visit. She stood on a crate while Molly sat on the floor pinning the hem of a dress. Molly moved the pin cushion. "The magenta color becomes ye. I can hem this while we have some tea so ye can take it home with ye. The other gown I will deliver to ye when I'm finished."

Grace turned slightly. "Ta. John knows when I come to see ye we will visit." A coy smile formed on her face. "Ye have been in mourning these past three months. Is it not time to put aside yer black and start wearing colors again?"

Molly stood. "Hmm. I hadna given it a thought. There ... 'tis all pinned. Take it off, and I will hem it." Molly went to the hearth and poured them tea while Grace changed back into her dress.

She called from the bedroom, "I just think 'tis time to put the black aside. Ye might wear the lilac muslin or the pale green. Both are so fetching on ye. And with Mr. Cummings around ..."

Grace came out from her room, handed her the gown and sat at the table.

Molly felt the heat rise to her face. "Mr. Cummings is my tenant."

Grace sighed. "We have been friends a long while, Molly MacGregor. Dinna tell me ye have not noticed the man is verra attractive ... and unattached. He seems to be a verra responsible and caring person."

"We have a business relationship, so stop listening to any gossip ye may have heard." Had Mrs. McGuire or Séamus been spreading lies?

Grace laughed. "I'm yer friend. Do ye really think I would listen to gossip? Ye cannot tell me that there is not an attraction between ye. I've seen the way ye look at each other at church. Lass, ye can do better than Séamus Macauley."

Molly shook her head. "Ye need not worry. I have no intention of wedding Seamus, and he knows it." She continued hemming the dress. "I know yer intentions are good, but the future is so uncertain."

"Please, just consider Mr. Cummings. Scott and his brother seem to get along verra well. I just want ye to have what I have found with John." Grace sat sipping her tea and giving her a knowing look.

"Is that all?"

"Nay. I think ye should wear yer lilac."

"Agh!" Molly put her finger to her mouth. "I stuck my finger, but I dinna think I got any blood on yer gown."

"'Tis magenta, so 'twouldna show anyway."

A loud knock on the door startled Molly.

She set aside the dress and opened the door. It was the landlord's agent. He handed her a document, nodded and left. She unfolded the paper and scanned the page. "'Tis the eviction notice I've been expecting."

Grace walked over to her and held her. "I'm so sorry, but I know ye and Scott will be fine."

The notice made it real, but they would be all right, especially if Katherine could be convinced to go with her to Coleraine—and if Grant and Keith also joined them.

After Grace left, Molly walked to the back of the cottage where Scott and Keith were cleaning the last of the fish they had caught that morning. Their pestering to go to the river had worn her down, so she and Scott both helped Keith to the river and back. Whatever fish they did not eat, she would smoke. How would Scott receive this news of the eviction and the changes that would follow? She needed to address it in a positive way, not as another loss.

Scott approached her, a serious expression had replaced his earlier joy. "I saw the man. Was that the 'viction paper?"

"What do ye know about that?" She had been so careful not to say anything around the lads, and Katherine would have done the same.

"Everyone has been talking about it. What will we do now?"

"We can chat about it later. I'm going in to cook the fish."

Clutching the paper, she sat at the table. The notice was like Katherine's. They were to be out by the end of June. Moving forward and changing their lives was no longer a choice. When Grant returned, she would go to Coleraine. Katherine and Grant could take care of the lads in her absence. Everything would fall into place. It had to.

She adjusted the peat bricks in the hearth and put the fish in the skillet. Grant should be back from Coleraine in the next day or so.

Sharing her thoughts with him on relocating had been a good idea, and he wasted no time to seek employment. But she needed to wait until he spoke to Katherine about it before she mentioned anything. Katherine was very fond of the Cummings brothers and was sure to reconsider her earlier wild idea of venturing across the Atlantic. God-willing, Grant and she would both be able to secure work soon, and there would be no need for goodbyes. She had been wrong to judge him because he was a Highlander. He'd been nothing less than kind, well-mannered, and generous with Scott and her. Truth was, she enjoyed his company—perhaps too much. The romantic notions he inspired were confusing. Even Grace had noticed. She'd let her guard down and must be more careful in the future.

Scott came through the door with the rest of the fish. "Smells good. I'll go get Keith."

"As I told ye the other day, 'twill take two of us to help him move around for now. We dinna want him falling or twisting his leg. When he is more surefooted, he will be able to use the stick to help him walk."

During dinner, she steered the conversation to fishing and hunting. Best to avoid the eviction for now.

"Thank ye for the meal, Miss Molly." Keith pointed to his empty place at the table. "Do ye think Grant will be back soon? He said he would only be gone a few days at most."

"Aye, he said to expect him in the next day or so. 'Tis good to see yer appetite has returned. Scott and I will help ye to Scott's pallet so ye can read the books Miss Katherine brought for ye. I need to get back to work."

She had not been sewing for much more than an hour when there was a knock at the door. Katherine came in wearing a grin but sobered quickly when she spotted Keith and Scott.

"Have ye a few minutes to take a walk? I wanted to chat with ye."

"Aye, a break would be nice." Molly got up and set her sewing aside. "We will be back in a few minutes." Katherine must have something to share, but not with the lads.

When they had walked about twenty feet down the lane, Katherine stopped. "Have ye gotten yer eviction notice?"

"Aye, just did and like ye, I have till the end of the month also to vacate."

"Well dinna fret, lass, yer sure to get another notice soon." Katherine pulled a document from her pocket. "'Tis from the landlord. He said there would be more information comin, and here 'tis." Katherine's face lit up as she read part of it. *"With little or no flax to harvest and the mechanization of spinning, I'm aware of the precarious position this puts on dispossessed tenants. In light of this, I will offer subsidized passage to North America this summer only."*

Katherine folded it again. "'Tis an answer to prayer and a sign from God Almighty. I wondered how I would come up with funds for the passage and now 'twill be taken care of."

Molly bit her lip. Grant would need to be mighty persuasive to convince Katherine to stay now. And how would he receive that news? Would he still want to work near Coleraine if Katherine went to America?

Grant rode home with the information about securing passage to America he had sought in Coleraine. The cost was not great, and he had some funds, but could they gather enough resources for their passage in time?

Katherine's cottage was on the way, and she would be pleased to learn of his news. He was eager to get home to Keith, but it could wait an additional half hour. Would she have any insight on how to encourage Molly? He had spent enough time anticipating how he would approach the lass. With God's help, he would find favor with her.

Katherine was outside gathering laundry when he arrived. Her smile and wave made him laugh. "I'm so glad to see ye."

"I was only gone three days." He dismounted and tied the horse to a post.

"Grant, I must show ye the notice from the landlord. The Lord must have moved his heart for 'tis a generous offer he is providin."

He followed her inside the cottage where she handed him a document. "Look. See what it says here."

He read through the notice twice and shook his head. "'Tis amazin—unexpected— 'n an answer. I stopped to tell ye what I learned in Coleraine about passages to America. I never dreamed the landlord would give ye the means."

"'Tis an answer to prayer for sure."

"Does Molly know about this?"

"Aye. I fear she is going to take some convincin. Ye needs to declare yerself."

He waved the parchment. "How is Keith?"

"Saw him yesterday and he is on the mend. She is takin good care of the lad."

"I wanted to tell ye what I found about the ships goin to America. Looks like we either depart from Belfast or Londonderry for a Philadelphia port of entry." He showed her the notes he took. "'Tis surprisin how many ships are transportin folks from Ireland to America in the next six weeks."

"So many ships? All leavin by mid-August?"

"There are more transports to New York, but Molly's brother lives in Philadelphia. Do ye think that might tempt her? The port at Philadelphia also makes travel to Gavin in Virginia easier.

"But now we shall have the funds." The sparkle in Katherine's eyes warmed his heart.

"I'm needin to get home."

"So, go … and do yer courtin."

"I'm askin for yer prayers again."

"Ye have them."

CHAPTER 15

GRANT APPROACHED THE MACGREGORS'. Was it excitement about approaching Molly with a proposal or fear of rejection that was making him sweat? Keith was not in the hut, and no one answered the cottage door. He walked around the cottage, but no one was in sight. The lad could not have gone far with a broken leg. He got back on the horse and rode toward town. Keith and Scott were sitting on the back of a wagon just beyond the church. "What are ye doin here?"

Keith laughed. "Glad yer home. Miss Molly had to make a delivery to the parsonage."

"We were tired of being stuck at home," Scott added. "So we came along for the ride." Scott looked at the parsonage door and frowned. "Molly said she wouldna be long, but 'tis been awhile."

"Be patient. I will get home 'n feed 'n pasture the horse. Ye will be back soon." He kicked the horse into a gallop. Taking a dunk in the river before supper was a must before courting the fair Molly.

The wagon was back by the time he finished bathing and reached the hut. He shivered as he set down the wildflowers he'd picked on the way back up the hill. Had there ever been a chillier summer? He smoothed back his hair, put on a clean shirt, and picked up the violets, cowslip, and bishop's weed. *"God, I'm needin the right words to tell her what she means to me. Please give me favor in her heart. Open her mind to comin to America with us."*

He came through the cottage door, and Molly stood, her eyes alight. "We are glad yer home."

She took his breath away standing near her work table, lovely in a lavender dress that set off her trim figure, blue eyes, and golden hair. Nice to see her in something other than her mourning clothes. He offered her the wildflowers he carried. "I thought ye might like these."

"Ta." She smiled and put them in a vase, then drew close to him. "Could we go for a walk?" she whispered.

That was encouraging—and he had not even said anything yet.

Lord, Yer good.

Scott and Keith were sitting on a low rock wall whittling when they left the cottage. Molly called to them. "Lads, we will be back soon. Then I will fix supper."

Her gait was brisk, suggesting she had something she wanted to say. Best hold back a bit and let her share what was on her mind.

She gave him a shy smile. "Was yer trip to Coleraine successful?"

"Aye, 'twas. 'Tis good to see Keith doin well 'n not in pain. Thank ye for takin care of him."

"The doctor came by yesterday. He said the break was healing, and the swelling is down. Scott has been helping him." She laughed. "Those lads are thick as thieves."

They were silent a minute, then she turned to him. "There were two things I needed to speak with ye about. Yer aunt received another notice from the landlord. 'Tis unbelievable, but he is offering his tenants payment for passage to America this summer." Molly shook her head, and the dreaded furrow returned to her brow. "Katherine was thrilled. I fear 'twill be harder to convince her to come with us to Coleraine."

What was she talking about? He reached for her hand and led her to a fallen oak on the slope overlooking the river. "Do ye care to sit?"

She nodded and sat on the trunk. "The other thing is … I dinna know when ye begin yer job, but I received my eviction notice and need to get to Coleraine to find employment. If ye must start work immediately, I'm sure Katherine would help with the lads. If we both had employment in Coleraine, it may encourage her to go with us."

He sat a few feet away on the trunk, his legs on the opposite side of hers. She thought he went to find work in Coleraine. Now what?

He swallowed hard. "The lads are close 'n we all love Katherine. 'Tis also my desire we all remain together …"

A look of relief replaced her worried expression. "I'm sure she will listen to ye. She thinks the world of the two of ye."

He held up his hand. "However, there is some confusion. I didna find work in Coleraine. I went there to find out about transport to America."

She leaned back, eyes wide. "But … I thought we talked about both of us finding employment in Coleraine so we could find places to live and …"

"That was yer plan, lass, not Katherine's or mine."

She put one hand to her lips. The anguish in her eyes tore at his gut.

He took her other hand in his. "I care for ye, Molly MacGregor, with all my heart."

Hurt and confusion crossed her face, yet she did not pull her hand away.

"I would be honored if ye would be my wife. We can be together, as a family, 'n settle in America. The transports sail from Belfast and Londonderry to Philadelphia." He reached for her other hand now which had moved from her chin to her chest. He held both hands in his, caressing the backs of them with his thumbs. "I favor the peaks 'n the glens, but if city life suits ye, we can settle in Philadelphia. If the peaks 'n the glens are more to yer likin, we could travel on to Virginia with Katherine. Say aye, sweet lass. Be my wife 'n let me love ye 'n care for ye 'n Scott."

Molly pulled her hands away and stood, pain etching her face. "I'm sorry. I cannot go with ye to America."

He stood, bit his lip, and nodded as she turned and dashed back toward the cottage. Rebuffed. He'd been foolish to think she cared for him. Katherine had also misjudged her feelings. He needed to get Keith and leave the hut, save them both further embarrassment.

Shaking, Molly headed to the cottage, tears running down her cheeks. What had just happened? How could she have misunderstood his intent on going to Coleraine after they had discussed the plan? Had he not gone to Coleraine at her suggestion? But he never had actually agreed with her. She shook her head. And the proposal. She had handled it wretchedly, impulsively—without honoring his feelings. As she neared the cottage, she stopped. Facing the lads like this would only prompt questions she couldn't answer. She strode toward the river to gather her thoughts.

She stopped when she was far enough to not be visable from the cottage. Leaving Aghadowey and going to Coleraine was enough of a change but going across the sea to America? Terrifying. Yet Katherine was willing, nay, excited by the prospect. Ewan and Gavin had gone there—and survived. She cried out. "Are Ye going to help me, Lord? I'm afraid. What should I do? I dinna want to lose Katherine." She put her hands on her hips. "I dinna want to lose him...and he and Scott will go with Katherine."

She paced back and forth several minutes before sitting on a log.

The memory of Grant holding her hands and declaring his affection warmed her. Why did she not tell him she cared for him also? All of this was so new to her. All because of fear—fear of change. What was it Ma had said about fear?

"There is no fear in love; but perfect love casteth out fear: because fear hath torment."

Lord, I asked Ye to make a way for us—and it appears Ye had—and I missed it.

"I do care for ye, Grant Cummings." She walked back to the cottage. She must apologize and try to make amends.

Grant lifted Keith down from the pony. "Lean on me lad, and I'll help ye inside."

Keith moved his arm allowing him to aid him to the door. "Ye have not said why we had to leave in such a hurry. We could hae waited till after supper."

How could he explain to the lad that it was best for all of them to leave now? Besides, in a day or so they would leave for one of the ports. "Everything will work out fine, lad. Ye'll see."

Katherine opened the door, her eyes shifting from Keith to him. A frown formed on her brow as she ushered them indoors. "Here, sit in this chair. Yer just in time for some cock-a-leekie." Once Keith was situated, she turned toward him. "Well?"

He shook his head. Not the best time to let her know of his disastrous proposal. "I'm needin to see to the horses, Aunt, then I will be in."

"I will go with ye."

Once outside he removed the packs and led them to the pasture. "Do ye mind puttin us up tonight?"

"Of course not. What happened?"

"I declared my love 'n the lass was not inclined to accept my offer." He put both hands up. "We misjudged her feelins."

"What did she say, if ye dinna mind sharin."

He glanced back toward the cottage before fixing his gaze on her. "She said, 'I'm sorry. I canna go with ye to America.'" He shook his head. "I said nothin to Keith about it. Figured it best we leave. There are ships sailin regularly. I have some funds, and with what we get for the horses, we should have enough to pay our passage. Ye will need to learn how the landlord will fund yers."

She stood silent holding on to the fence rail. "'Tis not right. I know she cares for ye. Somethin else is goin on here. Let me speak with her."

"Aunt, ye dinna need to do my biddin for me. She was not unkind, just plain spoken."

They went inside and sat down to supper. They had not finished eating when a knock at the door drew their attention. "'Tis late fer company, Aunt."

Katherine looked relieved. "Not at all. My guess 'tis just right."

Katherine opened the door. Molly stood there with a pensive expression and breathing heavily. "Been expectin ye." Katherine faced him. "Would ye kindly bring me a bucket of water from the well?" She handed Molly the pitcher off the table. "I need the pitcher filled also. Here, take a light." She handed him a lantern.

"'Tis only just dusk, Aunt."

"Take yer time." She closed the door behind him.

He gazed at Molly. "'Tis surprising to see ye." She was beautiful even with reddened eyes.

They walked toward the well. "I was not expecting ye and Keith to leave."

"How could we not leave given the circumstances?" Why had she come—just to have them return to the hut for a few days?

She shook. "I had to come … and tell ye … I was wrong. I do care for ye. If ye will forgive me … still have me, I want to be yer wife."

He put the lantern on the stoop by the well and drew her to him. Holding her close he leaned down and met her lips with his. How long had that desire floated through his mind? Since she shared her cottage rules. But here she was, returning his kisses. She was crying again. "'Tis somethin wrong, lass?"

"Nay, nothing. I'm trying not be afraid anymore. I feel at home … with ye."

"Can ye feel at home with a Highlander who loves ye … 'n go to America?"

"Aye … I will go wherever ye goes." She hugged him, and looked up at him, smiling now.

"Take my hand, lass. Come 'n we will tell Katherine we will all be off to America."

Author's Note

In 1816, millions of people throughout the British Isles as well as Europe experienced much colder and wetter weather that resulted in poor harvests and higher food prices and led to famine and increased disease. These unexplainable weather conditions caused many to migrate to America seeking better living and employment opportunities.

What wasn't known at the time was that the harsh weather was the result of a large volcanic eruption at Mount Tambora, Indonesia, in April of 1815 which spewed millions of tons of dust, ash, and sulfur dioxide into the atmosphere. 1816 became known as the year without summer.

Janet is a wife, mother of two sons, and grandmother of eight who lives in the historic triangle of Virginia (Williamsburg, Jamestown, Yorktown) with her husband. Her debut novel, *A Heart Set Free* was the 2016 Selah Award winner for Historical Romance. The second book in the series, *A Heart For Freedom* was released 2017. A lifelong student of history, her love of writing fiction grew out of a desire to share stories that communicate the truths of the Christian faith, as well as entertain, bring inspiration, and encouragement to the reader.

https://JanetGrunst.com
https://colonialquills.blogspot.com/
https://www.facebook.com/Janet-Grunst-Author-385405948228216/
https://twitter.com/janetgrunst

The Violinist

By

Jennifer Lamont Leo

This story is dedicated to my father,
Donald Lamont,
and our long line of Scottish forebears.

Chapter 1

Sandpoint, Idaho
May 1915

CALLAN MACTAVISH NEVER SAW it coming.

Last thing he recalled, he was chopping a tall white pine, lifting his ax high overhead and bringing it down hard. Far above, the tip of the towering pine swayed against the cobalt sky. He'd watched it, satisfied it would fall cleanly onto the pole-ribbed skid road, just as he'd intended. He yelled "Timber!" at the same moment that somebody else hollered something he didn't quite catch.

From there his memory grew fuzzy. A tremendous roar. Lars Bergstrom shouting at him, waving his arms.

Then nothing, until he awoke in the Page Hospital in Sandpoint, trussed up like a hog and aching from head to toe. But alive.

"The villain wasn't the tree you was cuttin on," Lars explained later as he sat next to Callan's hospital bed, rearranging a handful of playing cards. "The villain was that ponderosa pine behind you, the one bein felled by Bob's team. Durn thing changed direction as it fell, went completely cattywampus. Nothin nobody could do to stop it. Thankfully, you was the only one hit." He glanced up. "Well, maybe *thankfully* ain't the right word, but you get my meanin. We thought you was a goner for sure. But you're lookin better today. Rummy." He splayed the cards onto the bedside table.

"Nay, thankfully's right. I'm still in one piece." Callan's jaw clenched as he laid down his cards. Every part of his body hurt. Nonetheless, he thanked God for the pain. Pain meant he wasn't paralyzed, hadn't lost a limb or worse. For the second time, his life had been spared, despite his ability to attract trouble like iron filings to a magnet. *Why Lord?* he'd prayed more than once since waking in the hospital. *Not that I'm ungrateful, but why do Ye keep sparin me?*

"At least you lost no fingers this time," Lars said. "I seen your hand, how you got bit by the crosscut witch sometime in the past. So've I." He held up his hand to show where the tip of the thumb was missing. "And so have half the fellers up at the camp. Hazard of the trade."

Callan glanced at his own right hand. Where the middle and ring fingers were supposed to be, now were only stumps, the result not of this latest accident but an earlier one. An incident he tried very hard not to think about. At least he hadn't lost his card-shuffling ability. He picked up the deck. "Another round?"

Before Lars could answer, a young red-haired nurse entered the room. She set on the table a pair of denim pants, a plaid flannel shirt, and a pair of socks, all laundered and neatly folded, that Callan recognized as his own.

"Hey, you're upsettin our game," Lars teased, gracing her with his most endearing smile. Callan rolled his eyes.

"I'm afraid your card-playing days are over, Mr. Bergstrom." Her pretty face wore a stern expression, but her twitching lips gave her away. "Mr. MacTavish here is being released."

"Nurse Crandall, say it ain't so. You mean to tell me this is goodbye?" Lars clutched his chest with great drama. "I feel a pain comin on. Could it be my heart breakin clean in two?"

"Don't quit your day job. You'll never make it on the stage." She turned her attention to Callan. "The doctor has approved your release, but you're not to go—"

"I know, I know. He told me himself." Callan held up a hand. "I'm not to be goin back up to the camp just yet."

"Not until Monday. The doctor wants you to stay close by for a couple of days, just to make sure you're out of the woods. So to speak." The nurse grinned. "Meanwhile, the bill has been sent to the company. Eat a good meal, get plenty of rest."

"That's why I'm here." Lars stood and bowed deeply. "I've been assigned to stay with him, then help him find his way back to camp come Monday. A nice little holiday for me, but in the meantime, I'll have a bit of time to kill. What time do you get off work?" He winked at

Nurse Crandall. A faint blush rose in her cheeks.

"Why, Mr. Bergstrom, that's none of your concern." But by the way she said it, Callan wagered she'd be strolling through town on Lars' arm before the day was through. He grinned and shook his head. His flirtatious friend had a way with the ladies—unlike himself. A bonny face tied his tongue in knots. Not that there were many bonny faces to be found in the logging camps where he'd spent the last three years.

When the nurse left the room, Callan got out of bed and slowly dressed himself, wincing. Lars took hold of his arm as if to help him walk out of the hospital until Callan shrugged him off. "I'm not an old codger. Just a bit banged up, is all."

"Sure. And that's why the doc wants you to stick around." Lars' tone was cynical, but he released his friend's arm. "You look a fright. Let's settle in at Mrs. Donovan's, then get you cleaned up."

They ambled through the dusty streets to a large house shaded by pines. A sign beside the doorbell read *Rooms to Let, Bridget Donovan, prop.* The gray-haired Irish landlady greeted them affably, but her eyes narrowed when she got a good look at Callan's bruised face.

"Been in a fight, have ye?" She crossed her arms. "I don't allow brawlin in me house."

"No brawlin," Callan promised. "Just an accident."

"Hmmph." She hesitated as if weighing whether or not to believe him. "Well. Come along then." She turned and led the way toward a flight of stairs.

"Ain't you got a room on the ground floor?" Lars said. "My friend here's in no condition to be climbin up and down stairs."

"Nothin but me own quarters," the landlady said with an aggrieved air.

"Upstairs is fine," Callan muttered. His bruises had him on thin ice and he didn't want to test her patience.

In a sparsely furnished room, Lars dropped a sack onto one cot, then collapsed on the other. "Brought some things from the camp you might be needin. A comb. Your Sunday suit. Your book."

"My book?" Panic gripped Callan's chest. Had Lars discovered his private journal? The one stuffed in his locker, in which he sketched pictures and scribbled lines of verse? He'd almost gotten punched in the face for it once back in Minnesota, by a barely literate lout who claimed poetry was for sissies.

"Yeah. That one you been readin before lights out."

"Robert Burns." Relief washed over Callan. Lars might give him guff for reading poetry but wouldn't find it half as strange as writing it.

Lars shrugged. "Took a peek at it on the way down. The man's no Zane Grey. But there's no accountin for taste. You ready for a shave? You need it."

Lars led the way to a barbershop where they both got haircuts and shaves. Thus dandified, they went next to a general store, where Callan picked up a few personal items he needed, like ink and soap and licorice.

As he stood in line to pay for his purchases, over the pungent odors of tobacco, pickling vinegar, spices, and coffee, the scent of violets swirled around him. He turned. A bonny blond-haired lass of about twenty stood behind him, wearing a dress the soft pinky-purple color of Highland heather. She glanced up, and for a split second their gazes met and held.

"Are you deaf?" The rough voice of the cashier broke the spell. Callan quickly handed over some cash, heat rushing to his face, while the proprietor clattered the coins into an enormous bronze cash register. Never had he expected to see such a fetching lass standing right behind him in a rough-and-tumble town like Sandpoint. A fancy painted lady, maybe, but not a little slip of a thing looking for all the world like a breath of springtime. He longed to steal another glance but didn't dare in case he was observed.

Too late. When they were back out on the wooden sidewalk, Lars nudged him. "I saw you givin that young miss the eye."

"I wasna givin anybody any eye," Callan said crossly.

"Here she comes. Why don't you say hello to her?"

"Nay, I—"

But before Callan could stop him, Lars was lifting his hat, addressing the two women—the young one in pink and her brown-haired companion, who looked slightly older and a whole lot haughtier.

"Good day, ladies." Lars made a great sweeping bow. "How are you enjoyin this lovely May weather?"

"Nay, Lars." Callan hissed from the sidelines, mortified.

"Move along," the older woman said briskly to the younger. "Pay them no heed."

"Can we interest you ladies into takin a walk by the shore?" Lars called after them. While the women appeared not to have heard him, the younger one glanced back over her shoulder, pinning Callan in her long-lashed gaze until the older one tugged her arm and hastened her down the sidewalk.

"Lars, whatta ye think yer doin?" he chided, his heart pounding like the cannons in the "1812 Overture." "Those are *ladies* yer addressin." To the women's stiffened backs he called out, "Beggin yer pardon, ladies. Apologies on behalf of my friend here." The women quickened their pace.

Lars waved one hand as if brushing away flies. "Aw, forget 'em. Come on, let's go play some cards."

Callan stepped back. "Nay, thank ye. A man could squander his bankroll at the gaming tables."

"Or double it," Lars countered. "Suit yourself then. See you later."

Lars turned and headed back toward the tavern they'd visited earlier. Eager to stretch his muscles after days spent lying in a hospital bed, Callan ambled up and down the streets of the small town, looking into shop windows and getting his bearings, until he grew weary and turned back in the direction of the rooming house. Even the silent feature playing at the Gem Theater held less appeal for passing the time than his trusty volume of Burns. The only sight worth seeing would be a certain blond lass, and no lady of her quality would be spending Saturday night away from her own parlor, wherever that was. The question of where that parlor might be occupied his mind all the way home.

Chapter 2

ROSE MARCHMONT NEARLY LOST her footing as her sister, Daisy Tanner, grabbed her elbow and propelled her across the street. Though Rose's senior by only a few years, Daisy assumed the full authority and protectiveness of a mother hen.

"The first rule of living in Sandpoint is 'don't pay any heed to the lumberjacks.' They're uncouth, unsavory, and generally unwashed. And they swarm the town like cockroaches on Saturdays, particularly during the warmer months. We ought to have chosen a different day to do our shopping."

"All of them are like that?" Rose asked, thinking that the sandy-haired logger they'd just whirled away from didn't look unsavory at all. Neither did his blond friend, to be honest, although she didn't appreciate his cheeky attitude. Fresh! But she'd encountered coarser treatment on the streets of Chicago.

"All of them," Daisy said brusquely. "You'd best steer clear. Believe me, in the two years I've lived in this town, I've endured more catcalls and improper suggestions than in my entire life prior. And that's no compliment to my charms ... more to the loggers' lack of them." She relaxed her grip on Rose's arm. "You'll find Sandpoint to be a rough town, I'm afraid, but every day the trains bring new residents from all walks of life. Robert and I know some much more suitable young men to introduce you to if you're so inclined."

"I'm not at all inclined," Rose replied. "Mother and Father shipped me out to this godforsaken wilderness to help me recover from a romance, not to start another one."

"Well, they were right to do so," Daisy said firmly. "Jeremy Pyle isn't worthy of a single one of your tears, and the change of scenery will do you a world of good. It wouldn't do any harm to consider looking for a suitable husband while you're here. Robert and I are thrilled to have you stay with us. But I won't let you remain cooped up in the house day and night with no social life. It isn't wholesome for a young, pretty girl to stay cooped up with only her violin for company."

"I won't be cooped up. With any luck, I'll have some students soon to occupy my time."

"Besides," Daisy continued, "Sandpoint is not a godforsaken wilderness. It's a burgeoning town with a couple churches and a Sunday school and everything."

"Spoken like the wife of a prominent First Avenue haberdasher."

"I mean it. It may not ever become a great city like Chicago, but it'll be a fine place in its own right. Just give it a few years. But in the meantime, watch out for those lumberjacks—they're a sorry lot."

When Callan returned to the rooming house, the place was empty except for the landlady, who frowned at him and told him to wipe his feet. He was the only logger in town, it seemed, who didn't indulge in whiskey and women. As an outsider, loneliness wasn't an unfamiliar feeling. Moving from logging camp to logging camp, always the odd man out, he kept to himself. Most of the time he didn't mind; he enjoyed his own company. But every so often, on soft spring evenings like this one, the longing to be back in his own country, maybe strolling with a pretty lass on the banks of a *loch*, hit so hard, he could taste it.

Back in his room, with Lars still out carousing who-knows-where, he stretched onto his cot before the open window and tried to read Burns. But the words failed to hold his attention. He laid the book aside, undressed, stretched out again, and closed his eyes, letting the warm spring breeze flow over him, ruffling his hair and carrying his thoughts back to the heather-dotted fields of his homeland. As he drifted off, the wind through the larch and alder trees outside the window whispered a dreamy, romantic song. It was almost as if the breeze carried the sweet strains of a Mendelssohn violin concerto along with the scent of lilacs.

His breath hitched. His eyes flew open.

It wasn't his imagination. There truly was a Mendelssohn violin concerto floating in on the breeze.

Bolting upright, he peered out the window into the inky blue dusk but saw nothing. No fiddling troubadour wandered the wooden sidewalks. No magical violin-playing pixie perched in the trees. But most definitely the notes of a Mendelssohn concerto swirled around, sweetening the very air of a town more accustomed to the nerve-jangling rhythms of ragtime.

But where was the music coming from? This was no crude country fiddling, but a polished and practiced performance. Perhaps the neighbors next door owned a Victrola—one remarkably free of scratches and pops.

No matter. He lay back in the narrow bed and pulled the blanket over himself. To hear such a beautiful sound was a blessing, pure and simple, whatever its origin. He closed his eyes and let the music lift his spirit and soothe his soul. In his mind's eye, he could picture the notes dancing and changing color, now blue, now purple, the colors of twilight, of homesickness. He could practically taste them, now sweet, now spicy, now mellow. Swallowing the ache in his throat, he savored each passage of the familiar piece, lost in memories, until he slipped into sleep.

In the cozy back parlor of her sister's house, Rose let the bow linger on the final note of the concerto, then lowered the violin to her lap. Mendelssohn was one of her favorites, but playing it again felt a little painful, like stretching a dormant muscle. When she'd performed the piece for Jeremy, he'd yawned, glanced at his pocket watch, as if he found the listening tedious. Or perhaps it was just *her* he'd found tedious. In any event, she should have known their courtship was doomed from the start. They had so little in common. But his charm and good looks, and her amazement at gaining the notice of such a man, dulled her better instincts. She wouldn't make that mistake again. She stood and stretched, then walked over to the piano, lifted the bench lid, put away Mendelssohn and pulled out Mozart.

Daisy opened the door and poked her head into the room. "Care to join Robert and me in a game of whist? You've earned a break, don't you think?"

Rose shook her head. "I need to practice, so I'm ready to take on students. I'm afraid my musical skills grew rusty while I was …" *While I was spending all my time with Jeremy.* "While I was busy with other things. I don't want to disappoint anyone who might hire me for lessons."

"I doubt anyone could be disappointed in you, Rose. This isn't Chicago, with a music school on every corner. A small town like Sandpoint is desperate for a teacher."

"Apparently no one's told them how desperate they are. I haven't had a single inquiry yet."

Daisy rested against the doorframe. "It takes time. Robert has posted your notice in his store and several other places around town. I'm sure you'll get students as soon as word gets around. Plenty of people think Sandpoint could use some higher culture and will want their children to learn music. And from a teacher trained at the prestigious American Conservatory of Music. What could be better?"

"I hope you're right." Rose toyed with the handle of her bow. What would those fine citizens think if they knew she'd thrown over her conservatory training for Jeremy Pyle, who'd promptly thrown *her* over for a simpering brewery heiress?

"Don't stay up too late." Daisy gently closed the door.

Rose unfolded the Mozart score, praying her sister's reassurances of eventual success were true. While Daisy and Robert regularly assured her their home was hers for as long as she wished, she wanted to earn her keep and not wear out her welcome. The longer she could stay in Sandpoint, far away from Chicago and Jeremy, the better. Earning money by giving music lessons would make that possible. But not if nobody wanted them.

As her fingers flew over the neck of the instrument and her right arm pulled the bow, her mind flew unbidden to the sandy-haired logger she'd seen in town. No doubt a lumberjack would find her love of classical music as ridiculous as tone-deaf Jeremy had. A logger's musical repertoire, if he had one, was likely limited to a few bawdy drinking songs and odes to Paul Bunyan.

Still, she thought she'd seen a flicker of something fine in his gray-green eyes. *Noble* was perhaps too strong a word, but that was the word that stuck in her head. In spite of Daisy's dire warnings about woodsmen, Rose hoped she'd cross paths with him again.

Chapter 3

THE NEXT MORNING THE shriek of a train whistle startled Callan awake. Sometime during the night, Lars had returned from his carousing. Callan had a vague memory of bumping, scraping, and muttered oaths. Now his friend lay snoring on his cot, no doubt the worse for liquor and cigars.

In the distance, a church bell pealed. Callan rose carefully, wincing at his wounds. He washed in the communal washroom down the hall, combed his hair, and dressed in his one-and-only good suit, a somber blue serge he'd purchased in a Halifax haberdashery, specifically for churchgoing. The jacket fit snugly—too snugly. Three years of working in the woods had built his physique, made his arms and shoulders brawny and hard. Perhaps he'd need to find a tailor skilled enough to let out the seams.

Leaving his companion dead to the world, he walked down the street to the church he'd spotted on his walk the previous day. The service was just starting as he entered and slipped into a back pew. He pulled a hymnal from the rack, but soon found he didn't need it—the opening hymn was a familiar one.

> How firm a foundation,
> ye saints of the Lord,
> is laid for your faith
> in His excellent Word.

Sometimes when he got to singing hymns, Callan forgot himself and his own cares and just sang out loud to his Lord. So, he felt abashed when, after the *amen*, several people glanced at him with discreet curiosity. He had a strong baritone voice, and a good one, that made people sit up and take notice. He forgot that sometimes, working out in the middle of nowhere, belting out an old Scottish ballad with no one around to hear but the birds and squirrels. As the congregation took their seats, one particular face held its gaze on him a little longer. Glancing up, he was startled to see the winsome face of the bonny lass he'd noticed in town the previous day. The one in the dress the color of Highland heather, who'd been dragged off by her companion before Callan had found the presence of mind to say hello. Maybe he'd have a chance to do so after the service, even though the stern-faced companion was still permanently attached to her elbow.

When he worked up the nerve to glance at her again, she'd turned her attention to the pulpit. He admired her profile, at least what he could see of it beneath her bonnet: a small, straight nose, pale pink cheeks, determined chin, and curls the color of sunshine. Today she wore blue. He couldn't see her eyes, but from what he'd seen yesterday, he'd wager they, too, were blue—as blue as the lake on a clear day, most likely. Thoughts of what he'd say to her and how he'd say it filled his mind, making it difficult to concentrate on the words of the preacher up front.

After the last note of the closing hymn faded, he remained in his pew as others filed out, pretending to look up something in the red hymnbook until out of the corner of his eye he saw the bright blue of her skirt approaching down the center aisle. Then he picked up his hat and prepared to step out of the pew directly into her path, as if entirely by chance. He meant to slip out smoothly, but at the last second his boot caught on the edge of a kneeler, and he stumbled full force into the lass, nearly knocking her over.

"Goodness," she exclaimed as she righted herself.

"I beg yer pardon," he blurted, sure that his face was as red as the hymnal cover. "My apologies."

As she lifted her startled eyes to his, he was rendered mute. Not a mere blue, as he'd thought, but a startling sapphire color, framed by thick lashes.

"N-nice service, wasn't it?" he said as soon as he managed to untie his tongue.

"Yes. Yes, it was," the girl responded in a low, musical voice, like cool water over river rocks.

After that sparkling exchange of wit, her brown-haired companion said, "Please excuse us," but in a friendlier tone than previously. Perhaps she didn't recognize him in his serge Sunday suit instead of the flannel shirt and work pants that had marked him as a woodsman the day before. His bruised face still would give him away, however, so maybe she was simply in a kinder frame of mind, being in church and all.

In any case, she didn't yell or whack him with her reticule, which he counted as progress.

The sweet-faced blond woman, her sourpuss friend, and the smartly dressed man who accompanied them—apparently the friend's husband or beau—swept down the aisle and out the door with the rest of the congregation. Callan followed. At the double doors at the back of the church, he paused to shake hands with the minister.

"Looks like you were in quite a scuffle," the man said, squinting at Callan's face.

"What? Oh, nay, 'twasna a scuffle. 'Twas an accident up in the woods."

The minister nodded. "I see. Which lumber outfit are you with?" He must have thought Callan an idiot when he was unable to form a coherent answer. Because just at that moment, the blond lass glanced back over her shoulder and favored the bashful Scotsman with a shy smile.

He lived on the memory of that smile all through the noon meal with Lars, and through the long days of chopping, felling, and hauling timber in the woods once the boss deemed him fully recovered. Because at the end of that week, dangling before him like a carrot before a pack mule there'd be another trip to town, another church service, and another chance of being favored with that smile.

Funny. I didn't think loggers went to church.

That thought popped into Rose's mind as she helped her sister peel potatoes for Sunday dinner, but she opted not to voice it and thus open the door to another of Daisy's screeds. But she didn't have to, because Daisy introduced the topic herself, in a roundabout way.

"I noticed there was a stranger in church today," Daisy said. "That man who practically toppled you over after the service. I wonder who he was."

Rose blinked. How could her sister not know? Maybe she hadn't gotten a good look at his banged-up face. Or maybe he appeared different in his church clothes. Either way, Rose wasn't about to clue her in. Instead she said, "We ought to have introduced ourselves. I was so startled, I wasn't thinking clearly."

After a brief pause, Daisy said, "You're right. We should always make an effort to greet visitors to our church. I suppose we were caught off guard." She shrugged. "Well, I'm sure Pastor Nolan took care of it." As though welcoming strangers was a chore to be sloughed off to others.

"He was rather nice-looking, though, wasn't he?"

"I suppose so, but he had no wife with him," Daisy sniffed. "He was probably a traveling salesman or such, passing through on the railroad. I give the fellow credit for going to church, but I doubt we'll be seeing much of him."

Rose wiped the paring knife with a cloth and studied her sister. "Have you heard that the Pinkerton Agency is hiring lady detectives? Perhaps you should apply."

Daisy's forehead creased. "Me? Why?"

Rose sweetened her tone. "Because, apparently, you're able to tell everything about a person before you've so much as been introduced. The Pinkertons could use a person with that level of skill."

Daisy's face colored. "I'm only trying to make sure you meet the right sort of people while you're here. The sort of men who shop in Robert's store, for instance," she said as her husband walked into the room. "Right, Robert?"

"Right." Robert offered his usual affirmative response to any suggestion his wife made. "What are we talking about?"

"Introducing Rose to suitable young men. Surely you must have some nice young, single customers at your haberdashery."

"All my best customers are suitable," he said. "Suit-able. Get it?"

Rose giggled, but Daisy cast a withering look.

"Will dinner be ready soon? I'm famished." He snatched a carrot stick from the relish tray.

"Five minutes," Daisy said, administering a gentle slap to his thieving hand.

Rose set a basket of rolls on the table. "As I've told you, Daisy, I'm not in the market for a beau. At any rate, if no students sign up for music lessons, I won't be staying in Sandpoint long enough for it to matter. I'll have to move to a bigger town where I can earn a living."

"Not on your own, you won't," Daisy said. "You can either live here with Robert and me or go back to Chicago and live with Mother and Father. Those are your options."

"I won't go back to Chicago. Not as long as Jeremy still lives there, which likely will be forever." She filled the water glasses from a white hobnail pitcher. "But if I can't teach music, I'll be wasting my education. All those years at the conservatory, and for what? So I can fade away in some backwater town?"

"So you can marry a good man and rear lovely children and teach music to *them*," Daisy declared. "Now come sit down, you two, before dinner gets cold."

The following Saturday, when several of his crew descended into town for a rowdy night out, Callan joined them for the ride down. He claimed the same cot near the window in the room he shared with Lars. If the neighbor chanced to play the Victrola again, he'd be in a good spot to hear it.

After supper, as dusk settled over the lively town and his mates headed for the tavern, he took a long solitary walk, hoping to catch a glimpse of the blond girl. No such luck. Maybe he'd see her at church the next day. At the general store, he bought a bag of licorice, then returned to Mrs. Donovan's, stretched out on his cot, picked up a copy of *Moby Dick* that he'd borrowed from the camp library and began to read.

Sure enough, along about eight thirty, the sweet notes of a violin wafted through the azure twilight. He closed *Moby Dick* and set it aside. This evening's selection was a Brahms sonata. It wasn't generated by a Victrola, after all, but by an actual violinist, for the musician stopped, repeated a short passage several times, then started over again from the beginning. The mysterious violinist was skilled and exacting, rehearsing difficult passages until they were flawless. Callan crossed his arms behind his head, closed his eyes, and let the gorgeous notes soak into his soul like a refreshing rain after a parched season of crude loggers' ditties.

After a short while, he sat up. This was stupid. He should just go over there and find out who was playing. Maybe he and the violinist could strike up an acquaintance. At the very least, they'd have in common their taste in music, which was not shared by anyone else in the logging camp or even in the town, as far as he could tell.

But before he boldly knocked on some stranger's door, he wanted to get an idea of what sort of person he'd be dealing with. He left the rooming house by the front porch and walked around to the side lawn. Scanning the building next door, he approached a single open, lighted window toward the back of the house where the music sounded the clearest.

He pressed himself against the clapboard siding and leaned over to peer in the window. He had intended to just grab a quick glimpse of the player to determine whether man or woman, old or young, friendly- or intimidating-looking, before approaching the front door like a proper visitor. But in the same moment that the violinist's identity registered in his startled brain, he stepped on the tail of a stray cat, which let out a bloodcurdling yowl, ricocheted off his shin, and sped into the night.

The sonata screeched to a halt. A sharp female voice called, "Is someone out there?" Quick footsteps tapped across the wooden floor. A calico-clad arm pushed aside the lace curtain, and a lovely face framed by blond hair—the face he'd been watching for all day—appeared in the window.

There was no use trying to run. Callan stood exposed in the gloom, a sheepish grin on his face.

"Hello."

"You!" The girl's voice rushed out in a mix of surprise and horror. "What are you doing, creeping around outside my window? Are you trying to see in? Are you some kind of peeping Tom?" Her pitch rose along with her indignation. She raised her violin as if ready to clobber him with it.

"Nay!" Callan held up his hands. "Nay, lass, I wasna tryin to look in. Well, I was, but 'tis not what ye be thinkin." His brogue thickened in his agitation.

"What, then?" In the light of a nearby table lamp, a rosy color stained her cheeks. She liked to take his breath away, even more than she had in the church.

"I—I was just—" A score of excuses scrolled through his mind, from collecting wildflowers to getting lost on the way home, each one lamer than the last.

"Well?" She placed one hand on her hip. The other still gripped the neck of her violin, as if ready to use it as a weapon, if needed.

"Rose?" called a woman from the front of the house. "Who are you talking to in there?"

The girl wheeled around. "No one, Daisy. Just—just scolding myself for messing up a passage. Mister Brahms is giving me trouble tonight."

Rose, thought Callan. Her name was Rose. And apparently, she was more clever about making up excuses on the spot than he was.

"Yer name suits ye," he said when she turned back to the window.

"Does it now?" She didn't sound impressed. "Are you drunk?"

He chuckled in spite of himself. "Nay, lass. Sober as a lawman. And

I'm sorry for givin ye a fright."

She regarded him coolly. "You're Scottish."

"Am I now? Thank ye for tellin me." He gave a little bow. "Aye, I come from a small town not far from Loch Lomond. Ye know the song?"

She nodded.

He gave a little bow. "Callan MacTavish, at yer service."

She lifted an eyebrow. "So, Mr. MacTavish of Loch Lomond. How did you come to be lurking outside my window?"

"I dinna mean to lurk. 'Tis just that I was sittin upstairs there"— he gestured toward the top story of the rooming house—"hearin the beautiful tunes ye were playin, and I couldna help myself. I had to see for myself who it was makin an instrument sing like that."

"*Shh*. My sister will hear you." Her expression softened. In a slightly mollified tone, she continued. "Well, you can't very well creep about in the lilacs like a common burglar."

His spirit lifted. "Are ye welcomin me inside, then?"

"No. I can't. Besides, it's much too late for you to be calling."

"Perhaps I could call on ye tomorrow, then. I just want to hear ye play." While not the entire truth, it wasn't a complete lie either. He did want to hear her play. And he didn't want to scare her off completely by suggesting anything more.

A small crease appeared between her eyes. "I don't think that will work, either. My sister, she … she doesn't trust loggers."

"I'm not comin here as a logger," he reasoned. "I'm here as a fellow music-lover."

"I don't think that will make any difference." Rose hesitated. Suddenly her expression cleared. "Unless …"

"Unless what?" He was ready to climb the castle walls, to slay a fire-breathing dragon if he had to, if it meant getting to spend time in the company of this fetching lass.

"Unless you sign up for music lessons."

"What?"

"*Shh!*" She leaned forward over the sill. "If you sign up for music lessons, Daisy won't think twice about letting you call on me. She'll view it as a business arrangement."

"But I dinna need lessons. I just want to listen."

She straightened. "Lessons are the only way. Daisy will never agree otherwise to your calling on me."

While music lessons weren't remotely what he had in mind, he heard himself agreeing. Anything to see her again.

"Next Saturday, then," she said. "After supper. Let's say seven o'clock." She turned her head as if listening for a sound. "My sister's coming. Now shoo."

She withdrew from the window as suddenly as she'd appeared. He walked back to the boarding house on air, whistling Brahms.

But later, as he climbed into bed, it was no longer Brahms he heard floating through the window, but the sweet, melancholy strains of "Loch Lomond."

Chapter 4

THE NEXT DAY, CALLAN rose early and dressed in his Sunday suit with an eagerness inspired by much more than the prospect of a rousing hymn or bracing sermon. As he stood in front of the mirror, wielding a comb to tame an unruly cowlick, Lars stirred in bed.

"Off to church again?" he rasped in a voice thick with sleep. "Man, we're up before the sun six days a week. Why don't you take the seventh off? Day of rest and all that."

"'Twould do ye a world of good to come with me," Callan admonished. Lars grunted and rolled over, wrapping the blanket more tightly around himself.

Callan hastened to the church where Rose was again seated with her sister and brother-in-law. He took a seat in the rear of the church so he could watch her. Once or twice he caught her glance, and she smiled. He planned to speak to her after the service. But the three of them hurried out before he could do more than tip his hat to her. Disappointed, he met up with his mates for a meal in a café. Over beef stew and biscuits, they encouraged him to join them on a fishing expedition out on Lake Pend Oreille before heading back up the mountain.

"We've rented a boat for the afternoon. We aim to bring back plenty of salmon for Cook to fry for supper."

"Nay, thank ye," Callan said. "Just leave me a pole and line. I'll stick to fishin from here on the shore."

Lars looked at him as though he were daft. "Suit yourself, but you won't catch much standin on the pier. The bitin's better out in the middle of the lake."

"I prefer to stay here," Callan said firmly. "That way if fishin fails to hold my interest, I can find some other way to pass the time." He half-hoped that loitering around outside Rose's house would somehow cause her to appear on the sidewalk and take a walk with him. On the other hand, such behavior might get him arrested as a masher and banished forever from her presence. It was probably safer to stick to fishing.

"You're a funny duck," Lars said, but he didn't argue. As Callan watched the small steamer pull away from the dock with his friends aboard, he felt a tug of regret. In fact, he used to love fishing. He'd passed many a sweet afternoon catching lake trout as a lad in Scotland. But that had been a long time ago. These days no promise of fish—not even a bounty of fresh salmon to give them all a break from the endless pork and beans—could entice him to climb in that boat and venture out onto the deep, dark water.

"What's the hurry?" Rose asked as Daisy and Robert hustled her out of the church. She'd hoped to talk to the tall man with the sandy hair, but her sister refused to linger. "Can't we stay a few minutes and visit with people?"

"We must get home." Daisy sounded harried. "We have a guest coming for Sunday dinner."

"Who?"

"An acquaintance of Robert's named Miles Godfrey. He's an attorney for the railroad."

By the description, Rose expected to meet a portly, gray-haired man of distinction, but he turned out to be no older than Robert, although his gaunt frame, spectacles perched on a long thin nose, and formal demeanor gave the air of a much older man. He brought to Rose's mind an illustration of Ichabod Crane from her childhood copy of *The Legend of Sleepy Hollow*, an awkwardly built gentleman, receding of both hairline and chin.

"Mr. Godfrey enjoys music like you do, Rose," Daisy said when she introduced them, her voice weighting the fact with significance. "I thought after dinner you might play something for us."

The man's eyes lit up behind his spectacles. "I'd be delighted to hear you play."

Rose nodded politely. She didn't particularly enjoy performing on command, but entertaining a guest was the least she could do to repay her sister's hospitality.

During dinner she found that Mr. Godfrey did indeed know a lot about music—so much so that he totally dominated the conversation with his strong opinions, declaring ragtime "odious," Debussy "of questionable taste" and Bartok "a talentless hack." He also had much to say, none of it positive, about the new strain of music bubbling northward up the Mississippi from New Orleans.

"It's called 'jass,'" he explained, "or, as some say, 'jazz.'" He curled his lip as if detecting a foul odor.

"I've not heard it yet," Rose admitted, "but I'm curious about it. A professor at the conservatory was going to share with the class a recording made by a man named Jelly Roll Morton, but I—I left school before getting to hear it." What else had she missed out on by leaving the conservatory?

Mr. Godfrey scrutinized her through his spectacles. "Think of a brass band gone berserk, all trying to play at once, and not even the same song," was his lofty pronouncement. "Just a lot of noise."

If Daisy had hoped that a shared interest in music would spark an "understanding" between Rose and Mr. Godfrey, she was mistaken. Not to mention he possessed none of the rugged appeal of a certain sandy-haired, square-jawed lumberjack. Even so, after dinner, she kept her promise to play for their guest. She set up her music stand in the front parlor and took a seat, then played a series of short melodies. When she'd finished, the assembled group sat dumbfounded.

"Goodness, Rose," Daisy said. "I've not heard you play those pieces before. Why, they sounded positively … gypsy-like." Her face contorted as though she were having trouble deciding whether she approved or not.

"That was splendid, Rose," Robert said, and Rose cast a grateful smile at the effort, her brother-in-law being a man of few words.

"Magnificent, Miss Marchmont," Mr. Godfrey exulted, his eyes aglow behind his spectacles. "Such technique! Such exquisite tone! You must tell me who wrote that mysterious, haunting composition."

Rose attempted, but not very hard, to keep the smugness out of her voice. "Bartok."

At the end of the evening, Mr. Godfrey prepared to take his leave. "Thank you for a delightful afternoon." He turned to Daisy. "Dinner was delicious. You are most kind."

"Not at all. You must come again." She retrieved his hat from the rack.

"Glad you could join us, Godfrey," Robert said heartily, pumping the guest's hand.

Mr. Godfrey turned to Rose and took her reluctant hand in his damp one. "Miss Marchmont, there will be a concert of the visiting Seattle Symphony on Saturday next in Coeur d'Alene. I would be most honored if you would accompany me."

"Oh, thank you, Mr. Godfrey," Rose said, "but I regret I have another engagement on Saturday."

"I see." His mouth drooped under his waxy mustache. "Perhaps another time, then." He released her hand and clapped his hat on his head.

"Goodnight, Mr. Godfrey."

He started down the porch steps, then suddenly turned back, smiling. "Miss Marchmont, I just remembered. I believe there will be a repeat performance of the symphony concert at three o'clock Sunday afternoon. Perhaps you'd like to attend that one instead."

Rose scrambled for a plausible excuse. "Oh, I don't think—"

"She'd love to," Daisy interjected. "Wouldn't you, Rose?"

At that moment, Rose could have cheerfully wrung her sister's neck. "But don't we have something *else* planned for next Sunday?" she said meaningfully, hoping Daisy would take the hint.

"Not a thing, other than church," Daisy chirped. "How thoughtful of Mr. Godfrey to invite you."

"It's all settled, then," the man said with an air of satisfaction. "I'll join you at church. We'll have to leave directly after the service to make it to Coeur d'Alene in time to enjoy a bite to eat before the concert." He gave Rose a smug smile and tugged the end of his mustache. "You'll get to ride in my new automobile."

Rose worked up a weak smile. *Goody, goody.*

"Oh, won't that be delightful, Rose," Daisy said, her eyes alight. "You haven't heard a good concert since leaving Chicago."

"Delightful," Rose repeated, devoid of enthusiasm.

"I'll see you Sunday, then." Miles trotted down the steps, whistling.

When Robert had closed the door behind their guest and retreated to the safety of the parlor and his pipe, Rose wheeled on Daisy. "Why did you do that?"

Daisy blinked. "Do what?"

"Accept an invitation on my behalf."

Daisy thrust out her lower lip. "Because if I'd waited for you to do it, we'd have stood here half the night."

"Did it ever occur to you I might not want to go?"

"Why not? Miles Godfrey is a perfectly nice man who appreciates music as much as you do. You'll enjoy the concert."

"The concert, perhaps. Mr. Godfrey's company, I'm afraid not."

"Oh, Rose, don't be so stuffy. An eligible gentleman doesn't come along every day."

"I'm not looking for one."

Daisy sighed. "Honestly, Rose, it's just one afternoon out of your lifetime. Perhaps Mr. Godfrey isn't the most scintillating man on earth. But still waters run deep, as the old proverb says. Maybe you'll like him better once you get to know him."

Rose crossed her arms. "I'd rather decide for myself whom to get to know better, thank you very much."

Daisy glanced upward as if appealing to the Almighty for help. "Left to your own devices, you're liable to choose some ruffian from the wrong part of town. You're going to that concert with Mr. Godfrey, and I won't hear another word about it."

Rose conceded with a sigh. She did love the symphony. Perhaps the performance would be absorbing enough that she could lose herself in the music and not have to interact too much with the man sitting beside her.

The following day—the weekly washday—Rose helped her sister haul baskets of wet laundry from the basement washtub to the backyard clothesline. Wanting to broach the subject of Callan MacTavish, she chose her moment carefully. Washing the laundry tended to put Daisy in a grumpy mood, but hanging things to dry usually cheered her up, especially on a pretty spring day like this one. Rose waited until her sister smiled and remarked, "Just look at those gorgeous tulips," before speaking.

"Guess what," she said with practiced casualness as she took a wet towel from the basket. "It looks as if I might be getting my first music student."

"Really? That's wonderful news. Who is it?" Daisy lifted a wooden clothespin and pegged a pillowcase to the line.

Rose spoke carefully. "A Mr. Callan MacTavish."

Daisy quirked an eyebrow. "MacTavish? I don't know the name. Is he local?" She glanced at Rose. "And 'mister'? A grown man? I thought you'd be teaching children."

"That's what I thought, too," Rose said, shaking out the folds of her favorite white blouse with the pin-tucked front. "But I'm not exactly in a position to be choosy. I need paying students, and Mr. MacTavish is prepared to pay."

Daisy's brow furrowed. "Teaching a grown man to play the violin seems rather … unconventional." She pinned a damp dishcloth to the line. "But I suppose a student is a student. Since he's an adult male, though, take care that he only comes over when Robert and I are at home. It's not proper for you to be in the house with him by yourself."

"He's going to come on Saturday nights after supper. You're almost always at home then."

Daisy huffed, blowing a stray strand of hair out of her eyes. "Yes, we are, but Saturday nights are meant for relaxing with friends and family or for going out with nice men like Mr. Godfrey, not giving music lessons."

"I don't mind," Rose said. "It's the only night Mr. MacTavish is in town."

"I see. Is he a salesman or something, on the road throughout the week?"

"No."

"What, then?"

Rose bit her lip, then added in a rush. "You see, he spends all week up in the woods. He only comes down on Saturdays. He's a logger."

"A logger!" Daisy gaped at her. "One of those rough men who take over downtown every week?" She shook her head. "No. Absolutely not. What have I told you? Those loggers are nothing but ruffians. I won't have one tracking his dirty boots through my house."

"This one's different," Rose insisted. "He's polite and well spoken, not at all like the others."

Daisy eyed her suspiciously. "You've spoken to him? When?"

"Last Saturday." Rose's face heated. "He discovered I'm a music teacher and … and wanted to talk about music. He's quite fond of Brahms and Beethoven. Does that sound like a ruffian to you?"

"Well, no," her sister admitted. "But if he's so refined, what's he doing working in the woods? Why isn't he a professor or a dentist or something less … rugged?"

The conversation started to grate on Rose's nerves. "I'm sure I don't know why he's not a dentist," she said dryly. "I didn't think to ask him. The conversation didn't delve into his personal motivations. He wants to study music, he's willing to pay for lessons, and I'm looking for students. That's as far as we got." She stabbed a shirt to the line with vigor.

"There's no need to be prickly," Daisy said. "I'm just watching out for your best interests."

"For goodness' sake, my interests are doing fine on their own."

"Not if Jeremy Pyle is any indication."

Rose recoiled from the stinging remark. "What's Jeremy got to do with anything?"

Daisy pinned another dishcloth to the line. "I'm just saying that, apparently, you need a little guidance in the romance arena."

"Who's talking about romance? We're talking about music lessons. And by the way, if it relieves your mind at all, Mr. MacTavish is a churchgoer, too," Rose added. "Remember, we saw him there on Sunday and the Sunday before that. You even commented on him once."

Daisy thought for a moment. "You mean that tall, clumsy fellow in the back pew?" She sounded relieved and disappointed at the same time.

Rose pressed on. "Daisy, I'm going to be teaching the man how to play the violin, not marrying him. And having one music student will make it easier to attract some others, don't you think?"

At last, Daisy relented. "Oh, I suppose it's all right. As long as he's willing to pay top dollar for taking up your time." She peered at Rose over the clothesline. "But mind you toss him out the door if he acts improperly toward you in the slightest."

"If he tries anything of the sort, I'll give him the boot," Rose said. "But you need to promise me something in return."

Daisy picked up the empty laundry basket. "Like what?"

"Promise me you'll give him a fair shake, and not make judgments about him before you get to know him."

Daisy considered this, then nodded. "Agreed. I will strive to be fair and just. Even if he is just a lumberjack."

Chapter 5

THE FOLLOWING SATURDAY, IN the large upstairs room at Mrs. Donovan's rooming house, Lars and Mick watched as Callan stood before the crooked mirror, brushing the lint from his blue serge suit.

"Who are you goin to see, all spiffed up like that?" Mick asked. He elbowed Callan out of the way so he could see his own image in the mirror as he combed macassar oil through his dark hair.

"A young lady," Callan said, "and I'm needin to make tracks. She starts chargin at seven sharp." The words sounded wrong the moment they left his mouth, but he was too late to stop them.

"You're payin to see a girl?" Lars' mouth gaped. "Man, you shouldn't have to pay. With your strappin good looks, you'd have no trouble convincing a young lady to pass some time with you. Even Mick here, with a face like a gargoyle, managed to get a date with Trixie."

"Who you callin a gargoyle?" Mick said, grabbing Lars in a good-natured headlock.

Callan's face heated. He raised his voice. "Nay, I'm not payin for her company. Not like that. Get yer minds out of the gutter."

Mick released Lars and slapped his own knee in amusement. "Goldarn it, man, if we're so thick-headed, you'll have to explain it to us, then."

Callan adjusted his shirt collar in the mirror. "The situation's a wee bit complicated."

"Bet it is," Lars said. He and Mick chuckled and poked each other in the ribs.

Annoyance prickled the back of Callan's neck. "Nay, 'tis not what ye think." Hearing Rose jested about in such a coarse way, even if the men had never met her, made his fists clench. He paused, collected his wits, then sighed. They were bound to find out the truth sooner or later. "If ye must know, I'm takin a music lesson."

His friends gaped at him for a moment, then burst into gleeful laughter.

"Saturday night in a whole town filled with shiny lights and even shinier women, and you're taking a music lesson?" Mick turned to Lars. "You weren't kidding when you said he was different from anybody else."

Lars shrugged. "Leaves more fun for the rest of us."

Callan paid them no mind. Let them waste their time in boozing and brawling. He had better things to do.

On the short walk between the rooming house and the house next door, he plucked a rose from the landlady's garden and hastily flicked off the thorns with his thumbnail. *A rose for a Rose.* Pleased with his little verse, he knocked on the neighbors' door and was admitted by Daisy. She greeted him coolly but cordially, then spotted the long-stemmed rose.

"No need to bring flowers to your music lesson, Mr. MacTavish. It's not a social call." He caught a note of warning in her voice.

With his free hand, he removed his hat and inclined his head. "I dinna wish to offend, ma'am." He held the stem toward her. "I just thought a bright bloom like this one might add a wee bit of color to the parlor."

"I see." She took it from him. "Well, that's very thoughtful of you, then. I'll find a vase." She gestured toward the back of the room. "You can go straight on back, through that doorway. Miss Marchmont is waiting for you."

He entered the back parlor, hat in hand. Rose smoothed her skirt as she stood to greet him.

"Good evening, Mr. MacTavish."

She wore a black skirt and black-and-white striped blouse with puffed sleeves that stopped at the elbow. Her blond hair was tied in back with a black grosgrain ribbon. In her slender arms, she held a violin and bow.

"Good evenin, Miss … Marchmont, I believe your sister said."

"That's right."

Two wooden folding chairs were set up in front of a black metal music stand. She invited him to sit in one, and she took the other.

"Now. Shall we begin? You can use this old violin." She held the instrument toward him. "It belonged to my father until he bought himself a new one. He's a big man like you, so it should fit you and be comfortable for you to play. Try it out. Just hold the violin under your chin like so, and …"

Gently he pushed the instrument away. "Thank ye, but I willna be needin a violin."

"Oh? Do you already have one?" She looked confused. "Why didn't you bring it with you?"

"Nay, I dinna have one."

Her expression tightened. "Then how do you propose to learn how to play?"

He shook his head. "Like I told ye, I'm not here for lessons. I'm happy to pay an hour's fee only to hear ye play."

She regarded him distrustfully for a moment, then said, "Nonsense. Here, take the bow in your right hand." She thrust it at him.

"Ah, there's the rub," he said. He lifted his right hand so she could get a good look at it. When she saw the two stumps where there once were fingers, her cheeks turned pale. Slowly she lowered the bow to her lap.

"Oh, my." Her sapphire eyes glistened in the lamplight.

"So ye see, 'tis quite impossible for me to play that thing." He tried to give her his most heart-melting smile, the one that in his youth had earned him an extra meat pie or sweet biscuit from the neighbor ladies in his village. "Let me just listen to ye play, and I'll be a happy customer."

She sat up and squared her narrow shoulders. "You're wrong, Mr. MacTavish. It's not impossible for you to play. You'll just have to handle the instrument a little differently, that's all." Again, she held out the bow. "In fact, I recently read an article in an academic journal that said that learning a musical instrument can be very beneficial to people recovering from injuries."

Again, he pushed it away. "T'ain't recoverin I'm doin, lass. I'm afraid my circumstance is a permanent state of affairs."

She persisted. "You can still hold the bow, thus. Just balance it carefully between your thumb and … and your remaining fingers. Like this." She demonstrated, holding the bow using only her thumb, index finger, and little finger. The other two she held out of the way. "Now you try it."

She leaned toward him, so close he could breathe in the light violet scent of her hair. She placed the end of the bow into his fist and firmly moved his remaining fingers into position. Then she let go of the bow. It thudded to the carpeted floor.

"'Tis no use," Callan said. "I canna do it."

"Yes, you can," she insisted, sounding every bit the determined teacher chiding a reluctant pupil. "Try again."

"Nay." He picked up the bow from the floor, then handed it back to her. "You need not try to fix me, lass. Just play for me. I want to hear you play."

"But you're paying good money for—"

He held up his hand and closed his eyes. "Just … play."

She pushed out her lower lip. Then she stood, walked briskly over to a table, and replaced the violin in its case. He thought she was going to order him to leave, but instead, she opened a second case and pulled out a different violin.

"My father's old violin is too big for me," she explained as she sat back down. "Mine's a better fit." She looked expectantly at Callan. "What do you want to hear?"

"Brahms." A warm sensation filled his chest. She was going along with his wishes. He could hardly believe his good fortune to be given a private concert by such a fine musician, and a comely one too.

She reached toward the music stand and flipped open a score, then lifted the instrument and settled it under her chin. As opening notes of the Brahms sonata filled the room, Callan closed his eyes, the dull ache in his heart both sharpened and soothed at the same time. He didn't know if this strange effect was caused by the music or by the nearness of her. Or both. But he didn't care. He just let the notes wrap around him like a blanket.

Far too soon, a sharp rap came on the door, and her sister's voice said, "The hour is up. The lesson is over. Time to be on your way, Mr. MacTavish."

He started as if woken from a dream, yet he knew he hadn't been sleeping. Just floating along with the music.

"Aye," he called. "I'm goin."

He stood and reached for his hat. "Thank ye, Miss Marchmont. May I come for another lesson next week?"

She looked at him with wide eyes, as if she, too, were surprised at the effect her playing had had on both of them.

"Yes," she said. "And since we'll be working together, you may call me Rose."

"I'm Callan." He reached into his billfold, pulled out some bills, and handed them to her. She walked over to a small desk, wrote him a receipt, and tore it from the pad. He folded it and put it in his breast pocket.

"Here," she said, handing him the case that held her father's violin.

"Take it with you. I'm not going to need it."

"What about yer other students?"

"I have a child-sized violin for them. If they ever come."

"They will. Yer an excellent teacher."

"How would you know? You haven't seen me teach."

He looked at her with tenderness. "I just know. I can tell."

She straightened her spine. "Well, if that's the case, I must give you an assignment. Your assignment during the week is to practice holding the bow. I'm sure you can learn to do it if you try. I *know* you can. I have confidence in you."

"'Tis no use," he said, but he accepted the case anyway. Seeing it sitting in his bunkhouse locker would be a pleasant reminder of her all week long.

After he'd gone, Rose watched him cross the lawn and disappear into the rooming house. Such a strange man. So unlike anyone she'd ever met. And yet … he made her laugh. His soft, warm Scottish burr made everything he said sound intriguing. And if she could help him regain some dexterity in that damaged hand of his, well … her heart swelled at the thought she might be able to help him.

She brooded, however, about accepting his money when she hadn't taught him a thing. Certainly, Daisy would find it very strange and would not approve at all of the unusual arrangement. And yet he seemed to take such pleasure in simply listening. And who wouldn't want to help an injured man regain the use of his hand if such a thing were possible? Especially a kind, good-looking man who, unlike Jeremy, had sat through the whole sonata without once yawning, fidgeting, or checking his watch.

"How did the lesson go?" Daisy's voice broke into her thoughts. "Sounds like you did most of the playing."

Rose thought quickly. If she told the truth, that she wasn't actually teaching Callan anything, Daisy might forbid her to continue the lessons. But if it weren't for the lessons, Rose wouldn't be permitted to see him at all.

"Yes," she said presently, "his skills are really quite … rudimentary. He acted as if he hadn't seen a violin in his life. At least he appreciates music, so he's probably not tone-deaf. But he's experienced a terrible injury to his bowing hand. A hazard of working in the logging camps,

I suppose."

"Maimed, is he?" Daisy clucked her tongue. "And you with your tender heart. Mind you don't make a charitable project out of the poor man."

"I won't. I don't know if I can help him, anyway. But I wanted him to hear what might be possible to achieve if he worked hard at it. At any rate, we'll need to proceed slowly." Rose hoped that explanation would satisfy her sister's curiosity about how the "lessons" sounded to an outsider.

"Well, he seemed pleasant enough," Daisy said with indifference. "And I know you well enough to know you won't give him false hope, either of his musical potential or anything else."

Rose's mood lightened. Daisy hadn't forbidden the lessons to continue. Now if only she'd stop eying Rose as if reading the very thoughts in her head. Because if she could, she was certain to disapprove.

Callan's heart leapt when he saw Rose seated with her family at the front of the church. This time she was dressed in a green-and-white checked frock—a fresh, springtime green that reminded him of apple trees. He caught her gaze over the congregations' heads, and she smiled. As had become his custom, he chose a seat near the back to more efficiently intercept her after the service, this time without stumbling into her like a clumsy ox.

During the service, he tried to keep his mind on higher things. But after the last "amen," he strode toward the vestibule at the back, praying for something clever to say. With impatience, he nodded to the passersby. At last, Rose approached with her family.

"Good morning," she said warmly.

He swallowed. "Good morning, Miss Marchmont. Lovely day, isn't it?" Immediately he chided himself. Could he not think of anything more interesting to talk about than the weather?

"Quite." She stopped and turned to her sister. "Daisy, may I present Mr. Callan MacTavish? Mr. MacTavish, meet my sister and brother-in-law, Daisy and Robert Tanner." She smiled. "Mr. MacTavish is my new violin student."

Daisy nodded at Callan and said brusquely, "I know that, Rose. I met him the other day, remember?"

"I know you did, but Robert hadn't," Rose replied evenly.

"How do you do, Mr. MacTavish," Robert said, extending his hand. Callan shook it.

"How d'ye do, Mr. Tanner. I'm so enjoying my lessons. Yer sister-in-law is quite a talented teacher."

Before Robert could reply, a tall, thin man with a mustache and spectacles rushed up to them. "So sorry to interrupt, Miss Marchmont, but it's time for us to be going," he said. "We don't want to be late for our engagement." Before Callan's astonished eyes, the stranger extended a sharp elbow to Rose. She took it in her white-gloved hand.

"Goodbye, Mr. MacTavish," she called over her shoulder as the man steered her toward the exit. "See you on Saturday." And she was gone.

Callan stood in shock. It hadn't occurred to him that Rose might have a beau. She'd never mentioned having one, but of course, Callan hadn't thought to ask. Stupefied, he turned to say something to the Tanners, but they too had moved on. Listlessly he shook the minister's hand, then walked alone down the street, back to Mrs. Donovan's. In the empty room, he changed his clothes and gathered up his belongings, feeling strangely dejected. Of course, a pretty lass like her would have men taking her places. He shouldn't have expected anything different. Even so, a burning sensation smoldered in his chest, but he pasted on a grin as he met his mates for a hearty meal and a few more hours of leisure before heading back up the mountain.

Once again, his friends wanted to make the most out of the sunny afternoon by going fishing. Callan again demurred, preferring to return to the rooming house where he could sit on the porch and read.

By now the landlady, Mrs. Donovan, had figured out that Callan wasn't the rough-and-rowdy type of logger she was accustomed to and had taken a sort of motherly interest in his well-being. She beamed with pleasure to have him while away the afternoon on her porch.

"You just rest here in the shade, Mr. MacTavish," she said as she handed him a frosted glass of lemonade. "No sense getting your fair skin burned to a crisp out there on the lake with the other fellows."

He thanked her kindly for the lemonade. But he wasn't inclined to tell her that his fair skin had nothing to do with his decision to stay behind. To be sure, there was his strong aversion to going out on the water. But even more than that, his mind was preoccupied with questions about the young lady next door. Where in the world had she gone? And who in blazes was the bloke she had gone there with?

Chapter 6

"Dɪᴅ ʏᴏᴜ ᴇɴᴊᴏʏ ᴛʜᴇ concert?" Miles Godfrey asked Rose as they motored homeward in his fancy car.

"Yes, I did. Thank you very much." The stirring passages of Beethoven's Eroica Symphony still rang in her ears. The concert had been wonderful and her escort courteous, if a bit stiff. He knew good music and could discuss it intelligently. And riding in his elegant automobile had been a treat.

He touched the tip of his mustache. "Then I have a delightful surprise for you. At intermission, I visited the box office and succeeded in getting seats in a balcony box for the entire summer season of Sunday afternoon concerts of the symphony orchestra. Six concerts in all."

"You did?" Delight and dismay did battle in her heart. Not many symphony orchestra concerts came to northern Idaho, and the prospect of attending a whole summer's worth of them made her head spin. But the thought of attending them all with Mr. Godfrey cast a pall over her joy. What if he'd gotten the mistaken notion that she liked him as more than a friend? Still, it was awfully generous of him to buy the tickets. If all they did together was attend the concerts, they'd spend most of their time listening to music, not talking. Maybe that would be all right. Conversation would be limited to the automobile trips there and back. It might be worth it to hear good music. Hearing the music of the masters played by world-class musicians surely would make her a better instructor, should she manage to get some students. And it wasn't as if she had a full social calendar. Since coming to Sandpoint, she'd found that the hours between Sunday lunch and bedtime generally crawled, with little to do but read books and practice her violin.

"Well? What do you say?"

The gentleman's voice interrupted her thoughts. He stole anxious glances at her as he drove. She cleared her throat. "How thoughtful of you, Mr. Godfrey. Yes, I'll look forward to the concerts."

"Splendid." The twitch of his mustache as he smiled caused a slight wave of revulsion to course up her spine.

"Of course, you mustn't feel obligated to take me as your guest every time," she added hastily. "Surely a cultured man such as yourself has many other friends who enjoy music just as much as I do. I won't expect to be taken to every concert."

"What a generous creature you are," he said. "But I wouldn't think of taking anyone else."

When they reached Sandpoint, he parked the automobile next to the curb in front of the Tanners' house. Rose waited while he got out and walked around to the passenger side to open her door. As he escorted her up the walk, she thought she glimpsed Callan sitting silently in the dusky shadows of the porch next door. Was he spying on her? What nerve! Should she smile and wave, or take no notice? Would he think she was being courted by Miles? And was that a good thing or a bad thing?

Amid these flustered thoughts, she extended her hand to her escort. "Thank you for a lovely afternoon. I shall look forward to next week's concert." She shook his hand with her gloved one, stiffening her elbow to hold him at bay lest he get any ideas.

If he was disappointed not to have gotten a goodbye kiss, he did not show it. "Good night. I'll see you next Sunday." He held open the screen door, and she went inside, then he descended the porch steps, whistling.

As his motorcar puttered down the street, she cracked open the screen door and peeked in the direction of Mrs. Donovan's porch. But no one was there. The rocking chair sat empty. The ersatz spy had been a product of her imagination.

Well, that's a relief, she told herself. What right had the brash Scotsman, anyway, to be monitoring her comings and goings?

But as she turned from the door and climbed the stairs to her room, she gave one more peek out the little side window on the landing. Just to make sure.

In the back of the camp-bound rig, Callan endured some ribbing from his friends for the violin he carried.

"What's that you got there?" Lars asked. "Some new kind of saw?"

"A lure to summon stray cats with, more like," Mick teased.

To Callan's relief, they soon tired of the topic and moved on to discussing their morally questionable activities of the previous night.

His music lessons with Rose—or, more accurately, private concerts—were a sacred thing that he didn't fancy sharing with anyone, least of all his boorish campmates who didn't know a grace note from a guy line.

But his mood had lifted over the course of the afternoon. Indeed, he'd wished all manner of unpleasantries on the man she spent the afternoon with. But it cheered him up considerably that, from his hidden vantage point in the shadows of Mrs. Donovan's porch, he hadn't seen her kiss him goodbye.

As the summer evenings lengthened, so did the workdays of falling, bucking, and loading logs. Even so, there was still plenty of daylight left after evening chow. As was his habit, while his fellow loggers spent evenings fishing and hunting squirrels and swapping tall tales around a campfire, Callan took advantage of the empty bunkhouse to read and sketch and daydream. Now he'd added one other task best done away from prying eyes.

After an exhausting day in the woods, he bolted his supper, then returned alone to the bunkhouse. He read a couple of chapters of *Moby Dick* until he was sure his campmates were otherwise occupied. Then, with no one around to poke fun or ask intrusive questions, he reached into his locker, pulled out the violin case, opened it, and pulled out the bow. He tried to hold it the way Rose had shown him but clumsily dropped it, time and time again. Finally, he gave up. 'Twas a daft idea, that a man with two missing fingers could play the violin. Muttering a mild oath, he put the bow back in the case and snapped the lid, shoved the case back into his locker, and pulled out his leather journal. He opened it and lifted out a piece of paper folded inside—the receipt from his first music lesson. He liked to look at it, at the way her signature swirled gracefully across the bottom. *Rose Marchmont.* When he lifted it to his face, he caught a faint whiff of her violet scent. Just four more days until he'd see her again. But of course, it was possible she already had a beau, he reminded himself. Still, she wasn't formally engaged to that skinny bloke. At least, not yet. Callan was banking on the fact that since she hadn't kissed the man, she wasn't serious about him. And that meant Callan still had a chance to win her over if only he could convince that vinegar-lipped sister of hers he was a decent sort.

All at once the fragile scrap of hope shriveled in his chest like paper in a campfire. What good would winning her over do, when he had nothing more to offer than a life moving from logging camp to logging camp? Maybe her sister was right. Being a logger's wife wasna suitable future for a fine, highly educated woman like Rose Marchmont.

At the noisy clatter that signaled his mates' return, he folded the receipt, slipped it into the journal, and stashed the book in his locker. Then he joined his companions for a boisterous evening around the card table.

But later, as he lay in his bunk reading *Moby Dick* by the light of a smoky lantern, he found the fingers of his left hand—the hand that remained whole and intact—involuntary tapping the book's cover as they drummed out a half-forgotten pattern, the intricate fingering of the Brahms sonata.

Chapter 7

LEST THE SOUND OF Rose playing solo for an hour should raise her sister's suspicions, she devised a plan. During Callan's lesson time, she would play her violin for a while, Mendelssohn or Bach or the Brahms that he liked so much. Then she'd pause and scratch out some random passage, then say, "Well done, Mr. MacTavish. That's the way," or "Try it again, please," or "Let's try our scales, shall we?" loud enough for Daisy to hear in the next room if she happened to be listening.

"In other words, we're deceivin poor Mrs. Tanner under her verra own roof." Callan's voice was stern, but his eyes twinkled with amusement.

A warm tingle crept up Rose's neck. "Well, yes. I suppose so," she stammered. "But she's practically forced us into it. If she found out you're not a genuine music student, you'll be out on your ear."

He lifted an eyebrow. "Out on my what?"

She laughed. "Your *ear*. You'll be dismissed. Sorry, I'm afraid I picked up a bit of slang at the conservatory, along with my lessons."

"I see." He regarded her thoughtfully. "Ye had some fun at school then."

Warm memories filled her mind. "Yes, I loved it."

"Then why did ye leave?"

His question doused her mood like a spray of cold water. In no way was she prepared to explain about Jeremy to this inquisitive Scotsman. Surely, he'd make some joke about the situation, or worse, pity her. Abruptly she lifted the violin from her lap.

"I should play."

He cocked his head. "But I enjoy talkin with ye. Canna we just talk?"

"Our agreement is you pay to hear me play. What would you like to hear?"

He sat back. "The Brahms again. Please."

"Very well." For Daisy's benefit, Rose spoke distinctly in the direction of the closed door. "Pay attention, Mr. MacTavish. It should sound like *this*." She tucked the instrument under her chin and played, letting the ache in her heart flow out through the strings.

When the hour was over, she lowered the violin and looked at Callan. He swallowed hard, and his eyes held a shimmer she hadn't seen before. Clearly, the music had touched him deeply. Her own heart softened. Jeremy's eyes had never looked like that.

"That was magnificent," he said, his voice thick. "Ye play with such deep feeling. It makes me wonder what ye think about while ye play."

If he only knew.

He cleared his throat. "I've been meanin to ask ye somethin."

"Yes?" she said, a bit breathless.

"I've been tryin to acquaint myself with the literature of this great country. I've finished *Moby Dick*. Have ye another book to recommend?"

"Oh." Sighing, she stood and put her violin away, then walked over to a bookcase and ran her finger across the spines, reading the titles. She selected one, pulled it from the shelf and handed it to Callan.

"Nathanial Hawthorne," she said. "Another early nineteenth century author and a good one."

He glanced at the cover. "Thank ye." He set the book aside. "I've another question."

"You're full of questions tonight."

"This one's different. Might ye join me for a walk after church tomorrow?"

Joy coursed through her veins, only to be chased immediately by disappointment. "Oh, I'd love to, but I'm afraid I can't. I've committed to going to a concert with a—a family friend."

"I see. How about the following week?"

She cringed. "The concerts are a weekly series. Six in all." This was terrible. He was going to think she was putting him off.

He straightened. "Well, sometime when yer not otherwise engaged, I'd like to find a spot on yer schedule."

"I'm not engaged at the moment," she said, and immediately felt her face grow warm at her presumption.

His eyes lighted. "Aye? But what about yer sister?"

She thought for a moment. "It's a warm night. I'll tell her we're going for ice cream and offer to bring some back. She adores ice cream."

The plan worked. Delighted by the prospect of ice cream, Daisy gave her permission for the pair to walk downtown and back. Never had a stroll to First Avenue and back taken as long as it did that night. Rose and Callan spoke of many things. Of Rose's life back in Chicago. Of her experiences as a student at the conservatory. Of Callan's adventures in logging camps across North America. At the ice cream shop, Rose said, "Let's get chocolate mint. It's Daisy's favorite flavor. What are you getting?"

"Nay, none for me."

Rose looked at him in surprise. "You're not getting any?"

"Nay," he said, smiling down at her. "I just wanted to walk with ye, that's all."

At the Tanners' doorway, Callan said, "Well, good night."

Rose's shoulders sagged. "You won't stay for ice cream?"

"Nay," he murmured. "'Tis getting late. I don't want yer sister to be angry with me fer keepin ye out." He grinned. "I want her to say yes the next time. And the next."

She was glad the darkness hid her blush. "Good night then," she said with reluctance. When at last she went inside, Daisy took the carton from her and opened it. "It's practically melted," she complained. "But you were sweet to get chocolate mint. I know you prefer strawberry. Robert, come and have some ice cream."

But Rose, bustling around gathering dishes and spoons, barely heard a word she said.

Each Saturday after that, Callan took special care to turn up for his lesson well-dressed, well-groomed, and armed with additional ammunition: a pint of chocolate mint ice cream. And each week Daisy accepted the gift with cool politeness. "Thank you, Mr. MacTavish. You shouldn't have." But by the look on her face, he could tell she was pleased.

He wished Daisy could move past her prejudice against loggers and see him for who he really was. One hour a week spent in Rose's company was not nearly enough. He longed to treat her as a proper suitor should, the way that skinny fellow had—to invite her to dinner and concerts and picture-shows, to spend not just an hour with her, but all of Saturday, and Sunday too. But such a development would be impossible without Daisy's approval. One sultry August day, between passages of a Bach concerto, Rose and Callan's hushed conversation turned to his memories of Scotland.

"When do you plan to go back?" she asked.

Never, he thought, but such a response would only raise more questions he didn't feel ready to answer. He shifted his weight on the hard wooden chair. "Takes many a dollar to cross the ocean, lass. Perhaps I'm savin up." That was true as far as it went, but it didn't touch on the heart of the matter.

"Well, I hope you get to go soon. I'm sure your father must miss you terribly."

Before he could reply, there was a rap on the door, and Daisy poked her head into the room.

Startled, Rose sprang into action. She plucked at a violin string and proclaimed, "So you see, Mr. MacTavish, by plucking the string instead of bowing, you achieve the effect of—Yes, Daisy? What is it?" She frowned as if Daisy were intruding upon a pivotal moment in Callan's musical education.

"Sorry to interrupt," Daisy said. "I just wanted to ask if Mr. MacTavish will do us the honor of having Sunday dinner with us tomorrow."

"Surely that could have waited 'til we were finished," Rose snapped.

But Callan couldn't hide his grin. Daisy had invited him to Sunday dinner. Perhaps the skinny bloke with the fancy automobile was now out of the picture.

Later that evening, after Callan left, Rose sought out Daisy on a back-porch rocker, savoring the dark, sultry summer evening.

"Come and sit awhile, Rose. Get a breath of fresh air. It's so stuffy inside."

Rose drew up a chair and sat beside her, listening to the crickets chirping in the bushes. A cat paced across the yard, its eyes shining silver in the dark. Several blocks away, a train whistle blew. Finally, Daisy asked, "How did Mr. MacTavish's lesson go tonight?"

"Fine." In the dim light of the moon, she studied Daisy's profile. Had her sister caught on to the sham music lessons that were, in reality, private recitals interspersed with conversation? Was she toying with Rose, waiting for her to confess? But Daisy's expression betrayed no emotion.

Rose cleared her throat. "Speaking of lessons, I've heard from a few parents, inquiring about music instruction for their children. Two want piano, and another wants violin. All of them said they're planning to sign up when school begins. That's only a few weeks away."

"That's excellent news. See? I told you it would only take a little time. Maybe summer wasn't the most opportune time to try to sign up new students. With the exception of Mr. MacTavish, of course."

Rose worked up the nerve to say what was really on her mind. "Daisy, I'm pleased that you invited Mr. MacTavish to dinner tomorrow. But I must admit, I'm surprised as well. May I ask what made you change your mind about him?"

Daisy brought her rocking chair to a halt. "I haven't changed my mind about him," she said in a strained tone. "He's still a logger, and I don't approve of loggers calling on my sister."

"So why did you invite him to dinner?"

"Because he has been a faithful student of yours for going on three months now. I just thought it was high time we showed the man a little hospitality. In gratitude for his loyalty. I assume he's making progress, in spite of his disability?"

Rose nodded mutely, grateful that the darkness hid her blush. The Scotsman was making progress, all right, but not the musical kind. He was making progress on winning her heart.

"Well, then," Daisy continued. "Seeing as how Mr. MacTavish has such a strong interest in classical music, I've invited Mr. Godfrey to dinner tomorrow as well."

Rose's shoulders drooped. "Oh, Daisy, you didn't."

Daisy's eyes widened. "What's the matter? I only thought the two gentlemen might enjoy getting to know one another. Mr. Godfrey is extremely knowledgeable about music."

"He's extremely *opinionated* about music. That's not the same thing."

Daisy resumed her rocking. "Now that the summer concert series has ended, I don't understand why you refused his offer to continue your subscription into the fall."

"I don't want to go to concerts with him, nor anywhere else. He bores me to tears." She felt a rush of guilt and sighed. "Truly, I don't mean to seem ungrateful. The concerts have been a pleasant interval in the week. And Miles was always a perfect gentleman. It was a nice way to spend one afternoon a week, for six weeks. But honestly, if I have to continue going forever, I'll simply shrivel up."

Daisy looked troubled. "But he's a good friend of Robert's."

"I can't help that."

"There are worse things in a relationship than being bored." Daisy paused, and Rose wondered if she was thinking of her own marriage to the placid Robert.

"Mr. Godfrey is well established in his practice and would be a good provider. And you wouldn't necessarily be bored with him, either. I'm sure he'd have no objection to your continuing to teach music after your marriage; thus, you'd have plenty to keep you occupied."

"Our *marriage*?" Rose laughed. "Now you're really jumping the gun, sister." She stood. "If you'll excuse me, I must get my beauty sleep. Goodnight."

She swept up the stairs, indignant. How dare her sister try to plan her life! If that's how it was going to be, she might as well go back to Chicago. She knew her mother, too, would press her to settle down, but at least Chicago's pool of eligible suitors offered a wider selection of fish than Mr. Godfrey.

She changed into her nightgown of handkerchief linen, soft and thin, and washed her face. The smear of cold cream and splashes of cool water soothed her flushed skin. She removed her hairpins and combed her hair, then approached the bed. The August night being too hot for a blanket, she folded it and placed it neatly over the brass railing at the foot of the bed. Then she turned out the lamp, crawled between the sheets, and snapped up the shade covering the screened window beside her bed, which faced Mrs. Donovan's next door. A lamp burned in an upstairs window. She pictured Callan lying there reading, waiting for his friends to stagger home from the bars. He'd finished Melville, he'd told her, and had moved on to Hawthorne. He was familiarizing himself with the whole canon of American literature, he'd explained, to further his understanding of his adopted homeland. As the Hawthorne had been her suggestion, she hoped he was enjoying it.

She lay back against the pillow and smiled into the darkness. Was there anything more appealing than a man who appreciated both classical music and good literature? Especially one who sought out a lady's opinion, and then followed it?

She pictured him lying there, holding his book in the warm circle of lamplight. Just across the lawn. A few feet away, really. All alone in the empty rooming house on a Saturday night, reading. And she alone, too, when they could be out strolling together in the moonlight, or sitting on the front-porch swing, talking about Hawthorne.

She sighed. What a waste of a perfectly good moon.

She snuggled under the sheet and closed her eyes. But it was a long time before she slept.

Thoughts of dinner with Rose's family kept Callan from following the sermon the next morning, and he missed his chance to speak with her after the service. So when he arrived at their home, the shiny automobile parked in front took him by surprise. He was even more startled to find the skinny fellow with the spectacles standing in the front parlor like he owned it. Callan's hopes crumbled to the floor.

Rose jumped up from the sofa with a wide smile as Callan entered the room. "I'm so glad you could make it." Something in her tone made him feel as if he'd somehow come to her rescue.

Daisy stepped forward to perform her duty as hostess. "Mr. Godfrey, meet Mr. MacTavish. Mr. MacTavish, Mr. Godfrey."

Godfrey acknowledged the introduction with a stiff nod, but Callan stepped forward and thrust out his hand. "How d'ye do," he said with a grin. Rose should see he could be a good sport, even if his rival was a cold fish.

Godfrey returned a weak handshake, peering at Callan through his spectacles as if he were an insect to be flicked out of the way.

"Mr. Godfrey is an attorney with the railroad," Daisy said. "And Mr. MacTavish is employed by a local lumber concern."

"What she means to say is, I'm a lumberjack, workin up in the woods," Callan clarified cheerfully.

Daisy's face reddened.

Callan's first impression of Miles Godfrey was that he had all the personality of a poached egg. Why would Rose's family approve of a worm like that? Well, with any luck, Rose had a mind of her own.

Over roast chicken, potatoes, and green beans, he politely answered Daisy's inquiries.

"Where in Scotland are you from?"

"I grew up in the countryside near Dunoon. Near Loch Lomond."

"Ah, she of the bonny, bonny banks," Godfrey drawled in a fake Scottish accent.

"Aye, that one." Callan cast a suspicious glance at the interloper. Was he trying to make Callan look foolish?

"What does your family do there?" Daisy inquired.

"My father is a … a teacher." He declined to specify "music teacher" to avoid further inquiries on that point. "My mother died when I was verra young."

"Any brothers or sisters?"

"Nay."

"It must be lonely for your father, then, back in Scotland all by himself."

Rose interjected, "Daisy, I'm sure our guest must be tired of being grilled, don't you think?"

"Oh, I dinna mind talkin about my homeland." But the questions ceased, and the rest of the meal passed pleasantly if a little stiffly.

Over their dessert and coffee, Callan turned to Rose. "'Tis such a beautiful day out, Miss Marchmont. Can I entice ye to go for a walk before my ride leaves?"

Rose smiled at him. "I'd like that very much."

Mr. Godfrey sat up straighter. "I'm sure Miss Marchmont would prefer to do something a little more out of the ordinary."

Robert sat back in his chair, unbuttoned his vest, and patted his belly. "I propose that we all celebrate this perfect summer day by heading down to the city docks and taking a ride on an excursion boat. The *Northern* will be launching at three o'clock."

"Oh, let's!" Rose clapped her hands. "Doesn't that sound fun, Mr. MacTavish?"

Callan's palms grew clammy. "Nay. I'm—I'm afraid I'm prone to seasickness."

"Oh. That's too bad." Her face registered disappointment, but she did not press the issue.

"I'd be more than delighted to accompany you on the boat, Rose," Godfrey said. His satisfied look chafed worse than Callan's stiff collar.

I'll bet you would. He stabbed a fork into his slice of cake.

Rose regarded him thoughtfully for a moment, then shook her head. "No, the rest of you can go on the boat. I accept your invitation for a walk, Mr. MacTavish."

Daisy's mouth opened, trout-like, but Robert said, "That sounds fine." He smiled at his wife down the length of the table. "It's been a long time since we went on a boat excursion, hasn't it, dear?"

"I'd love to go, Robert," Daisy said, folding her napkin. "But we wouldn't want to leave our guest."

Callan mentally filled in the rest of the sentence: *We wouldn't want to leave our guest alone with my sister.* Disappointed but understanding the situation, he said, "Rose, there's no reason ye canna join yer family and Mr. Godfrey." He pushed back his chair. "I'll need to be heading back up the mountain soon anyway."

"No, I prefer to stay with you," Rose said firmly. "We will enjoy our walk."

"Verra well."

Robert looked at Mr. Godfrey. "You'll join us, won't you, Godfrey?"

Mr. Godfrey looked irritated. For a moment Callan was afraid he'd invite himself to join him and Rose on their walk. But he said, "No, thank you. I have some other things to take care of this afternoon."

He and Callan followed Robert onto the front porch while Rose and Daisy cleared the table and did the washing-up. They seated themselves in large wicker armchairs. Robert lit a pipe and offered the tobacco pouch to Miles, who accepted and filled his pipe and then to Callan, who declined. Callan could think of nothing to say, and Robert, as host, was of no help in that regard. The two of them puffed their pipe smoke in Callan's face as they all three sat in awkward silence.

At last, the ladies appeared, and the men stood. Robert offered his arm to Daisy. Callan and Godfrey stood awkwardly on either side of Rose. They all walked together to the sidewalk, where Godfrey said his goodbyes, got into his fancy car and sped away. Daisy and Robert turned one way and headed toward the city docks while Rose and Callan proceeded the other way down First Avenue, the town's principal street. They looked in the windows of the closed shops, then strolled along the residential streets, talking all the while.

As they walked, Callan drew one of her hands up through his arm and laid his other hand on hers. Was he imagining this, or did she really feel about him the way he did about her? He smiled into her sapphire eyes and kept his hand close over hers.

"That's too bad about your getting seasick on boats," Rose said. "You must have had a rough crossing when you came to America."

"Aye," Callan said quietly. "Ye could say that."

"There must be some remedy you could take. Some medicine to settle your stomach."

"Nay. There's not a medicine to cure what ails me."

"Well, you'll have to do something when the time comes for you to go home to Scotland for a visit. You can't spend the entire voyage lying ill in your cabin."

He slowed his pace and glanced at her in surprise. "Who says I'm goin home to Scotland?"

"Why, no one. But you will need to eventually, won't you?"

"Nay," he said sadly. "I canna go back."

"But your father ..."

"Rose." He stopped walking. "I'm never goin back to Scotland. Not now, not ever. Now, please, can we talk about something else?"

"Of course." She looked stricken, and immediately he regretted his harsh tone. She continued in a soft voice, "I'm sorry, Callan. I didn't realize it was a sore subject."

"Never mind," he said. "Let's go back to First Avenue and see if we can find someplace open to get a Coca-Cola."

They found a soda fountain and seated themselves at a table while a waiter bought them frosty glasses of cola. But the tense exchange had cast a pall over the lighthearted afternoon. Soon after, he escorted her home, and they said goodbye with promises to see each other the following Saturday.

Seated in the back of the rig heading up to the camp, while his mates boasted of their Saturday night exploits, Callan gazed at the mist-mantled mountains, his mind far away, thinking of the similar landscape surrounding the *lochs* of his beloved homeland. If he were going to keep growing closer to Rose—something he very much wanted to do—he'd eventually have to talk to her about Scotland. And America. And everything that had happened in between.

Chapter 8

AT FIRST, IT WAS the devil's own business just holding onto the bow. The infernal thing slipped from his grasp, skittered wildly across the strings, and resisted any attempt to create a pleasant sound. But once he'd conquered the bow, practicing the violin became more rewarding. And yet, Callan didn't share that news with her. As far as she was concerned, they still spent his lesson times just getting to know each other. Although she was the reason he was able to even pick up the instrument and make an attempt, he didn't feel ready to share the music that was slowly coming back to life in his own soul.

On Saturdays, he rode down the mountain with his mates, then parted ways with them and went to see Rose. Daisy remained staunch in her opposition to Callan calling on Rose socially. But she allowed the music lessons to continue, and her disapproval of their friendship had lessened as she'd gotten to know him for who he really was instead of her idea of a lumberjack.

They had their music "lesson," then they'd walk out, weather permitting. On Sundays, he'd see her again at church before heading back up the mountain. Callan and Rose were getting to know each other quite well, and Callan, at least, was falling in love. He wasn't quite sure how she felt. Sometimes he was certain she returned his affections. But there was always the simpering Miles Godfrey, not to mention that disapproving sister of hers, hovering in the background. Even so, once in a while, Daisy invited him for Sunday dinner. That had to count for something.

One autumn Sunday, Rose and Callan went for a walk after lunch. The wind picked up and shook the crisp branches, rattling the dry leaves, and the pines whispered softly. He drew her arm through his as they walked.

"Rose, I've somethin to tell ye. A big order for lumber has come in, so we'll be workin seven days for a while. I willna be able to come into town as often. And when the snow starts fallin heavy, well, I may not be able to come down at all."

"Oh, but surely you'll come down for Christmas, though, won't you? You'll spend Christmas with us?"

"Aye, if I can, I will. But ye mustna count on it too much. Ye must keep yourself busy with other things."

The snow did fly, well before Thanksgiving that year. Between the weather and the big order to fill, the crew was unable to make it down the mountain every Saturday but spent their weekends in camp. To fill the long evenings, they'd ask Callan to play a jig or a reel or a schottische or a polka, the folk tunes of their various homelands. He'd oblige, and they'd dance around the bunkhouse, burning off energy, until the boss called, "Lights out."

Callan missed Rose with an aching intensity, especially whenever he practiced the violin. But practice he did, determined to play well for her the next time he saw her.

The day before Christmas, the boss called a holiday. Horse-drawn sleds carried all the loggers who wished to go—which was most of them—down the mountain into town. Callan and his mates took their accustomed room at the rooming house. After greeting Mrs. Donovan, he dropped his bag on a cot and raced next door to see Rose.

"She's out, I'm afraid," Mrs. Tanner said when she answered the door. "She's gone to a Christmas concert in Coeur d'Alene."

"With Miles Godfrey, I'll bet," Callan snapped in spite of himself.

Mrs. Tanner got a strange look on her face. "No, with the youth from the church. She and another young lady are acting as chaperones." She hesitated, then added, "If you must know, my sister hasn't been spending any time with Mr. Godfrey. Since you've been gone, she's barely seen anyone at all, outside of family and church activities. She has plenty of students now, and they keep her very busy."

"'Tis good," Callan said.

Daisy bit her lower lip. "The fact is, Callan MacTavish, Rose is not interested in spending time with anyone else but you. It's 'Callan this' and 'Callan that.' She will be thrilled you've come home."

Callan's heart leaped. "And you, Mrs. Tanner?" he said cautiously. "What do *you* think of my comin home?"

She studied him for a long moment. Then her face broke into a wide grin. "I think you'd better start calling me Daisy." She pulled the door open wide "And I think you'd better come in out of the cold."

In the warm, steamy kitchen, Callan stood at the stove with an apron tied over his white Sunday shirt, stirring a pot of gravy. His stomach growled as he inhaled the delicious scents of roast turkey, onions, cinnamon, and nutmeg. Seated at the kitchen table, Robert sliced radishes for the salad. Daisy flitted between them, giving orders.

"That's right, Callan. Don't let the gravy stick to the pan. Slice them thinner, Robert."

The kitchen door opened and Rose entered, accompanied by a blast of cold air. She tugged off her gloves, her cheeks rosy from the cold.

"I'm back. The concert was wonderful. We—"

Her eyes lighted when she spied Callan. "You're here!"

Callan crossed the room in two strides. In Daisy and Robert's presence, he stopped short of sweeping her into his arms but contented himself with pumping both her cold little hands in his.

"Rose," he breathed. "Merry Christmas."

They grinned stupidly at each other for a moment before Daisy screeched, "Callan! The gravy!"

He returned to his post at the stove. "Yer sister has pressed me into service," he said.

"So I see. I'd better get cracking, too." She unwound her scarf, hung her coat on the parlor coat rack, returned to the kitchen, and grabbed an apron.

After dinner, the family relaxed in the front parlor. The garland-festooned white pine in the corner scented the air.

"'Tis nice to have Christmas in a home again, with a family," he remarked, lifting his punch cup.

"We're happy you could join us." Daisy sounded like she meant it.

Rose played some Christmas tunes on the violin, and they sang along. When she took a break to drink some punch, Daisy said, "Now you play something, Callan."

"What? Me?" He gaped at her.

"Yes," she urged. "Show us what you've been learning through all those months of lessons."

The time had come. He'd keep up the charade no longer.

Rose gasped, but he smiled and winked to reassure her.

"You needna worry, lass," he whispered. "I've bin practicin."

Her brows lifted. "You have?"

He shrugged. "Not much else to keep a man busy at camp of an evenin. Besides, my teacher is a stern taskmaster. I want to impress her with my diligence."

Rose glanced around uncertainly. "But all I have is my own violin. It's too small for you."

"I'll manage."

He stood, tucked the violin under his chin, picked up the bow in his injured hand, and pulled it over the strings. He made a show of tuning the instrument, then launched into a sweet, melodic rendition of "Auld Lang Syne."

The assembled company sat speechless. Callan played masterfully. His right hand bowed skillfully in spite of his missing fingers, and his left hand expertly fingered the strings. From the corner of his eye, he saw Daisy lean toward Rose.

"You were able to teach him to do that in just a few months?"

Wide-eyed, Rose shook her head. Catching her eye over the neck of the violin, Callan couldn't tell whether she verged on laughter—or tears.

Rose sat astonished as rich, splendid music poured forth from the instrument. When had he learned how to do that? Surely not from her.

When he'd finished, stunned silence filled the room. Then Daisy and Robert broke into applause. Rose couldn't make her hands and arms move.

"That was quite impressive," Daisy said. "Rose, you've done a wonderful job of teaching him."

"I've done nothing." Rose's voice was flat. She sounded near tears.

"Shall we take a walk outside, Rose?" Callan suggested gently. "Ye look as if ye could use some fresh air. And I think we have some talkin to do."

"Don't stay out too long," Daisy admonished. "It's icy out there."

Bundled in their coats and gloves, they walked in the moonlight, boots crunching on the crisp snow.

"You lied to me," Rose said.

"How did I lie?"

"You said you didn't know how to play the violin."

"I said nothin of the kind."

"But you asked to take lessons."

"I took lessons so I could be with ye, Rose. I dinna see any other way."

"You must think I'm a fool."

"Yer not a fool, Rose. Far from it. Yer ... yer everythin to me."

They'd reached the edge of the lake. Standing side by side, they looked out over the vast expanse where the moon glittered on the ice.

"Rose, I have somethin to tell ye. Somethin I havena told anyone, these three long years." The low tremble in his voice signaled he was on the verge of confessing something weighty. Her breath hitched. Some past scandal or legal entanglement? Or worse, another woman back in Scotland, or at some lumber camp? Someone with a prior claim on his heart? She stifled her instinct to flee, not at all sure she was ready to hear whatever he was about to say. "You don't need to tell me anything."

"Ye deserve to know."

But instead of saying anything more, he walked further down the shore where a wooden bench lay forlorn and forgotten. He brushed the snow from it and sat, leaning his elbows on his knees, and stared out over the icy lake shimmering in the moonlight.

Rose followed him, unsure whether he welcomed her company or wanted to be alone. She tentatively sat on the bench next to him, half expecting him to get up and move away, but he barely seemed to notice.

"I was a violinist, back in Scotland," he said. "Quite good at it, too. As a boy, my da taught me to play. When I grew older, I studied under the finest teachers in Glasgow."

She blinked and swallowed the sudden impulse to laugh that bubbled in her throat. Was this the dire confession? That he already knew how to play the violin? That he'd hoodwinked her into thinking he couldn't play a note? So what? But his grave expression told her there must be more to the story than that.

"So what happened?" she gently prompted.

"My da's ambition for me was to become a classical concert violinist, perhaps join the Royal Scottish National Orchestra. I'm sorry to say, I disappointed him greatly. I wanted adventure, so I sought it by playin in dance orchestras from Glasgow to Inverness. I loved travelin, bein on the road. 'Twas the life." His voice lightened and his mouth curved into a melancholy smile.

"I'd have thought your father would've been so proud," Rose said. "You were earning a living with your music."

His smile faded. "My father thought that sort of playin was beneath me, unworthy of all those years of classical trainin. We had a terrible row about it the last time we were together. But I paid him no heed, for I was too excited, havin just received a welcome bit of news. You see, a bunch of musicians, includin me, had received a great honor—we'd been hired by the White Star Line to be the official orchestra performin on board the greatest ocean liner ever built—the R. M. S. *Titanic*."

Chapter 9

ROSE GASPED. "YOU PLAYED aboard the *Titanic*," she whispered.

"Aye," he said. "That I did." He cleared his throat. "Until now, I dinna like to talk about it. Too painful."

Rose placed her gloved hand on his arm. "You don't have to if you don't want to. But sometimes it's good to talk about things."

"Aye. I'll talk about it now. With ye."

"All right." She squared her shoulders. He'd been brave; now she would too. For him.

He sat in silence for a few minutes, as if gathering his thoughts. Then he drew a deep breath. "'Twas over the moon we were. She was the finest steamship afloat. Unsinkable, they said. Aye, she was a beauty. Enormous black steel hull risin higher than the Highland hills. I couldna believe my good fortune in bein allowed to play music on such a vessel. Of course, our accommodations were modest. Four men to a room with two iron bunk beds on a long hallway of identical rooms. But 'twas good enough for me."

"What a marvelous experience." Rose sighed. Then her breath hitched. "I mean, the *ship*. The ship must have been marvelous. Not … not …" She clamped her lips.

He took her hand in his and pressed it gently, "'Twas. 'Twas marvelous. First, we played on the Southampton dock even before the passengers boarded, lively tunes for gettin 'em in a good mood. Then we played near the bottom of the Grand Staircase, greetin them as they came aboard and got settled into their cabins. We played durin dinner, and after for those who cared to dance. The object, we were told, was to keep the passengers constantly entertained, no matter what time of day or what they were doin."

He looked at the sky. "'Twas a night much like this one. Frosty and clear, stars danglin above our heads like crystals spilled over black velvet. We played for dinner, same as always. At one point durin the evenin, we felt a jolt and a shudder under our feet.

"'Nothing to be concerned about,' the steward said. So we picked up our playin, and the passengers picked up their dancin. I remember feelin the floor tilt, and it felt to be vibratin. But I dinna think nothin of it.

"Sometime later the stewards came back and told us to get ourselves up on deck. Nothin to worry about but shake a leg even so. We heard shouts, people bangin on doors, footsteps thunderin.

"Our band leader grabbed the arm of a passin steward. 'What's happened?'

"'Ship's hit an iceberg,' he said, real quiet-like so as not to panic anybody. 'Best you and your boys come up on deck now.'"

Callan paused and looked at Rose. "Am I goin on too long?"

She shook her head. "No," she whispered, her breath frosted. "Go on."

"I followed the rest of my bandmates through the ship. The frigid air slapped our faces as we stepped out onto the deck. But 'twasna the cold that stole the breath from our bodies. 'Twas the sight of the great iceberg that done it, risin out of the dark sea like the Loch Ness monster. Hairs stood up on the back of my neck. Panic had spread throughout the ship, people cryin and screamin, hysterical women bein herded into lifeboats The officers were makin the women and the bairns go first, draggin 'em to the lifeboats even if they dinna want to leave their husbands behind."

Rose's throat constricted. "What did you do? Did you try to get in a lifeboat?"

Callan shook his head. "Nay. They dinna let men in the boats, and anyhow, I guess we thought our turn would come. The captain urged us to keep playin, to try to calm everybody down. 'We must lift their spirits,' he said. So, at first, we chose lively, cheerful music. Ragtime and upbeat dance tunes, like we played when they were first boardin. None of us sought to get off the ship. Pretty soon we learned there were no more lifeboats, anyway. We knew we were goin to our deaths. Our leader prayed for us, then we sat on deck and continued to play. All I can say is that God must have been with us, for us to be so calm. Toward the end, somebody asked us to play hymns to comfort people, so we did. Some of the crew sang along. Some of the passengers too."

In his rich baritone voice, Callan sang softly the words of the old hymn.

There in my Father's home, safe and at rest,

There in my Savior's love, perfectly blest;
Age after age to be nearer, my God, to Thee.

His voice cracked on the final note. Then he fell silent and dropped his head as if in grief, or maybe in prayer. Rose waited for him to continue, her heart shattering at the unimaginable horror he'd endured.

"There was no more to be done," he whispered hoarsely. "The captain said, 'Well, boys, ye've done yer duty, and ye've done it well. Ye know the rule of the sea. 'Tis every man for himself now, and God bless ye.'

"All at once, there was a great crunchin sound. The entire ship listed hard. I remember slidin along the deck, chair and all, and fallin, fallin, fallin.

"I hit the icy water full impact, fully clothed. I dinna remember what happened next. I must have gone unconscious for a while, in God's mercy. When I got my bearings, I was bouncin around amid chunks of ice and thrashin bodies. All around people were cryin, some groanin, some still and silent, but the great ship was gone, all of her. I heard later that she'd broken clean in two and slipped into the sea."

Rose hugged herself, her throat tight with unshed tears. "I can't imagine the horror."

Callan folded his arms as if to quell the shivering. She longed to reach out to him, to wrap him in her arms but didn't dare. He stood and walked a few steps away, staring out over the icy moonlit expanse of the lake.

"Someone told me later that I'd been dragged underwater, sucked down when the ship went under, only to be blown back to the surface when the ship's boiler exploded. I've no idea, but 'tis as reasonable an explanation as any.

"I managed to hang on to an overturned rubber raft, along with several other men. Somehow, we stayed alive until a rescue boat pulled us from the frigid water, and we wound up on board the *Carpathia*. Passengers and crew of that ship gave us blankets and dry clothes to wrap ourselves in." He sat down and put his head in his hands. "Over fifteen hundred people died, Rose. Why not me? Why did I survive?"

Rose put her hand on his shoulder. "Because obviously, God has a purpose in saving you."

"What purpose? So I can wander around North America like a ghost?" He raised his head, then lifted his right hand. "I was the only member of the orchestra who lived. The only one. All the rest, gone.

And I dinna lose my fingers in a loggin accident like I let people think. I lost them to frostbite because of that night."

Rose nodded silently. No words of comfort or reassuring platitudes seemed adequate.

"We landed in New York, and I've been on this continent ever since. After I'd recovered from the ordeal, I wanted to go home to Scotland, but I couldna bring myself to set foot onto a ship. Each time I tried, I froze, utterly incapable of movin my legs up the gangplank. So you see, I canna get on another boat. Not now, not ever.

"So I wound up joinin a loggin crew in upstate New York, then Nova Scotia. Turns out I had a knack for it. Violinists have strong arms and shoulders. I worked my way from Eastern Canada to northern Idaho. And here I am."

Rose laid her hand on the sleeve of his coat. "But you can't ever go back?" she whispered.

He pulled off his glove and laid his bare hand over her gloved one.

"Nay, lass. I'd love to go back and see my homeland again. To fix things with my da. He knows I'm alive. I've written to him. But he's old and too weak to travel, and I still canna bring myself to step foot onto a ship. If I canna even manage a fishin boat on Lake Pend Oreille, how will I ever manage to board a great ship out on the ocean?"

Rose lifted his damaged hand to her lips and kissed it.

"Maybe God's purpose for saving you was that you be here, now. Maybe He gave you back your music so you can share it for His glory. Not for adventure or fun or seeing the world, but for Him."

He studied their clasped hands. "Aye, He gave me back my music." He gazed at her tenderly. "With no small effort on yer part, too."

She turned to face him directly, her voice gaining strength. "You're still a violinist, Callan. And a good one. Good enough to play for others, to play concerts all over the world, and to tell people your story. To give them hope that they, too, can face their difficulties with God's help."

He shook his head sadly. "Ah, Rose, that's a bonny little dream, but it canna be. Aye, I can play again. But how can I travel the world givin concerts and tellin my story when I canna even get on a ship?

"The music has come back to you. And so will your ability to sail."

"How d'ye know?"

"We'll take it slow, the same way you got your music back. Step by step, with me beside you all the way. You'll go to Scotland. And when you do," she said, "I'll go with you."

"Ye will?"

She tilted her head. "You'll need an accompanist, won't you?"

"I believe I would, lass," he said, his eyes crinkling with amusement.

Her mind whirled with plans. "We'll go to Scotland first, of course. You've met some of my family. I'd like to meet yours."

"Hold on there, lass. Yer gettin ahead of yourself."

The air froze in her lungs, making it hard to breathe. Once again, she'd jumped to conclusions, gotten the wrong impression about someone's feelings for her. When would she learn?

"You don't want to go?" Her voice quivered in spite of her effort to sound neutral. "Or you don't want to go with *me*?"

"Ah, lass, there's nothin I'd rather do than take ye to Scotland."

Her breathing eased. No mistake, after all.

"But it wouldna be proper for us to be travelin together, ye and I."

"Why not?"

"Because we're not married. Yer sister would have a fit."

Really? *That* was the problem? "Well, then." She stared at her gloves.

"Well, then," he parroted. Gently he lifted her chin, so she faced him. A dimple quirked at the corner of his mouth. "I guess there's nothin for it but for ye to marry me."

Heart pounding, she looked him straight in the eyes. "Do you mean it?"

"I do."

A laugh bubbled up from her chest. "Then I do, too. I mean, I will. Marry you."

He swept her up off the bench and into his arms. "Now yer sister really will have a fit," he said, laughing. "How soon can we be married?"

"Right away. The sooner, the better."

He set her on her feet, and together they sat on the bench. His arms went around her and drew her close, her head on his shoulder, her face close to his.

"I love ye, Rose Marchmont," he said. Then he lowered his head and pressed his lips to hers. "I can do anythin, with ye by my side. Even get on a ship. And then we'll go home, lass—to *our* home—together."

Author's Note

This story is a work of fiction. All of the characters in this novel, including Callan MacTavish, are entirely fictional. The sinking of the *Titanic* was, of course, all too real.

The professional musicians aboard *Titanic* included a violinist from Scotland named John Law Hume. Twenty-one years old at the time, Hume perished in the sinking, as did all of the other musicians.

"Many brave things were done that night, but none were more brave than those done by men playing minute after minute as the ship settled quietly lower and lower in the sea." (Lawrence Beesley, *Titanic* survivor)

Hearing the story, I imagined what might have happened if Hume had survived the sinking and ended up in America. Thus, *The Violinist* was born.

With deepest thanks to:
My husband, Thomas, for his support, enthusiasm, and cheerful
willingness to discuss my characters as though they were real people
My editor, Pegg Thomas, without whom this story would not exist
My steadfast writing partners: Anita Aurit, Melissa Bilyeu, Cassandra
Cridland, Terese Luikens, and Grace Robinson
Olivia Luther and the Bonner County Historical Society in Sandpoint,
Idaho, for their enthusiastic support and research assistance

With a passion for all things historical, Jennifer Lamont Leo
captures readers' hearts through stories set in times gone by. Her first
novel, *You're the Cream in My Coffee*, won the Grace Award for women's
fiction and a Carol Award from American Christian Fiction Writers.
She is also a copywriter, editor, and journalist. An Illinois native, she
grew up listening to stories about Chicago's vibrant history. Today she
writes from the mountains of northern Idaho. Visit her at A Sparkling
Vintage life (JenniferLamontLeo.com/blog) and Miss Marjorie's Jazz
Age Journal (MarjorieCorrigan.blogspot.com), as well as on Facebook,
Twitter, and Pinterest.